THE
WORLD'S FAIR
QUILT

Also by Jennifer Chiaverini

Canary Girls

Switchboard Soldiers

The Women's March

Mrs. Lincoln's Sisters

Resistance Women

Enchantress of Numbers

Fates and Traitors

Christmas Bells

Mrs. Grant and Madame Jule

Mrs. Lincoln's Rival

The Spymistress

Mrs. Lincoln's Dressmaker

The Elm Creek Quilts Novels

The Quilter's Apprentice

Round Robin

The Cross-Country Quilters

The Runaway Quilt

The Quilter's Legacy

The Master Quilter

The Sugar Camp Quilt

The Christmas Quilt

Circle of Quilters

The Quilter's Homecoming

The New Year's Quilt

The Winding Ways Quilt

The Quilter's Kitchen

The Lost Quilter

A Quilter's Holiday

The Aloha Quilt

The Union Quilters

The Wedding Quilt

Sonoma Rose

The Giving Quilt

The Christmas Boutique

The Museum of Lost Quilts

THE WORLD'S FAIR QUILT

An Elm Creek Quilts Novel

JENNIFER CHIAVERINI

WILLIAM MORROW
An Imprint of HarperCollinsPublishers

THE WORLD'S FAIR QUILT. Copyright © 2025 by Jennifer Chiaverini. All rights reserved. Printed in the United States of America. No part of this book may be used or reproduced in any manner whatsoever without written permission except in the case of brief quotations embodied in critical articles and reviews. For information, address HarperCollins Publishers, 195 Broadway, New York, NY 10007.

HarperCollins books may be purchased for educational, business, or sales promotional use. For information, please email the Special Markets Department at SPsales@harpercollins.com.

FIRST EDITION

Designed by Nancy Singer
Quilt ornament © nielsd96/stock.adobe.com

Library of Congress Cataloging-in-Publication Data has been applied for.

ISBN 978-0-06-338175-9

25 26 27 28 29 LBC 5 4 3 2 1

To my family, with all my love

THE
WORLD'S FAIR
QUILT

1

September 2004

Soft morning sunlight filtered through the leafy boughs of the tall elms behind Elm Creek Manor as Sylvia nudged open the back door and lugged a five-gallon glass dispenser of fresh apple cider outside onto the landing. After catching her breath, she carefully descended the four stone stairs to the gravel parking lot, nearly empty now during the off-season, with only the Elm Creek Quilts minivan and the few vehicles belonging to the manor's year-round residents basking in the sunshine or keeping cool in the shade, according to their drivers' preferences.

Awaiting Sylvia at the foot of the stairs was a much smaller four-wheeled contraption better suited for her current errand: a sturdy red wood-and-steel wagon with rugged wheels, slat sides, and a long handle with a secure grip. Just minutes ago, she had placed a container of apple-oatmeal muffins and a sleeve of paper cups at one end. Now she muffled a grunt as she carefully set the heavy dispenser beside them, bending her knees to prevent strain to her lower back. After checking to make sure the dispenser's spigot remained tightly closed, she grasped the wagon's handle, gave it a firm tug to get the wheels turning, and set off for the orchard.

The wagon rattled cheerfully over the hard-packed dirt and gravel, but an axle squeaked and a bit of rust flaked off in Sylvia's palm when she adjusted her grip. She made a mental note to ask Matt McClure, the estate's young caretaker, to give the wagon a tune-up when he could spare time away from the apple orchard. She supposed it was a wonder the antique contraption still rolled along at all, but things had been built to last back in the day when her father had brought the shiny new wagon home for her younger brother—1932, if memory served. The gift had been a surprise in more ways than one. Before the dreadful stock market crash, the Bergstrom family could well have afforded to celebrate a birthday with a delightful new toy, but such expenses had become extravagances during the Great Depression, what with so many of their formerly wealthy customers suddenly penniless and the family horse-raising business in precipitous decline. "You were supposed to buy yourself a new pair of boots," Sylvia's great-aunt Lydia had reproached Sylvia's father afterward, but she fell silent when she spotted Sylvia eavesdropping in the doorway.

Sylvia smiled wistfully to herself, remembering how her father had patched his worn boots and carried on, perfectly satisfied with his choice. What were a few blisters compared to his son's joy? Richard had loved that wagon, and when he wasn't careening wildly down the steep slope behind the stables, his imagination transformed it into a speeding locomotive, a pirate ship, a rocket to the stars.

If Richard had survived the war, perhaps he would have passed it on to his own children one day, but that was not to be.

Over the decades the once-beloved wagon had been entirely forgotten, slowly rusting away in a corner of the barn amid a tangle of antique farm tools. Only a few months ago, Matt and Joe, the husband of another resident Elm Creek Quilter, had discovered it while making room to expand Joe's woodshop. Struck speechless from astonishment, flooded by memories, Sylvia could only nod when Matt asked if he could fix it up for his own children. Now it was nearly as shiny and sound as when Richard had first taken it for a spin, with only a few dings and dents to remind her of her brother's boyish misadventures.

Matt and Sarah's eighteen-month-old twins were still too young for the wagon, but in the meantime, Sylvia found it quite useful for transporting heavy or awkward things around the estate—including, that morning, refreshments for her hardworking friends. Though the worst of the summertime heat and humidity was behind them, it was still rather warm for mid-September, and she suspected the more senior members of the construction crew would appreciate an excuse to take a break.

And if Sarah playfully accused Sylvia of trying to delay the orchard's grand opening—well, Sylvia was used to her younger friend's fond teasing by now, and she wouldn't take offense. Hadn't Sylvia agreed to Matt's "Pick-Your-Own" scheme, despite her misgivings? She wanted his new venture to succeed as much as anyone did—in fact, she was counting on it. Sarah was responsible for the company's finances, and if she said their accounts were tilting dangerously toward the red, it must be true. Elm Creek Quilt Camp was the most popular quilter's retreat in the country, but recently, unexpected financial difficulties had beset them. They still broke even every month, and at the height of the quilt camp season they eked out a modest profit, but their operating expenses rose every year, and the nineteenth-century manor badly needed essential repairs and upgrades.

"We could raise tuition," Sarah had tentatively suggested earlier that summer, tucking a long strand of her reddish-brown hair behind her ear as she studied a meticulously detailed spreadsheet. "We could offer fewer classes or simpler meals—"

"Absolutely not," Sylvia had interrupted, although when Sarah's expression turned dejected, Sylvia wished she had at least let her younger friend finish her thought. "A week at Elm Creek Quilt Camp must remain within the budget of an average quilter, and we've worked too hard to establish our excellent reputation to lower our standards now."

"Then we need to find other sources of revenue," Sarah had replied, her tone reasonable but firm. "The only other alternative is to take on debt, and I'd rather not resort to that unless we have no other choice."

"Certainly not," Sylvia had replied, a faint tremor in her voice betraying her sudden emotion. She and Sarah had worked too hard to bring the estate back from near insolvency to risk losing it now. Elm Creek Manor had been in the Bergstrom family since Sylvia's great-grandfather, his wife, and his sister had immigrated to Pennsylvania from Germany in the 1850s. They and their descendants had labored tirelessly to establish Elm Creek Farm and Bergstrom Thoroughbreds—prosperous, widely respected enterprises that had sustained the family through three wars, an influenza pandemic, the Great Depression, and innumerable personal losses.

Or so it had been for four generations.

When Sylvia's elder sister, Claudia, had assumed control of the Bergstrom estate after their father passed, she and her spendthrift husband had driven it to the very brink of bankruptcy. It was a small mercy that Sylvia had not witnessed the decline. In the early summer of 1945, Sylvia had fled Elm Creek Manor, reeling from grief and anger after Claudia had refused to break off her engagement to the man whose cowardice had led to the deaths of their younger brother, Richard, and Sylvia's first husband, James, in the war. Irreparably estranged from her sister, Sylvia had built a life of her own in Sewickley, near Pittsburgh. Fifty years later, when she inherited the estate upon Claudia's death, she had returned to find the manor in such wretched condition that she had contemplated cutting her losses and selling the estate—the manor, the furnishings, and every last acre of forest, creek, and wildflower meadow.

Fortunately, before Sylvia could make a decision she would later regret, she had hired Sarah McClure, then a young, unemployed accountant new to Waterford, to help her clean out the manor and prepare it for sale. One prospective buyer had spoken of turning the manor into an apartment complex for students of nearby Waterford College, and Sylvia had been tempted to accept his offer. In all the months the estate had been on the market, no one else had suggested a more appealing plan, and as a retired teacher, it had pleased Sylvia to imagine students enjoying such a beautiful, comfortable home.

Sylvia had been very close to signing away her ancestral estate when Sarah had become suspicious of the developer's plans and secretly investigated his company. When Sarah learned that the developer intended to raze Elm Creek Manor and build condos on the property, Sylvia had immediately broken off negotiations. At a loss for what to do next, she had asked Sarah to help her find a way to bring the manor back to life. Sarah's ingenious and unlikely suggestion was to turn Elm Creek Manor into a retreat for quilters, a place for them to stay, to learn, to find inspiration, and to enjoy the companionship of other quilters.

How fortunate it was that Sylvia had accepted Sarah's proposal—otherwise her beloved home would now be rubble in a demolition landfill, and the local quilters she and Sarah had invited to become founding members of the faculty would not have become her dearest friends. Together they had restored the once-neglected manor to the elegance Sylvia remembered from her youth. Indeed, in many ways Elm Creek Manor was even more wonderful than before, for rather than belonging to only one fortunate family, it had become a second home to quilters the world over, if only for one glorious week each summer. At Elm Creek Quilt Camp, aspiring and longtime quilters alike could explore their untapped artistry and take creative risks within a nurturing, supportive community.

What a blessing indeed it was that Elm Creek Quilts had prospered, or Sylvia might have been more than a hundred miles away when Andrew Cooper, her younger brother's childhood friend and fellow soldier, pulled up in his motor home for the surprise visit of a lifetime. She had been astonished to discover that he had never forgotten her, and they had quickly resumed their old friendship. In time their feelings had grown deeper, and they had fallen in love and married.

Sylvia often paused in the middle of a busy day to marvel at her good fortune. To think that in her golden years, she had forged cherished new friendships, founded a thriving business, rediscovered the artist within herself, fallen in love with a dear, long-lost childhood friend—and somehow still felt as if the best was yet to come.

But that would not be so if Elm Creek Quilts did not regain solid financial footing.

It was too beautiful a morning for such anxious thoughts, so Sylvia set them aside with the same deliberation with which she steered the wagon around an errant tree root. Her good mood was quite restored by the time she reached the bridge over Elm Creek, which murmured a familiar melody as it flowed over rocks and fallen branches on its winding journey through the Bergstrom estate. She was halfway across when she detected the distant, industrious noise of hammers, drills, and circular saw. The sounds grew ever louder as she reached the opposite bank and continued along the gravel road, glancing over her shoulder now and then to confirm that the dispenser had not toppled over and crushed the muffins.

Slowing as she descended a low hill, she passed the red banked barn her great-grandfather had built so long ago, and the green, shaded forest behind it, resonant with birdsong. Up ahead, the gravel road curved left and disappeared into the shade of the leafy wood, a route she had traveled countless thousands of times and knew well. What still jolted her with its unfamiliarity was the new fork continuing straight ahead along the southern edge of the orchard. The extension had been completed a few days before, but only once had Sylvia followed it to its terminus at a new gravel parking lot between the orchard and the forest.

"Our customers will park here," Matt had explained as he showed her around, a worn, sun-faded baseball cap tugged low over his unruly blond curls, his smile endearingly hopeful as he searched her expression for signs of approval. He stood about a head taller than Sarah, with a muscular build, a ready grin, and a perpetually sunburned nose from spending nearly all his time working outdoors. "It's closer to the orchard, so they won't have to carry their heavy bags full of apples very far. This will also leave the lot behind the manor open for quilt campers and visitors."

"And for those of us who live here," Sylvia had reminded him, resting her hands on her hips as she inspected the scene. "You'll need to put up a sign at the intersection so drivers know to turn left for the orchard, right for quilt camp."

"Joe's on it," Matt had assured her. "I told him it didn't have to be fancy, but knowing Joe—"

"It'll be a work of art," Sylvia had finished for him. "A master craftsman like Joe wouldn't settle for anything less."

But when she reached the fork and found no evidence of a sign yet, she wondered if she should encourage Joe to lower his standards just this once, to sacrifice artistry to efficiency and necessity. She didn't want crowds of confused would-be apple-pluckers pounding on the back door of Elm Creek Manor at all hours every autumn weekend until the first frost, interrupting her meals or quilting or conversation at the most inconvenient moment.

Grimacing at the thought, she paused to admire the orchard, what she could see of it from its southeast corner, acres of thriving trees heavy with fruit. Although she still worried that entrusting the harvest to paying customers would prove to be a lamentable mistake, her heart gladdened as she inhaled the sweet, tantalizing fragrance drifting on the intermittent breeze.

Throughout her youth, she had found solace and joy in the orchard, nurtured through storms and droughts by generations of Bergstroms before her. Her mother had taught her to observe the trees through the changing seasons, to watch in wonder and awe as buds formed on the bare branches, faint green leaves deepened and grew lush, blossoms burst forth and sweetened the air with their perfume, and apples, gold and red and green, ripened in the sun. Whenever Sylvia had passed the orchard on horseback, on a solitary stroll, or even through the window of a car, she had found reassurance in the orchard's promise that patience and endurance would be rewarded. She remembered well how in the darkest, loneliest days of her life, she had walked alone through the orchard, brokenhearted and angry, certain that her future held only bitterness. And yet, somehow, among the trees her ancestors had planted, she had found her grief easing. As the breeze had moved through the budding branches, it had seemed to whisper a promise that one day she would taste sweetness again.

Was it any wonder she felt protective of the orchard in a way her younger friends couldn't possibly understand?

Sighing, she tugged the wagon's handle and continued on her way. Matt cared about the orchard too, she reminded herself. In the few years he had served as caretaker of her estate, Matt had patiently restored the neglected orchard to an even greater abundance than she remembered from childhood. Their harvests yielded more than enough for their household use, so Matt had begun selling the surplus to local grocers, restauranteurs, and a dried fruit company, earning profits he reinvested into the orchard. Earlier that summer, she had risen early to meet him in the orchard before breakfast to discuss the upcoming harvest of the early fall varieties. As they strolled through the rows of trees, the fragrance of apples sweet and heavy in the warm summer air, Matt had updated her on his experiments with organic farming and his plans for expansion the next season. Sylvia had congratulated him on a job well done and had instructed him to proceed as he thought best. "I have no intention of interfering in what is obviously working exceptionally well," she had assured him. He had taken her at her word, and she could hardly fault him for that. He had never given her reason to doubt his stewardship, and it would be unfair to start second-guessing him now.

A few paces down the new road, the sound of familiar voices and laughter reached her in the brief pauses between construction cacophony. A smile came to her lips as she imagined her friends' delight when she turned up with a surprise delivery of sweet apple treats, and she picked up speed in anticipation.

When she reached the new parking lot, she shaded her eyes with her hand and turned in place until she spotted her friends on a gentle, grassy slope beside a wide footpath leading to the nearest rows of trees. From the look of things, Matt, Joe, and her own dear Andrew were nearly finished building the market stand, a one-story, square structure with half-walls open on four sides, wide counters, and a pitched roof with a generous overhang to provide customers with cooling shade on bright, sunny days, or shelter from an unexpected cloudburst when ill-timed but essential rain caught them by surprise.

Sylvia's admiring gaze lingered on Andrew, her husband of almost three years, who stood solidly halfway up a ladder leaning against the market stand roof. He cut a fine figure in his sturdy tan work trousers and navy blue T-shirt, neatly tucked in. His steel-gray hair was cut short, and his eyes were such a rich, clear blue that they seemed to shine for Sylvia even through his wire-rim glasses, which he wore when reading the newspaper or tying flies. For the task at hand—nailing shingles in place, if she was not mistaken—he had donned a pair of plastic safety goggles instead. Despite his limp, a remnant of his wartime service, Andrew carried himself with almost military precision, but although his bearing gave him a stern and measured air, he was the kindest and gentlest of men, and she loved him dearly.

At a safe distance, but still close enough to observe and to call out teasing suggestions to the toiling men, were Sarah; her twin toddlers,

Caroline and James; and Joe's wife, Gretchen, all seated comfortably on a faded Nine-Patch quilt spread in the shade of a stand of elms. Gretchen was showing Caroline how to make a daisy chain, except with dandelions. Sarah and young James were rolling and bouncing a ball back and forth, although James frequently forgot the game in his fascination with the construction site a few yards away.

The rattle of the wagon drew Gretchen's attention, and she rose, smiling, with young Caroline in her arms. "Wave to Auntie Sylvia," she instructed cheerfully, and the golden-haired girl obliged, welcoming Sylvia with a bright smile and an energetic wave of a chubby fist. Gretchen Hartley was in her late sixties, with gray hair cut in a pageboy and a thin frame clad in comfortable light blue capris and a yellow long-sleeved T-shirt rather than the prim skirts and blouses she wore for teaching. Although she had joined the Elm Creek Quilts faculty only two years before, she was one of their most experienced quilters, with flawless technical skills and a passion for traditional quilting that equaled Sylvia's own. She and Joe had been married for more than forty years, and anyone who saw them together could tell that they were absolutely devoted to each other. When they first met, Gretchen was studying to be a teacher, the first of her family to attend college, while Joe had gone straight from high school to a Pittsburgh steel mill, where he soon worked his way up to machinist. They had been married only a few years when a devastating workplace accident had left Joe with a broken back. Although his doctors warned the couple that Joe would never walk again, he had resolved to prove them wrong. Thanks to his union, Joe had received disability payments and a modest pension, which Gretchen had supplemented by working as a home economics teacher, leading workshops at quilting guilds, and, for a time, managing the most successful quilt shop in western Pennsylvania. As for Joe, as the years passed and he regained his mobility, he had built a second career as a skilled carpenter and expert restorer of antique furniture, a successful business he had re-

THE WORLD'S FAIR QUILT 11

located to a new woodworking shop in the estate's red barn when Gretchen joined the faculty of Elm Creek Quilt Camp.

Yet for all his experience, Joe was not the foreman this morning. That honor belonged to Matt, not only because the market stand was his idea, but because Matt had spent many years working for his father's construction firm in Uniontown. His father still hoped Matt would eventually come to his senses, resign from Elm Creek Manor, and take over McClure Construction so he could retire, confident that the company he had built from nothing but a toolbox and ambition would endure. It confounded the elder McClure that his son had ambitions of his own, and that while Matt was willing to drive three hours to Uniontown to pitch in on crucial projects when he could be spared from his duties at Elm Creek Manor, he always returned to Waterford.

"Hank is actually a very nice person except for this one incredibly annoying thing," Sarah had confided to Sylvia soon after the twins were born. "He has plenty of employees who want the work, but as far as he's concerned, only Matt will do."

"Perhaps it's fortunate that Uniontown is one hundred thirty miles away," Sylvia had observed.

"One hundred thirty-five," Sarah had corrected her, as if every mile mattered.

"What did you bring us?" Sarah called to Sylvia now, rising and holding out both hands to help little dark-haired James climb to his feet. Spotting Sylvia, James grinned widely and began toddling her way, releasing Sarah's fingers and picking up speed as he headed downhill.

"Slow down, sweetie," Sylvia cried out as the boy's gait became increasingly unsteady, but in two quick strides Sarah caught him from behind and swept him into the air. He shrieked with joy, and for a moment the hammering clamor fell silent as the men looked up from their work, Matt looking mildly alarmed, Joe and Andrew smiling indulgently.

Andrew's gaze traveled to Sylvia, and when their eyes met, his face lit up with affection. "What's in the wagon?" he asked, tucking a hammer into his belt and removing his safety glasses before descending the ladder.

Sylvia tugged sharply on the handle to get the wagon rolling again as her friends met her at the edge of the new parking lot. "Fresh apple cider from our first press of the season," she proclaimed, gesturing grandly to the dispenser. "Also, the last of Anna's apple-oatmeal muffins."

"Not the last ever, I hope," said Sarah, kneeling to steady the wagon as James, back on his own two feet, grasped the top edge and attempted to haul himself over the side.

"Heaven forfend," Sylvia replied as her friends gathered around the wagon and began helping themselves. "No, only the last of this batch. When camp resumes in March and Anna returns as our full-time chef, I'm sure she'll keep us well supplied with delicious treats again."

"I doubt we'll have to wait that long," said Andrew, pausing to rest a hand on Sylvia's shoulder and kiss her cheek before pouring himself a cup of cider. "Mark my words, in another week or two, we'll find Anna in the kitchen testing a new recipe she's invented, offering us samples and asking us if something needs less salt or whether she should add more chocolate."

"The answer to the last question is always yes," said Sarah, breaking a muffin in two and handing one half to each twin. "Lucky for us, the oven in Anna's apartment is too small for most of her baking pans."

Lucky for them, Sylvia thought, but unfortunate for Anna and Jeremy, her husband, a graduate student in history at Waterford College. When the couple had married in March, Sylvia had invited them to move into Elm Creek Manor, but they had declined, explaining that Jeremy needed to be close to campus. Sylvia took them at their word, but she suspected the newlyweds also wanted more privacy than living in the manor would allow. It was just as well. During quilt camp season, they needed every available room they could spare for paying guests.

"Since you're here, Sylvia, let me show you around," said Matt, devouring a muffin in two huge bites and rubbing his hands briskly to brush off the crumbs.

"I'd be delighted," Sylvia replied.

When Andrew gallantly offered her his arm, she took it, and together they followed the burly caretaker up the footpath to the market stand, which, she had to admit, was shaping up quite nicely. "This is where we enter," he said, swinging open a low hinged door that wasn't visible from the parking lot. "There's plenty of room to move around, and since the stand is open on all sides, we can have four workers helping customers at the same time."

"Apparently you're anticipating vast crowds," Sylvia remarked, the smell of fresh wood and sawdust tickling her nose as she strolled around the small, square building.

"Maybe not during our first season, but eventually." Matt gestured to the market stand's four counters. "We'll sell bags here, or customers can bring their own. Sarah got a good deal on reusable bags made from recycled plastic bottles. Eventually, we might upgrade to a version with our logo printed on the sides."

Sylvia regarded him, curious. "Do we have a logo?"

"Not yet. I figured we could adapt the Elm Creek Quilts logo. The name too. I was thinking Elm Creek Orchards. Or Bergstrom Orchards, if you prefer. Or we could call it Elm Creek Farm, as your great-grandparents did."

Sylvia mulled that over. "I'm touched by the homage to my great-grandparents, but I think I like Elm Creek Orchards best. May I take a day or two to consider it?"

"Of course," said Matt. "Take all the time you need."

"Not too much time," said Andrew. "We should decide on an official name before we advertise."

"Yes, of course," Sylvia said, wondering what they could spare for an advertising budget. She didn't want to complain, not with Matt and Andrew smiling at her, clearly hoping she would be pleased by all that they had accomplished thus far, but it pained her to imagine how many bushels of apples they would have to sell before they recouped their expenses. Likely she didn't need to imagine; the exact figure was probably recorded in one of Sarah's spreadsheets.

Matt thumped the nearest counters with an open hand. "I figured we could set up one set of scales here, and another on the opposite side. Customers will stop by on the way from the orchards to the parking lot, we'll weigh their bags, give them the grand total, and we'll attach a wristband to the bag—you know, like those Tyvek admissions bracelets you get at a concert—to show that they've paid."

Tyvek wristbands—yet another expense. "The concerts I attend require tickets, not wristbands or bracelets, but I think I know what you mean," Sylvia said. "But this is all rather dependent upon the honor system, isn't it? There's nothing to prevent people from strolling right past with their bags full of apples without paying, isn't that so?"

Matt hesitated. "When you put it that way, yeah, we are kind of counting on people's honesty and goodwill. I figure most people are generally decent, and they wouldn't want to steal apples from a small family orchard."

Sylvia shrugged. "Perhaps. Perhaps not."

"We could erect some barricades," said Andrew, giving her a wry, sidelong glance. "Set up security cameras. Hire a few bouncers."

"Don't tease," she retorted. "Whoever is working the stand will just have to keep a sharp eye out. I suppose the loss of a few apples here and there is the cost of doing business. After all, we'll never account for the overly eager customers who munch on an apple or two while they're picking."

Matt's smile faltered. "I think we can spare a free apple or two per customer, don't you?"

"Consider them free samples," said Andrew. "Once folks have a taste, they'll want to buy more."

"Assuming they pick only the ripe ones," countered Sylvia. "If they pick apples before they're ready—"

"I have a plan for that," Matt broke in. "We're going to make a sign with a map of the orchard. Every week, we'll update it with markers to indicate which varieties are ripe. We'll also explain the system to customers when they purchase bags. Just to be safe, we'll rope off the rows of trees that aren't ready to be picked yet, are past peak ripeness, or have already been picked clean."

"That's another thing," said Sylvia, ignoring her husband's increasingly deepening frown. "Picking the apples. Most people have no idea how to pick an apple properly. They grab one and give it a good yank, damaging the branch and shaking loose other apples that fall to the ground, wasted." She mimed the proper technique. "One is supposed to gently lift and remove the apple, as if one is unhooking it."

"I think Matt knows that, honey," said Andrew.

"Well, of course *he* does, but we're talking about amateurs running amok in my orchard."

"Running amok? Sylvia, honey—"

"Andrew, it's okay. She makes a fair point." Grimacing, Matt removed his hat, ran a hand through his blond curls, and tugged his cap back on again. "Okay, how's this? We'll put up another sign explaining how to properly pick an apple, with photos."

"Yet another sign?" Sylvia turned to gesture toward the gravel road—and was surprised to find her other friends gathered around behind her, watching the exchange with expressions that ranged from puzzlement to exasperation. Even the twins looked bemused. "We don't even have a sign marking that intersection yet."

"I'm on it," said Joe reassuringly. "It'll be in place by tomorrow afternoon. I'll start the new sign immediately after that."

Gretchen smiled and raised a hand. "I volunteer as apple-plucking demonstrator."

"And I'll take the photos," Andrew chimed in.

It seemed they had an answer for every possible objection. "Even so," said Sylvia, deflated, "I can't imagine how we'll possibly be ready to open a week from Saturday. Perhaps we should postpone."

Matt and Sarah exchanged a look of wide-eyed alarm. "We have to open then," said Sarah. "I've accounted for it in our budget."

"And the fall varieties are going to be ready for harvest," said Matt. "If our customers don't pick them, I'll have to do it myself. I didn't hire a crew for this part of the season."

"We went over the schedule a few days ago," Sarah added, regarding Sylvia quizzically. "You said everything looked good. Nothing's changed, but now you seem worried. What's wrong?"

"Nothing's wrong," Sylvia said, a bit flustered. "I'd simply rather be ahead of schedule than running behind. We have much to do and little time to do it."

At that moment, the sound of a car approaching drew her attention. Shading her eyes with her hands, she watched as a small compact car emerged from the woods, slowed as it approached the new intersection, and turned right toward the manor, disappearing from view behind the sheltering trees before it reached the bridge. "This is exactly what I was afraid of," she declared, gesturing to the car as it drove out of sight. "Apple pickers are showing up early and going the wrong way, all for the want of a sign."

"That was Gwen's car," said Sarah, infinitely patient. "She must be here on quilt camp business."

"On a weekday morning, with college back in session? Very unlikely." And yet the car had looked familiar, even at a distance. "I suppose I should see what's going on. Andrew, dear, would you bring the wagon back when you're finished?"

"Sure, honey," said Andrew, his expression troubled. She thanked him with a tight smile and hurried off before he could ask her what was bothering her, really.

Oh, she had made such a mess of things, she scolded herself as she retraced her steps to the manor. She had brought refreshments to show everyone that she supported Matt's scheme, but she had probably convinced them of the exact opposite. She vowed to make it up to them, especially to Matt. She would decide on a name for the orchard by the end of the day, wholeheartedly endorse any logo Matt recommended, and pay for a half-page ad in the *Waterford Register* out of her own pocket. If she showed enough enthusiasm, her friends might remember only the cider and muffins, and none of her fretting and frowning.

The sounds of construction resumed while she strode briskly across the new parking lot, but they faded behind her as she crossed the bridge over Elm Creek. All at once the manor came into view—three stories of gray stone and dark wood, its unexpected elegance enhanced by the rambling, natural beauty of its surroundings. Sure enough, Gwen's fuel-efficient hatchback was parked in the shade of the elms on the near side of the lot, but someone else was sitting on the bottom step leading up to the back door to the house—Gwen's lovely, auburn-haired daughter, Summer.

"Hello, dear," Sylvia exclaimed as Summer rose and bounded across the lot to meet her halfway. If Gwen would have been an unexpected visitor, Summer was only slightly less so. She was newly enrolled in the Waterford College Master of Library and Information Sciences program, and Sylvia would have assumed she was as busy on campus as her mother, a professor of American Studies. "What a delightful surprise!"

"I called, but no one picked up," Summer replied. "I figured you were around somewhere, so I decided to come by anyway."

"I'm sorry no one was here to meet you. It's rare to find no one at home at Elm Creek Manor." Sylvia gestured vaguely to the west.

"Everyone else is up at the orchard, working on the market stand, or watching others work, as the case may be."

"I'll stop by to see them on my way out," Summer said as they headed to the manor, side by side. "How's construction going?"

"Oh, fine, fine." Sylvia didn't want to linger on the topic. "How are you, dear? Is your semester off to a good start?"

"Yes, it's been great, actually," said Summer, her face lighting up with a smile. "I really like my professors, my classes are interesting, and I love working in Rare Books and Special Collections."

"I figured you would. You've spent so much time there through the years, delving into archives, researching one historical mystery or another." Sylvia paused at the foot of the back stairs to regard her young friend fondly. "And how is the quilt exhibit at Union Hall? You're still the official curator, correct?"

"Officially, yes, but now that the gallery is complete and I'm back in school, the docents from the Waterford Historical Society have taken over the daily tasks." Summer hesitated. "Actually, that's what I wanted to discuss with you, the quilt exhibit."

"Oh? Is there a problem? Has attendance dropped off since the grand opening gala?"

"No, not at all. We're seeing more visitors every week, thanks to word-of-mouth and positive reviews in the press. There's no problem with the exhibit. Well, there's an *issue*, but it's so minor it doesn't even qualify as a problem."

"Don't leave me in suspense, dear." Sylvia leaned against the railing and studied her, curious. "An issue that isn't a problem. What is it, then?"

Summer sat down on the top step, her gaze level with Sylvia's. "When Sarah loaned her quilt to the exhibit—you know, the twelve-block sampler she made when you taught her how to quilt—"

"Yes, of course. I know the one." Sylvia wasn't likely to forget it, ever. Stitch by stitch, as Sylvia had taught Sarah how to quilt, she had shared stories from her past as well as quilting lore. Those stories and the other confidences had not only bound them together in friendship, but had also inspired Sarah to save Elm Creek Manor from the malicious real estate developer's wrecking ball. It was no exaggeration to say that Sarah's Sampler had changed both of their lives for the better.

"I'd love to keep Sarah's Sampler in the exhibit longer. It's a classic example of the sampler as an instrument of learning, and everyone at the historical society loves the story behind it." Summer pulled a face, comically woeful. "But when Sarah loaned us the quilt, I promised that I would return it to her before the weather turned colder."

"A reasonable expectation on Sarah's part," Sylvia remarked. "She made it for her bed, not for a museum wall."

Summer gestured from the clear, sunny sky above to nearby trees, whose leaves were only beginning to take on their autumn hues. "I know it doesn't seem like it today, but it's nearly fall, and I'll need to return Sarah's quilt to her sooner rather than later."

"Which will leave an empty wall in the Union Hall gallery." Sylvia offered her a knowing smile. "Am I correct to assume you'd like me to provide you with a replacement?"

"Yes, I was hoping you would." Summer clasped her hands together in her lap and regarded Sylvia expectantly. "Actually, I have the ideal quilt in mind."

Sylvia hesitated, reluctant to disappoint her. "I've already loaned you the Log Cabin quilt my great-aunt Gerda Bergstrom made, and we discussed my other antique quilts when you were planning the exhibit. As I said then, those that would suit the exhibit's theme of having some significance to local history are too fragile for me to loan out."

"We didn't discuss *all* of your antique quilts," Summer reminded her. "My mom mentioned another quilt you showed her about two years ago, one you made with your sister. She said it would be perfect for the exhibit."

"A quilt I made with Claudia?" Sylvia gave a dry laugh. "That would be a rare thing indeed. We usually didn't get along as well as sisters should, and that made us very poor quilting partners."

And yet, they *had* worked together from time to time when they were young, on especially important projects—a crib quilt for Richard, a wedding quilt for his bride, a few others. The memories they evoked filled her with regret. If only she and Claudia had not squandered so many opportunities to be kind to each other, to be tolerant and forgiving, to admit their mistakes and reconcile—

Sylvia gave her head a little shake to drive the melancholy thoughts away. "Which quilt was your mother referring to?" she asked. "Did she describe it to you—the style, the block pattern, the colors? Did this quilt perhaps have a name?"

"She said it had a pieced border surrounding about a dozen appliquéd scenes, and that you and Claudia made it when you were in your early teens," Summer said. "As for a name, she called it the World's Fair Quilt."

2

January 1933

As icy snow crystals scoured the windows of her room on the third floor of Elm Creek Manor, Sylvia lay on her side on her bed propped up by pillows, contentedly lost in *The Tenant of Wildfell Hall*. Suddenly, a distant metallic thud resounded from elsewhere in the manor, followed immediately by her great-aunt Lydia shouting, "Richard David Bergstrom!"

An answering call followed in a calmer voice, likely her great-aunt Lucinda's, but not a peep from Richard. Sylvia sighed and turned a page.

Moments later, she heard footsteps swiftly approaching in the hallway outside her room. The door burst open, and there stood her younger brother, panting. "Hide me?" he begged, darting inside without waiting for an answer and slamming the door behind him.

Barely glancing up from her book, Sylvia raised the edge of her quilt and gestured beneath the bed. Flashing a grateful grin, Richard scampered across the room and ducked out of sight, jostling the mattress, muffling grunts of discomfort as he collided with books and boxes of keepsakes and whatever else she had forgotten down there.

Sylvia released the quilt and rolled over onto her back, adjusting the pillow behind her head.

She managed to read another page before two sharp knocks sounded on her door. Before she could respond, it opened—Did no one in this family understand the rules of a closed door?—and Claudia stepped inside, her hand lingering on the doorknob. Nearly fifteen, she was two years older than Sylvia, but she seemed to believe she was far wiser and more mature, more like the youngest of the grown-ups in the household instead of the eldest of the children. This was a frequent source of irritation for Sylvia, who was nearly as tall as her elder sister, definitely more clever, and absolutely certain they should be treated as equals.

"Is he in here?" Claudia asked, craning her neck to study every corner of the room. Her thick light brown hair rippled in shining waves down her back, held away from her pretty oval face by an emerald headband that set off her green eyes. The elder members of the family claimed that Claudia was the very image of Great-Grandmother Anneke Bergstrom, a known beauty, but they respected their ancestors too much to blame any of them for Sylvia's appearance. Her darker brown hair, "the color of wet tree bark," as Claudia put it, always looked unruly no matter how vigorously she assailed it with comb and brush. Her eyes were the color of faded denim, sometimes appearing more blue, sometimes gray. Her mother had fondly called them the color of the sky before a storm, smiling as she smoothed Sylvia's untamed locks away from her face and kissing her brow.

With Mother gone, no one had said anything nice about Sylvia's eyes in more than two and a half years.

Raising a finger, Sylvia read to the end of the paragraph before marking her place with a scrap of fabric and setting the novel aside. "Is *who* here?"

"Richard, obviously," Claudia retorted, exasperated. "You must have heard Great-Aunt Lydia calling for him."

Sylvia furrowed her brow and shook her head. "I heard something, a bang and then a shout."

"The bang was Richard crashing into the foyer wall in his wagon. He left a hole in the plaster."

Sylvia winced. "Is he okay? How's the wagon?"

"I don't know about the wagon, but considering how fast Richard sprinted up the stairs to flee the scene of the crime, I'm sure he's fine. But he won't be for long if he doesn't come out and accept responsibility."

Accepting responsibility was very important to Claudia, but Sylvia figured the longer Richard eluded capture the better, to give their great-aunt's anger time to subside. Still, she decided not to say so rather than provoke her sister, who didn't seem any happier to be searching for Richard than he would be to be found. Claudia adored their younger brother as much as Sylvia did, and if she caught him, she would only reluctantly drag him off to face Great-Aunt Lydia's justice.

Maybe Richard ought to go willingly. It wasn't as if he would be spanked or sent to bed without supper, not so close to his sixth birthday, not even for the crime of careening around the foyer in the wagon he knew was meant for outdoor play. Richard could be mischievous—especially on a day like this, with a fierce winter storm confining him to the house—but he was good-natured and kind. More than anything, he wanted to make their father, their uncle William, and their aunties proud. It was little wonder that none of the grown-ups could bear to bestow any punishment upon him more serious than a stern lecture.

With a pointed look for her sister, Sylvia gestured around the room. "I don't see him in here. Do you? Feel free to check the wardrobe." She picked up her book and shifted to a more comfortable position, but when Claudia didn't leave, she added, "Do you mind? You interrupted me in the middle of a chapter, and I want to finish before dinner."

"Aren't you going to help me look for him?"

"No, but I'll wish you good luck. Shut the door behind you when you go, would you?"

Scowling, Claudia stepped back into the hallway and yanked the door shut with a bang. Sylvia read on, listening for Claudia's footsteps receding down the hall.

A minute passed, and then another. Eventually Sylvia heard scuffling beneath her bed, followed by Richard poking his head out from beneath the quilt. "Is she gone?" he asked in a stage whisper. His tousled hair was the color of dark honey, the same as their mother's.

"For now."

"Good." Richard scrambled out from his hiding place, rubbing his nose with the back of his hand. "I couldn't hardly breathe under there. Did one of the barn cats get in the house?"

"That's not cat fur," Sylvia said as he brushed himself off. "Those are dust bunnies."

"No wonder I had to pinch my nose so I wouldn't sneeze. Don't you ever clean?"

"You're a fine one to talk. Have you seen your own room lately?" Sylvia set down her book and swung her legs over the side of the bed. "For goodness' sake, Richard, why were you riding your wagon in the foyer? You're almost six. You know better."

"I couldn't ride it outside, could I?" Richard gestured to the window, where icy snow pummeled the glass so fiercely it was as if a giant were flinging gravel at it. "Father said we had to stay inside until the storm passed. If I'd left my wagon outside, it would've gotten buried."

"Fair point, but that doesn't mean—"

"I only meant to bring it inside to keep it safe, but the marble floor in the foyer looked so smooth, I just had to see how fast the wagon would go on it." He spread his hands helplessly, his blue eyes earnest. "There must have been some snow on the wheels, and I guess it melted, and then the wheels slid, and then—crash."

"You're lucky it wasn't your head that hit the wall."

"I was careful." Something in her expression made him hastily add, "But maybe not careful enough."

"Obviously not, since you left a hole in the plaster." She patted the bed, and he took a seat beside her. "You can't hide in my room forever. Want my advice?"

He shrugged, glum. "I guess so."

"Go to Great-Aunt Lydia and tell her what you told me. Apologize for breaking the rules and promise to fix the wall. Father or Uncle William will help you. Then promise never to ride your wagon in the house again."

His face fell. "But that means I won't get to ride until spring!"

"Ride your sled instead. Outside."

"My sled is too small. I can't even fit my legs on it. It's like trying to slide downhill with two anchors dragging behind me."

Sylvia could see how that would be a problem. "You can borrow my sled."

He brightened. "Really?"

"Yes—after the storm passes, and after you make things right with Great-Aunt Lydia."

He hesitated, wincing, but then he nodded. "Okay. Will you come with me?"

"Sure." She stood up and held out her hand to him. "Let's get it over with."

Richard took her hand, but he released it the moment they stepped into the hallway, and he fell a pace behind as they headed for the stairs. Sylvia glanced over the railing to the foyer floor far below, but although she heard a murmur of voices, she didn't glimpse anyone. No doubt the aunts were conferring in the parlor, well aware that Richard would eventually turn himself in, if Claudia didn't find him first.

They headed downstairs, Richard's pace slowing with every step until Sylvia had to pause halfway and wait for him to catch up. "You can't even see the hole from here," he said, gesturing vaguely, too quickly for her to know where to look. "That's how small it is."

Sylvia smiled wryly and tousled his hair before continuing down the grand oak staircase, lightly resting her fingertips on the banister, worn smooth by the hands of the many Bergstroms who had inhabited the manor before her. It had been polished by the seat of Richard's trousers too, for he occasionally saved time and gained a thrill by sliding down the curved oak rail, although this was also forbidden. On their left, on the far side of the foyer, the black marble floor that had so tempted Richard ended in two long stairs descending to the tall double doors of the front entrance. On the wall opposite the staircase were the double doors to the ballroom, while on their right, an identical set led into the banquet hall. The newer, grander wing of the manor included not only the three-story foyer, banquet hall, and ballroom, but a vast library on the second floor, and the children's playroom on the third, as well as bedrooms and suites for the family and guests. Their grandfather David Bergstrom had added the new wing to the original farmhouse when their father was a boy, after Bergstrom Thoroughbreds had become one of the most successful horse farms on the East Coast. It was the only home Sylvia, Claudia, and Richard had ever known.

Once, not very long ago, Elm Creek Manor had been home to the entire extended Bergstrom family, grandparents and aunts and uncles and cousins all living together happily, mostly, and working for the family business. As far back as Sylvia remembered, though, a good many of the bedrooms went vacant except when relatives returned for important occasions like weddings or Christmas. Some of their father's brothers and cousins had found other work in other cities, and several cousins and aunts had married and moved away with their husbands. Two of their father's brothers had been killed in the Great War, and a sister and a sister-in-law had perished in the Spanish flu epidemic soon thereafter. Sylvia had never met those Bergstroms, but she had seen photographs and had heard so many stories that it often felt as if she had known them. But even though Elm Creek Manor was less bustling than it once had been, it still felt far from empty. Father, Claudia, Sylvia, and Richard called it home, of course, as did the great-aunts Lucinda and Lydia, who had never married. Father's youngest brother, William; his wife, Nellie; and their three children completed the family circle still residing on the ancestral estate.

The cook, the housekeeper, and the caretaker lived in the manor too, but the farmhands and grooms stayed in the mews north of the manor near the round pen and the pasture. Great-Aunt Lydia said the Bergstroms kept on more staff and hands than they could afford, but Father refused to send anyone away. "Where would they go? How will they make a living?" he asked, and of course no one had a good answer. Father and Uncle William paid what wages they could, with promises to make it up to them when times got better. In the meantime, if the staff and hired hands were content to work for room and board alone, Father and Uncle William would at least do that much for them.

But at the moment, no one else from their rather large household was there to observe as Richard led Sylvia across the foyer and showed her the hole in the plaster. To Sylvia's relief, it wasn't much larger than the wagon's handle grip. "It's not so bad," she said in an undertone, and her brother brightened a trifle.

Together they followed the murmuring voices into the older, west wing of the manor, the original gray stone farmhouse built by their great-grandfather Hans Bergstrom in 1858. Sylvia suspected Richard was tempted to turn left and flee down the hallway past the kitchen and out the back door, heedless of the snowstorm, but she nudged him toward the first room on the right, the formal parlor, where visitors were welcomed with coffee or tea, and if they were very lucky, some of Great-Aunt Lucinda's delicious cookies or Great-Aunt Lydia's scrumptious cakes. Sometimes the ladies of the family sewed and chatted there in the warmth from the fireplace and the bright glow of lamplight, but mostly the parlor was reserved for company. When it was just family, the Bergstrom ladies preferred the cozier west sitting room off the kitchen for its natural light and brighter, more modern colors.

Placing her hands on her brother's shoulders, Sylvia steered him toward the doorway, then gave him a gentle push forward. Richard squared his shoulders and stepped into the parlor.

All at once, the murmuring voices fell silent as Great-Aunt Lydia, Great-Aunt Lucinda, and sweet Aunt Nellie too all turned to regard him from their seats, resting their needlework in their laps, a sure sign that a serious conversation was about to begin, as unmistakable as the room they had chosen to deliver their inevitable judgment. Grandmother Elizabeth had brought the parlor's overstuffed sofas, embroidered armchairs, beaded lamps, and ornate cabinets to Elm Creek Manor when she married Grandpa David. Her new in-laws had looked askance at the antique furnishings, but to spare her feelings they had arranged everything in the little-used parlor and proclaimed it too fine for everyday use. Yet over time, as their affection for Elizabeth grew, the other Bergstrom ladies had acquired a nostalgic fondness for the Victorian décor. The parlor was still one of their more formal rooms, but Father had installed a very modern radio in the corner, which Great-Aunt Lydia concealed with a Grandmother's Fan quilt when it was not in use. Aside from the radio, what Sylvia liked best about the parlor were the tall windows that looked out upon the front verandah and the broad, wildflower meadow beyond, now covered with snowdrifts, sweeping downhill between the house and the dense forest of oak, maple, pine, and elm.

What none of the Bergstrom children liked about the parlor was that it was often where they were summoned to take responsibility for something.

"Hello, Richard," said Great-Aunt Lucinda, raising her eyebrows at him. "We were just talking about you."

Richard gulped and clasped his hands behind his back. He looked to Aunt Nellie for sympathy, but when she smiled sadly and shook her head, it was clear whose side she was on.

"Come in and sit down," said Great-Aunt Lydia, her voice a bit sharper than her sister's. "We need to have a little chat." Her gaze shifted to Sylvia. "Alone. Close the door, would you, dear?"

Sylvia nodded and obeyed. She didn't even think to wish her brother good luck first. The best she could do was to press her ear against the closed door and listen as he offered a sober confession, just as she had counseled him.

"What are you doing, Sylvia?"

Startled, Sylvia spun around to discover her nine-year-old cousin Alice peering up at her curiously. "Nothing," she quickly replied, scooting away from the door. Hoping for the best for her brother, she returned upstairs to her bedroom and her book.

She didn't see Richard again until suppertime, when he barely looked up from his plate and the grown-ups' conversation was unusually subdued. It was only afterward that Sylvia learned her brother's fate. The wagon would be banished to the barn until spring, and it would never enter the house again. With his father's guidance, Richard would repair the hole in the wall with plaster and paint. For the next two months, twice a day on Saturday and Sunday and immediately after school the rest of the week, he would report to the stables, where he would muck out the stalls and take care of any other tasks the hands assigned him.

Even though it was obvious his disgrace weighed on him, Sylvia thought Richard accepted his punishment rather well. She understood why too. He enjoyed working with Father, so repairing the wall would be fun. Also, he loved horses as much as Sylvia did, hanging around the stables, looking on without getting in the way, eagerly helping with any small tasks the indulgent stable hands could safely entrust to him. For the two months of his sentence, he would surely be diligent, industrious, and cheerfully occupied—and Sylvia figured maybe that was the point. If he hadn't been so bored this morning, he wouldn't have been racing his wagon in the foyer in the first place.

Claudia, who was afraid of horses and would have been absolutely miserable in his place, felt terribly sorry for him. The day after the incident, while Father and Richard were spreading a drop cloth on the black marble floor beside the damaged wall, she found Sylvia in the playroom, sitting cross-legged in the window seat and piecing an eight-pointed star from rich blue and snowy white fabrics. "Richard is heartbroken," Claudia announced, standing over Sylvia with a magazine clutched to her chest.

"I really don't think he is," Sylvia replied, threading a needle.

"Well, I do, and I think we should cheer him up by finding him the perfect birthday gift. If we put together all the allowances we've saved up, we should have enough to get him something nice."

Sylvia wished she had thought of it first. "I don't have much saved," she admitted, moving her fabric scraps, scissors, and thread out of the way so Claudia could join her on the window seat. Money was so tight that the sisters received only a nickel a month, and Richard a penny.

"It'll have to be enough." Claudia sat down with the magazine on her lap and gave it a resolute pat. Now Sylvia could see that it wasn't a magazine at all, but the Sears, Roebuck & Co. catalog, an excellent place to search for the perfect gift—another idea Sylvia wished she could claim as her own.

After some nudging and scooting apart until both sisters were comfortable, they spread the catalog open on the seat between them. "Maybe a nice football," Claudia mused, slowly and carefully turning the pages, one by one, admiring the illustrations and skimming each caption.

"No, not a football." Impatient, Sylvia tugged the catalog closer and swiftly flipped through ladies' garments and farm tools, searching for toys.

"You're going to tear it."

"No, I won't," Sylvia retorted, but she did slow down a bit rather than prove her sister right. A few more pages, and—"There," she said, tapping an illustration triumphantly. "A Flexible Flyer Racer. It's perfect. He's outgrown his old sled. He'll love this one."

"That *would* make up for not being able to use his wagon," Claudia conceded, studying the advertisement. "All right, we'll get him a sled. Does it have to be a Flexible Flyer Racer, though? Look at these Firefly Coasters on the opposite page—"

"They're too small."

"But they're much cheaper."

"Father always says you get what you pay for. See what it says here about the Racer? 'Improved Construction, All-Steel Front. More Effective and Easier Steering. High Grade Steel Runners—'"

"Thanks, I can read. But did *you* read *this*?" Claudia tapped twice on an alarming bit of print: The Racer cost $6.00. "I have two dollars and fifty cents. How much do you have?"

Sylvia would have to count to be sure. "I think I have about a dollar fifty."

Claudia pointed to the facing page. "The Firefly Coaster Number Twelve is only three dollars and thirty cents. It's forty-five inches long, so it wouldn't be too small for him."

"But it's not as well made. Look at the runners and the support braces. We'll save money today, but if the Firefly falls apart, we'll have to buy him a new sled for Christmas."

"If it falls apart after one winter, Father will return it to Sears and demand a refund." Yet Claudia continued studying the illustrations, frowning thoughtfully. "Maybe Father will give us an advance on our allowances."

"Or we could do some extra chores to earn the rest."

"Maybe, but there's another problem. Even if we somehow scraped together enough money and ordered a sled today, it wouldn't arrive in time for Richard's birthday."

Sylvia thought quickly. "We could ask Father to drive us to the Sears store in Harrisburg and we could buy one in person."

"In the middle of a snowstorm?"

"Not today. Tomorrow."

"We have school—if it isn't canceled again."

"On Saturday, then."

Claudia paused, apparently at a loss for additional objections. "I guess it wouldn't hurt to ask him."

Sylvia snatched up the catalog and bounded to her feet. "Let's ask him now."

"He's with Richard now," said Claudia, making a grab for the catalog, but Sylvia held tight. "You'll give away the surprise."

"Then I'll wait until he's alone." Sylvia tried to pull the catalog from her sister's grasp. "Let go."

"*You* let go."

The sisters pulled on opposite edges of the catalog, each stubbornly refusing to yield, until Claudia stumbled backward, Sylvia tumbled after her, and the catalog flew through the air, landing a few feet away, spine-up and pages splayed open.

"Now you've done it," Claudia grumbled, stooping to pick up the ill-treated wish book.

As her sister tried to straighten a newly dog-eared corner of the front cover, Sylvia glimpsed a familiar word. "Wait. What did that say?"

"What did *what* say?"

Before her sister could tighten her grip, Sylvia snatched the catalog away. "It was something about quilts." Swiftly she paged back until she found the full-page, multicolored advertisement on the inside front cover—and when her gaze fell upon a small, yellow text box at the bottom of the page, she drew in a breath, astounded.

"What is it?" Claudia demanded, peering over her shoulder. "Are those drawings of model buildings? What is that map supposed to be? Oh, I know. 'A Century of Progress.' 'Important Points of Interest at the Fair.' This must be about the World's Fair opening in Chicago this summer. Father told us about it, remember?"

"I remember he told us about the exposition," said Sylvia, "but he didn't say anything about *this*."

She pointed to the yellow-boxed text, then tapped the headline twice for emphasis. After taking in the first few words, Claudia gasped, so close to Sylvia's ear that Sylvia instinctively waved her away as if she were a buzzing gnat. Then both sisters held perfectly still, transfixed by the words on the page.

Century of Progress

QUILTING CONTEST

$7,500 IN PRIZES

Do you quilt? If you do, you'll be interested in entering Sears's great nationwide Quilting Contest, being held in connection with the Chicago World's Fair. Anyone may enter a quilt in this contest. At the close of the contest the winning quilts will be exhibited in the Sears building at the Fair.

For full particulars, write Sue Rogers, Home Advisor, for free circular 9452L. Address your letter to your nearest Sears mail-order house.

"Seven thousand five hundred dollars in prizes," Claudia breathed. "Can you imagine what we could do with that much money?"

"That probably wouldn't all go to one person," said Sylvia, thinking it through. "It says *prizes*, plural. There will probably be a grand prize, and then second and third prizes and so on."

"But even so—"

"Yes," said Sylvia. "Even so."

It was an enormous sum. They could buy Father a new pair of boots. They could buy Richard new clothes to replace those he was swiftly outgrowing. Father could pay the staff and the hands better wages, like in the old days before the Great Depression. Sylvia could save for college, because she was determined to go and her mother had told her she could. They could put money aside for a rainy day—although as Great-Aunt Lucinda said, if their days got any rainier they'd have to start bailing.

But it was not only the prize money. Sylvia felt a frisson of excitement race through her as she imagined one of her own quilts on display in the Sears Pavilion at the World's Fair—there it was, number seven on the map, nearly on the shore of Lake Michigan, right next to Soldier Field and diagonally across the street from the Field Museum. How thrilling it would be to be ranked among the best quilters in the country!

"Is there a children's division, like at the county fair?" Claudia asked.

Sylvia read the small announcement again, then skimmed the surrounding columns of text, which described the services that would be offered in the Sears building during the fair. "It doesn't say," she reported, shaking her head.

"I hope there's a children's division," said Claudia fervently. "We wouldn't stand a chance if we had to compete against older, more experienced quilters, especially if they're as good as Mother and the aunts are—as the aunts are, as Mother was—"

"Speak for yourself," Sylvia retorted, pretending not to notice her sister's mistake. Their mother's quilts were lovely and exquisitely made—and it was so unfair, so terribly wrong and unfair, that she would never make another. The family cherished the quilts Mother had left behind, remembering her graceful hands working the needle through the layers of soft fabric, remembering her sparkling eyes and gentle smile as she had sat at the quilt frame with the other Bergstrom women, laughing, chatting, and teasing one another as their tiny, meticulous stitches united the colorful pieced top with the smooth backing, a soft, fluffy layer of batting in between. Mother's quilts had already become precious family heirlooms, and someday Sylvia would show them to her own children and tell them about the wonderful grandmother they had never met.

But that wasn't something she could say aloud to her sister, not without breaking down in tears, not even now, after the sharp, fresh anguish of losing her mother had condensed into a dull, persistent ache of missing her every day.

"Speak for yourself," Sylvia repeated, less sharply, with a catch in her throat. "I'm not afraid to compete against the adults. I've been quilting for more than eight years. That's more experience than what some of those ladies have, I'll bet. But if you're afraid to try—"

"I'm not afraid," Claudia snapped, snatching the catalog from Sylvia for emphasis. "I'll prove it. I'll write to Sue Roberts today and ask for the official rules."

Suddenly inspiration struck. "I have a better idea."

Claudia rolled her eyes, but when Sylvia explained, she agreed it was a good plan.

They waited until evening after Richard had been sent to bed. Then they sought out their father in the library, his favorite place in the manor—and maybe Sylvia's too—where he often relaxed at the end of a busy day. French doors opened into the stately second-floor room spanning the entire width of the manor's south wing. At the moment the curtains were drawn against the cold, but during the day, light would spill in through tall diamond-paned windows on the east and west walls. Between the windows stood tall bookcases, shelves bowing slightly under the weight of hundreds of volumes. A fire burning in the large stone fireplace on the south wall made the library warm and snug, but when summer returned to the Elm Creek Valley, gentle cross breezes would keep the room comfortably cool even on the sunniest days. Sylvia thought they might find their father seated in the tall leather chair behind his large oak desk, where he wrote letters, kept the books, and managed his business affairs, but he was seated in one of two armchairs placed before the blazing fireplace, his feet resting on a footstool, his gaze fixed on the book resting on his lap. In the center of the room other chairs and sofas were arranged in a square, inviting visitors to sit and rest awhile, but the sisters quietly made their way around them and halted a respectful distance from their father, eager to speak to him, but reluctant to interrupt his reverie.

He glanced up from his book, offered them a fond but weary smile, and beckoned them closer. "What it is, girls?" he asked, marking his place and setting the book aside. "You both look rather determined."

Claudia promptly produced the Sears catalog, which she had been carrying behind her back. Their father listened as they explained how badly they wanted to get Richard the Flexible Flyer Racer for his birthday, but they didn't have quite enough money, although they were willing to work for it. They would also need Father—or Uncle William, or Great-Aunt Lucinda, whoever was available and willing—to take them to Harrisburg on Saturday morning before his party to buy the sled in person because if they ordered it the usual way, it wouldn't arrive in time for his birthday on Tuesday.

"And while we're there," Sylvia said, taking the catalog from her sister and paging back to the inside front cover, "we want to pick up the rules for this quilt contest. We want to enter and we think we can win."

Father's brow furrowed, and it looked to Sylvia as if he was trying to hide a smile. He was, the sisters agreed, very handsome for a man his age. He was tall, fit, and usually tanned from working outside with the horses, though not so much now, in midwinter. He had a kind smile, blue eyes like Sylvia's, and thick curly hair that had once been so dark brown it was almost black, but over the past three years had become threaded with gray. "You can't both win," he pointed out. "I don't want any resentment between you. Would you be good sports about it, win or lose?"

Sylvia and Claudia exchanged a quick look. "We figured one of us could take first place and the other second," said Sylvia, although they hadn't discussed it. "That means more prize money for the family."

"I see." He nodded thoughtfully. "Do you think you have a chance? I have to assume the best quilters in the country will be vying for the purse, not to mention the glory."

"We think we have a very good chance," said Claudia, "even if there isn't a separate children's division and we have to compete against the grown-ups."

"Mother taught us everything she knew," Sylvia chimed in.

"Maybe not everything," Claudia quickly amended. "But we've been quilting since we were little, and we're not afraid to try."

Sylvia shot her a sidelong look, feeling an unexpected flicker of admiration. Father respected courage, so that was the perfect thing to say.

"All right, then," he said, after mulling it over a moment longer. "You may enter the contest, and I'll make up the difference for the cost of the sled. But if I take you girls to Harrisburg on Saturday morning, Richard will want to come along. He'll see the sled, and that will spoil your birthday surprise."

Sylvia's heart sank, but Claudia shook her head slightly as if this was no problem at all. "He has to stay home and help get ready for his party. He can't go. He'll understand."

"But if we go without him, he would be so disappointed," Sylvia objected. "I don't want that."

"I may have a solution," Father said. "I'll go to Harrisburg tomorrow, while you children are at school. I'll bring the sled home and hide it under my bed, where Richard would never think to look. We'll keep it a secret until you two give it to him after his birthday party. What do you say?"

"That's a wonderful idea," Claudia exclaimed, clasping her hands together.

"Thank you so much," said Sylvia, flinging her arms around her father. "You're the best father ever in the whole, entire world!"

He chuckled and patted her on the back. "The whole, entire world? Not just Pennsylvania?"

"The whole, entire world," Sylvia repeated emphatically, her voice a bit muffled against his chest. "Only—could you please, please, be extra sure to bring home the quilt contest rules too, since we won't be there to remind you?"

"Yes, Sylvia," he said, his laughter a low rumble in her ear. "I'll be extra sure."

3

September 2004

For a moment, Sylvia could only gaze back at Summer, speechless. The quilt she and Claudia had made for the Chicago World's Fair so many years ago was perhaps the last one she would have expected her young friend to request for the Waterford Historical Society's exhibit.

And considering how fervently Sylvia had once longed for that particular quilt to be displayed among the nation's finest, where hundreds of thousands of fairgoers could have admired it, she couldn't explain why she hesitated to loan it to a much smaller, local exhibit now.

"Why don't we discuss this in the kitchen?" she said, gesturing to the back door. "There's fresh apple cider in the fridge."

"Sounds great." Rising from her seat on the stairs, Summer opened the door and held it for Sylvia, then followed her into the back foyer. Pausing to adjust to the dimmer light and the unusual hush of the unoccupied manor, Sylvia gave herself a little shake and led the way through the first doorway on the left.

Nine years ago, when Sylvia had returned to Elm Creek Manor after a fifty-year absence, she had found it in a dreadful state, with the kitchen particularly dismaying. Claudia had left rubbish everywhere, a startling sign of how she had changed through the years. The most modern appliances had dated from the 1940s, except for one rickety microwave, which could have been the first model ever invented from the look of it. Poor lighting, clogged pipes, broken stovetop burners— the list of essential repairs and recommended upgrades had gone on for pages, but as they prepared to launch Elm Creek Quilt Camp, Sylvia had settled for making the place clean and functional. For the first few years, the Elm Creek Quilters had taken turns cooking three tasty, satisfying meals a day for their dozens of quilt campers, but adapting to the kitchen's "charming quirks," as Sylvia had euphemistically put it, had been a perpetual struggle. Two years ago, when they realized they couldn't do without a professional chef any longer, Anna had joined the staff on the condition that the kitchen would be thoroughly renovated. Sylvia had been all too happy to assent. After camp had ended for the season, contractors had gutted the space, knocking out a wall and expanding into the adjacent sitting room, once the Bergstrom women's favorite place to quilt. At first Sylvia had been reluctant to give up the room that held so many fond memories, but when she examined the blueprints, she realized that the remodel couldn't be completed otherwise.

Now, where the sitting room had once been, there were state-of-the-art appliances, marble counters, efficient workstations, a central island, spacious cabinets, and a walk-in pantry. In the half of the room closer to the entrance, eight cozy booths lined the walls. A dark walnut refectory table with two long benches on either side—a well-made, much-loved heirloom from the manor's early days—stood between the booths and the cooking area. On the wall above the nearest booth hung a bright, cheerful quilt Sylvia and Anna had sewn from scraps of fabric from Great-Aunt Lydia's collection of cotton feed-sack aprons, an appliquéd still life of fruits and vegetables framed by blocks evocative of the room in which it was displayed: Corn and Beans, Cut

Glass Dish, Honeybee, and Broken Dishes. The kitchen had become the perfect place to create nourishing, delicious meals, but it was also a cozy gathering spot for faculty and campers alike to catch up with friends over a cup of tea and a snack any time of day.

Sylvia gestured to her favorite booth, where a west-facing window looked out upon the parking lot and the tree-lined creek beyond it. As Summer took a seat, Sylvia went to the cupboard and retrieved two glasses. "How are your classes going?" she asked as she continued on to the refrigerator for the pitcher of apple cider. "I imagine it must be rather exciting to start a new graduate program, even though you already know Waterford College so well."

When she turned around to the counter to pour, she found Summer smiling a bit quizzically, and Sylvia remembered that she had already asked a nearly identical question before they had come inside. "It *is* exciting," Summer replied, too kind to draw attention to Sylvia's distraction. "It's quite a leap to change both my program of study and my university midway through graduate school, but I'm absolutely certain I made the right choice."

"That's wonderful, dear. I'm so pleased for you." Sylvia crossed the room, put the glasses on the table, and sat down in the booth opposite her young friend, who promptly poured. "How does it feel to be living at home with your mother again, back in your old bedroom?"

"It's actually really nice." Summer set down the pitcher and gestured as if to take in the whole manor. "Nothing beats living here, of course, like I did this past summer, but my mom's house is so convenient to campus, I'm saving a ton on rent, and my mom and I are having a lot of fun together. We take turns cooking dinner and we share each other's quilting supplies, just like old times."

"I'm sure your mother is as delighted with the arrangement as you are." Sylvia paused to sip her apple cider. "Probably more so. And are you still seeing that nice young man from the library? Enrique, I believe his name is?"

"Yes, his name is Enrique, and, yes, we're still seeing each other, but please don't ask me where it's heading because it's much too soon to tell." Amused, Summer patted the tabletop briskly, a little drumroll to signal an end to that particular topic. "So, about that quilt—"

"Of course, dear." Sylvia took another sip of cider, then folded her hands on top of the table. "Let's get down to business. You're considering my World's Fair quilt for your exhibit at Union Hall. I'm certainly honored, but I admit I don't understand why you wish to include it. The Bergstrom family is already well represented in the gallery, and surely you have other options."

"None that I'd prefer to your quilt," said Summer. "It's a remarkable historical artifact. My mom said it's beautifully made too, especially considering that you and your sister were so young at the time. You might have been the youngest participants in the contest, and you were almost certainly the youngest to proceed as far as you did."

"I've often wondered whether we were," Sylvia admitted. "I suppose there's no way to know."

"You'd be surprised what one can find in the library. If we had a list of the participants' names and hometowns, we could search census records for birth years and calculate their ages." Summer leaned forward and rested her arms on the table. "Is that why you have misgivings about lending the quilt, because it's one of your early works?"

"Who says I have misgivings?"

Summer pressed her lips together as if attempting to smother a laugh. "I'm sensing some reluctance. Or maybe you're concerned that people will mistake Claudia's work for yours? You've said that she wasn't exactly the most skilled quilter ever."

"That's one way to put it." And yet, until Summer brought it up, it hadn't occurred to her that anyone might attribute Claudia's work to herself. Sylvia could distinguish her own quilting from her sister's at three paces in poor light. "Claudia rarely matched her points properly, her seam allowances could vary by as much as an eighth of an inch, and she chopped off the tips of her triangles with impunity." She paused to reflect before amending, "But that was mostly when she was younger. Eventually she overcame most of her bad habits and became a rather decent quilter."

"Is that why you and your sister rarely collaborated? Because there was such a difference in your abilities? Wait, no, that can't be it. You always said the women of your family would piece blocks or work together around the quilt frame. I can't imagine you were all equally skilled, and yet you still enjoyed quilting together."

"We did enjoy it, very much so, and our talents, interests, and styles ran the gamut. Learning from one another, especially passing down knowledge between the generations, was very important in our family." Sylvia traced a line of condensation down the side of her glass and sighed. "Loving cooperation was the rule among the Bergstroms, but Claudia and I were the exception."

"Why do you suppose that was?"

Sylvia shrugged. "I suppose it all comes down to sibling rivalry. Claudia was very pretty, and I was not. She was two years older, but I did better in school. And yet our teachers liked Claudia best. Everyone did."

"Everyone?"

"How could they not? Claudia was outgoing and cheerful, while I was sulky and sensitive. I used to think that it must have been a terrible disappointment to our mother, to have a child like me after doing so well the first time."

"Sylvia," Summer exclaimed. "I'm sure your mother never felt that way."

"Likely not," Sylvia acknowledged. "I'm simply explaining how I felt as a girl. I was the better quilter, which made Claudia jealous. Claudia was considered superior to me in virtually every other way, which made me frustrated and resentful. You might not understand this, dear, being an only child yourself."

"I always thought it would be rather nice to have a brother or a sister."

"I suppose it usually is. Claudia and I both got along well with our younger brother, for example." Sylvia fell silent, remembering. "Quilting was an especially fraught subject for me and Claudia, going back to our very first quilting lesson."

"You were—how old? Six or seven?"

"Five," Sylvia corrected. "I was five and Claudia was seven. I'm sure I've told you this story before."

Summer shook her head. "No, you haven't. You might've told Sarah, but you haven't told me."

"Haven't I?" Sylvia paused to gather her thoughts. "Well, one winter day when I was in kindergarten and Claudia second grade, it snowed so terribly that we couldn't go to school. Claudia was relieved because she needed the extra time to study for a spelling test, but I fretted, glaring out of the nursery windows and stomping about, annoyed that the other children would learn something and I would fall behind."

Summer looked bewildered. "The nursery?"

"The playroom, dear. We called it the nursery back in the day." Sylvia smiled to herself, remembering. "My mother assured me that none of the other children would be going to school that day either, but I was not consoled until she promised to teach us something new herself. 'But not reading or math,' she said, to my surprise. 'It's time you two girls learned to quilt.'"

"A momentous day," remarked Summer, smiling. "The launch of the brilliant career of a master quilter."

"You flatter me, dear. Since rotary cutters and strip piecing hadn't been invented yet, my mother taught us to piece simple Nine-Patch blocks the old-fashioned way, using stiff cardboard templates. We carefully selected the prettiest light and dark fabrics from our mother's basket of scraps, cut out the little squares with scissors, and sewed them together using a running stitch. By late afternoon we had each finished several small blocks." Sylvia sighed. "We were having a wonderful time, but it couldn't last."

"Why not?"

"Because my mother had us working together on a single quilt, rather than each of us working on our own. In hindsight, I'm sure she thought it was practical for two young beginners to help each other, but as the hours passed, it slowly dawned on us that only one of us could use the quilt at a time."

Summer winced. "Let me guess: You and Claudia didn't like taking turns?"

"No, but it bothered me much more than my sister."

"Why so?"

"Because Claudia *always* got to be first in everything simply because she was the eldest. I always came second, always—but I was determined that this time would be different. I counted the blocks in my pile, and then those on the floor by Claudia's side. I had finished four, but she had finished only three. So I announced that since I was doing more of the work, I should get to use the quilt first. It was only fair."

"Maybe you should've suggested flipping a coin instead."

"That never occurred to me. Nor to my sister, I suppose, since she retorted that she would match me block for block. We argued back and forth for a while, but eventually my mother admonished us to stop bickering. We would share the work and the quilt equally."

"And that put an end to it?"

"Of course not. As soon as our mother left the room, the race was on. We scrambled for fabric, fought for the scissors, and pieced our blocks with the biggest stitches you've ever seen. I blazed through my sewing, but Claudia couldn't keep up the pace. She struggled to thread her needle. Sometimes she had to pick out stitches after sewing the wrong side of one piece to the right side of the other. She was obviously frustrated, but I didn't feel a single pang of sympathy. I was too determined to win."

"Oh, Sylvia, no," teased Summer. "Poor Claudia."

"Yes, poor Claudia, indeed. Suddenly she flung down her sewing and burst into tears. 'It's not fair,' she sobbed. 'You always do everything best. You always beat me. I hate you!' And with that, she fled the room."

"Wait. She said she *hated* you?" Summer's eyes widened. "That must have stung. Did you go after her, try to make up?"

"No. I barely glanced up from my work except to count the blocks Claudia had scattered as she ran away. There were six. I had nine, including the one I was still working on."

"Congratulations, I guess?"

"Hardly. My mother must have heard my sister's outburst, because moments later, she entered the room and asked me what was going on. 'Nothing, Mother,' I said, perfectly innocent. 'I'm just sewing, like you told us to.'"

"What a perfect little angel."

"Oh, my mother knew better, I assure you. She told me to tell Claudia I was sorry, and to behave nicely. When I protested that I hadn't done anything wrong, she frowned at me, a sad and disappointed frown. I felt simply awful. She never looked at Claudia that way."

"Poor little Sylvia."

"Yes, poor little me," she replied, pulling a face to show she wasn't proud of her younger self. "I found my sister in her room, face down on the bed, sobbing into her pillow. I couldn't leave without obeying my mother's instructions, so I took a deep breath and said, 'Mother said to say I'm sorry, so . . . I'm sorry I sewed faster than you.'"

Summer laughed. "You didn't!"

"I did. I know, I know. That wasn't the apology I was supposed to make, but at least I was honest."

"What did Claudia say?"

"Oh, you know how children are. She called me a mean brat and ordered me out of her room." Sylvia shrugged, rueful. "One could hardly blame her. Word of the incident quickly spread among the family, and I was in disgrace. Claudia didn't speak to me for the remaining two days we were snowed in. When school resumed, she finally forgave me and let me help her with her spelling."

"So after you made up, you finished the quilt together?"

"Oh, heavens, no, not together. Claudia never touched those Nine-Patch blocks again. Eventually I put all of the blocks together and finished the quilt on my own. I offered it to Claudia, but when she said sleeping under it would give her nightmares, I gave it to my cousin Elsa, who had just turned four." Sylvia glanced at Summer's empty glass. "Would you care for more cider? I believe this is one of our best pressings yet."

"I would," said Summer, reaching for the pitcher.

As Summer refilled their glasses, Sylvia's thoughts returned to those days long ago when she and Claudia had quarreled and played and argued and helped each other, shifting between tentative friendship and heated enmity, often several times within the same day. "After that bad beginning, my sister and I didn't attempt to make another quilt together for two years," she said, remembering. "Then, when I was seven and Claudia was nine, our parents told us that they were going to have another child. My goodness, but we were excited. Claudia looked forward to helping Mother take care of the baby, I was eager for a new playmate, and of course, we both wanted to welcome our new brother or sister with a crib quilt."

Summer's eyebrows rose. "Dare I hope that you two learned your lesson from the Nine-Patch fiasco and cooperated nicely?"

Sylvia shook her head. "Ordinarily I believe hope is a very good thing, but in this case, yours would be misplaced. Claudia said that she should be in charge of making the baby's quilt because she was the oldest. I said I should be in charge because I was the better quilter. So Claudia said, 'If that's the way you're going to be, I'll make the quilt all by myself.' Naturally, I piped up that I would make my own quilt for the baby too."

"If that would keep you from arguing, why not? A baby needs more than one quilt."

"You underestimate our ability to argue. We merely changed the point of contention. Now we fought over whose quilt the baby would use first. Naturally Claudia said hers, since she was the oldest. My, how that argument infuriated me. Claudia would always be the oldest, and nothing could ever change that, so she would always use her status as the eldest sibling to justify every privilege."

Summer's brow furrowed slightly. "Didn't you ever get any special treatment for being the youngest? My friends who have younger siblings used to complain about that all the time."

Sylvia paused to consider. "No, I didn't, perhaps because I wasn't the youngest child in the household. That distinction belonged to my cousin Peter, although the new baby would be taking over that role soon."

Summer nodded, but a slight frown suggested that she didn't think this was fair.

"So, I countered Claudia's argument by declaring that the baby should use the quilts in the order that they were finished," Sylvia continued, "which obviously meant that my quilt would be first. Well, that just made her angry. As our argument escalated, our mother intervened. She decided that we would work together on a single quilt."

"Because that worked so well the last time."

"Yes, my thoughts exactly. Claudia and I pouted and complained, but our mother insisted, so we had to go along. We agreed that I would pick the block pattern and Claudia could select the colors. I chose Bear's Paw."

"That's a rather complicated pattern for two young girls, don't you think?"

Sylvia shrugged. "It's true that we would have many triangle points to match, but I figured that since there were no curved seams or set-in pieces, Claudia couldn't ruin it too badly. Then it was Claudia's turn to choose the colors. 'We'll use pink and white,' she declared, 'with a little bit of green.' Well, I didn't like this at all. 'What if it's a boy?' I asked. 'It's a baby,' Claudia retorted. 'It won't care. You picked the pattern. I get to pick the colors. You can't pick everything.'"

"She's not wrong," Summer noted.

Sylvia shrugged. "Perhaps not. But again our mother intervened. 'Compromise, girls,' she said, and she shook her head and gave me that sad and disappointed frown again. I don't think Claudia ever received one of those looks. 'Okay,' I said to my sister. 'Then you pick the pattern and I'll pick the colors.' I should have known better. You'll never guess what she chose."

"I wouldn't even try. How bad was it?"

"It was dreadful! It was quite possibly the worst block she could have chosen."

"Because it was super difficult?"

"Not only that. She picked Turkey Tracks. Turkey Tracks! Obviously, I immediately declared that this was a terrible idea."

Summer pulled a face, bewildered, but then she sat back in her seat, a faint smile playing at the corners of her mouth. "Oh, I get it. The superstition. The Turkey Tracks block is also called Wandering Foot."

"Precisely. Our grandmother had told us the old stories, so Claudia should have known better. If you give a child a Wandering Foot quilt, they'll never be content to stay in one place. They'll always be restless, eager to leave home before they're ready, roaming around, never settling down." When Summer regarded her skeptically, Sylvia added, "I'm sure many of these old tales have no basis in reality, but sometimes there's a kernel of truth in the folklore. Either way, why take unnecessary chances?"

"Sure," said Summer, nodding. "Fair point."

Sylvia suspected Summer was only humoring her, but she didn't mind. "Perhaps I was too credulous as a girl, but the idea of giving a baby a Wandering Foot quilt troubled me. I told Claudia I'd rather use the Bear's Paw pattern and any colors she wanted, but she had made up her mind to use Turkey Tracks and would not budge. Resigning myself to it, I selected the nicest blue and yellow pieces from my mother's overflowing basket, with a cream off-white fabric for the background. If we had to make a Wandering Foot quilt, and I didn't see any way out of it, then at the very least I was going to make it from my lucky colors." Sylvia offered a self-deprecating laugh. "Listen to me go on. Bad luck blocks, good luck colors. Perhaps I'm a bit superstitious after all—or at least I was as a girl."

"How did the quilt turn out?" asked Summer. "Did you finish this one?"

"Oh, yes. Despite my concerns, it was quite charming in the end, soft and warm, and very cheerful with all those pretty blues and yellows. More to the point, Claudia and I managed to complete it without mishap or serious argument."

"Well done, Bergstrom sisters. Your mother must have been pleased."

"I believe so." Sylvia mulled it over for a moment, then sighed. "Unfortunately, I fell back into old bad habits the next time we worked on a quilt together."

"Oh, Sylvia," Summer chided her playfully. "Say it isn't so."

"I would if I could, dear." Sylvia paused, thinking. "Let me see. This would have been the following year, about eight months later. My mother had spent the previous two years working on a beautiful appliqué quilt as a twentieth wedding anniversary gift for my father—"

"I know the one you mean," Summer broke in. "Elms and Lilacs.

It was one of the five quilts Claudia sold after you left Elm Creek Manor. You and Andrew eventually found it at that boutique in Sewickley."

"Found what was left of it, you mean." A quirky artist had made several very expensive quilted jackets from her mother's long-lost masterpiece. Andrew had bought Sylvia the last one. If not for Summer's internet sleuthing skills, Sylvia would not have even that precious remnant.

Elms and Lilacs was Sylvia's favorite of all her mother's quilts; indeed, it was quite possibly her favorite out of all the quilts she had ever seen. A masterpiece of appliqué and intricate, feathery quilting, the Elms and Lilacs quilt displayed her mother's skills at their finest. The circular wreath of appliquéd elm leaves, lilacs, and vines in the center gave the quilt its name; a graceful, curving double line of pink and lavender framed it. The outermost border carried on the floral theme with elm leaves tumbling amid lilacs and other foliage, and intertwining pink and lavender ribbons finished the scalloped edge. The medallion style allowed for open areas, which her mother had filled with elaborate hand quilting.

"Elms and Lilacs was truly my mother's finest work," said Sylvia. "I wish you could have seen it. My sketch didn't do it justice. My mother appliquéd each lilac petal and elm leaf by hand, using fabrics in the new pastel hues that were coming into fashion. She quilted around the floral motifs in an echo pattern, as if the leaves and petals had fallen into a pond and had sent out gentle ripples. In the open areas, she had quilted feathered plumes over a fine background crosshatch. Every stitch and scrap of fabric she had put into that quilt had a meaning. The foliage was inspired by Elm Creek Manor, and the lilacs represented the cornerstone patio, which my father had built for her."

"You've always said the cornerstone patio was your mother's favorite place on the estate."

"But did I ever tell you that I helped my mother finish her quilt?"

Summer's eyes widened. "No, never."

"Because of her declining health. Otherwise my mother might not have let me help. Let *us*," Sylvia amended. "Claudia helped too."

She smiled, remembering how her father and Uncle William had struggled to disassemble the quilt frame and carry it from the west sitting room upstairs to the nursery. Her mother had hidden her work from their father while she was completing the top, but in order to preserve the secret, she had to quilt the top unobserved as well. She explained that she wanted to quilt in the nursery so she could keep an eye on the children while she worked, a reason all the more believable because it was true.

It soon proved to be a bit *too* true. Mother could hardly make any progress, because as soon as she sat down and slipped her thimble on her finger, young Richard would toddle over and demand to be picked up. She would laugh and settle him on her lap, but she would barely manage to put a few more stitches into the quilt before he would squirm and try to grab the scissors.

"I remember the day my mother agreed to let us help," said Sylvia, cupping her hands around her glass, now empty, still pleasantly cool to the touch. "It was in May. I remember that clearly because her long-estranged mother, recently widowed, came to live with us in June, only a few days before my parents' anniversary. But she's not a part of this story, and she was not a pleasant woman, so let's say no more of her."

"A story for another day," Summer agreed, nodding to encourage her to continue.

"As I was saying, it was a May afternoon. My mother and we three children were upstairs in the nursery, but she couldn't get anything accomplished because Richard kept distracting her. 'Let Mother quilt,' Claudia scolded him. 'Don't be naughty.' I protested that he wasn't being naughty; he was just being a baby. 'But Mother needs to finish her quilt,' Claudia retorted.

"'I need to play with Richard too,' our mother interjected, before the argument could escalate. At that moment, inspired, I suggested that we help her by taking turns. One of us could work on the quilt while the other two played with Richard. My mother agreed that this was a fine idea. Delighted, I reached for the thimble and thread—just as my mother asked Claudia to take over for her at the quilt frame."

"So Claudia got to go first yet again."

"Alas, always. But that was all right, because my mother and I had a delightful time playing blocks with Richard. After ten minutes that felt like twenty, I gave my mother a look of such woebegone hope that she agreed that I could take my turn. Claudia relinquished the needle with a pout, but she took one of Richard's favorite storybooks from the shelf and offered to read it to him. He climbed onto her lap, stuck a finger in his mouth, and stared at the pictures while Claudia told him the story. I listened along for ten happy minutes as I worked on the quilt, until my mother's turn came again. Again and again we passed the needle from one to another. Richard was content, we girls were not squabbling, and my mother was pleased with our handiwork. She told us she was especially impressed with Claudia's quilting stitches, which she said were showing great improvement."

In the significant pause that followed, Sylvia offered her younger friend an abashed grimace.

"So, Claudia's skills had improved?" asked Summer, puzzled. "Had she been practicing, hoping to catch up to you?"

Sylvia began to reply, but embarrassment brought her up short. She tried again. "Not exactly."

"Then what was it?" Summer paused. "No. You didn't."

"Maybe, maybe not. It depends what you think I did."

Summer folded her arms and rested them on the table. "Did you pick out Claudia's stitches when she and your mother weren't looking?"

"Yes, but as I told Claudia, only the bad ones." Sylvia offered a faint shrug. "It wasn't my fault that most of them were bad."

Summer burst out laughing. "I shouldn't laugh. I know I shouldn't. But Sylvia, it's too funny."

"I wish my sister had thought so." Sylvia sighed and shook her head. "Naturally, Claudia was terribly upset. I tried to explain that since the quilt was an anniversary gift for Father, it ought to be as perfect as possible, and I was only trying to help. They didn't accept my rationale. My mother ordered me to apologize to Claudia and then to go to my room and think about what I had done."

Sylvia still remembered stammering out an apology, her face burning from shame and frustration. But a few weeks later, she knew her mother had forgiven her when she allowed her to help bind the quilt, completing the gift just in time for her parents' anniversary.

"Elms and Lilacs was my mother's last quilt," Sylvia said, wistful. "It was so beautiful, and we cherished it so. Even now I cannot fathom how Claudia could have sold it."

"When Sarah and I helped you search for your mother's missing quilts three years ago," Summer ventured, "you said that Claudia must have been absolutely desperate for cash."

"Well, yes," Sylvia acknowledged. "But I myself couldn't have parted with it for any sum—although I would have gladly loaned it to you for your exhibit at Union Hall. If ever a quilt deserved to be displayed and admired—" She gave herself a little shake. "Except I'm forgetting the most important criterion. Your exhibit is meant to showcase quilts with important ties to local history, not the finest examples of quilting from the region. For all its beauty, Elms and Lilacs wouldn't have qualified."

"But the quilt you and Claudia made for the World's Fair does," Summer said.

"To be perfectly frank, dear, I'm not sure why you think so."

"Why?" Summer echoed, surprised. "For all the same reasons you told my mom about the Sears National Quilt Contest when she was searching for a new research topic. This was the largest quilt contest ever held, and it hasn't been equaled since. Twenty five thousand quilts were submitted, which, given the population at the time, means that roughly one of every two thousand American women participated. The twelve-hundred-dollar grand prize was an enormous sum back then, more than the average per capita income."

"It's still a rather nice sum today."

"Then there's the theme of the World's Fair, 'A Century of Progress,'" Summer continued. "Don't you remember what you told my mom about the way some quilters interpreted that theme through their designs?"

"I don't recall precisely."

"You told her that all of those expressions of optimism and hope in such difficult times deeply impressed you. The quilts submitted to the contest revealed how the concept of progress was imagined and defined by a people still recovering from World War I and struggling through the Great Depression. These theme quilts captured the mood and the values of a nation during one of the most difficult periods of its history. And then when you consider Eleanor Roosevelt's role in the contest, and the controversy that erupted when the story behind the grand prize winner came out, and how the winning quilt mysteriously vanished—"

"I'm not disputing that the quilt competition was an important historical event," Sylvia interrupted. "It's certainly one of the most significant episodes in the history of American quilting. What I fail to see is how my quilt, mine and Claudia's, is important to local history. Our small successes didn't even merit a few lines in the Waterford newspaper. Although we were interviewed too, if I recall correctly."

"Really?" For a moment Summer looked puzzled, but she quickly shook it off. "I can't explain *that*, but I absolutely believe that the participation of two local girls in such a significant national event meets the definition of local history. You were part of something truly unprecedented, a historical event that's been nearly forgotten but deserves to be remembered. Your quilt will enlighten and inspire everyone who sees it—and if you're willing, I'd love to include it in the exhibit at Union Hall."

Sylvia paused to think, impressed—and a bit flummoxed—by her younger friend's spirited request. "I never thought of it that way," she admitted. "Maybe our quilt is more remarkable than I realized. It was always special to me and Claudia, of course, and we were proud of our achievements, but I never considered them historically significant."

"Maybe you should."

"Maybe I should indeed."

The kitchen fell silent as Sylvia rested her chin in her hand, thinking. In the distance she heard cheerful voices and the metallic rattle of Richard's old wagon. A glance through the open window revealed the construction crew, their supervisors, and the twins making their merry way across the bridge to the manor, no doubt hungry for lunch, their appetites whetted by hard work despite the tasty snack she had delivered earlier.

Sylvia did not want to make her decision in front of an audience, nor did she relish the thought of everyone chiming in with an opinion while she was still trying to sort out her own feelings on the matter.

"I've taken your words to heart, dear," Sylvia said, rising from the booth. "I'd like to sleep on it. May I give you my decision tomorrow?"

Summer rose too and nodded, smiling to hide her disappointment. "Of course," she said. "Take all the time you need."

Sylvia managed a smile of her own. She accompanied Summer to the back door, where they parted with a promise to speak again in the morning.

4

January 1933

Two days after the snowstorm, when the Bergstrom children came home from school and were tumbling out of their winter gear in the back foyer, Father beckoned to Sylvia and Claudia from the butler's pantry across the hall from the kitchen. While Richard and their cousins raced to the kitchen for warm apple cider and cookies, Father quietly explained that he had just returned from Harrisburg, where he had bought Richard the new Flexible Flyer Racer for his birthday. "I hid it beneath my bed," he murmured, glancing toward the doorway in case Richard should suddenly appear. "It's too large to wrap, but perhaps you girls could tie a red ribbon around the steering bar before you give it to him on Saturday."

"I'll look for one in the box of Christmas decorations in the attic," Claudia said. "Thank you, Father."

"Yes, thank you," Sylvia chimed in. "Did you remember to get the rules for the quilt contest too?"

"Hmm. Let me see." Their father frowned thoughtfully, patting his pockets. Sylvia felt a momentary frisson of alarm before he smiled to show that he was only teasing. "I left them on the kitchen table."

Quickly Sylvia thanked him and darted into the kitchen, with Claudia following close behind. They found Richard, Elsa, Alice, and Peter seated on benches at the refectory table, cheerfully answering Aunt Nellie's questions about their day while Great-Aunt Lydia poured each a steaming mug of fragrant warm cider and Great-Aunt Lucinda set a plate of cookies in their midst. From the doorway, Sylvia spotted a folded paper on the table at her own usual place. She hurried over, snatched it up, and scrambled to a seat on the bench. On the front of the brochure, a fashionably dressed woman with dark bobbed hair and a demure smile sat at a quilting frame pulling needle and thread through a Log Cabin quilt. Overlaying the lower half of the quilt was a banner announcing, "Sears Century of Progress Quilt Contest." Below that, dramatic boxed text promised "$7,500 in Prizes."

Claudia sat down beside her, pressing so close as she read over Sylvia's shoulder that Sylvia had to shrug her off and scoot an inch away. "What does it say?" Claudia demanded in an undertone. "You know Father brought that home for both of us."

"I *know*," Sylvia retorted sharply, drawing a sidelong look from Great-Aunt Lucinda. "Here," she said in a more pleasant tone, opening the brochure on the table between herself and Claudia. "Let's read it together. Oh, look at that headline. 'Think What Winning the Grand Prize Would Mean!'"

"I can hardly think of anything else," said Claudia fervently, inching closer. "Read the rules carefully so we don't miss anything."

"Why don't you read them aloud?" said Great-Aunt Lydia as she poured Claudia a mug of cider, and then one for Sylvia. "I believe we're all interested."

"I'm not," Peter mumbled around a mouthful of oatmeal cookie.

"Then you don't have to listen," said Great-Aunt Lucinda, ruffling his hair. "Go on, girls. How is this national quilt contest going to work, exactly? It seems like a rather ambitious undertaking to me."

Sylvia and Claudia exchanged a quick glance, enough for Sylvia to know that Claudia shared her sudden worry. "Are you planning to enter the contest too?" Claudia asked tentatively. Sylvia braced herself for the affirmative. Their aunts were excellent quilters, and Sylvia wouldn't stand a chance against any of them.

Great-Aunt Lucinda smiled and shook her head. "No, I think not." But Sylvia's relief was promptly quashed when she added, "One quilt from the Bergstrom family will suffice."

"Yes, I quite agree," said Great-Aunt Lydia, returning the saucepan of apple cider to the stovetop to keep warm. "What would people think if we Bergstrom ladies competed against one another?"

This time the look Sylvia and Claudia shared was wide-eyed and apprehensive. Which of the sisters' two quilts would be chosen as their family's entry? What about their plans to win the grand prize and first runner-up?

"Why should anyone give it a second thought?" asked Aunt Nellie, taking a seat between Peter and Alice. "We Bergstroms compete against each other in quilt contests every year at the county fair. As long as the rules don't restrict it to only one entry per family—"

"Well, let's find out." Great-Aunt Lucinda gestured to Claudia. "Take it from the top, dear."

Claudia inhaled deeply as if steeling herself. "'Quilters may enter the Sears Century of Progress Quilting Contest by submitting a patchwork quilt of original or traditional design never previously exhibited in their local retail store or mail-order house,'" she read aloud. "'Quilts must be recently made. The Quilt Contest is not intended as an exhibition of heirloom quilts.'"

"That's too bad," said Great-Aunt Lucinda, shaking her head in feigned sorrow. "Eleanor's Elms and Lilacs would surely take the highest honors, without any of us needing to sew a single stitch more."

"We could *pretend* it was new," Elsa piped up.

"Enter a contest on false pretenses?" said Aunt Nellie, appalled. "We most certainly could not."

"Go on, Claudia," prompted Great-Aunt Lucinda.

Claudia nodded and found her place on the page. "'Each retail store will award a first prize of ten dollars, and second and third prizes of five dollars. Each mail-order house will award five ten-dollar prizes.'" She glanced up at the aunties for confirmation. "So you have to win at the local level before you can move on to the next round?"

"That's what it sounds like," said Great-Aunt Lucinda as the other aunties nodded.

With her sister's gaze averted, Sylvia tugged the brochure a bit closer to herself. "'The entire country has been divided into ten regions which mark the second step to the national prize,'" she read. "'The centers will be at Chicago, Philadelphia, Boston, Kansas City, Minneapolis, Memphis, Atlanta, Dallas, Los Angeles, and Seattle.' Ours must be Philadelphia."

"Obviously. It's closest." With a pointed glare, Claudia placed a fingertip on the brochure and pulled it back to the midpoint between them. "'The three winning quilts in each region will be sent to Chicago, where they will compete for the national prizes. A bonus of two hundred dollars will be presented to the grand national prize winner if the original design of her quilt commemorates the Century of Progress Exposition.'"

A two-hundred-dollar bonus! Without a doubt, Sylvia would include the World's Fair theme in her quilt somehow. "'At the conclusion of the Fair,'" she read aloud, "'the quilt winning the first grand prize will be presented to Mrs. Franklin D. Roosevelt!'"

"The First Lady!" Great-Aunt Lydia exclaimed. "Can you imagine making a quilt for the White House?"

Great-Aunt Lucinda shook her head in wonder. "I'd certainly be proud to have one of my quilts there. Perhaps even the president himself would use it."

Sylvia and Claudia exchanged another quick, wary look. Great-Aunt Lucinda seemed rather keen on entering the contest now, regardless of what she had said earlier. Sylvia resumed reading aloud, but in a dull monotone, hoping to trick her great-aunt into losing interest. "'The first, second, and third grand prize–winning quilts will be exhibited together with the regional prize–winning quilts in the Sears Century of Progress Exposition building, which will open in Chicago on May 27.'"

"Another great honor," said Aunt Nellie, taking up a napkin to wipe apple cider and crumbs from Peter's mouth as he winced and tried to duck out of reach. "Think of all the thousands of fairgoers who will admire those quilts."

"Hundreds of thousands, maybe," said a wide-eyed Elsa, who lately had been learning a lot about numbers in school. "Those quilters will be famous!"

Sylvia felt her heart pound a bit faster. How proud her family would be if she took the top honors! Their sorrow and worry could be forgotten for a moment. The prize money would benefit them all. Claudia would be jealous, of course, but Sylvia would be gracious in victory.

"That explains how the competition will be structured," said Great-Aunt Lucinda, leaning back against the kitchen counter and folding her arms, "but what about the rules for the quilts themselves?"

"There are always rules," said Great-Aunt Lydia, nodding sagely.

Sylvia and Claudia turned back to the brochure. "'The contest is open to everyone except employees of Sears, Roebuck and Company and the judges of the contest,'" Claudia read aloud. "'Quilts must be of the contestant's own making and must never have been exhibited before.'"

"'Quilts must be of adequate size for a single or double bed. All entries must be filled, backed, and completely quilted.'" Sylvia paused, bemused. "Well, obviously. It's not a quilt if it doesn't have batting or backing. Then it's just a quilt *top*."

"'Only one quilt may be entered by a contestant,'" read Claudia, glancing up at the aunts hopefully. "It doesn't say anything about only one entry per family."

"I thought not," said Aunt Nellie triumphantly, while Great-Aunt Lydia nodded and Great-Aunt Lucinda shrugged, conceding the point.

"'Sears will not be responsible for loss to quilts due to agencies beyond their control.'" Now it was Sylvia's turn to look to her aunties for answers. "What does that mean?"

Great-Aunt Lucinda waved a hand dismissively. "That's just legal talk. If the delivery truck carrying the finalists' quilts to Chicago plunges into Lake Michigan, or if the Sears Pavilion goes up in flames and takes the quilts with it, Sears doesn't owe the quiltmakers a penny."

"Is that likely to happen?" asked Claudia anxiously.

"Not at all likely," Great-Aunt Lydia assured her, shooting Great-Aunt Lucinda an exasperated look. Great-Aunt Lucinda offered an unrepentant grin in reply.

"Participants have to fill out and sign an official tag and sew it to the lower right-hand corner of the quilt," said Sylvia, moving on to the next section. "They say, 'It may be obtained at any Sears retail store.'" One tag was printed on the back of the brochure, she noted, but only one. They would have to get a second one for Claudia—and maybe a third for Great-Aunt Lucinda.

"Oh, this part is important," said Claudia, pulling the brochure closer to herself so Sylvia had to crane her neck to see. "'Quilts will be judged on the following basis: Design, twenty points, ten for suitability, ten for beauty.' Beauty I understand, but what do they mean by suitability?"

"I don't know," said Sylvia. "Maybe whether it meets the size requirements and has all three layers?"

"Maybe. 'Color, thirty points, fifteen for beauty, fifteen for harmony. Workmanship, thirty points, fifteen for beauty of quilting, fifteen for perfection of stitching. Materials, ten points. General appearance, ten points.'" Claudia pushed the brochure toward Sylvia, wincing. "Golly, that's a lot to worry about."

"What do you expect, for that sort of prize money?" asked Great-Aunt Lucinda. "They can't make it too easy, or everyone and their grandmother would enter."

Sylvia picked up the brochure and read the last rule. "'Decision of the judges is final.'"

"That means no whining if you don't win," said Great-Aunt Lydia, giving Sylvia and Claudia each a pointed look in turn. "You must be good sports, regardless of the outcome."

"We're good sports," Claudia protested in a small voice, and Sylvia nodded. That was almost always true. They were good sports everywhere and with everyone, except with each other.

"Mama, can I go play?" Alice piped up plaintively. Apparently she'd had enough of quilt talk.

"Yes, you *may*," said Aunt Nellie, her emphasis a gentle correction. "Take your dishes to the sink first."

"May I go to the stables?" Richard asked eagerly as his cousin scampered off.

"Yes, in fact, you *must*," said Great-Aunt Lydia. "There are stalls to be mucked out and you're still serving your punishment."

Richard jumped up from the bench, unsuccessfully attempting to hide a grin. He was halfway to the door before he remembered his own dishes and hurried back to take care of them. Then he darted from the kitchen, and they soon heard him in the rear foyer scrambling back into his coat, boots, and mittens, and then the door opening and closing behind him.

With a sigh, Great-Aunt Lucinda settled onto the bench Richard and Alice had abandoned. As she reached across the table for the brochure, Claudia turned to Sylvia and offered one of her best, most indulgent big sister smiles, well practiced and rarely authentic. "Since I know how particular you are about colors, you can have the first choice of Mother's fabrics," she said. "I don't mind choosing from whatever is left over."

Her words were generous, but Sylvia noticed the quick flick of her eyes toward their aunties as she spoke, and she knew Claudia was just trying to show off how mature and unselfish she was. "Thank you," replied Sylvia, her smile warm and her voice sweet. "Since you're the eldest, you should get to use the quilt frame. I'll be fine with my lap hoop."

"Thanks," said Claudia, a bit brittlely. "How thoughtful. If you'll all excuse me, I'm going to do my homework, and then I'll begin planning my quilt."

"I think I'll do the same," said Sylvia, rising and gathering up her mug and cookie plate. Claudia quickly grabbed her own, hurrying so she would be the first to the sink.

Great-Aunt Lucinda was studying the brochure. "Are you two determined to make your own separate quilts instead of working together on one?"

Sylvia set her dishes into the sink with a clatter, her eyes meeting Claudia's over the faucet. "Yes," they replied in unison.

"You might want to reconsider."

Sylvia's heart dipped. "Why?" asked Claudia.

Great-Aunt Lucinda held open the brochure and pointed to a paragraph on the back. "I think you overlooked an important detail," she said as the sisters hurried back to the table. "'All quilts must be submitted to their local Sears store, or must arrive at a mail-order house, by midnight on May fifteenth.'"

"What?" exclaimed Claudia. "Are you sure?"

"It's all right here," said Great-Aunt Lucinda, handing her the brochure.

"That doesn't give you much time," Great-Aunt Lydia remarked. "One would almost need to have a quilt already in progress to finish before the deadline."

"That's not fair," said Sylvia.

"It's not unfair if the same deadline applies to everyone," Aunt Nellie pointed out. "Challenging, yes, but not unfair."

"I'd give serious thought to collaborating on a single entry if I were you," Great-Aunt Lucinda advised, handing the brochure to Claudia. "You'd be more likely to finish before the deadline, and you might learn something about setting aside your differences and working together."

Sylvia and Claudia exchanged a look of commiseration. They both knew that if they took her advice, they would lose more time in argument than they could ever hope to make up by collaborating. And they had no time to spare. They were in school all day, except on weekends, and they were responsible for chores around the house. Sylvia also worked for the family business, exercising the horses and helping her father with the office work however she could. Neither of them had an abundance of free hours to spare for quilting.

Sylvia muffled a sigh, not wanting to appear a poor sport. Like Aunt Nellie said, all participants had the same amount of time to make their quilts. But four months was such an awfully brief period in which to create a masterpiece.

She raced through her homework, but for the rest of the day and throughout the next, the quilt contest was never far from her thoughts. She briefly considered entering her current work in progress, a lovely Snow Crystals quilt in shades of blue and snowy white, which she could definitely finish before the deadline. But within minutes, she dismissed the idea. Surely the judges would favor quilts that commemorated the Century of Progress theme, and the two-hundred-dollar bonus was very tempting.

"One thing I don't understand about that theme," she mused

aloud at dinner the following evening. "What's so special about the century from 1833 to 1933?"

"That's what *you're* supposed to tell *them* through your design," said Great-Aunt Lucinda, amused.

"What's so hard to understand?" asked Claudia, shrugging. "A century is a hundred years, and it's nineteen thirty-three."

"I know that," retorted Sylvia, frustrated. She knew she wasn't explaining herself well. "It just seems like an odd hundred years to celebrate."

"I see what you mean," her father said from his seat at the head of the table. "You'd prefer round numbers—the century from 1800 to 1900, for example—or something less arbitrary, such as 1776 to 1876."

"Yes," said Sylvia, glad to be understood. "That's exactly it."

"It's not arbitrary," said Uncle William, helping himself to more creamed chicken and biscuits. He was shorter than her father, with the same gray-blue eyes but lighter hair, and a more rounded, boyish face. "Chicago was founded in 1833. Obviously the World's Fair theme is meant to honor the city's centennial."

They all looked at him, surprised, even the youngest children. "How did you know when Chicago was founded?" asked Great-Aunt Lucinda.

Uncle William shrugged. "Everyone knows that."

Sylvia hadn't, but it gave her an idea. She would create a design that celebrated Chicago too. That wouldn't be easy since she'd never visited the city, but she could look up pictures and facts in books. It would be foolish to squander any opportunity to impress the judges.

The next day was Saturday, but although Sylvia didn't have school, she couldn't spend the day quilting either. The morning passed in a scramble of last-minute preparations for Richard's birthday party. At noon, six of his closest friends arrived for hours of fun, including lunch, games, a wild romp in the snow, and Great-Aunt Lydia's delicious apple cake.

After the party ended and Richard's rambunctious friends departed, the family gave Richard his gifts. To Sylvia's delight, the Flexible Flyer Racer was far and away his favorite. He, Peter, and Uncle William immediately set out for the steep hill by the orchard to test it out. Richard invited Sylvia to come along too, but although she was tempted, she instead went to the library and settled down on the sofa nearest the crackling fireplace with her notebook, sketchpad, and colored pencils. The day had passed in such a whirlwind of activity that she'd barely given a passing thought to her quilt design. She was determined to make up for lost time.

She opened to the first blank page in her notebook and wrote "Progress" at the top. When a cascade of brilliant ideas failed to immediately appear, she underlined the word twice, sat back in her chair, and tapped her chin with her pencil.

The most obvious idea would be to create several images tracing the history of the city of Chicago from its earliest Native American settlements to the arrival of European settlers, and then through important stages in the city's growth. But she couldn't include anything before 1833, which might leave out some of the most interesting bits. She didn't really know much about Chicago history either, and every moment she devoted to research was one she couldn't spend sewing. Furthermore, this idea had come to her so quickly that it had no doubt occurred to many other quilters too, and she didn't want her quilt to get lost in a crowd of look-alikes. Muffling a sigh, she wrote down "Pictorial history of Chicago" at the top of her list. It didn't really appeal to her, but she ought to keep it in reserve in case she couldn't think of anything else.

Fortunately, she almost immediately did so. A similar idea, but different enough that she needn't worry quite so much about copycats, was to trace the progress of the United States as it grew as a nation. She could make appliqués of the forty-eight states, embroider a star upon each to mark its capital, and arrange them in a pleasing pattern,

maybe a graceful oval, with a pieced border all around. Newly hopeful, she set notebook and pencil aside, leapt up from her seat, and
hurried over to the bookcases between the tall north-facing windows
where various books on American history were shelved. Finding the
one she sought, she took it down, sat cross-legged on the floor, and
opened the heavy volume on her lap, turning pages until she came to
a list of states and the dates they were admitted to the union. "Well,
that won't work," she murmured aloud. Twenty-four states, including
her own Pennsylvania, were admitted before 1833, which meant she
couldn't really include them and still remain true to the Century of
Progress theme.

This was going to be harder than she'd thought.

What about science? She had learned quite a lot about science in
school, and the Bergstrom library was full of books about scientists
and scientific discoveries. Using appliqué, she could depict Charles
Darwin's theory of evolution, Louis Pasteur's discoveries about germs,
Gregor Mendel's studies of peas and inherited traits, Marie Curie's
discoveries of radium and polonium—maybe she was listing things
out of order, but she could sort that out later. Some discoveries and
inventions might be very hard to illustrate in appliqué, but it was still
an excellent idea, the most promising she'd had yet. With a flourish,
she added "Scientific progress" to her list.

After a moment's pause, she wrote "Inventions" on the next
line. Discoveries were not the same thing as inventions and so qualified as a fourth idea. She could appliqué pictures of the telegraph
and the telephone, the electric light and the radio, the automobile and
the airplane. Pencil flying over the page, she swiftly jotted down
as many technological marvels as she could think of, including a few
that might have appeared decades too early. That was something
else she could look up later. What was most important, and encouraging, was that there was an abundance of possibilities to choose
from.

Maybe too abundant. So many marvelous inventions had come about since 1833 that winnowing them down might be overwhelming. Perhaps she should focus on one particular type of invention, or one category of scientific discovery. Pencil and pad in hand, she rose and paced about the room, thinking, pausing once to gaze out the windows at the snowy landscape in front of the manor. Far to her left, trudging along through the drifts that covered the path through the trees to the north gardens, she spied Richard pulling his new sled, Uncle William and cousin Peter following behind. Much nearer, a black delivery truck was pulling into the circular driveway in front of the manor. "Transportation," Sylvia exclaimed, delighted. She could appliqué scenes of vehicles popular in 1833 and newer ones that had come along in the century since, including cars and airplanes. If she emphasized the transition from older forms of transportation to modern, she needn't limit her design to things that had been *invented* in the past century; it would be enough that the train, or the steamboat, or the bicycle, had been used in that time. Best of all, these images would be far easier to illustrate in fabric and thread than, say, the theory of evolution.

Satisfied—and relieved to have hit upon the perfect idea so soon—she returned to the sofa and switched to her drawing pad and colored pencils. She had sketched a few rough appliqué concepts when the French doors swung open and Claudia entered, a pencil in one hand and a composition book in the other. "I've been thinking about what Great-Aunt Lucinda said," she said. "I was looking at the calendar and making a schedule—"

"A schedule?" Sylvia echoed. They knew when they had to begin—immediately—and they knew when their quilts were due. Every day in between, they would have to work nonstop as fast as they could. What more did they need to know?

"Yes, a schedule, how much time to budget for design, piecing, quilting, and shipping, given how long those things usually take."

Claudia tapped the notebook with her pencil twice for emphasis. "If you'd done the same, instead of rushing headlong into designing, you might have figured out the same thing I did."

"If you'd begun brainstorming designs instead of poring over calendars and timetables, you'd be a step ahead, like me." After a moment, Sylvia reluctantly added, "What did you figure out?"

"There just isn't enough time." Claudia flopped into an armchair, dejected. "We have less than four months to make an entire bed-size quilt from start to finish. Sometimes I need several months just to piece a top."

"Same here, and several months more to quilt it," Sylvia acknowledged reluctantly. If she didn't have school and chores and could devote herself entirely to sewing, she might be able to pull it off, but the quality of her work would surely suffer. She'd end up with a quilt that was finished, but lacking the perfection required to win the grand prize. As for Claudia, even that modest achievement would be out of reach.

"I don't like it any more than you do," Claudia said, "but Great-Aunt Lucinda is right. The only way either of us will be able to enter a finished quilt in the contest is if we work together."

Sylvia slumped against the back of the sofa, dispirited. She'd much rather work alone, but then again, if she didn't have to worry so much about racing to meet the deadline, she could focus on beauty of quilting and perfection of stitching. If Claudia did her very best work, it might be good enough.

And in the end, submitting a less-than-perfect quilt would be better than entering no quilt at all. That prize money would mean too much to their family.

"It's the only way," Sylvia admitted, resigned. "We have to collaborate on a single quilt to have any chance at winning that grand prize."

"At least the aunts will be happy to see us working together."

"That's another thing. I'll agree to work together on one condition."

Claudia pulled a face. "Fine. What?"

"You can't boss me around because you're the eldest. We work together as equals or not at all."

5

September 2004

Sylvia had taken a loaf from the breadbox and was cutting generous slices when she heard the back door open and her friends come noisily in, chatting and laughing, not quite drowning out the rumble of Gwen's car as Summer drove away. Evidently they had lingered outside to chat for a few minutes before Summer departed, and in all likelihood, the apple orchard had not been the only topic of conversation.

Sylvia sighed, preparing herself for well-meaning but difficult questions about why she had not immediately agreed to lend her World's Fair quilt to the Waterford Historical Society's exhibit. She knew Sarah would see it in very simple terms. Summer, a dear and trusted friend, had asked to borrow the quilt; the quilt was not otherwise engaged or too fragile for public exhibition; as a general rule Sylvia enjoyed displaying her quilts in shows and in museums; therefore, the only response that made any sense was yes. But it was *not* that simple, and Sylvia's inability to express precisely *why not* was proof enough of that.

"How goes the construction?" she asked as she rinsed off a couple of tomatoes in the sink, raising her voice to be heard over her friends' happy clamor.

"We're nearly finished," Matt said cheerfully as he lifted James into his high chair. "Andrew finished shingling the roof, and Joe and I placed the last countertop. I need to oil the door hinges, set up the bins for the bags, and hang a few signs, and we'll be good to go."

"I'll finish making the road sign this afternoon," Joe added, taking Sylvia's place at the sink while she carried the tomatoes to the cutting board on the opposite counter. "I might not have time to set it up until tomorrow, but you can rest assured it'll be there before the customers arrive on Saturday."

"I have every confidence in you," Sylvia replied, carefully slicing the tomatoes into juicy, red circles. Soon everyone except the toddler twins was pitching in to help prepare the meal—washing up at the sink, setting the table, taking sandwich fixings from the refrigerator, putting on a fresh pot of coffee, refilling the pitcher of apple cider, and raiding the pantry for jars of pickles and bags of chips. As they gathered around the refectory table, with the McClures at an overflow booth to accommodate the twins' high chairs, the conversation was lively and cheerful, and Sylvia's heart was light. Although she often missed the bustle of quilt camp during the off-season, she never wanted for companionship. Though she was not related to a single person gathered around that table—except for Andrew, by marriage—she never doubted for a moment that she was among family.

"I spoke with Summer on her way out," said Sarah, assisting Caroline with a spoonful of applesauce. "She said she asked to borrow another one of your quilts to replace my sampler in the Union Hall exhibit, but you told her you needed to think it over."

There was no mistaking the unasked question in Sarah's voice, nor the sudden, expectant hush that fell upon the gathering. "Well, of course *you're* hoping I'll consent, Sarah," said Sylvia airily, spearing a pickle with her fork. "You want your own quilt back before the weather turns colder."

"Actually, I'm hoping you'll consent because that would help Summer, and because your World's Fair quilt sounds amazing." Sarah set down the spoon and wiped a bit of applesauce from her daughter's cheek. "I can't believe you never showed it to me, or even told me about it."

"I assumed you'd heard through the grapevine. Didn't you know Gwen wrote an article about it for an academic journal?"

"So I'm told." Sarah threw Sylvia a wry glance before turning back to Caroline, who was straining to reach her sippy cup. "Academic journals aren't my usual genre of choice."

"Mine either," Sylvia admitted. "If Gwen would revise her piece for a quilt magazine, I imagine it would garner more interest in the quilting community. The *Journal of American Studies* is probably a bit obscure, except among academics." As her friends exchanged glances, she added, "Just to be clear, I did read the article. Gwen's subject wasn't the quilt Claudia and I made, but rather the Sears National Quilt Contest as a historical event and social phenomenon."

Matt's brow furrowed. "Gwen didn't write about your quilt? Did you ask her not to?"

Sylvia laughed lightly. "No, no, that's not it at all. Gwen mentioned our quilt in a paragraph about several entries from Pennsylvania. Thankfully, she gave it no more attention than it deserved."

"I'm sure it deserved at least a page," said Andrew stoutly. "Maybe the editor didn't give Gwen enough space."

"All the more reason to include your quilt in Summer's exhibit," said Sarah. "At Union Hall, it would be appreciated and admired by quilt lovers and history buffs alike."

"Perhaps," said Sylvia. "Yet some might wonder whether it belongs there."

"Of course it belongs," said Gretchen. "The Sears National Quilt

Contest was truly unprecedented. Gwen isn't the only scholar who thinks so. Years ago, when I was still working at Quilts 'n Things in Sewickley, two quilt researchers published a book about the competition, and we could hardly keep it in stock. The authors also created a traveling exhibit of several contest entries they had been able to acquire. I'm certain they would have been delighted to include the quilt you and Claudia made, if they had known it existed."

"A book and a traveling exhibition?" said Sylvia, a bit taken aback. "Really? How extraordinary!"

"Whatever you decide about the Union Hall exhibit, you should definitely write to those two historians about your quilt," said Gretchen. "They'll want to document it for their archives. I have a copy of their book upstairs in my room. I'll get you their names and addresses later."

Sylvia didn't know quite what to say. "It seems like a lot of fuss and bother, but if you really believe they'd be interested—"

"I know they would be. They included their contact information in the book for precisely this reason."

Sylvia shook her head, still uncertain. "But the quilt Claudia and I made didn't earn any of the grand prizes. It's nothing special, except to us."

"You're a master quilter," protested Sarah, always her champion. "Every quilt you make is special."

Gretchen reached across the table to squeeze Sylvia's hand. "You're wrong, Sylvia. Every quilt submitted to the contest is historically significant—and yours is especially important to *local* history."

Turning to the others, Gretchen proceeded to tell them about the quilt contest, including several details Sylvia had forgotten long ago. While her friends listened, fascinated, Sylvia's doubts began to fade.

Perhaps her World's Fair quilt was more valuable than she realized. Not monetarily or artistically, she didn't mean that. She had made many other, much finer quilts through the years, quilts that had won prizes, had been photographed for books and magazines, and had been acquired for museums. She wouldn't have thought that the humble creation of two teenage girls, which had not even qualified for the finals of the grand and glorious contest they had naively hoped to win, deserved any special attention.

Perhaps she was wrong.

When Gretchen finished her tale, Sylvia started from her reverie to find everyone regarding her expectantly, as if they were awaiting a grand speech or a heartfelt confession.

"Well?" Sarah prompted.

Sylvia sighed, finished the last morsel of her sandwich, and wiped the corners of her mouth with her napkin. "I told Summer I would think about it and give her my answer in the morning, and that's precisely what I intend to do." A muffled sigh went up from the table, and Sylvia had to laugh. "Just for that, I might wait until tomorrow *evening*. Let's leave it there, shall we? Don't you all have work to get back to?"

"How do you like that?" said Andrew, feigning indignation. "She's tossing us out."

"I would never," Sylvia assured him, patting his shoulder affectionately. "Not before you help me clear the table."

Everyone laughed or groaned or both—except for James, who looked around, bemused, wondering what was going on, and Caroline, who was thoroughly engrossed in pulling off her socks. While Sarah and Matt cleaned up after the twins, the others carried dishes to the sink or began putting away the lunch fixings, chatting about their plans for the afternoon.

"We sure do get spoiled during the camp season," Joe remarked, making his way around the counter with a stack of plates in one hand and a coffee mug in the other. "I miss Anna's delicious buffets, and her banquets, and the dessert tables—"

"Oh, man, those dessert tables," breathed Matt, laying a hand on his stomach and gazing heavenward.

"There might be a package of cookies in the pantry," said Gretchen helpfully.

Matt shook his head. "It's not the same."

"I miss Anna's company more than I miss her cooking," said Sylvia, and everyone quickly chimed in, in agreement.

"I also miss having Anna's staff around to take care of the cleanup for us," said Sarah, lifting Caroline from her high chair, balancing the toddler on her hip, and trying to wipe up spilled applesauce with a paper towel clutched in her free hand. "Still, at least we only have to carry our dishes across the kitchen, not all the way from the banquet hall like during the camp season. That's best left to the professionals."

"We should give them all a raise," said Gretchen, retrieving the broom from the pantry.

"I'd love to, but we can't afford it," Sarah replied, with a quick, sidelong glance for Sylvia, which she pretended not to notice.

"Sales from the apple orchard will help with that," said Matt, sweeping James up in his arms, heedless of the applesauce handprints his son left on his shirt.

"*After* we replace the ballroom carpeting," Sarah reminded him, "and fix the west wing plumbing, and upgrade the electrical wiring so we never have another short when all of the classroom sewing machines are running at the same time—"

Sylvia quickly interrupted. "Speaking of the apple orchard and carrying burdens long distances—"

"Were we?" asked Andrew, brow furrowing.

"Yes, of course we were." It was a strained segue, but Sylvia couldn't bear to listen to any more of Sarah's recitation of repairs the manor needed so badly. "Providing our customers with reusable bags made from recycled plastic bottles is an inspired idea, but some of our customers may find them too difficult to carry. The weight might not trouble you young people, but others may struggle to haul a heavy bag full of apples all the way from the orchard to the parking lot."

Joe scratched the faint scruff of beard on his chin. "We wouldn't want to discourage folks from filling their bags."

"Precisely." Sylvia wet a dishcloth in the sink, wrung out the excess, and returned to wipe down the refectory table. "My brother's old wagon came in handy earlier this morning when I brought you refreshments. Wouldn't it be nice to have several others for our customers to use?"

"Instead of bags?" asked Gretchen.

"No, not at all. Our customers would put the bags of apples in the wagons. Think of how much easier it would be to haul a heavy load."

Some of her friends nodded thoughtfully, but Sarah was regarding her, bemused. "I love the idea, but new wagons will cost us. You were fairly emphatic before about not going over budget."

"It doesn't have to be an *armada* of wagons, nor do they have to be the top-of-the-line, deluxe models," said Sylvia. "We could check yard sales, Goodwill, and St. Vincent's, for starters. As long as they're functional, they'll do."

"Even if they're only mostly functional, we could repair them," said Andrew, looking to Joe and Matt, who nodded in reply.

"I'm in," declared Gretchen with a grin as she loaded cups into the dishwasher. "I love a good yard sale, and a thrift store dig can be a treasure hunt if you approach it with the right attitude."

"If you say so," said Sarah dubiously. "For me it would be a chore, but if you honestly don't mind—"

"Sarah hates shopping," Matt explained, unnecessarily, because they were all quite familiar with Sarah's quirks by now. "She's much happier working with spreadsheets and ledgers."

"And I can't abide paperwork." Gretchen feigned a shudder. "That's why we all make such a good team, don't you think? Each of us contributes our different strengths, interests, and experiences to achieve our shared goals."

"That's so inspirational, we should put it on our website," Sarah teased, and Gretchen playfully swatted her with a dish towel.

Working together, they soon finished tidying up, as if eager to prove Gretchen right. Afterward, Joe set off for his woodshop to complete the road sign, Matt and Andrew returned to work on the market stand, and Gretchen accompanied Sarah upstairs to the nursery to play with the twins for a while before putting them down for a nap, assuming the children cooperated.

Sylvia lingered in the kitchen after they all departed. It was her turn to make supper that evening, so she mixed up a marinade for chicken breasts and put together an orzo and chickpea salad, following Anna's recipe to the letter. Setting out some frozen bread dough to thaw—also courtesy of Anna, whose baking instructions were written in neat cursive on an index card taped to the package—she placed her dinner-prep utensils into the dishwasher and turned it on.

Satisfied that all was in order, she fixed herself a glass of lemon ginger iced tea, retrieved a new quilting magazine from the stack of mail on the hall table, and carried them both through the manor and out the front entrance to the verandah, where she settled into an Adirondack chair with a contented sigh. From this side of the manor, she could hear no construction noise, only birdsong and the hum of honeybees in the wildflower meadow. It was a lovely place to relax and read, especially on a gorgeous early autumn day boasting sunshine and the lingering warmth of summer. The wide stone verandah ran the entire length of the front of the manor, with white columns supporting a roof far overhead. Two stone staircases near the center gracefully arced away from each other, forming a half circle as they descended to the ground. The driveway at the foot of the stairs encircled a fountain with a large sculpture of a rearing horse at its center, a symbol of the Bergstrom family that was reflected elsewhere on the estate, including on the fine china that graced the banquet hall tables on special occasions.

Sylvia was engrossed in an article about the "quilting renaissance" of the 1970s when one of the tall double doors opened and Sarah stepped outside, a manila folder tucked beneath her arm. "Did the twins go down for a nap peacefully, or was it a struggle?" Sylvia inquired, closing the magazine and setting it on a nearby footrest.

"About as you would expect," said Sarah, settling wearily into the chair beside Sylvia's. "James gave me a sweet kiss, cuddled up with the quilt you made him, and fell asleep right away. Caroline remained standing in her crib, holding the rail, bouncing up and down, and singing. I think it was singing. Anyway, she eventually wore herself out, and now she's asleep too."

"Good. Now you have a precious few minutes to yourself."

"Maybe more than a few, since Gretchen offered to listen to the baby monitor for me." Sarah rested the folder on her lap and drummed her fingertips on it, as if she had something to say but wasn't quite sure how to begin. "You know, your suggestion about the wagons is brilliant."

"Brilliant?" Sylvia's eyebrows rose. "Good, perhaps. Very good, even. But surely not brilliant."

Sarah allowed a small smile. "Maybe I'm just glad to see you finally taking a more active interest in Matt's project. Can I be honest with you?"

"You usually are, I trust."

"It's been difficult for him, working so tirelessly to launch Elm Creek Orchards under the cloud of your disapproval. It's not clear to any of us why you gave the project your blessing only to express misgivings about every decision."

"Goodness," Sylvia murmured, taken aback. Her friends had been talking about her, worrying and wondering? "I certainly never meant to be overly critical."

"I know you didn't," Sarah hastened to assure her. "That's why I'm sure there must be something else going on with you, especially since you didn't seem to want Summer to borrow your quilt. You're usually so gracious and generous when it comes to supporting any of your friends' endeavors. This isn't like you."

"I haven't yet made up my mind about the World's Fair quilt," Sylvia reminded her, "and this business about the quilt is an entirely different matter from Matt's scheme for the orchard. You're searching for connections that don't exist."

"Are you sure?"

For a moment, Sylvia felt unsettled. She lifted her hands and let them fall to her lap. "As sure as I can be."

"Okay." Sarah nodded, her gaze falling to the folder she held on her lap. "If you say so."

"Sarah, dear—" Sylvia reached out to rest her hand on her younger friend's forearm. "I'm sorry if I seem to lack enthusiasm, especially if it has caused you or Matt or our friends any worry. It isn't Matt's scheme that troubles me, but rather the—well, the *necessity* for such a dramatic rescue plan."

Sarah shook her head, puzzled. "We're not on the verge of bankruptcy if that's what you're worried about."

"Not at all. You've explained our financials so clearly that I have an excellent sense of where we stand." Sylvia sighed. "It's not that I don't want to earn more income from the orchards than we have in the past, or that I think Matt's scheme will fail. It's simply that I don't want to *need* additional profits from the orchard. I wanted Elm Creek Quilts to thrive on its own. I wanted our quilt camp to succeed so marvelously that we needn't ever fear a single repair bill—that *you* needn't ever fear anything, after I'm gone."

"Oh, Sylvia," said Sarah, face falling. "Elm Creek Quilts *is* a marvelous success, and you aren't going anywhere."

"Really, Sarah," Sylvia reproached her gently. "I'm merely mortal, after all."

Sarah pursed her lips and shook her head, clearly unwilling

to discuss the inevitable. "If we raised our prices by ten dollars per camper per session, we might be able to get by on our camp income alone."

"I don't want to raise our prices," Sylvia reminded her, "and I suspect Matt would be terribly disappointed if we called his scheme to a halt at the last minute. It's not just about the income for him. He wants to launch a business of his own, just as we Elm Creek Quilters did."

"That's certainly true. He's thoroughly enjoying himself. He's brimming over with ideas and plans for later this season and even next year."

And Sylvia was determined to stop spoiling it for him. "It doesn't matter whether the estate generates income from one venture or another or many, as long as we earn enough to compensate our people well and pay our bills on time," she said firmly. "I'll be sure to tell Matt how proud I am of him, and how excited I am to see what the future holds. I'll do everything I can to make our opening day a big success."

"I'm glad to hear you say that," said Sarah, smiling, "because I need your help."

"Oh?"

"I'd like your opinion on the orchard's logo." Opening the folder on her lap, Sarah removed several colorfully printed pages and arranged them neatly on top of the nearest footrest, covering up Sylvia's magazine. "These are our four finalists. Which one do you like best?"

"Let me see." Sylvia studied the designs carefully. All of them were striking, but some were prettier, others easier to read, and two managed to be both. She spent another long moment deciding between the two. "This one," she said at last, pointing to the nearest design. "I like that you've used the same typeface and the river design from the Elm Creek Quilts logo, and simply replaced the elm with the trio of apple trees. There is continuity between the two logos, and yet enough differences to set them apart."

"That was Matt's favorite too," said Sarah, clearly pleased that they agreed. "That settles it. We can finalize our ad and email it to the local papers before close of business."

"I'm glad we reached consensus so quickly," Sylvia remarked as Sarah gathered up the pages and returned them to the folder. "My sister and I would have spent the next hour or two arguing, each of us choosing our favorite and fighting passionately for it, until someone with better sense persuaded us to compromise. We never could agree on anything."

"Never?" echoed Sarah. "Not quite. You've told me plenty of stories that prove otherwise. What about that time you and Claudia made apple strudel from Gerda Bergstrom's legendary recipe? Or when you welcomed your brother's bride into the family by teaching her how to quilt? Or, something a bit more pertinent, like when you worked on your World's Fair quilt together? You finished the quilt, so you obviously must have agreed on a design, right?"

"I suppose so," admitted Sylvia, "but compromise never came easily to us."

"But you got there, didn't you?"

"Yes." Sylvia paused to think. "Our World's Fair quilt was the first project Claudia and I collaborated on after our mother's death. I suppose we made an effort to get along in her memory."

"Sounds like a historical event worth commemorating."

Sylvia laughed lightly. "Oh, yes, Claudia and I cooperating was as momentous as Armistice Day and the fall of the Berlin Wall."

"Maybe not, but all the same—" Sarah shrugged and rose. "Well, anyway. I think it's worth remembering. Need help with dinner tonight?"

"Thank you, dear, but I have things well in hand. Besides, you cooked last night and I'm sure the twins will need you."

"Don't they always?" Sarah sighed wearily, but her smile revealed that she didn't mind being needed, not in the least. "I'll see you inside."

Sylvia gave her a little wave goodbye and took up her magazine again, but she didn't open it. Nothing remained of her iced tea but a few melting ice cubes, so after a moment of thoughtful contemplation, she gathered her things and returned inside. As she crossed the foyer, she thought she heard one of the twins babbling upstairs, and when she reached the kitchen, through the open window came the distant sound of a hammer pounding a steady rhythm.

She was quite alone, so she picked up the phone and placed a call, which was answered on the second ring.

"Hello, Summer, dear," Sylvia greeted her friend. "I'm giving you my answer earlier than I promised but later than I should have. Yes, you may include the World's Fair quilt in the Union Hall exhibit. The honor is all mine."

6

January–March 1933

Sylvia and Claudia spent their precious last days of January mired in debate over the design of their World's Fair quilt. Their perpetual arguing so annoyed the other Bergstrom women that the sisters were banished from the cozy west sitting room, "Until you girls sort out your nonsense," as Great-Aunt Lucinda put it. Father and Uncle William didn't like to hear them bickering in the library either, so the girls were forced to retreat upstairs to the nursery. It soon proved impossible to conduct the business of serious artistic creation with the other children romping around, peering over their shoulders at their sketches and interrupting with questions and laughter, so they withdrew to Claudia's bedroom. Claudia decreed it, and Sylvia complied. She preferred to save her voice for more important arguments.

Claudia's bedroom was on the second floor next to Sylvia's. They were almost mirror images of each other, with identical furniture, lamps, and windows arranged with a wall between them. Both rooms were decorated in fashionable pastel hues, but Claudia favored bright pinks, clear greens, and yellows, while Sylvia preferred cooler greens, blues, and lavenders. Claudia's room was tidier, naturally, her clothing and linens tucked away in the bureau and wardrobe, her dressing table uncluttered, and her toys and belongings organized in gingham-lined baskets stacked on shelves.

Sylvia secretly admired her sister's apparently effortless order and tried to impose it on her own room, but tidiness was not its natural state and cheerful disarray inevitably resumed. Sylvia's dressing table doubled as a desk, with books and papers and sketchpads scattered about. Fascinating souvenirs from the forest and the creek bank littered her bureau, and photos of friends and sketches of future quilts were thumbtacked to the walls all around. Whenever she was in a hurry to clear away the clutter, she shoved things under the bed or into drawers, with little logic applied to what went where. If the room appeared properly sorted from the doorway when her father came around to check, that was good enough for her.

Sylvia wouldn't admit it aloud, but it truly was more restful to work in her sister's uncluttered room. She silently vowed to keep her own in better order. As Claudia claimed her dressing table and chair, Sylvia carried her sketchpad, notebook, and pencil case to the bed.

Suddenly Claudia yelped, seized her by the elbow, and pulled her away.

"What's the matter?" Sylvia asked, glancing about wildly, expecting to discover that her sister had saved her from sitting on a spider.

"Don't sit on my Sunbonnet Sue quilt. Ever."

"Why not? You do."

"Hardly ever." Claudia steered Sylvia toward the wall near the dressing table and released her arm. When Sylvia just blinked at her, uncomprehending, Claudia pointed to the floor. Frowning, Sylvia sat down, resting her back against the wall. "I know how to be gentle," Claudia said loftily as she returned to her dressing table. "You'd probably tear off half of the appliqués."

Sylvia thought that unlikely. Grandmother Elizabeth had made that quilt, and her stitches were famously tiny, precise, and strong. Sylvia would never criticize their beloved grandmother's handiwork, but in her opinion, fewer appliqués could only improve the quilt's appearance. She thought Sunbonnet Sue was the most insipid and trite of all quilt patterns—a girl in profile clad in a billowing dress, one rounded arm at her side, the side of one shoe visible below her hem, her head entirely concealed by an enormous sunbonnet. What exactly was Sue supposed to be doing, thinking, or looking at? It only made matters worse to put two dozen of them on the same quilt top, distinguishable only by the different calico prints for their dresses and bonnets, all of them staring blankly in the same direction. Sylvia much preferred the quilt Grandmother Elizabeth had made for her own bed, a Broken Star Log Cabin pieced from soft blues, greens, and creams.

The sisters settled down to work, Sylvia in the vaguely annoying position of having to look up at Claudia as they resumed their ongoing debate about the design of their quilt. Claudia had brainstormed an entire list of ideas before they had reluctantly agreed to collaborate, just as Sylvia had. Each had expected the other to abandon her own ideas in favor of her sister's, and both had been unpleasantly surprised to discover that her sister would prove stubbornly resistant.

"They call it the Century of Progress Quilting Contest in the announcement," Sylvia reminded Claudia for at least the millionth time. "We really ought to include the theme in our design."

"It's not required." Claudia held out the pamphlet, but Sylvia folded her arms rather than take it. She already knew the rules by heart, or nearly so, certainly better than Claudia did. "There aren't any extra points awarded for making a theme quilt."

"If the theme doesn't matter, why would they offer a bonus if the grand prize winner is a Century of Progress quilt?"

"I don't know. To make it more challenging, maybe? We *do* know how the entries will be evaluated." Claudia raised a fist and ticked off the criteria by opening it one finger at a time. "Design, color, workmanship, materials, and general appearance. The rules don't say anything about awarding points for theme."

"The *theme* is part of the *design*, and the design is worth twenty points." Sylvia inhaled deeply, trying to contain her exasperation. "Claudia, listen. I honestly believe that our best chance to get a perfect score in design is to create an original pictorial quilt inspired by the Century of Progress theme."

"And *I* honestly believe that we stand a better chance of impressing the judges if we use a traditional pattern and flawless, intricate sewing and quilting."

Sylvia managed not to retort that no one had ever described Claudia's handiwork as flawless. "I agree we should sew as perfectly as we can—on an original theme quilt, not a traditional pattern that everyone has already seen before."

"It would be a huge mistake to waste time chasing novelty when there are already thousands of traditional quilt blocks to choose from."

Sylvia's temper flared. "I'm not 'chasing novelty.' I'm pursuing originality, and I bet the judges are seeking it."

Claudia fixed her with a hard, appraising look. "Your problem is that you're only focusing on the bonus we'd get *if* we won the grand prize. You're paying no attention to everything we need to do just to make it into the finals."

"I am too paying attention to all of that," Sylvia snapped back. But was she paying *enough* attention? Maybe she was so dazzled by the thought of that extra two hundred dollars that she had lost sight of the fundamentals. The judges' criteria did seem to emphasize the basic elements of the quilting arts, flawlessly executed.

What would their mother advise if she were there? Sylvia imagined her reading the pamphlet, studying the rules carefully, and offering her gentle wisdom.

Just this once, Sylvia longed to hear her say, "Compromise, girls."

"Maybe I am getting ahead of myself," she admitted, almost regretting it when Claudia's face lit up in triumph. "It's true that we have to make it through the first two rounds before the bonus prize even matters. What do the rules say about who the local and regional judges will be?"

Quickly Claudia consulted the brochure. "'Local and regional judges will be experts chosen by Sears. The judges for the national contest . . .'" Claudia's voice trailed off as she read silently, and then shook her head. "I don't recognize their names, but they include the director of the Art Institute of Chicago, the needlework editor of *Good Housekeeping*, a quilt designing expert, the home advisor for Sears Roebuck—"

"So some of them are definitely quilt experts, but others are probably more familiar with other kinds of art, and some are businesspeople who might not know much about quilting at all."

Claudia shrugged and closed the brochure. "That's what it sounds like."

Sylvia puffed out her cheeks and blew out a long breath, thinking. "You're right about the design—but I'm right too," she quickly added, before Claudia celebrated too much. "We need flawless handiwork to appeal to the quilters among the judges, but we also need a sparkling, original design to impress the artists, and something about the World's Fair theme to win over the Sears people."

"Fine. The design can't be all one thing or another, not if we want to impress all of the judges." Claudia thrust out her lower lip in a pretty pout as she always did when untangling the threads of a difficult problem. "Maybe we should take bits from your favorite idea and bits from mine and put them together."

"A compromise," said Sylvia, resigned. She preferred to design her quilts according to artistic inspiration, not strategy, but with their deadline approaching and so much prize money at stake, what else could they do?

After another twenty minutes of intense discussion, the sisters decided that Sylvia would design a central medallion comprised of several individual appliqué blocks depicting progress in transportation technology from colonial times until the present day. Meanwhile, Claudia would create a wide border of stunning pieced blocks to frame the appliqué center.

"And if it's originality you're after, I've designed something you should like." Claudia leafed through her sketchbook, held it open to a well-illustrated page, and handed it over. "It's an original block in the traditional style. I call it Star of Progress."

"The name is perfect," Sylvia acknowledged as she studied the diagram, so neatly drawn in pink, green, and butter yellow pencils that Claudia must have used a ruler. Claudia's design was an eight-patch block, and it resembled a Sawtooth Star with a smaller Sawtooth Star in the center, where a solid square usually belonged. In the middle of each of the four sides, a small Flying Geese unit fit between the larger Sawtooth Star's points, creating the illusion of brilliance and sparkle. Each corner was a four-patch comprised of two solid background squares opposite two half-square triangles—a pieced square made up of two right triangles, one dark and one light, sewn together along the longest edge. Sylvia couldn't help admiring the block. Her sister had taken a simple, traditional pattern and made it far more complex and interesting. And yet piecing it required only straight stitches and abutted seams, no set-in pieces or curved sewing, so Claudia would not have to struggle.

That was what made what Sylvia had to tell her all the more difficult.

"This block will make an excellent border," Sylvia said carefully, "but I don't think it's an original design. But that's fine. It doesn't have to be."

Claudia's brow furrowed. "What do you mean?" She snatched her sketchbook back and studied her drawing, frowning. "I'm sure I've never seen this block before."

"Like I said, it doesn't matter. Weren't we just saying that we should combine traditional and original? It's too bad we can't use your name, though, because Star of Progress would be—"

"It's an original block and I'll prove it." Marking her place with her finger, Claudia closed the sketchbook, tucked it beneath her arm, and left the room without looking back.

Heaving a sigh, Sylvia rose from the floor and followed after her.

She hung back a few paces as she descended the stairs after her sister, following along silently as Claudia strode down the west wing and through the kitchen, where Aunt Nellie was helping the cook prepare dinner. She halted just inside the doorway to the west sitting room, since their banishment had not yet been rescinded. Peering over her sister's shoulder, Sylvia glimpsed Great-Aunt Lydia seated at her sewing machine on the other side of the room, her back to them as she stitched two bright strips of feed sack cotton together. Great-Aunt Lucinda sat in a chair by the window, frowning in concentration as she rooted through her sewing basket for a particular spool of thread.

"May I ask you both a question?" Claudia asked, opening her sketchbook and turning the drawing toward them. When the great-aunts glanced her way, she did a slow quarter turn from one to the other so each could take a good look at the page. "Have you ever seen this block before?"

"I don't recall that I've ever made it, but it looks familiar," said Great-Aunt Lydia thoughtfully, turning in her chair for a better view. "Odd Fellows Block, perhaps?"

"Odd Fellows *Patch*, I think," said Great-Aunt Lucinda, slipping off her reading glasses and peering at the block studiously.

"Almost, but not quite," declared Great-Aunt Lydia, triumphant. "It's Odd Fellows Chain!"

"Yes, I remember now," said Great-Aunt Lucinda, nodding. "Hortense from the quilt guild made an Odd Fellows Chain quilt for her brother-in-law a few years ago. It was her own private joke, because she found him to be a rather odd fellow."

Great-Aunt Lydia nodded too, smiling. "I remember trying to explain that the name comes from the Odd Fellows fraternal order, but she preferred her own interpretation."

As the aunties laughed together, Sylvia hung back, shifting her weight and wincing, wondering if she should make a quick and stealthy exit before Claudia realized she had witnessed her embarrassment. But she couldn't resist lingering to see what would happen next.

"Are you sure?" Claudia wailed, darting into the room, first to Great-Aunt Lucinda and then to Great-Aunt Lydia, so they could inspect her sketch more closely. "Are you absolutely sure?"

"Yes, dear," said Great-Aunt Lydia, admiring the drawing. "It's a very nice rendition."

"But I was trying to make an original design," said Claudia, tears in her voice. "For our World's Fair quilt, to impress the judges."

Sylvia took a deep breath. "I told her it doesn't matter," she ventured, stepping into the doorway.

"I'm sure it won't," said Great-Aunt Lucinda, offering Claudia a reassuring smile. "What was it the brochure said about what the judges will be looking for? Beauty, perfection of stitching, fine materials, etcetera. I don't recall anything about an original block design meriting extra points."

"Design," said Claudia flatly. "That's twenty points."

"It's a striking block," said Great-Aunt Lucinda. "When made in attractive colors with your very best handiwork, it will surely deserve full credit for design."

"Besides, this block gives us a great name for our quilt," said Sylvia, daring to cross the threshold since Claudia had defied the ban and survived. "Now we can call it 'Chain of Progress.'"

Claudia whirled upon her, but as she drew in a breath, gathering steam for an argument, she unexpectedly halted. "I actually like that," she admitted.

Sylvia heaved a sigh, relieved that the matter was settled at last.

For several days thereafter, as soon as the sisters returned home from school, they raced through their homework and reconvened in the nursery, where they ignored the younger children's noise and worked out the general plan for their quilt top, taking turns drawing and erasing on a large pad of blank newsprint paper fastened to an easel. When they were satisfied, they quickly settled upon a color scheme of rich pastels, light enough to suit the modern style, but dark enough to be bold and striking. To their delight, their aunties invited them to choose from among the very best fabrics in their own stashes rather than drawing upon their mother's scrap bag, their usual source, which had become rather depleted through the years. Then, after agreeing to check in with each other daily, Sylvia and Claudia parted company to work on their separate sections independently.

First, Sylvia began transforming her sketches into appliqué patterns, working from illustrations in books in the Bergstrom home library. When she needed a break from drawing, she switched to sewing. By mid-February, she had sewn blocks for a canoe, a sleigh, and a hot air balloon, and she had drawn patterns for several more. When she couldn't find any suitable pictures for a stagecoach, a blimp, a locomotive, or several other ingenious ideas crowding her imagination, she turned to the Waterford Public Library on the town square. After school, instead of catching the bus home with her siblings and cousins, she would walk to the venerable Greek Revival building and ask her favorite librarian for help finding the pictures she needed. Sometimes she worked in the library's reference section, opening a heavy volume on a table and glancing back and forth between an illustration and her sketchbook as she carefully reproduced the image in colored pencil. On other occasions, if a book had many designs she wished to reproduce, she would borrow it, proudly presenting her library card at the circulation desk, behind which a splendid antique Album quilt was displayed. At home, she would work at her father's oak desk in their own library, which she decided ought to boast a quilt on the wall too. Perhaps Chain of Progress would be that quilt, maybe with a magnificent ribbon from the Chicago World's Fair pinned to it.

Richard was happiest when Sylvia worked at home. After he finished his chores and tired of playing outside with his sled, he would join her in the library with his own drawing pad and pencils, a lingering flush in his cheeks from the cold. To her amusement, he tried to help by providing his own drawings of automobiles, airplanes, and massive locomotives, which she admired profusely and promised to consider including in the quilt, although she knew they wouldn't suit. Richard proved to be very helpful, though, as an excellent source for ideas. He seemed to have an infinite number of vehicles committed to memory, and whenever she found herself at a loss, he could recite a half dozen options without pausing for breath.

One day, Sylvia returned home from the library to find Claudia waiting for her in the foyer, bursting with news. "Great-Aunt Lydia is teaching me to use her sewing machine to piece my blocks," she said, fairly bouncing with excitement. "She says it's the only way I'll ever finish in time, and my seams are so much neater this way."

"That's great," said Sylvia, only a little envious, because whatever benefited the quilt benefited them both. "I wish her sewing machine could do appliqué too."

"It's all right," said Claudia, resting a hand on her shoulder. "If I finish my blocks before you finish yours, I'll help you."

"Thanks," Sylvia murmured. She really wanted to do them all herself, but she'd rather finish on time with her sister's help than finish too late on her own.

Thanks to the sewing machine and the much simpler assembly required for the Odd Fellows Chain blocks, Claudia completed two identical blocks for each unique, complex appliqué block Sylvia made. But the disparity in difficulty was not the only reason Sylvia lagged behind her sister. They both had school and chores, but Sylvia also worked for Bergstrom Thoroughbreds, as often and as much as her father and uncle allowed. She loved to feed and brush the horses, but her very favorite task of all was to exercise them, especially when her father permitted her to take them out of the riding arena or the round ring and ride cross-country through the estate. Even a short ride was exhilarating—the sense of freedom and power as the horse carried her over the meadow, the almost mystical connection and trust she felt sparking between herself and the horse. With the wind in her face and the sound of hoofbeats in her ears, she felt a part of the natural, wild world, not merely a traveler passing through it. After a ride and a cooldown, Sylvia even enjoyed the meticulous, essential duties that followed: carefully removing the tack; brushing the horse's coat, mane, and tail; clearing debris from the hooves; checking all over for any injuries or sore spots; and feeding and watering. She performed each act with gratitude, sometimes even murmuring her thanks aloud, so softly that only she and the horse could hear.

After the horses were comfortable in their stalls with fresh bedding, if Sylvia wasn't needed in the house, she often lingered to help with other tasks. One afternoon in early March, she was sweeping the stable entrance while her father and uncle mended tack. When her father asked about her school day, she dispensed with that subject in a few words and chattered on about the World's Fair quilt instead.

"I still haven't decided how I'm going to arrange my blocks," she mused aloud as she swept a cloud of dirt and straw out the doorway. "I suppose I can't really say for sure until I make all of them and know what vehicles I have to work with. My favorite idea so far is to arrange them in pairs, with the older vehicle on the left and the modern version on the right to show progress. So I'd have the canoe on the left paired with a steamboat on the right. Next to that, I could have a pair of blocks with a horse-drawn gig on the left, an automobile on the right." She paused, resting both hands on the top of the broom. "But what if all of my blocks don't naturally divide into pairs?" With a cheerful shrug, she resumed sweeping. "It's fine. I'll figure it out."

"Interesting concept, progress," said her father from his workbench, where he was mending a saddle with his leatherworking tools. "A canoe is an ancient form of transportation, but I can't agree that a steamboat, while more technologically advanced, necessarily represents progress."

"No?" Sylvia finished sweeping and returned the broom to its nook in the wall. "But it's faster, more powerful, able to haul more cargo—"

"Fair enough, but one wouldn't get you very far on Elm Creek, would it?"

"I guess not." Even the ferry was restricted to the deepest, broadest part of the creek near Widow's Pining, where it was as wide as a river.

"Some waterways are better suited for a canoe, some for a steamboat," Uncle William remarked as he hung up newly cleaned tack on pegs. "A canoe is an engineering marvel, ideal for its place and purpose. That's why the design hasn't changed much over the centuries. It's already near perfect."

"I suppose that's true," said Sylvia. Maybe she should reconsider the arrangement of her blocks. Fortunately, she hadn't stitched them together yet.

"And furthermore," said Uncle William, his face lighting up with a mischievous grin, "what's the big idea, suggesting that autos are an improvement over horses? I can't believe a Bergstrom girl would say such a thing."

Sylvia felt heat rush into her cheeks. "I never said that." But in a way, she had, hadn't she? "It's just that an automobile is more techno-logically advanced than a carriage."

"You said 'progress,'" Uncle William teased.

"You did. I heard it too," her father remarked.

"I love horses, and you both know it," she protested, looking from one to the other, her face burning. "I don't ever want cars to replace horses, not completely anyway. Like you both said, sometimes one thing is better suited for a certain place and purpose than another."

"I'm relieved to hear you admit that," said Uncle William, com-ing over to chuck her beneath the chin fondly. "I'd hate to see you take the Ford on a tear across the meadow the way you rode Daffodil just now."

"I wouldn't," said Sylvia indignantly, although it did sound like fun.

Her father heaved a sigh and rose from his stool, leaving the saddle on the workbench. "Most days I'm skeptical of the modern world's concept of 'progress.' It emphasizes technological advances rather than moral development," he said as he put away his tools. "Labor-saving devices and other modern marvels may do more harm than good if they aren't accompanied by progress in justice, equality, and ethics."

"Well said, brother," said Uncle William, his merry grin turning into something else, a look of respect and admiration.

That evening after supper, Sylvia found herself working more slowly than usual, her thoughts wandering, her stitches less swift and sure. Not a thread of her finished blocks or a pencil stroke of her sketches had changed, and yet they didn't please her as much as they had the last time she had admired them.

Throughout the next day, Sylvia found herself mulling over her father's words when she was supposed to be paying attention to her teachers. After school, she walked to the Waterford Public Library to return her library books and to search for another with an illustration of a dirigible. Usually she practically skipped and flew to the library, but today her feet seemed to drag. Her heart wasn't really in her design anymore, and she didn't know what to do about it.

In the library, as she slipped the books into the returns bin at the circulation desk, she glanced up at the lovely antique quilt displayed on the wall above it. She had seen the quilt so many times through the years that she almost didn't notice it anymore, but this time she lingered to admire it, drawing as close as the barrier of the desk allowed. The quilt's green, Prussian blue, and Turkey red calicoes were faded, but still pretty, stitched together into sixty-one traditional Album blocks, each eight inches square, all arranged in an on-point setting and surrounded by a Stacked Bricks border. The muslin center rectangle of each block was inscribed with a name, the names and penmanship unique to each block. The ink had faded away long ago and, in some places, had deteriorated the muslin fabric, but the black embroidery over each signature remained. Sylvia knew that nearly a century before, local women had made the quilt, Authors' Album, to raise money to build the very library in which she stood. Then, and now, those signatures made the quilt unique and priceless. Sylvia felt a bit awestruck as she read the names she could puzzle out at that distance—Washington Irving, James Fenimore Cooper, Elizabeth Barrett Browning, Walt Whitman, Frederick Douglass, William Cullen Bryant, Henry David Thoreau, Elizabeth Cady Stanton, Henry Brown, fifty-two others—the most renowned authors, artists, and politicians of the mid-nineteenth century, or so her favorite librarian had once told her.

A thrill of inspiration raced through her like an electric current—brilliant, delicious, and a bit scary. The people who had signed patches for Authors' Album understood progress as her father did—not in creating better, faster machines, but in advancing ideas, in improving lives, in striving for justice, dignity, and liberty for all people. *That* was true progress—and that spirit was what she longed to capture in fabric and thread.

It was a pity she'd have to scrap all the blocks and sketches she'd already made, and Claudia would probably fret about the time wasted, but the end result would be worth it. She'd make Claudia understand why she must start anew. Inspiration was beckoning, and she must follow where it led.

7

September 2004

Sylvia woke to a cool, intermittent breeze stirring the curtains and the music of birdsong, a chorus of blue jays, cardinals, and swallows greeting the sunrise, as well as an occasional robin reminding its kin that they must prepare to fly south soon. She and Andrew had left the window open only slightly the night before in deference to the forecast, which had predicted that the lingering summer heat would surrender to autumn at last. "Prime apple-picking weather is on the way," Andrew had said as he leaned over to switch off the bedside lamp. Sylvia hoped he was right.

Sitting up in bed and stretching, Sylvia glimpsed clouds in the eastern sky through the window, barely pink with the new light of dawn, which was arriving noticeably later every day. Andrew's side of the bed was empty, so evidently he had risen earlier without waking her. Now he was likely in the kitchen reading the newspaper over breakfast, unless he had already finished and was carrying his rod and tackle box to his favorite fishing spot on the west bank of Elm Creek.

Sylvia dressed in a light sweater and slacks and set out to join her husband, pausing at the top of the grand oak staircase to savor the brief, reverential stillness that descended upon Elm Creek Manor in the early mornings. Not every morning, she noted, smiling to herself as she grasped the smooth banister and descended to the foyer. When quilt camp was in session, the manor would be bustling even at this early hour with eager campers who couldn't wait to begin another day of quilting and fellowship with friends new and old. On other occasions, the twins broke the silence before dawn calling out for their parents, although kindhearted Gretchen often let the young couple sleep in and hurried to answer the children's summons herself. The Hartleys had not been blessed with children, but before moving to Elm Creek Manor, Gretchen had spent many years volunteering at a Pittsburgh shelter for pregnant homeless teens. Now the McClure family was the beneficiary of all her experience and kindness. Gretchen had known and loved the twins all their lives, and she had even attended Sarah's childbirth classes with her when Matt had been away in Uniontown working for his father's construction company.

Sylvia smelled coffee brewing as soon as she crossed from the foyer into the west wing, so when she entered the kitchen, she was a bit surprised to find it empty. Only a newspaper spread open on the refectory table suggested that Andrew and Joe had shared it over breakfast not long before. Though the enticing aroma lingered, the coffeepot too was empty, so Sylvia put on a fresh brew and enjoyed a piece of toast spread lightly with apple butter while she waited. When the coffee was ready, she filled two travel mugs—one with cream and sugar for herself, the other with sugar only for Andrew—and carried them out the back door and down the four steps to the rear parking lot.

Outside the air was cool and misty, dew lingering on the grass, the breeze carrying a hint of autumn crispness as it rustled the elm boughs high above and sent fallen leaves scuttering across the gravel lot. With a mug in each hand, Sylvia crossed the bridge over Elm Creek without spilling a single drop. Andrew's favorite fishing spot, a large, round, flat rock on the creek bank beneath a willow tree, had been her favorite secluded hideaway as a child. Whenever she had needed time alone to think or to cool her temper after an argument with her sister, she had stolen away to the willow and the rock. The musical burbling of the creek never failed to soothe her, and sometimes even now—as an octogenarian well aware of her good fortune to be one—she favored the private spot for quiet contemplation.

But she was happy to share it with her dear Andrew.

She knew better than to scare away the fish by calling out to him when she spied him through the willow branches, that familiar, worn fishing cap on his head, a tackle box on the rock by his side. She approached quietly, but her footfalls alerted him when she was still some distance away. He glanced over his shoulder, and his face lit up at the sight of her. "There's my girl," he said, his voice low. Shifting his fishing rod to one hand, he patted the rock beside him.

Sylvia gladly took the offered seat, handed him his coffee, and rested her head upon his shoulder as he drew her closer. "Catch anything?"

"Not yet, but fishing isn't just about catching."

"So you always remind me."

"That's because it's always true."

She smiled, and they sat in companionable silence for a while, sipping their coffee and watching minnows draw close to the hook and dart away into the shadows.

"The manor was quiet this morning," Sylvia remarked, shifting to a more comfortable position on the rock. "No one else seems to be up yet. I hope that means the twins let Sarah and Matt sleep in."

"Joe's up. I saw him at breakfast." Andrew inclined his head toward the red barn. "Afterward, he said he was heading over to the woodshop to finish the road marker for you."

Sylvia felt a pang of chagrin. "I hope he didn't get up early especially for that. I think I might have been a bit too peevish yesterday, with all my caveats and second-guessing."

"Peevish? You?" Andrew shook his head and adjusted the line, his eyes on the bobber. "Not at all. You were raising sensible questions. No one got their feelings hurt."

"I'm not so sure about that." Sylvia sighed, remembering Matt's crestfallen expression after she found fault with his loose security at the market stand checkout. "Yesterday afternoon, Sarah gave me a bit of a talking-to and set me straight."

"Is that so?"

"Quite so." Sylvia stretched out her legs before her and leaned back, resting her weight on her hands. "Sarah and Matt are two very clever young people. If they believe they've come up with a scheme to see us through our little financial crisis, the least I can do is let them try."

"They *are* the future of the business," Andrew reminded her. "The future of the entire estate, for that matter. The only way they're going to learn how to run things on their own is by doing it."

"And without us looking over their shoulders every minute, finding fault." For the most part, that was how Sarah already ran Elm Creek Quilts. In the beginning Sylvia and Sarah had divided the administrative tasks between them, with the exception of managing the website and other internet activities, a role Summer had eagerly undertaken. In recent years, though, Sylvia had essentially retired from the day-to-day business operations, serving mostly as an advisor to the faculty and staff, and as primary hostess and master of ceremonies for quilt camp.

Perhaps it was time for her to officially turn over everything to the younger generation. She could keep only her more ceremonial roles and mentoring, which she knew no one wanted her to give up.

"From now on, I'm going to give Elm Creek Orchards my unconditional blessing," Sylvia declared. "I'll give encouragement freely, but I'll offer advice only if and when the younger folks ask for it."

"I'm sure Sarah and Matt will appreciate that," said Andrew, "but if you see them driving off a cliff, you should feel free to warn them, even if they don't ask for your opinion first."

"Very well," Sylvia agreed, amused. "I'll warn them of impending disaster if I see something they don't, but otherwise, I'll leave them to it. In fact, I'll go one step further."

"Meaning?"

"I'm going to schedule a meeting with Sarah and invite her to share more of her ideas for generating additional revenue. She's mentioned a few things now and again, but I haven't really listened." Sylvia was too embarrassed to admit that she often changed the subject whenever Sarah tentatively ran an idea by her. Worse yet, sometimes she dismissed Sarah's proposals with a brusque critique without giving them the attention they deserved—or rather, without giving her dear friend and colleague the attention and respect *she* deserved.

But no longer. It was remarkable how energized she felt, choosing optimism over negativity. And wasn't she already practicing this more enlightened approach to new ideas by allowing Summer to borrow her quilt for the historical society's exhibit?

"Did I tell you Summer is coming over later this morning to see my World's Fair quilt?" Sylvia asked.

"You did." Andrew leaned forward as the bobber dipped slightly, then scowled comically when it did not move again. "Do you need my help bringing it down from the attic?"

"Thanks, but no. Summer and I can manage." She laughed softly, mindful of the timorous fish. "I may find myself with more helpers than I need if word gets out. Sarah wants to see the quilt too."

Yet Sarah might have her hands full with the twins and with submitting various advertisements and website announcements for the orchard's grand opening. They seemed to be cutting it a bit close given that the big day was little more than a week away—but, Sylvia reminded herself, she would trust that Sarah knew what she was doing.

This hands-off approach might take a bit of practice to master.

Sylvia and Andrew contemplated the bobber a while longer, listening to the birds, the creek rushing over smooth stones, and the wind in the trees. Once or twice, Sylvia thought she heard the distant whine of an electric screwdriver or a hammer pounding nails in the vicinity of the market stand. Andrew must have heard the construction noise too, for he downed the last of his coffee, drew in his fishing line, and began packing his gear. "I thought I'd offer Joe a hand installing that sign," he said. "After that, I'll see if Matt needs any help finishing up the market stand."

"Sounds like a plan." Sylvia smiled her thanks as Andrew extended his hand and helped her to her feet. "As for me, I'll see about fixing us all a nice lunch after my meeting with Summer, something other than the usual sandwiches." A sudden cool gust of wind sent brown and gold leaves falling all around them. The seasons were changing, no question about it. Perhaps she should ask Anna for some of her autumn squash recipes.

They parted at the bridge with a kiss, Andrew for the woodshop in the red banked barn, Sylvia, an empty mug in each hand, for the manor kitchen. This time she found the room bustling with cheerful activity and happy noise, for Gretchen and the four McClures had all come down to breakfast. Sylvia jumped right in to help, pouring a bowl of cereal here, filling a sippy cup there, moving Matt's coffee mug out of reach when James lunged for it. Then she settled down at the refectory table with a second cup of coffee to catch up on the morning gossip.

Late the previous night, she soon learned, Sarah had received an email from Bonnie, a founding Elm Creek Quilter who spent most of her time on Maui at a new quilt camp she had launched with an old college friend. After rhapsodizing about the gorgeous weather and the exquisite traditional Hawaiian appliqué quilts members of a local guild had displayed for a special camp program, Bonnie had asked Sarah to remind her friends of their standing invitation to visit. It was a tempting offer Sylvia and Andrew had accepted the previous

February. Sarah and Matt intended to go the moment the twins were old enough to leave for a week in someone else's care.

"They're old enough now," said Gretchen. "They're ready."

"Yes, but I'm not," said Sarah.

"Don't wait until they're teenagers to enjoy time alone as a couple," Sylvia advised. "Seize the day."

"Sounds like good advice to me," said Matt to Sarah, hopeful, but Sarah merely smiled.

There was more news from another distant Elm Creek Quilter. Only moments before Sylvia returned from the fishing rock, Maggie Flynn had called to check in from a bed-and-breakfast somewhere in Nebraska between Lincoln and Omaha. During the off-season, Maggie spent most of her time traveling from quilt shop to quilt guild, lecturing and teaching, often accompanied by her boyfriend, Russell, an accomplished modern quilter based in Seattle. Occasionally Russell worked at Elm Creek Quilt Camp as a visiting instructor, but for much of the year, the couple's careers kept them apart. They both considered the arrangement far less than ideal. Sylvia and Sarah had privately agreed that whenever a full-time position became available, Russell would be the first person they'd ask to join the faculty. Sylvia only hoped they wouldn't lose Maggie in the meantime, if another arts center with teaching positions for both of them beckoned the couple away.

After breakfast was finished and many hands made light work of tidying up, Sylvia joined Gretchen in the playroom to keep the twins happily occupied while Sarah worked in the office and Matt on the market stand. It was nearly eleven o'clock when Sylvia remembered her appointment. On the way downstairs, she stopped by the library to invite Sarah to the quilt reveal, but Sarah was caught up in a struggle between accounts payable and receivable and regretfully declined. Instead Sylvia returned to the kitchen alone to ponder the possibilities for lunch. She hoped Summer might join them. If she remembered correctly, Anna had left some vegetarian soups in the freezer that would do nicely.

She had just opened the deep-freezer door when she heard Gwen's car rumbling over the gravel just outside the window. Quickly she stretched deep into the freezer to retrieve two tubs of Anna's signature roasted red pepper and tomato bisque and shut the door with her hip. She was setting the rock-solid containers on the counter when she heard the back door open and close, followed by voices in conversation. Apparently Summer had not come alone. Perhaps her mother had joined her.

Curious, Sylvia rubbed her very cold hands together and came around the counter to greet the new arrivals. Summer entered the kitchen first, smiling over her shoulder not at Gwen but at—"Anna," Sylvia exclaimed. "What a delightful surprise! It's been too long."

Anna laughed, her dark eyes sparkling. "It's been two weeks," she said, shrugging her long, dark French braid over her shoulder. She had a well-stuffed reusable grocery bag hanging from each shoulder, and Summer carried a third.

"As I said, too long." Sylvia hurried forward to take one of Anna's bags. "Here, let me help. What do we have here? Oh, my. Butter, sage, and—What's in these containers?"

"Lunch," Summer declared, smiling. "When I told Anna I was paying a visit today, she asked to come along, and you know she's incapable of arriving empty-handed."

"I missed this wonderful kitchen," said Anna with a sigh as she set her bag on the refectory table next to the one Sylvia had taken. "The kitchenette in our apartment is functional, but just barely. I don't have any counter space to speak of, and Jeremy has taken over the table with his books and dissertation notes."

"How can an artist like you work in such conditions?" Summer teased.

"I can't, which is why I'm here." Anna retrieved a spotless white

apron and her favorite toque from the pantry and swiftly put them on.
"I've nearly perfected my new recipe for butternut squash ravioli with
browned butter sage sauce, but I've already fed Jeremy two variations
this week. I can't ask him to taste-test another, so I thought I'd ask
you all instead."

"I already told her we'd accept," Summer told Sylvia.

"And gladly. Butternut squash ravioli sounds marvelous." While
her friends unpacked the grocery bags, Sylvia furtively returned the
frozen soups to the deep freezer to enjoy another day. "Would you
like some help with the cooking?"

"Thanks, but I've got this covered," said Anna as she retrieved a
large stainless-steel pot from a low cupboard and placed it in the sink
to fill with water. "You two go on and take care of that quilt. Summer
is just about bursting from anticipation to see it."

"I am," Summer admitted, linking her arm through Sylvia's.
"Shall we?"

"Before I change my mind?" Sylvia asked, amused, as Summer
steered her from the kitchen into the hall.

"Something like that."

They walked in step down the west wing and into the foyer, but
they brought themselves up short at the foot of the grand staircase;
when Sylvia turned to head upstairs, Summer continued forward
toward the ballroom, and their linked arms anchored them in place.
"This way," Sylvia prompted, inclining her head toward the stairs.

Summer glanced to the ballroom door and back to Sylvia, per-
plexed. "It's not in the cabinet with the rest of the heirlooms?"

"No, dear." Sylvia understood why Summer might assume so. The
ballroom, once the setting for the Bergstrom family's most elegant
parties and celebrations, now served as the center of Elm Creek Quilt
Camp Day. Movable partitions divided the expansive space into class-
rooms, each filled with an assortment of sewing machines, overhead
projectors, felt design boards, ironing stations, cutting tables, and

other accoutrements of the quilting arts. At the far end of the room was a raised dais that provided a stage for special guest speakers during the day and for entertainment programs in the evenings. In the southeast corner stood a rectangular quilting frame, large enough for three quilters to sit at comfortably, and four to sit more snugly, on each of the longer sides. Nearby was its more modern counterpart, a longarm quilting machine, currently unplugged and silent, with nothing layered on the rollers. Longarm Quilting was one of their most popular workshops, and successive groups of quilters managed to complete two or three quilts each season.

The most recent addition to the room was a superb cedar quilt cabinet, expertly crafted by Joe for storing the manor's most precious quilts. Broad and solid, sanded to a satin-smooth finish inside and out to avoid snagging fragile fabrics, lined with acid-free material to protect the quilts within, the cabinet offered spaces for small quilts folded on the bias as well as larger pieces stored on rolls.

It had never occurred to Sylvia that the World's Fair quilt belonged there among the manor's most cherished heirlooms, but now that seemed like an oversight. "It's upstairs in the attic," she admitted, "where your mother and I first found it."

"Oh, okay," said Summer, nodding, a slight frown of puzzlement appearing and quickly vanishing. "Let's go find it."

Sylvia led the way to the third floor, then down the hall to the narrower, steeper staircase that led to the attic. Easing the trapdoor open, she climbed upstairs into the attic, where faint sunshine leaked through the roof ridge vent, but the air smelled stale and lifeless. Sylvia could not make out anything distinctly in the feeble light, though she could almost feel the weight of the looming jumble of old furniture and the accumulated possessions of four generations pressing in on all sides.

The attic was the one area she and Sarah had not cleaned and organized upon Sylvia's return to Elm Creek Manor after her long absence. Only occasionally did Sylvia make her way up to the attic to retrieve a particular item—a long-lost heirloom she had suddenly remembered, perhaps, or the boxes of Christmas decorations. Joe came more frequently in hopes of finding an intriguing piece of antique furniture to restore. Sylvia often told herself that eventually she simply must set aside a few days to sort through all the clutter, preserving what was most meaningful and parting with the rest, but it would be a dusty, wearying, tedious job, and she gladly seized any excuse to put it off.

Still, she wouldn't necessarily have to tackle the work alone. Sarah thrived on uncovering the secrets of the Bergstrom family, Summer loved historical research, and Gretchen had only recently compared thrift store browsing to a treasure hunt. Her friends would likely be willing, perhaps even eager, to help her clear out the attic if she asked. It would be a relief to have the Herculean labor over with. And who knew what fascinating heirlooms they might discover along the way?

"Would you get the light, please?" Sylvia asked, gesturing to the wall behind Summer.

A faint click followed, and then the overhead light came on, steady and sure. Matt had installed it a few years before, and it illuminated the attic much better than the single bare bulb it had replaced, but even now the sloped ceiling and the mounds of trunks, cartons, and sheet-draped old furniture cast deep shadows into the corners of the room. Directly before them stretched the newer, longer south wing of the manor; to their right lay the older, shorter west wing. In the attic the seam joining old and new was more evident than below, the colors of the walls subtly different, the floor not quite even.

"Now, where to begin?" mused Sylvia. Previous searches through the years had revealed a pattern within the clutter. The newest items were closest to the stairs, as if Claudia or her husband had merely stood on the top step and shoved the boxes inside. Moving deeper into the attic was like stepping back in time, although occasionally, a misplaced object juxtaposed the past and present: an electric lamp missing its shade rested on top of a treadle sewing machine; a pile of Sylvia's schoolbooks sat on the floor beside a carton of polyester fashions from the seventies. For the most part, however, the pattern held true. Sylvia had found Great-Aunt Gerda Bergstrom's journal in the deepest part of the west wing, and she had discovered some of her mother's belongings in the middle of the south wing. The World's Fair quilt was more recent than either of those, but unless it had been returned to the place where she and Gwen had found it, the chronological pattern wouldn't help much now.

"Do you remember where you put the quilt after my mom finished her article?" asked Summer, picking her way carefully down one of the narrow aisles between boxes and trunks.

"I didn't return it to the attic; your mother did that for me. I recall her saying that she put it where it would be easily found again." Sylvia paused, turned away to cover a sneeze, and waved away dust motes. "I know where it ought to be. My concern is that it was moved afterward during a search for something else."

Summer bent with easy grace to open a large cardboard box, which was full of yellowed newspaper clippings. She looked as if she were tempted to browse through them, but instead she closed the lid and moved on to a nearby trunk. "Are you surprised that Claudia didn't sell your World's Fair quilt along with the others?"

"No, not really. Our handiwork wasn't as fine as our mother's, so I can't imagine that our World's Fair quilt would have sold for much. Also, Claudia rarely won ribbons for her quilts. She wouldn't have parted with one that had earned such a distinction." Sylvia paused to think. "I recall that it was stored in a large, beige, flat box with a removable lid, not the brown cardboard type with flaps that fold down."

"Flat and beige. Got it."

Sylvia's gaze fell on a walnut bureau, and a memory stirred. "We originally found the box over there," she said, gesturing. "I suspect it's more likely to be on the top strata rather than buried lower, since it was so recently excavated."

"But you're sure it's up here?" Summer asked. "You didn't stash it beneath your bed or in a closet?"

"I wish I had, dear."

But since she hadn't, they focused on the boxes and trunks surrounding the bureau. They found numerous papers, books, china, clothing, and assorted items Sylvia no longer had any use for, so she began to set them aside, generally organized by type, to be discarded or donated later.

Summer soon discovered a bundle of Storm at Sea blocks pieced from the pastel cottons common to the late 1920s and early 1930s. After a quick examination, Sylvia recognized Claudia's signature flaws, including the poorly matched seams that Sylvia never would have permitted in her own work. "You're on the right track, dear," said Sylvia approvingly. "At least you've found the proper era."

"Maybe I should call my mom and ask her if she remembers where she put it."

"Let's give it five more minutes before we trouble her." Sylvia paused to rest, hands on her hips, and turned slowly in hopes that a different angle would reveal something she had overlooked. That was when she spotted the box on a desk near the stairs. "There it is," she exclaimed, pointing. "In plain sight, if only I had thought to glance in that direction."

Summer quickly made her way to it, and lifted the lid. "Jackpot," she cried, replacing the lid. "What do you say we take this downstairs to the ballroom where we can examine it in better light?"

Sylvia had had quite enough of the cluttered attic, so she readily agreed. Summer carefully carried the box down all three flights of stairs while Sylvia followed along behind. In the ballroom, they covered a long table with a clean sheet, then carefully removed the quilt from the box, gently unfolded it, and laid it upon the table.

"Sylvia," Summer breathed, "it's marvelous."

"It's a nice quilt," Sylvia allowed. It was in fine condition for its age, a testament to the thoughtful care it had received, even during shipping and at the judging venues. Even so, a few stains and broken threads marred the green, lavender, rose, and ivory quilt, which was accented with appliquéd features in bold red, blue, and black.

"It's marvelous," Summer repeated more emphatically. "The pieced border is so striking, and these appliquéd scenes are so evocative. That's the Emancipation Proclamation, isn't it? And that's the suffrage meeting at Seneca Falls, and that—No way. Is that supposed to be the 1913 Woman Suffrage Procession?"

"It is indeed."

"I wrote my master's thesis about that," Summer reminded her. "It would've been nice to include your quilt in a footnote."

"One scholarly work about this quilt is quite enough, thank you." Sylvia watched as her young friend gazed at the quilt in wonder, drawing closer now and then to study an appliqué, or to examine a flaw in need of repair. "Now that you've seen this old thing, are you sure you still want to include it in your exhibit?"

"Even more sure than before," said Summer. "With your permission, I'd like to take it with me when I leave today to prepare it for display."

"Oh?" Sylvia felt an unexpected pang of loss. "Is that necessary?"

Summer nodded. "I have a workstation set up in Union Hall where I can inspect the quilt more thoroughly and take care of any necessary cleaning and repairs."

"Couldn't you work on it here?" Then Sylvia caught herself. "Of course you *could*, but it would surely be much more convenient for you to work at Union Hall."

"Yes, it would be." Summer offered her an understanding smile. "I promise I'll take excellent care of your quilt."

"I don't doubt that for a moment." Why did she suddenly feel so protective of a quilt she had consigned to the attic decades ago? After all, the World's Fair quilt had traveled much farther than to downtown Waterford and had survived unscathed. And it would be far better to display it where quilt aficionados and history buffs could appreciate it, especially since it would support the Waterford Historical Society's ongoing fundraising. These days Sylvia could certainly sympathize with the need to raise capital.

Yet as she joined Summer in admiring the World's Fair quilt, it was reassuring to note that the financial problems Elm Creek Manor faced now were very small compared to what her family had overcome in the Great Depression. She had found a way through tough times before and she could do so again.

"Of course you may take it today," said Sylvia, "and you may keep it for the exhibit as long as you like. If I miss my quilt, I can visit it in the gallery."

"It'll have Gerda's Log Cabin for company," Summer reminded her.

"And many other excellent quilts as well." Smiling, Sylvia patted Summer's forearm. "First things first. Shall we let the quilt air out a bit while we see how Anna's lunch is coming along? I don't know about you, but all that climbing up and down staircases has left me famished."

8

March–May 1933

"Y ou want to change your appliqué designs *now*?" asked Claudia, eyes widening in dismay as she bounded up from the window seat, sending triangles of muslin and pastel calico tumbling to the nursery floor. "But we had a plan."

"Your part of the plan won't change," Sylvia assured her, trying again to show Claudia her revised sketches, but her sister wouldn't even glance at them. "I'll simply swap out my new appliqué blocks for the old ones. Your pieced border of Odd Fellows Chain blocks will fit around the center exactly the same."

"But now you'll have to start completely over, and it's already March!"

Sylvia felt uneasy about this too, but she wouldn't let her sister know that. "I think with a few small alterations, some of the old blocks will work in the new design."

"A few small alterations?" Now Claudia snatched Sylvia's sketchbook and leafed through her most recent drawings. "I don't see how. The blocks are too different. This means most of the work you've already put into our quilt is going to be wasted, and for what?"

"I told you," Sylvia said patiently. "Social progress is a much better interpretation of the Century of Progress theme than pictures of bigger boats and faster trains. Our quilt will be so much more meaningful this way, and I bet the judges will reward that."

Even if they didn't, Sylvia wouldn't regret changing her design. She knew this version of their quilt would be so much better than the original, more interesting and pleasing to the eye and eloquent. How could she settle for the old design when the new one taking shape in her imagination was immeasurably more relevant?

Heaving a sigh, Claudia closed the sketchbook and returned it. "Is there anything I can say to get you to change your mind, aside from reminding you that now you're going to have to sew twice as fast if we're going to have any chance of meeting the entry deadline?"

Sylvia felt a nervous flutter in her stomach. Maybe she *should* check a calendar before committing, count the days, make a schedule like her sister's—"No, there isn't," she replied firmly before she talked herself out of it. "This is a far better idea. It'll make a much better impression on the judges."

The look Claudia threw her as she stooped to pick up her scattered fabric pieces was all too familiar, a sort of resigned exasperation intrinsic to elder sisters. "You know what definitely *won't* impress the judges? A half-finished quilt."

"I'll work double time," Sylvia promised, quickly bending to help her. "When you see the finished quilt top, you won't regret it. I promise."

"I already regret it." Claudia sank onto the window seat, clutching her fabric pieces on her lap. "But you're going to do whatever you want, just like always."

Stung, Sylvia pressed her lips together tightly and set the fabric triangles she had collected on the window seat beside her sister. She'd let Claudia have the last word. They couldn't afford to waste another minute arguing.

Lifting her chin and turning her back, she carried her sketchbook to the window seat on the opposite end of the room, sat crossed-legged upon the cushion, and dug into her sewing basket. After comparing her transportation-themed blocks to her new sketches, she set aside a few that could be adapted to her new designs fairly easily. From these, she selected the one that looked easiest and got to work.

By the time Great-Aunt Lydia called them for supper, Sylvia had made a very good start transforming her locomotive block into an appliqué still life depicting the Emancipation Proclamation. The next day, as soon as she completed that block, she tackled another, carefully picking out stitches and removing a few fabric shapes from her stage-coach block. Later that day and the next, she began adding several new appliqués to transform it into a float from the 1913 Woman Suffrage Procession. The design was far more complex than any she had attempted before, and it took her the rest of the week to complete it.

But complete it she did, making the most of every spare moment not already claimed by school, homework, chores, and working with the horses. Some days she stitched so quickly for so long that her eyes grew bleary and her fingers cramped. She finished a third block and started a fourth. Meanwhile, Claudia grew ever more swift and sure at Great-Aunt Lydia's sewing machine. Before long she finished enough Odd Fellows Chain blocks to make the border for one long side of the quilt. She sewed the blocks together and proudly displayed the long row for the family before carefully pressing it and rolling it loosely in muslin to keep it clean and tidy while she pieced more blocks. By then, Sylvia was on her fifth block, an embroidered scroll representing the Thirteenth Amendment.

In late March, spring arrived in the Elm Creek Valley, so the Bergstrom stables and training rings were busier than ever. Muddy pastures and trails meant more time needed for grooming the horses and cleaning their stalls, and Sylvia helped out as much as she could. The fair weather had brought a few itinerant laborers to the estate, some who had experience with horses and hoped to be hired on permanently, others who asked only for a day's work for a decent meal and a place to sleep. Sylvia's father and Uncle William hired workers as the need arose, but they could not take on everyone, and too often the ragged men were turned away with a meal and a respectful handshake. It seemed to Sylvia that the Bergstroms' longtime employees looked askance at the newcomers, their eyes sympathetic but their mouths set and unsmiling, a silent warning not to covet their places, which they would not give up without a fight.

By the first week of April, the lilacs surrounding the cornerstone patio were in full, fragrant bloom, beckoning Sylvia outside. When the weather was fair, she liked to settle down in one of the weathered teak chairs with broad armrests and sew, or read a book, or just be alone with her thoughts. The cornerstone patio had been her mother's favorite place on the estate, built for her by Sylvia's father to offer her comfort and beauty to console her in a difficult time. The cornerstone that had given the patio its name had been set in place by Hans Bergstrom in 1858 when construction had begun on the original farmhouse, and it was still visible through the foliage that had grown up around the northeast corner of the manor. The exterior door leading to the patio had been the manor's front entry until Grandpa David added the south wing, with its curved stone staircases, grand verandah, and tall double doors. The patio's gray flagstones were the same color as the fieldstones forming the manor's walls, and Sylvia's father had planted a profusion of bulbs around the edges of the broad rectangle they formed—dahlias, irises, and gladioli, bright bursts of color her mother had much admired. Rising above the perennials were tall, verdant lilac bushes and evergreens, enclosing the patio completely except for one arched opening on the northern side. Passing through it, one would emerge near the start of a gravel footpath that wound toward the north gardens, the gazebo, and beyond that, the stables.

The cornerstone patio was so full of memories of her mother that sometimes Sylvia had to set her sewing or her book on her lap and close her eyes, overcome by the ache of loss and loneliness. In moments when searing grief blindsided her, it seemed impossible, simply impossible, that her beloved mother was gone from them forever. Yet over the past year, whenever Sylvia spent quiet, contemplative moments in the beautiful place her mother had so loved, she felt a soft, quiet peace settle upon her, soothing her troubled thoughts. She could almost imagine that if she listened carefully, she would hear her mother murmuring words of reassurance and love.

Although Sylvia would always feel that her mother had been cheated out of the long, happy life she deserved, when her mother had reminisced about her life, she had never expressed anything but gratitude for the years she had been granted. She had been stricken with rheumatic fever as a baby, she had told her daughters matter-of-factly, but although she had recovered, the doctors had concluded that the illness had irreparably damaged her heart. For the rest of her life, which the doctors warned would be tragically short, she would remain fragile and delicate, prone to fevers and fainting. She would certainly not live to adulthood.

But Eleanor Lockwood *had* lived, in defiance of her doctors' predictions and her parents' expectations. She had lived long enough to marry and to bear children of her own and to enthrall her daughters with stories of growing up amid the wealth and privilege of turn-of-the-century Manhattan. Claudia had adored their mother's romantic descriptions of the Lockwoods' luxurious Fifth Avenue residence on Central Park, the elegant dresses she and her elder sister had worn, and the glamorous balls and society affairs they had attended. For her part, Sylvia had been fascinated by her mother's reminiscences of Grandfather Lockwood's stable of magnificent horses—including several Bergstrom Thoroughbreds. It was through their fathers' business dealings that Sylvia's parents had met as children and had become friends. Yet amid so many fascinating details, Sylvia was also intrigued by the things her mother had *not* said aloud, the sudden pauses and wistful expressions that suggested she believed her parents had neglected her in favor of her elder sister, Abigail.

"Maybe Mother's parents didn't want to get too attached to her, since everyone expected her to die at any moment," Claudia had speculated once, when she and Sylvia were alone.

"Maybe they were just cold, selfish, unloving people," Sylvia had replied. She had met Grandmother Lockwood for the first time when she was seven years old, and although their acquaintance had been brief, she had observed enough to convince her that this was the likeliest explanation.

As young girls, Eleanor and Abigail had spent little time in their parents' company, or so Sylvia had gathered from her mother's stories. The routine tasks of their upbringing had been entrusted to their beloved English nanny. Grandfather Lockwood's two passions were the business he had founded—Lockwood's, the famous department store on Fifth Avenue—and his stables, full of Thoroughbreds and Andalusians. But the Panic of 1893 struck his business a staggering blow, and as the years passed, it required every ounce of financial cunning he possessed to keep it solvent.

Yet as Grandmother Lockwood kept up appearances with fine clothes, lavish parties, and the necessities of society life, Grandfather Lockwood's debts mounted. By the time the Lockwood sisters were in their teens, their father had settled on a last recourse: He would marry off Abigail to the eldest son of another successful department store magnate, with whom he would create a partnership, infusing Lockwood's with much-needed cash and creating a bulwark against the competition.

Abigail had consented to the arrangement, but on the night before the wedding, she eloped with another man—Herbert Drury, her father's fiercest business rival. Drury was twice her age, a widower, and the father of her best friend, and no one had ever suspected any romantic entanglement between them. At first Grandfather Lockwood swore to bring Abigail home and force her to go through with her original engagement, but when it was discovered that the couple had already wed, Eleanor's parents ordered Eleanor to marry the jilted bridegroom instead.

Eleanor was shocked. She had always been told that her poor health meant she could never marry, but that was not her only objection. To her, if no one else, it was incomprehensible that she should simply step into her sister's role as if she were an understudy in a play, all for the sake of a business partnership. And, although no one else knew it, she was already in love with a different man altogether—Fred Bergstrom.

Her father had invited Fred to Abigail's wedding, and when Fred learned of Eleanor's plight, he urged her not to let anyone treat her as if she were property to be bartered between families. "If you're going to marry," he urged, impassioned, "marry for love. Marry me."

Eleanor knew her parents would never consent, so she too fled in the night to marry the man she loved.

Sylvia knew that Grandmother Lockwood had never forgiven Mother for her betrayal. There had been years of silence between them, punctuated by brief, scathing letters from New York, usually accompanied by newspaper clippings of the twice-jilted bridegroom and the young woman he had eventually married, the couple's gracious home, their trips to Europe, his business success. Her estrangement from her parents had pained Sylvia's mother, but she had never regretted her decision to marry Sylvia's father. The Bergstrom family had welcomed her with joy and affection, and the couple had enjoyed twenty-three happy, loving years together. Sylvia knew her father grieved the loss of his beloved wife and always would, but she was equally certain he would have married her all over again. Love and grief were the warp and weft of the fabric of a life, and it was impossible to have one without the other.

Sylvia thought of her mother often while she appliquéd her blocks for the World's Fair quilt, especially when she worked alone on the cornerstone patio. Sylvia knew her mother would have admired her daughters' handiwork, praised their ambition and creativity, and encouraged them to do their best and not to be daunted by their impending deadline. Most of all, she would have been pleased to see Sylvia and Claudia working together, cooperating and collaborating, the way she had always hoped they would.

Claudia completed her last Odd Fellows Chain block in mid-April, and the next day, she sewed them together in groups to make the remaining three borders. She came looking for Sylvia to share the good news and found her outside on the cornerstone patio. "How are you coming along?" she asked, folding her arms and casting an appraising look over Sylvia and the blocks stacked on top of the sewing basket beside her chair.

"I'm halfway through with this block," said Sylvia, not glancing up from what was turning out to be a very difficult seam on an all-too-narrow arc of fabric. "I have one more to do after that and then I'll be done."

"None too soon. Do you want me to start the last block?"

"No, no," said Sylvia—too forcefully, she realized, as soon as she spoke. "I mean, thanks, but I've got it. It would take longer to explain how to put it together than to do it myself."

Claudia regarded her dubiously. "I'm sure I can figure it out from your sketch."

Maybe she could, but Sylvia wouldn't have time to pick out her sister's stitches and do them over properly. "I know how you can help," she said, setting her block aside and wincing as she worked an ache out of the base of her right thumb. "You can start sewing my appliqué blocks together to make the center section. That will go fast on the sewing machine."

"All right, if you're sure that's all the help you need."

"I'm sure." Sylvia found the diagram in her sketchbook, handed it over, and placed the stack of quilt blocks on top. "Just remember to leave the bottom right corner free so we can add these last two blocks."

"Got it," said Claudia. "I bet I'll finish my part before you finish your last blocks."

"I bet you will too," said Sylvia glumly, resting for a moment as Claudia headed back inside with the precious appliqué blocks. Then she quickly got back to work.

Two days later, at the dinner table, Claudia announced that she had finished assembling the central appliqué section except for Sylvia's two blocks that were still in progress. But she did not beat Sylvia by much. By racing through her homework and staying up past her bedtime, Sylvia was able to put the last stitch in her last appliqué block before the day was through. She almost slept through her alarm the next morning and she stifled yawns in her classes throughout the day, earning a few stern frowns from her teachers and giggles from her friends, but it was worth it.

Yet the quilt was still far from finished.

Sylvia wanted to sew the last two blocks to the appliqué center herself, but Claudia pointed out that she was more experienced with the sewing machine and could get the job done more quickly. Sylvia couldn't argue the point. She looked on, trying not to sulk or to interject advice, as Claudia deftly attached first one block and then the other, pressed the seams, and began attaching the long borders.

But eventually waiting and watching became too tedious. "May I please have a turn?" Sylvia asked, trying to keep the impatience from her voice. "Let me sew on one border, at least. It can be one of the shorter ones."

Claudia shook her head, then flinched as a sharp click announced that she had sewed over a pin. "It'll go faster if I do it myself."

"Speed isn't everything. You'll break the needle if you keep sewing over pins like that."

"I know what I'm doing," Claudia retorted. But from then on, as she fed the fabric beneath the presser foot, she would ease back on the foot pedal as a pin approached the needle and remove it just before it would have passed over the throat plate.

Holding back a retort, Sylvia peered over Claudia's shoulder as she attached the second long side border. Great-Aunt Lydia's sewing machine clattered merrily until Claudia reached the end, backstitched to secure the seam, and snipped the threads. "Would you please not hover?" she grumbled as she raised the presser foot and eased the quilt top free.

Sylvia leapt forward to help. "I can press the seams for you," she offered, sharing the weight of the quilt as Claudia rose from her chair. "After that, you can pin the top border in place while I pin on the bottom border. If we work at the same time, we'll finish twice as quickly."

Claudia shrugged and agreed.

After Sylvia's turn at the ironing board, the sisters carried the quilt top to the kitchen and unfolded it upon the refectory table. Seating themselves on opposite benches and sharing a single box of pins, they swiftly but neatly pinned the last two borders to the top and bottom edges of the quilt.

Sylvia was not quite a quarter of the way along when she discovered a problem: Claudia's Odd Fellows Chain blocks varied in size, sometimes by as much as a quarter inch.

A casual glance would reveal nothing amiss if the blocks were scattered across a tabletop, but when the blocks were sewn together into a long strip, the mistakes of small fractions compounded over its length. Sometimes a block that was a bit too small would cancel out the mistake of a block that was a bit too large, but when Sylvia reached the end, she discovered that the bottom border was an inch too short for the width of the quilt.

She paused to think. Maybe the border *was* the proper length, but she'd made a mistake with her pinning. She stole a glance at Claudia, who was nearly finished pinning the top border in place, her brow furrowed slightly in concentration. Quietly, reluctant to draw the attention of her sister or of their great-aunts, who had arrived moments before to start dinner, she scooted down the bench and studied the corner where she had begun pinning. The border was aligned perfectly with the quilt top there, so she moved on down the edge, checking her work. Maybe she had added too much slack to the strip of pieced blocks. If not—but she didn't want to say anything until she was sure.

Just then Richard wandered into the kitchen. "Can I have something to eat?" he asked the great-aunts.

"Dinner will be ready in an hour," said Great-Aunt Lydia. When Richard groaned and clutched his stomach, she sighed and inclined her head toward the cellar door. "You may have an apple, but don't spoil your supper."

Richard grinned and darted off, returning moments later munching a crisp Cortland harvested from their own orchard the previous autumn. He wandered over to see what his sisters were up to, first passing behind Sylvia and tickling the back of her neck with the stem of his apple before rounding the table to study Claudia's work. "Is it supposed to do that?" he asked, gesturing with his apple.

"Do what?" asked Claudia, waving him back. "Don't get apple juice on our quilt."

"Sorry." He pointed with his free hand. "Is the part between those two pins supposed to stick out that way? It looks like a little hill of fabric."

"What are you talking about?" Claudia leaned forward, frowning in puzzlement as she ran her gaze over the section he indicated.

Sylvia leaned forward too, and that's when she saw it—an extra inch of fabric from the appliqué center forming a graceful arc between two pins, in a place where the pieced border was stretched taut. "It's not supposed to do that at all," Sylvia said, uneasy. "The border is supposed to lie flat against the edge of the quilt."

Great-Aunt Lucinda glanced up from peeling a potato. "Is the border too short, Claudia?"

"It can't be," said Claudia. "I multiplied the width of the block by the number of blocks, and the result is the same as the width of the appliqué center."

"That's the right math," said Sylvia, "but it only works if all of the blocks are the same size as the pattern."

Claudia shook her head, impatient. "Why wouldn't they be?"

Sylvia threw Great-Aunt Lucinda a pleading look, hoping she would intervene. "Did you measure each block after you made it, Claudia?" her great-aunt asked, setting the peeled potato on the cutting board and gesturing with the peeler.

Claudia's face fell. "No."

"The blocks aren't all the same size," Sylvia said in a rush, with all the relief of a confession. "I had the same problem with the bottom border. I thought maybe I made a mistake while I was pinning—"

"Maybe you did," Claudia retorted.

"No, it's just too short," said Richard, peering at it more closely. "That's why you have that sticking-out part along the edge. Can you stretch the border to make it fit, maybe?"

"No, I can't stretch it," Claudia snapped, color rising in her cheeks.

"Are you sure you cut your pieces the proper size, dear?" asked Great-Aunt Lydia, sprinkling parsley and sage on a chicken—a rather small chicken, Sylvia thought, considering how many hungry people would gather around the dinner table later.

"Yes, of course," said Claudia, wounded, a tremor in her voice. "I measured twice and cut once, just like Mother always told us to."

"Hold on, let's not get upset." Great-Aunt Lucinda wiped her hands on her apron and came around the counter to join them at the table. "If you're sure your block pieces are the correct size, then perhaps it's your seam allowances. If they aren't a consistent quarter-inch, a row of pieced blocks may end up shorter or longer than it should be."

Sylvia scooted out of the way as Great-Aunt Lucinda inspected the borders, first the one Claudia was pinning in place, and then Sylvia's. "Some of your seam allowances are too big," she said, indicating several places on the bottom border where the blunted triangle tips between two joined Odd Fellows Chain blocks betrayed a too-generous seam allowance. "You should pick out these seams and sew the blocks together again, taking care to keep to a quarter-inch. Do the same for the top border. That might be enough to correct the problem."

"What if it isn't?" asked Sylvia, rising from the bench. "What if the borders still don't fit?"

"Stretch them," Richard repeated helpfully, finishing the last of his apple and tossing the core into the trash.

"But redoing all that work will take hours, maybe days," Claudia lamented.

"Which is why you should have done it right the first time," Sylvia pointed out.

"*You* had to do *your* blocks over."

"That was an artistic choice. It wasn't to fix mistakes."

"Sylvia," Great-Aunt Lydia scolded. "That's unnecessary and unkind, especially considering how graciously Claudia accepted your decision to change your design at the eleventh hour."

It wasn't the eleventh hour, and Claudia hadn't been particularly gracious, but Sylvia knew better than to talk back to her elders. "I'll need my seam ripper," she muttered as she stalked off to fetch her sewing basket from the west sitting room.

The first step was to unpin the two borders from the quilt top, which the sisters did in disgruntled silence. Next they each took a border and a seam ripper in hand and carefully began picking out stitches. The work consumed the rest of the evening, with interruptions for dinner and chores. It was not until the next day that they were able to pin the separated blocks together again and begin reassembling the borders. To save time, one of them would pin while the other resewed seams, so Sylvia found a bit of satisfaction in being granted alternating turns at Great-Aunt Lydia's sewing machine.

Later that evening, when both borders were complete and neatly pressed, they returned to the kitchen, spread the quilt top on the refectory table, and tried again to fit the borders to it. This time Sylvia's border was only a half-inch too short, while Claudia's was three-quarters shy of the correct size.

"What now?" Claudia asked, sitting down heavily on the bench, a note of panic in her voice. "Should we trim the appliqué center?"

"Absolutely not," Sylvia exclaimed. She could well imagine how that would go. Claudia would cut a bit off one edge to make that border fit, but the other border would still be too short. So she'd trim a bit off the other side, but then the first border wouldn't fit anymore, and on and on it would go until there was nothing left of Sylvia's appliqué center.

"Sylvia's right. That's not the solution," said Great-Aunt Lucinda. "The appliqué center measures true, so keep that as it is. The borders aren't too far off the mark, so let's block them and see if we can't get an extra half-inch out of them."

"Block the blocks?" asked Claudia, bewildered. "What does that mean?"

"I'll show you."

With a hot iron and steam, and measurements marked with masking tape on the broad, thick wool pad she used for items too large for her ironing board, Great-Aunt Lucinda pressed and eased the pieced border into the desired shape. "The trick is to coax the fabric into place without distorting the block design," she explained as they watched carefully, hopefully, grateful that she knew so many tricks and techniques they never would have figured out on their own. "Your grandmother taught me, and now it's my turn to pass along her lesson to you."

Not long thereafter, when Great-Aunt Lucinda finished, the sisters discovered to their delight and amazement that both borders were exactly the right length. They thanked her profusely, then dashed off to pin the borders in place and then to sew them on, Claudia the top border and Sylvia the bottom.

"So you did stretch them after all," Richard remarked as he wandered into the west sitting room to check their progress. Sylvia laughed, but Claudia either didn't hear him over the merry clatter of the sewing machine or ignored him.

Another turn at Great-Aunt Lucinda's wool mat, and the quilt top was finished at last—but they had not even begun to quilt it, and it was already the first week of May.

Sylvia and Claudia had decided upon favorite quilting motifs for various sections of the quilt, so as quickly as they dared without sacrificing clarity and accuracy, they marked the feathered wreaths, scrolls, and crosshatch on the quilt top with the finest of pencil strokes. They had wanted to make the quilt entirely on their own, but with their deadline swiftly approaching, there was nothing else for it but to ask Great-Aunt Lucinda, Great-Aunt Lydia, and Aunt Nellie for help.

After removing a partially finished scrap quilt of Aunt Nellie's from the frame, the aunties layered the sisters' backing fabric, soft batting, and the finished top in its place. Then they all seated themselves around the quilting frame, threaded their needles, and got to work. Sylvia felt a bit uneasy that she and Claudia were accepting so much help, but the aunties assured her that the other participants were likely calling in friends and family to quilt their tops too. Quilters had finished tops in such a fashion since time immemorial, and the four brief months between the announcement of the contest and the submission deadline rendered any other approach all but impossible.

In the days that followed, the aunties and the sisters worked on the quilt as often as they could. Sometimes all five of them sat around the quilt frame, their needles darting swiftly through the fabrics and batting, uniting the three layers with elegant, intricate patterns of stitches. Sometimes Sylvia and Claudia came home from school and discovered, to their relief and their delight, that their elders had accomplished a great deal in their absence. Sometimes the sisters quilted together while the aunties attended to the usual work of running the household. They marveled at how neat and small the more experienced quilters' stitches were, and did their best to emulate them.

In the second week of May, Sylvia put the last quilting stitch into place, tied off the thread, and popped the knot through the backing so it nestled invisibly within the batting. Aunt Nellie, meanwhile, had prepared a long bias strip for the binding. After Great-Aunt Lydia sewed the strip to the front of the quilt all around with the sewing machine, the others took turns folding the strip over the raw edges and sewing it to the back with sturdy slip stitches.

Every day the quilt came closer to completion, and every day Sylvia's nervous excitement grew. The quilt was going to be so lovely, exactly as she had envisioned and hoped, but that would be a very small comfort if they finished too late.

At last, on May 13, the binding was securely in place, and the quilt was finished. Sylvia and Claudia scrambled to fill out the official entry form, but they hesitated before signing it, uncertain what to do about the requirement, clearly stated on the form, that "Quilts must be of the contestant's own making."

"It *is* of our own making," said Claudia.

"Yes," said Sylvia, "but the way the rule is written, it sounds like they mean one contestant for each quilt, not two, and certainly not a whole family."

"But like we said before, it would have been practically impossible for a single person to make an entire masterpiece quilt in only four months. Maybe the apostrophe is in the wrong place."

"Maybe," said Sylvia, dubious. She decided to assume Claudia was right, since the alternative was not to enter the contest. "What should we put down for the contestant's name? There isn't room to list all of us."

Claudia thought for a moment. "We'll put my name since I'm the oldest."

"That's not fair," Sylvia protested. "I did at least as much work as you did."

"Fine. We'll put 'Claudia Sylvia Bergstrom.'"

"That's ridiculous. No one would ever name their baby Claudia Sylvia."

"I've heard worse. Do you have a better idea?"

"Not really."

"Then Claudia Sylvia Bergstrom it is." With a flourish, Claudia signed the proper space using the pseudonym, but as she set down the pen, she suddenly looked uneasy. "I don't like it. It's a lie."

Sylvia rolled her eyes. "You say that *now*, after you signed in ink? You should've used pencil."

"I didn't think of it until now." Claudia pressed a hand to her stomach, looking queasy. "It'll be obvious to the judges that more than one person quilted our top. No qualified judge could possibly miss the differences between our quilting stitches and our aunties'. Theirs are so much smaller and consistent."

Sylvia thought her own stitches were actually quite small and consistent in size, but Claudia's definitely weren't. "So what should we do? Not enter?"

Claudia shook her head vigorously. "We've worked too hard. We're definitely going to enter."

"Then we'll just have to own up to it." Sylvia gestured to the pen, giving her sister a pointed look until she picked it up again. "Underneath your fake signature, you could add, 'Quilted by the Bergstrom Family.' The judges might accept that."

"Maybe." Claudia mulled it over. "Yes, that might work. Our

aunties did say that we surely wouldn't be the only contestants who got help with the quilting in order to finish in time."

She added the note, and as soon as she did, they both felt much better.

Finally the quilt was ready to submit, but there was no Sears store in Waterford, and if they sent it to one of the mail-order centers, it would never arrive in time. On the morning of May 14, they were debating their options over breakfast, when Uncle William offered to drive it to the store in Harrisburg. "I promised your aunt Nellie an outing to the city," he said, smiling fondly at them both and ruffling Sylvia's hair. "Tomorrow is as good a day as any."

They flung their arms around him and thanked him from the bottom of their hearts. Sylvia longed to go along with him and see the precious quilt safely to its destination, but she had school, and she knew Uncle William and Aunt Nellie wouldn't let their nieces down with so much at stake.

The next day, Sylvia and Claudia hurried home from school to find Aunt Nellie in the formal parlor, showing off a lovely new spring dress, an early birthday gift Uncle William had bought her in Harrisburg. "We turned in your quilt with hours to spare," she assured her nieces.

"Thank you so much, Aunt Nellie," said Claudia, sighing with relief.

"Yes, thank you," said Sylvia, giving her aunt a quick hug. She then raced off to the stables to thank Uncle William too.

Now the fate of the World's Fair quilt was in the judges' hands. All Sylvia could do was wait and hope.

9

September 2004

Two days after Sylvia entrusted Summer with the World's Fair quilt, she woke to an autumn morning so clear and crisp that after breakfast, she decided to extend her usual morning walk around the estate. Leaving the manor by the cornerstone patio door, she passed through the shrubbery arch and stepped onto the gravel path, which meandered through a dense grove of elm, sugar maple, and evergreen. The boughs overhead were touched with yellow-gold and burnt orange, and a scattering of fallen leaves crunched underfoot in the dappled sunlight that filtered through the branches.

Before long Sylvia emerged at the north gardens, an oval clearing surfaced in the same gray stone as the cornerstone patio. Just ahead of her were four round planters, each about fifteen feet in diameter and three feet high; the lower halves of their walls were two feet thicker than at the top, forming smooth, polished seats where visitors could rest and admire the chrysanthemums, sedum, purple coneflowers, and black-eyed Susans blooming amid decorative grasses. The planters were spaced evenly around a black marble fountain of a mare prancing with two foals, reminiscent of the rearing stallion in the center of the circular driveway in front of the manor. On the other side of the fountain was a gazebo, its posts and gingerbread molding gleaming white in the autumn sunshine as if it had been freshly painted only yesterday and not before the season opening of quilt camp months earlier. Beyond the gazebo, Sylvia glimpsed the garden terraces cut into the slope of the gentle hill on the other side, filled with rosebushes, English ivy, maiden grass, and asters. It was a lovely, picturesque setting, designed by the Bergstrom women at the turn of the previous century, constructed by their brothers, and beautifully, impressively restored by Matt after Sylvia's long absence from Elm Creek Manor.

Thinking of Matt, Sylvia lingered a moment to admire his artistry, and then continued through the garden to the arched stone footbridge over Elm Creek, which was wide enough for two people strolling side by side, or a single horse and rider. It was little used now except during the quilt camp season—like Sylvia, many guests of Elm Creek Manor enjoyed beginning their day with a brisk walk or a run—but once it had provided a shortcut from the manor to the stables, the riding arena, and the round ring. Those facilities, once so essential to Bergstrom Thoroughbreds, were long gone, sold off by Claudia and her husband along with scores of acres to support their spendthrift lifestyle. If not for the clever, surreptitious legal maneuverings of Richard's young widow, Agnes, who decades later would become a founding Elm Creek Quilter, the entire estate could have been lost.

Sighing, Sylvia gazed across the wildflower meadow to the stand of trees behind a post-and-rail fence that marked the boundary between her property and her neighbors'. She was fortunate indeed that the new owners—well, hardly *new* anymore—were a family of organic farmers, very pleasant people and good stewards of the land. The parcel could have been developed into an industrial site, or a big box store, or something even worse. She was immeasurably thankful for every acre of Bergstrom land that remained to her, and yet she missed the old buildings and pastures where generations of her family had raised their renowned horses, once admired throughout the country for their strength, beauty, and grace.

As her thoughts turned wistful, she reminded herself quite firmly that there was no point in brooding over what had been lost. She could learn important lessons from the past, but she mustn't stay stuck in it. Yes, Bergstrom Thoroughbreds was no more, but Elm Creek Quilts was thriving, and she had every reason to believe that the future of her ancestral estate was very bright indeed.

Turning, she walked parallel to the fence until she reached the orchard, intoxicatingly fragrant, with boughs green and lush and laden with sweet, ripening fruit. Diligent honeybees hummed over the windfall fruit scattered beneath the trees, and the mowed grass between the rows, still glimmering with dew, tickled her ankles as she passed. Eventually she came to the dirt service road running between the two halves of the orchard, which now led to the new parking lot. She smiled to herself, imagining couples, families, and cheerful groups of Waterford College students making their way up the hill in the weeks to come, full of anticipation for the pies and cobblers and sauces they would enjoy from the fruits of the Bergstroms' harvest.

She heard Matt whistling while the last rows of trees still blocked her view of the market stand. As she approached, she laughed aloud from surprise when she came upon her caretaker painting the orchard policies sign they had discussed, paintbrush in one hand, his other arm holding James securely on his hip.

"You need a third hand, Matt," she declared, hurrying forward to take the toddler from him. "Hello, sweetheart," she crooned to little James, smoothing his soft, dark hair away from his face and kissing him on the brow. "Are you helping your papa?"

"Papa," James agreed, pointing at his father. He too clutched a paintbrush in his fist, but Sylvia was relieved to see that it was merely for show; there wasn't any paint on it.

Sylvia drew closer to inspect Matt's work. "It's coming along nicely," she said, nodding approval.

"Thanks." Matt painted a final stroke, stepped back to study the sign, and shrugged. "It's not art, but it's legible. That's the important thing."

"Agreed."

"After it dries, I'll hang it where it can't be missed." He threw her a grin over his shoulder. "You'll be glad to hear that Andrew put up the road sign at the intersection. Now you won't have to worry about orchard customers getting lost and interrupting you at the manor."

Sylvia winced, remembering how ridiculously peevish she had been that day. "I suppose the occasional bewildered customer wouldn't be intolerably disruptive. Even so, the sign will save all of us a bit of bother. I'll be sure to stop to admire it on my way back to the manor." She smiled at James and shifted her weight, rocking him playfully back and forth. "Shall I take this little fellow with me so you can work undisturbed?"

"No, it's fine, let him stay. He's the best kind of disturbance."

"That's not what you were saying when he and Caroline weren't letting you and Sarah sleep through the night," Sylvia teased.

"Don't remind me. I don't think I could survive that much sleep deprivation ever again." Tossing her a grin, Matt stooped to rinse the brush in a bucket of water next to the paint can, drying his hands on his jeans as he straightened. Taking James from Sylvia's arms, he swung the boy into the air. "Say bye-bye to Auntie Sylvia, James."

Smiling brightly, James waved, and Sylvia waved back.

She continued on her way, crossing the new gravel parking lot and turning onto the road extension, where she spied the new sign from quite some distance away. "My goodness," she murmured as she drew closer. For all her joking about Joe's artistic tendencies, she had expected a simple rectangle board on a post, with neat text and painted arrows indicating directions. Instead Joe had fashioned a near duplicate of the venerable sign marking the turnoff from the state highway onto the forest road leading to Elm Creek Manor—four feet wide atop sturdy support beams, angled to be clearly visible to traffic from all three directions, with beautifully carved, freshly painted lettering. The only differences between the original road sign and the new one were the text and the age of the wood. Sylvia, with her fondness for tradition, was delighted by the homage.

After admiring Joe's craftmanship, Sylvia hurried on to the red barn, through the larger section devoted to Matt's caretaker's equipment, tools, and workbenches and onward to Joe's domain. It was a remarkably tidy woodshop, well organized, with ample lighting and a floor swept clean of sawdust and scraps. Lining the walls were various workstations and racks neatly filled with all manner of drills, saws, lathes, and hand tools. In the center was a large, scarred wood-and-iron table Joe had made himself. Joe and Andrew were standing before it, apparently engrossed in a fascinating discussion about a certain metal contraption overturned on the table, with assorted tools and cans of spray paint and rust remover scattered all around.

"You've gone above and beyond, Joe," Sylvia declared as she approached the men. "The sign is simply perfect."

"Glad you like it," said Joe. "I think it turned out all right."

"All right?" Sylvia threw Andrew a look of comic exasperation. "What I wouldn't give to hear him brag, just once, just a little."

"His modesty is part of his charm," Andrew replied, clasping his friend's shoulder and giving him a playful shake.

"Enough, you two," Joe grumbled good-naturedly. "It's a sign. It's not rocket science. Now, Sylvia, those posts are set deep, so you don't need to worry about them blowing over in a storm."

"That never would have occurred to me. It looks sturdy enough to withstand a hurricane." Sylvia drew closer, curious. "What's this you're working on? Oh, it's a wagon. I didn't recognize it at first, upside down."

"We're following up on your suggestion," said Andrew, smiling.

"This is only one of three wagons that Gretchen found at garage sales and secondhand stores around town," Joe said proudly. "She's on the trail of several more. We're fixing 'em up as they come in."

"This one had an axle almost rusted through, as well as a missing wheel, but we replaced them." Andrew pointed to the relevant places, near the front of the wagon. "After that, we'll give it a good cleaning and a fresh coat of paint."

"Gretchen made us a stencil," said Joe, gesturing to a piece of sturdy, translucent plastic at the other end of the table. "First, we'll spray the chassis with a nice red, then we'll stencil 'Elm Creek Orchards' in white."

"How wonderful," Sylvia exclaimed.

"We've finished one already, if you'd like to take a look." Andrew beckoned her to follow him to another workbench against the wall. There sat a bright, cheerful "Elm Creek Orchards" wagon in near perfect condition, except for a few dings in the chrome handle that gave it a bit of character.

"I love it," Sylvia declared. "I thought wagons would be useful for our customers, but I never imagined they'd be so charming too."

A slow smile spread over Andrew's face as she spoke, and for a moment she wasn't sure why. Then she realized it was because she had said *our* customers, not Matt's customers. She hadn't done so on purpose. Apparently, unbeknownst to herself, over the past few days she had gone from expressing misgivings about every decision, as Sarah had bluntly put it, to supporting Matt's project wholeheartedly.

It was a good change. She felt lighter, happier, more purposeful. She supposed she had just needed a little time.

"Gretchen plans to browse some more garage sales this weekend," Joe said. "I'm sure she'd appreciate the company if you'd like to go along."

"Perhaps I'll do that," said Sylvia. She liked the idea of contributing more to Matt's program than simply approving logos and suggesting signs.

In the meantime, she had other tasks requiring her attention. She and Sarah had agreed to meet for lunch at noon to discuss other possible ventures to raise revenue, but until then Sylvia would put the rest of the morning to good use. After bidding Andrew goodbye with a kiss, and thanking Joe again for the excellent road sign, she strolled back to the manor, refreshed and content.

Taking a box of sturdy garbage bags from the storage cabinet in the butler's pantry, she headed up three flights of stairs to the attic. A bit breathless from the climb, she switched on the light, planted her hands on her hips, and surveyed the room. Sorting the trash from the treasures was a long-overdue task, and it wouldn't get any easier the longer she waited. If she didn't put things in order while she was still hale and hearty, eventually the responsibility would fall to Sarah and Matt. She couldn't bear the thought of burdening them with such a difficult chore in her absence.

Contemplating the amount of work that lay before her, Sylvia decided to warm up with something easy. When she and Summer had searched the attic for the World's Fair quilt two days before, Sylvia had set aside certain items to be discarded or donated, so she began by placing the discards into garbage bags. Next she sorted the donations pile into categories—china and housewares here, clothing there, and books in neat stacks against the wall to examine more carefully later. She might add a few select volumes to the manor library rather than give them away. After that, she began sorting through the items that were sitting out in the open rather than tucked away in trunks and boxes. At least trunks and boxes could be arranged to give the *appearance* of order until she had time to examine their contents.

As the hours passed, she filled three large garbage bags with useless clutter—mostly rags and newspapers and rusted nuts and bolts that Claudia must have believed would be useful someday. To Sylvia's delight, she also discovered several charming decorative items that, once properly cleaned, would add lovely touches to some of the guest-rooms. After coming across numerous pieces of fine vintage clothing and china, she decided to take any such things to the consignment shop in downtown Waterford. She might not earn much from them, but every bit earned would help their bottom line.

She had made a respectable amount of progress when she spied a rocking chair along the wall halfway down the west wing. A few of the splats were missing, but it seemed sturdy enough, so she decided to treat herself to a brief rest. But as she made her way toward the chair, she realized that a dark space on the wall behind it, which she had assumed was a shadow, was actually water-stained plaster.

"Please let there be no mold," she murmured, stooping to push a cardboard carton out of the way so she could get close enough to inspect the wall. To her relief, she didn't see any spotting or smell any must, but unless she was very much mistaken, there was a leak in the roof above. Her heart sank. If the aged roof was leaking here, it very likely was leaking elsewhere too, the damage yet to be discovered amid the clutter and shadow.

She sank down gingerly into the rocking chair, which creaked beneath her weight but held. She would ask Matt to inspect the attic carefully so he could take any essential emergency measures before matters worsened. In any event, replacing the roof may have just leapt to the top of their list of urgent repairs.

She rested a few minutes more, then rose and put in another good half hour of work, starting with moving the rocking chair, an old dressmaker's model, and several trunks and cartons away from the wet patch on the wall, just in case it sprang a leak. Shortly before noon, she tied the filled garbage bags shut, carefully dropped them through the hatch to the floor below, and descended the narrow stairs after them. She knew Matt or Sarah would be more than willing to haul the bags down the last two flights and outside to the trash re-ceptacle for her later. As reluctant as she was to admit it, there were some tasks she simply wasn't up to anymore, but hauling trash was one she was quite happy to delegate.

After stopping by her room to freshen up, she went downstairs to meet Sarah for lunch, only to be caught by surprise as soon as she entered the west wing by the smell of stewing tomatoes, garlic, and basil. Perhaps Sarah was heating up pasta leftovers for lunch, she mused, but when she entered the kitchen, she found her seated at her favorite booth, papers and folders neatly arranged on the table before her. Anna stood at the stove dressed in her chef's toque and apron, mixing up a huge pot of something deliciously fragrant.

"Why, hello, Anna," Sylvia exclaimed, pleased to see her. "Are you canning stewed tomatoes? Mixing up a batch of pasta sauce? Dare I hope you'll have extra to share?"

"I'm sure I can set aside a serving or two." Anna smiled, but Sylvia detected fatigue and strain around her eyes. "I'm making *pappa al pomodoro*."

"It's a Tuscan tomato and bread stew," Sarah chimed in, her eyes bright with anticipation.

"It's for a dinner party I'm catering tonight." Anna paused to scoop up a bit of the rich, red mixture with her spoon, blow to cool it, and taste. "Needs more basil. What was I saying? Oh, yes. I hope it's all right that I'm using your kitchen for my side gig. The stove in our apartment finally called it quits this morning, and our landlord isn't returning our calls."

"Oh, what dreadful timing," said Sylvia. "Anna, dear, rest assured, this kitchen is at your disposal anytime you need it. To be honest, we all think of it as yours anyway."

"That's what I told her," said Sarah, "and not just because she's bribing me with tomato stew."

"This needs to simmer another ten minutes," said Anna as she tore a handful of basil leaves and tossed them into the pot. "After that, you can do me a favor and be my taste-testers."

"Did you hear that?" said Sarah to Sylvia. "*We're* doing *her* a favor."

"A likely story," said Sylvia, seating herself in the booth across from Sarah. "Shall we get down to business, or wait until after lunch?"

"Let's get to it." Sarah took two sheets of paper from a folder, set one on the table before her, and slid the other over to Sylvia. "Gretchen is watching the twins, but I don't want to impose on her any longer than necessary."

"I'm sure it's not an imposition. Gretchen adores the twins, as do we all." Sylvia skimmed the page, which appeared to be a list of potential revenue sources and schemes, complete with bullet points. She would need a strong cup of something to get through the details. "Shall I make us some tea first?" she asked Sarah, rising. "Coffee?"

Sarah chose coffee, and Sylvia tea. As their beverages brewed, they each took out a pen and settled back into the booth, the flavorful aroma of Anna's *pappa al pomodoro* an enticing distraction all around.

"Item number one," said Sarah, darting a quick wary look Sylvia's way. "Raising our prices."

"Sarah, dear, we discussed this. You know how I feel about keeping a week of quilt camp within the budget of an average quilter."

"I know, but it's a valid idea nonetheless, and I thought you might reconsider. If we raise tuition only ten dollars per camper, we could earn approximately six thousand dollars more over the season, depending upon enrollment. Ten dollars is negligible to the average quilter."

"Do you really think so?"

"I do. It's the equivalent of one yard of quilt-shop-quality fabric, and quilters have proven themselves willing to pay that."

The timer went off then, and while Sarah fetched their beverages, Sylvia removed her glasses and rubbed the bridge of her nose, thinking. "Very well," she said when Sarah returned to the booth, carrying their steaming mugs as well as spoons and napkins for their tomato stew. "I won't entirely rule out raising tuition, but I'd prefer to consider other options first."

THE WORLD'S FAIR QUILT 143

"That's reasonable." Sarah made a note on her page. "Keep in mind, we'll need to decide before we open registration for next season."

"That doesn't give us much time." Suddenly Sylvia remembered something else. "Remind me to tell you about the roof later."

Sarah's eyebrows rose. "The roof? Is something wrong with the roof?"

"Maybe. Probably." Sylvia waved it off. "Let's talk about it later. Item number two?"

Sarah winced. "Roof," she murmured, making another note in the top margin of her page and underlining it for emphasis. "Item number two: Extending the camp season into the fall."

"Hmm." Sylvia put her glasses back on and studied the agenda, but Sarah had not provided any more details there. "How far into the fall?"

"I was thinking we could stay open through November. We could take off the week of Thanksgiving so our faculty and staff could spend the holiday with their families, then wrap up the season the following week with Quiltsgiving."

Sylvia mulled it over. Quiltsgiving was the Elm Creek Quilters' own special holiday, so recently invented that the inaugural event had taken place only the year before. A few months after Gretchen joined the faculty in August 2002, she had approached Sylvia with an intriguing notion for how the Elm Creek Quilters might use their creative gifts to give back to the community. She proposed that they hold a special winter session of quilt camp dedicated to making quilts for Project Linus, a national organization whose mission was to provide love, a sense of security, warmth, and comfort to children in need through the gifts of new, handmade quilts, blankets, and afghans. Quilters who wished to participate would enjoy a week at Elm Creek Manor entirely free of charge, but rather than taking classes and working on quilts for themselves, they would make soft, comforting children's quilts for Project Linus. Sylvia and the other Elm Creek

Quilters had declared the idea absolutely ingenious. Soon thereafter, they had chosen the week after Thanksgiving for their special camp session, and the holiday had inspired its name.

"In some respects, it might be easier to continue through the fall instead of shutting down after Labor Day and restarting for a single week in late November," Sylvia acknowledged. "Do you suppose enough quilters would be interested in attending camp in the fall to justify the expense of staying open?"

"I'm certain they would be, going by our campers' evaluation forms and the many queries we've received through our website." Sarah leaned forward, folded her arms, and rested them on the table. "When we first launched Elm Creek Quilts, we chose late March through Labor Day with the Waterford College academic calendar in mind. Gwen and Judy were professors and Summer was a student, so they weren't available to teach in the fall."

"It was no simple matter for them to juggle both jobs in the spring either," Sylvia reminded her, "but they managed beautifully."

"And I give them so much credit for that. But after Summer and Judy resigned from our faculty—"

"I see where you're going," said Sylvia, nodding. "We hired new teachers who aren't affiliated with the college, and therefore don't have those same scheduling conflicts."

"Exactly. Nowadays it's really only an issue with Gwen. So I was thinking, when the fall semester begins at Waterford College, we could hire Russell to take over for Gwen."

"Now, that's a thought," said Sylvia, intrigued. "Our campers rave about Russell's Modern Quilting classes when he works as a visiting instructor. And I'm sure Maggie would enjoy having her boyfriend around on a more regular basis."

"As for me, I would have been thrilled if quilt camp had continued throughout the fall this year," Anna remarked as she set two fragrant, steaming bowls of *pappa al pomodoro* on the table before them. She deftly grated a generous portion of Parmigiano-Reggiano over each, drizzled on a bit of extra-virgin olive oil, and finished with a sprinkle of snipped basil. "During the off-season I take whatever catering gigs I can find, but I'd much rather have another few months of steady paychecks working here—but what I'd prefer shouldn't influence your decision."

"Why shouldn't it?" asked Sarah. "You're just as important as any other Elm Creek Quilter. *More* important, even."

"We couldn't run quilt camp without you, dear," Sylvia added, smiling fondly.

Sylvia had meant it as a compliment, but Anna's face fell. "Oh, I'm sure you'd manage just fine."

Something in her tone prompted Sylvia and Sarah to exchange a wary look across the table. "That sounds vaguely ominous," said Sarah.

"Is something on your mind, dear?" Sylvia asked, studying Anna over the rims of her glasses.

"Nothing that can't wait another day or two—or longer, even." Anna paused to wipe her hands on her apron, giving Sylvia the distinct impression that she was stalling. "You two have enough on your minds already."

Sarah slid down the bench and patted the now vacant seat. "Don't worry about us. We're expert multitaskers. You might feel better if you talk about it."

"What's troubling you, Anna?" Sylvia asked. "Perhaps we can help."

Anna hesitated before taking her place on the seat beside Sarah, but then she inhaled deeply and smiled. "Nothing's troubling me—in fact, it's the most wonderful news. It's still very early, and I wasn't going to say anything quite so soon, but—"

Sarah gasped. "You're pregnant!"

Anna nodded, radiant with joy.

"Oh, that's wonderful, dear," exclaimed Sylvia, reaching across the table to clasp her hand.

"Yes, Jeremy and I think so too." Anna laughed, a flush rising in her cheeks. "But when the baby arrives—in April—I probably won't be able to keep the same hours as I do now."

"Nor would anyone expect you to," Sylvia assured her.

"We'll work it out, whatever you need," said Sarah. "Believe me, I know how challenging it is to be a working mother, and I don't even have to commute. I think I can speak for everyone when I say we'll support you however we can."

"Hear, hear," said Sylvia, as Sarah made another note in the top margin of her paper. It was difficult for Sylvia to make out reading upside down, but it might have said "On-site daycare."

"Thank you," said Anna. "Thank you both. We'll just . . . see how it goes. But there's something else."

Sarah's brow furrowed. "Are you feeling okay? Is the baby—"

"We're both doing well," Anna quickly assured her. "That's not it. It's just that—well, you know Jeremy has been working on his dissertation for quite some time."

Sylvia and Sarah nodded.

"He's nearly finished, and he's on track to defend it in the spring." Anna paused for a moment, evidently choosing her next words carefully. "After he earns his doctorate, his goal is to become an assistant professor of history."

Sarah's smile turned uneasy. "Would he stay on at Waterford College?"

"That's not very likely." Anna laced her fingers together and rested her hands in her lap. "Typically, academic departments don't hire their own doctoral students for tenure track positions. They prefer to send their graduates out into the world, and to hire scholars from other universities for their own faculty, in order to encourage the exchange of ideas and things like that. That's what Jeremy says, anyway."

"What about Penn State?" asked Sarah, looking increasingly dismayed. "You could commute to Elm Creek Manor from State College. It's only about an hour's drive. You could bring the baby with you, and—"

"Sarah, dear," said Sylvia kindly, reaching across the table to give her a consoling pat on the arm. To Anna she added, "I'm sure Jeremy will earn his degree with honors, and that he'll find a wonderful position at an excellent university. My only regret is that apparently his success will mean that you'll be leaving us. I can't even begin to tell you how much you'll be missed around here."

"Thanks, Sylvia," said Anna, a catch in her throat.

"Could you tell Jeremy to take his time?" asked Sarah plaintively. "Maybe he could put off graduation a year or two?"

Anna laughed, but her eyes glimmered with unshed tears. "Sorry, no, I can't ask him to do that. He's ready to finish graduate school and move forward with his academic career."

"Of course he is," said Sylvia. "We wish only the best for him, and for you."

Sarah sank back in her seat, defeated. "You can't blame me for trying. Oh, Anna, I can't bear the thought of you leaving."

"I can't bear it either. Don't get me wrong. I'm very proud of Jeremy, and I've known all along that this was the plan, but I love Elm Creek Manor, and all of you, and—" Blinking swiftly, Anna pressed her lips together and shook her head. "We have months, maybe longer, before Jeremy and I might be moving away. Let's not feel sad about it until we know for sure."

That, Sylvia suspected, would be easier said than done.

"How can I possibly enjoy lunch after that news dump?" asked Sarah glumly, taking her spoon in hand and tasting her *pappa al pomodoro*. "Oh, wow. This is amazing."

Anna smiled and rose. "I'll be sure to leave a few gallons in the deep freezer before I leave town."

Sarah managed a smile, but after Anna returned to the stove, she savored another mouthful of stew, traded her spoon for her pen, and wrote "Hire new chef?!?" in the top margin of her agenda, which was getting rather crowded with increasingly frantic notes.

Sylvia suppressed a sigh and tasted her *pappa al pomodoro*, which was, as anticipated, absolutely delicious. If Jeremy's career did take Anna away from them, she would miss these scrumptious meals, but she would miss Anna even more.

A cloud hung over Sylvia and Sarah as they returned to the business at hand, but they carried on, forcing cheer into their voices and savoring every last morsel of their lunches. Sarah proposed several other interesting and ambitious schemes for raising revenue—acquiring corporate and local business sponsors for Quiltsgiving; remaining open throughout the winter as an artists' retreat for individuals and quilt guilds, offering lodging, meals, and facilities, without classes and entertainment programs; holding seminars for other quilting entrepreneurs who wanted to start their own quilt camps; and publishing their own line of Elm Creek Quilts quilt patterns, a suggestion from Gretchen, who had successfully launched a similar venture when she worked at Quilts 'n Things in Sewickley.

As they discussed the merits of each idea, the advantages as well as the potential risks, Sylvia reminded herself that change, whether deliberate or unexpected, was inevitable in life. How one responded to change—with optimism or timidity, resilience or resistance— determined whether it would bring about opportunities for growth and progress, or for disappointment and bitterness.

If she had learned nothing else in her eighty-plus years, it was that she should choose hope.

10

May 1933

With Chain of Progress safely delivered to the Harrisburg Sears store a scant few hours before the midnight deadline, Sylvia settled in for a nerve-wracking wait for the results to be announced. At first she tried not to think about the contest at all, focusing instead on schoolwork and chores she had neglected in the mad rush to finish the quilting and binding. She assisted the stable hands with exercising and tending the horses, wrote a theme for English class, played with Richard and her young cousins, and helped Great-Aunt Lucinda weed the raised beds and plant annuals in the north gardens. "It's in the hands of the judges now," she would say with a shrug and a smile whenever her friends caught her in the hallways at school or passed her a note in class asking how she could possibly bear the suspense.

How was she bearing it? Not very well, but she was determined not to let anyone know that her stomach was in knots, that she spent far too much time daydreaming about how her family might spend the prize money, and that her heart plummeted dizzyingly whenever she imagined how awful it would be if she and Claudia finished in last place.

Her outward show of nonchalance began to crumble on the evening of May 18, the day local winners had been chosen at Sears stores and mail-order houses throughout the country. The judges had made their decisions. Sylvia just didn't know what the results were.

"How will we find out, do you suppose?" Claudia asked Sylvia later that night, her voice hushed, since they were supposed to be in bed. They had brushed their teeth and put on their pajamas, but neither had been able to sleep. By some curious instinct, at the same moment they both had crept from their beds and had peered out into the hallway, startled and yet somehow not at all surprised to find the other peering back. They met in the middle to confer and commiserate.

"I don't know. A telegram, maybe?" said Sylvia. "That would be fastest."

"I wish the manor had a telephone," said Claudia, a frequent lament that had long predated the quilt contest. "That would be even faster."

"They'll probably notify us by mail. Unless—do you suppose they'll contact everyone, or just the winners?"

Claudia blanched. "I hope they contact everyone. How dreadful it would be to wait and wait and hear nothing, and be left wondering forever."

Probably not forever. The losers would eventually figure it out. If the dates for the local contest passed without a word from the officials either way, they must assume they hadn't made it past the first round.

The sisters whispered together a while longer, wondering aloud about their chances of making it through to the regionals, worrying that perhaps they had been disqualified after all for receiving help with their quilting.

"It wasn't cheating," Sylvia insisted. "I'm only thirteen and you're only fifteen. If we combine our ages, I bet that's still younger than most of the other participants. Why shouldn't we work together and get help from our aunties?"

"Because the rules don't say—"

Claudia abruptly fell silent at the sound of someone ascending the stairs. The sisters had time to exchange quick, alarmed glances before darting back into their rooms, closing their doors, and diving into bed.

All the next day, Sylvia tried her best to think about anything but the contest, to keep busy, to distract herself. After working so tirelessly on the World's Fair quilt for so many weeks, it felt strange not to be appliquéing small pastel cotton shapes to soft, ivory background fabric, eyes straining, neck aching, fingertips sore from needle pricks. At odd moments, she found herself feeling disconcerted, as if she ought to be sitting at the quilt frame working small, neat stitches through the three layers, thimble on her right forefinger above, left hand touching the backing below, wrists and fingers falling into the familiar rocking motion she had learned from her mother and had practiced faithfully ever after.

Friday passed. The weekend brought housework and, more to her liking, lots to do around the stables to prepare for upcoming visits from prospective customers. Sylvia didn't expect to hear anything from the judges on Sunday, and yet, as she helped Great-Aunt Lydia make supper, and while she finished her homework, she kept one ear tuned toward the front door in anticipation of a messenger's welcome knock.

"At this point I'd be grateful for any news, even bad," Claudia lamented later that night as they headed upstairs to bed. "No, I take that back. If it's bad news, I'd rather it got delayed in the mail, so we can be hopeful a little while longer."

"We haven't really been waiting *that* long," Sylvia reasoned as they reached the second floor landing and turned down the hallway toward their rooms. "The judging took place on Thursday. Someone in charge probably wrote letters announcing the results Friday morning and mailed them later that afternoon. That means our letter might be at the Waterford post office this very moment. If that's so, tomorrow morning it'll get sorted into our mail carrier's bag, and it could be here by afternoon."

"Announcing the results—" Claudia gasped and stopped short, putting a hand on Sylvia's arm to bring her to a halt too. "Of course Sears would want to announce the results as soon as possible. It's good advertising. Do you suppose the store manager posted the results in the front window? Maybe they even ran a newspaper ad?"

Sylvia's heart gave a little flutter. "Maybe." Could it be that even now, a large, brightly colored sign was propped up on an easel in the front window of the Harrisburg Sears, with Chain of Progress listed among the winners? The Bergstroms subscribed to the *Waterford Register*, not the Harrisburg paper, so if there *had* been an advertisement announcing the winners, they wouldn't have seen it.

Sylvia's eyes met her sister's, and she knew they shared the same thought. "We should wait until morning to ask him," Claudia said. "It's past our bedtime."

"He might be out at the stables when we come down to breakfast, and that means we wouldn't see him until after school." Sylvia darted off down the hallway, calling back over her shoulder, "The sooner we ask, the sooner he can take us."

"*If* he'll take us," Claudia retorted, hurrying after her.

Sylvia halted at the library doors and slowly eased one of them open. She expected to see their father at his desk, but the chair was empty. Without making a sound, she opened the door wider until she spied her father and Uncle William seated in the center of the room on opposite sides of the coffee table, papers and ledger books scattered about between them.

"It's not going to be enough," her father was saying, shaking his head as he looked from a document to an open ledger and back again.

Uncle William heaved a sigh. "We could try to get a mortgage—"

"Out of the question. I won't plunge this family into debt. Owning this land free and clear is the one advantage we have."

"It's just as well," said Uncle William, leaning back and lacing his fingers together behind his head. "There's not a single bank in the Elm Creek Valley that could afford to loan us all that we need."

"I'm sure we could find one or two that would—" At that moment, Sylvia's father glanced up and saw his daughters peering through the doorway. "Girls, what are you doing still awake? It's late."

A wary note in his voice told Sylvia that he wondered how much they had overheard. What *was* it she had overheard?

"We were just on our way to get ready for bed," said Claudia. "First, though, could we ask you a favor?"

Uncle William turned around in his seat and gave them an appraising look, amused. "Must be important if it can't wait until morning."

"It is." Sylvia strode confidently into the room, nudging Claudia forward as she went. If they lingered shyly in the doorway, their father would assume they believed their request was ridiculous and they expected him to refuse. "You probably noticed that we've been a bit anxious, waiting to hear about the quilt contest."

"That's understandable," said her father, sympathetic. "There's a lot at stake. I'm impressed with how patient you've both been."

Sylvia hoped their father wouldn't be too disappointed when he learned how very *not* patient they really were. "We've been trying," she said, pulling a face, "but honestly, our patience is pretty strained at this point."

"Well, naturally," said Uncle William, shaking his head, feigning distress. "It's been what, three whole days since the judges picked the winners?"

"Don't tease us," said Claudia. "It feels a lot longer."

"You'll surely hear something soon," their father said absently, his gaze returning to the ledgers. He rifled through a sheaf of papers, then glanced up again, eyebrows rising. "Was there something else?"

He obviously wanted to get back to work, so Sylvia plunged ahead. "If the judges mailed the participants a list of the winners, we really should have received it by now. Maybe our letter got lost in the mail. Claudia and I figure that the judges probably posted the results in the store too. We were wondering if maybe you could take us to Harrisburg tomorrow so we could see for ourselves."

"If you're too busy," Claudia broke in, "we can go by ourselves on the train. I promise I'll watch over Sylvia."

Sylvia shot her a look, astonishment quickly giving way to indignation. She never would have expected her sister to suggest they travel alone, something they had never done—and what nerve, to suggest that Sylvia needed her elder sister to mind her! She was only two years younger, but probably twice as clever.

But their father was shaking his head. "I'm sorry, girls," he said. "Tomorrow is a school day. You know that."

"But it's almost summer break," said Claudia. "We won't miss anything important."

Uncle William grinned. "Somehow I doubt your teachers would agree."

"We can make up any work we miss," Sylvia quickly chimed in, her heart sinking as she watched her father sigh and rub his jaw. She realized too late that they really should have waited until morning to ask. "I'll help Claudia with anything she doesn't understand."

"I think you mean *I'll* help *you*," said Claudia sharply.

Their father held up a hand. "Girls, please. It's late and we're all much too tired to argue. You may not go to Harrisburg tomorrow—not with me, not alone."

"How about with Uncle William?" said Claudia, turning a desperate, hopeful look his way. "Please?"

"Sorry, kid," said Uncle William. "Your father says you can't miss school, and he has the final say."

Claudia's shoulders slumped, and Sylvia heaved a sigh. "We thought it couldn't hurt to ask, but we understand," said Sylvia. She turned toward the door, and when Claudia didn't move, she took her sister by the arm and tugged to get her moving. "Good night."

"Good night, girls," said Uncle William.

But then their father said, "Wait."

The sisters abruptly halted. Sylvia felt a spark of hope.

"I'm sure you'll receive your letter in the next day or two," her father said, setting the papers down and sitting back in his armchair. "However, if you don't hear anything by Friday afternoon, I'll take you down to Harrisburg on Saturday."

"Saturday?" said Claudia. "But the regional judging takes place on Thursday. Our quilts could be in Philadelphia by Saturday. Please, Father—"

"Saturday is fine," Sylvia broke in, backing through the doorway and pulling Claudia along with her. "Thank you. Sorry for the interruption. Good night."

"Straight to bed," their father called after them.

"Yes, Father," Sylvia replied, tightening her grip as she steered her sister into the hall.

"Would you let go?" Claudia spluttered, yanking her arm free. That was fine by Sylvia; she needed both hands to shut the French doors before her father had second thoughts. "What's your hurry? Another few minutes and we could have convinced him."

"No, we couldn't have." Sylvia lowered her voice in hopes that her sister would do the same. "Didn't you see what was going on in there, what we interrupted?"

"What?" Claudia shook her head, exasperated. "They were talking about money, like always. What else is new? That's all anyone talks about these days—money, or the lack of it, or how to get more of it—"

"They were talking about debt and mortgages," said Sylvia, emphasizing each word. "That's serious. This wasn't just another talk about paying the grocery bill."

Claudia hesitated. "Well, what does it mean?" she asked flatly, her anger fading.

"I don't know, but it can't be good." Sylvia stalked off down the hall to her bedroom, thoughts churning.

The next morning, as Sylvia, her siblings, and cousins set off on foot through the forest to meet the school bus where the long, gravel drive intersected with the county road, Sylvia dropped back and gestured for Claudia to do the same. "I have an idea," she said after the younger children had moved several paces ahead, well out of earshot if the sisters kept their voices low. "I could telephone the Sears store in Harrisburg and ask if they've posted the results."

Claudia mulled it over, frowning. "I suppose that's better than waiting for the mail, but driving to the store today would be better."

"Well, Father ruled that out, so calling is the next best thing."

"But where would you call from? When?"

"From the pay phone at the pharmacy after school." Sylvia jingled the nickels in her skirt pocket, one for the call and two extra just in case. "You can tell everyone at home that I went to the library. I have to return a book anyway, so it won't be a lie. I'll catch the cross-valley bus afterward, and I'll make it home well before dinner."

"Maybe I should make the call." Claudia held out her palm for the coins. "I'm older and more responsible."

"Nope." Sylvia put on some speed to catch up with the younger children. "My nickels, my idea, my call."

Sylvia usually enjoyed school, but that day she couldn't wait for the hours to pass. When the dismissal bell finally rang, she bolted from her seat, gathered her things, offered breathless goodbyes to her friends, and hurried off, breaking into a run as soon as she left the building. Five minutes later she was entering the pharmacy, nodding politely to the clerk, and hastening to the telephone nook only to find a Fuller Brush salesman on the line, his back turned, a large case of wares on the floor at his feet. She pretended to browse the magazine racks while she waited for him to finish his call, resisting the temptation to clear her throat impatiently to remind him that someone was waiting. Eventually he hung up, put on his hat, and took his case by the handle. "Hey, there, little lady," he exclaimed in surprise as she darted around him to reach the phone. "Take it easy."

She pretended not to hear him, her hand trembling slightly as she took a nickel from her pocket and fed it into the slot. She kept her voice low and steady and, she hoped, mature as she asked the operator to connect her. Then she had to pay another nickel since Harrisburg was on another exchange. Before long a woman answered the ring, greeting her with a cheerful, "Sears, Roebuck and Company. How may I direct your call?"

"I—I'm not sure—" Sylvia took a quick, steadying breath. "I'm calling to inquire about the Century of Progress Quilting Contest. Could you please tell me who the top three finishers were at your store?"

"I'm sorry, miss. I don't have that information in front of me, but I'd be more than happy to find out. Would you prefer to hold the line, or shall I call you back?"

"I—I'm sorry, I can't really do either. I'm calling from a public phone."

"Oh, I see. Well, if you like, you can stop by the store on Market Square and see the winners for yourself. The prizewinning quilts as well as a selection of other particularly lovely entries will be on display in the housewares division for a little while longer. After tomorrow, the top three quilts will be sent off to Philadelphia for the regional contest. Isn't that exciting?"

"Yes, it is. Very." Sylvia felt her heart thudding nervously at the very thought of it. "I won't be able to stop by the store today. To be perfectly frank, I'm wondering about my own quilt. It's Chain of Progress, by Sylvia—by Claudia Sylvia Bergstrom. It has appliqué scenes of various historical events in the center, with a border of Odd

Fellows Chain blocks all around. Have you seen anything like that
in the exhibit?"

"That sounds familiar," the receptionist mused, "but I couldn't
say for sure. I do know, however, that all of the winners were notified
by mail last week."

Sylvia's heart plummeted. "Really? They were?"

"Oh, yes. Letters went out to the top three finishers the day after
the judging. We wanted to notify those contestants right away, since
their quilts will be shipped to Philadelphia soon."

"Of course." Sylvia closed her eyes and swallowed hard, disappointment a lump in her throat. "And . . . what about everyone else
who entered quilts but didn't place? Were they notified too?"

"Certainly. Their letters went out this morning, since those required a bit more time. There were far more of them to send, and it
was necessary to include instructions for picking up the quilts after
the store exhibit ends."

"I understand." Indeed, Sylvia now understood all too well. Good
news had flown swiftly to its destination; bad news was dragging its
heels, miserable. It was just as well their father hadn't agreed to drive
them to Harrisburg to receive the verdict in person. Still, it would
have been nice to see the exhibit. She wondered if the judges had considered their quilt to be "particularly lovely" enough to be included.

She thanked the receptionist for her help and hung up. Slipping
the strap of her satchel over her head, she trudged off to the bus stop,
remembering only after she boarded that she had forgotten to return
her library book.

Settling back in her seat, she watched the familiar scenery passing
by her window and silently rehearsed how she would break the news.
Claudia would be crushed, but Sylvia would remind her that Chain
of Progress was the best quilt either of them had ever made. They
had so much to be proud of, even if the judges hadn't honored them
with an award.

She rolled her eyes and folded her arms over her chest. No matter how she tried to phrase it, it sounded hackneyed and false. They had been eliminated in the first round, and it felt awful, and there was no finding a silver lining in it.

As the bus approached the intersection with the winding forest road to Elm Creek Manor, Sylvia pulled the cable running the length of the bus, signaling to the driver that she wished to disembark. She walked the rest of the way home, her footsteps slowed by the twin burdens of her own disappointment and her reluctance to deliver bad news. She barely noticed the verdant springtime beauty of the forest she loved so dearly, until birdsong and sunlight peeping through the branches overhead drew her attention, offering a bit of solace. When she reached the familiar fork in the narrow gravel road, she took the right branch leading to the manor's front entrance rather than the longer, winding way around back to the barn and the other outbuildings. She hoped to slip into the house quietly, but when she emerged from the leafy wood and it came into view on the other side of the wildflower meadow, she spied Claudia pacing the length of the verandah.

Of course her sister was keeping watch for her, anxious for news. Sylvia braced herself. She couldn't hide, so she might as well get it over with.

Claudia must have spotted her, for she froze for the barest of moments before breaking into a run—down the nearest of the twin curved staircases and around the circular drive, picking up speed as she hit the straightaway. Sylvia almost called out to her not to bother, that the news she was bringing wasn't worth any haste, but then she saw that Claudia was carrying an envelope—undoubtedly the much-anticipated letter from the Harrisburg Sears.

Claudia slowed as she approached and held up the envelope, which seemed rather thick. "It's here," she panted. "The letter from Sears—but maybe they told you the results over the phone?"

Sylvia shook her head. "I didn't learn much. What does the letter say?"

"I didn't open it yet. The aunties told me I had to wait for you. And here you are, finally, so—" Without another word, Claudia carefully tore open the flap and withdrew some folded pages.

"What does it say?" Sylvia demanded, darting closer to read over her sister's shoulder.

"Give me a minute." Claudia tucked the empty envelope between her elbow and her side as she unfolded the letter. A much smaller, narrow blue rectangle of paper fluttered free, but Sylvia quickly snatched it out of the air before it touched the ground. She barely glanced at it, so intent was she on the letter, which Claudia was holding at an angle that made it impossible for Sylvia to make out anything more than the salutation. Then Claudia gasped. "Oh, my goodness!"

"What? What does it say?" Sylvia snatched the pages from her sister's hand, read the first few lines—"We won first place! We did it! We won!"

"I was just getting to that part." Claudia snatched the letter back. "'We are pleased to inform you . . . First place in the local competition at Harrisburg . . . Quilt will advance to the regional contest in Philadelphia . . . Your check for ten dollars is enclosed—'" Her eyes met Sylvia's. "The check?"

Sylvia glanced at the slim blue paper in her hand. "Oh, this is it! Can you believe it? Ten dollars!"

"Be careful with that," Claudia warned, as Sylvia clutched it to her chest and spun around in place, her satchel swinging wildly from its shoulder strap. "If you tear it, they might not give us a replacement."

That brought Sylvia's whirling about to an abrupt halt, and she carefully returned the precious check to the envelope.

The sisters raced back to the manor, where they found their aunties and cousins and Richard waiting for them in the front foyer. They cheered and embraced when Sylvia and Claudia entered, showering them in congratulations and praise. Sylvia basked in their acclaim until she remembered that her aunties deserved their fair share of credit for the win too, for everything they had done to help her and Claudia finish the quilt in time.

But when she tried to tell them so, they laughed and refused to accept any laurels for themselves. "It's your quilt, girls," said Great-Aunt Lucinda firmly. "You envisioned it, you pieced every seam, and you appliquéd every appliqué. We helped with the quilting, but even then, we were following your instructions."

"Exactly so," said Great-Aunt Lydia, as Aunt Nellie nodded.

When their father and Uncle William came in from the stables, they too cheered the sisters' victory and congratulated them on a job well done. Later, as they had agreed, Sylvia and Claudia took their father aside and presented the check to him. "We wanted to repay you for making up the difference when we bought Richard the sled for his birthday," Claudia said.

"Whatever's left over, we'd like you to use for groceries or bills or anything else the family needs," Sylvia added. "We're old enough to contribute, even if you don't think we're old enough to understand when something's wrong."

She didn't mean to sound indignant—although she was, a little, maybe. She didn't like being treated like a child, as if she had to be protected from worrisome truths. But there must have been an edge to her voice, for her father's eyebrows rose, and his glance became a mild rebuke. Heat rose in her cheeks and she lowered her gaze.

"Thank you, girls," her father said, and his voice was kind. "Consider the debt cleared. The rest I'll set aside for your educations. Speaking of which—" He paused so long that Sylvia looked up again, curious. "I don't think yours will suffer greatly if you miss one day of class in order to view the quilt display in Harrisburg tomorrow."

The sisters gasped. "Really, Father?" said Claudia. "You'd let us miss school?"

"For such an impressive achievement, I think we can make an exception to our usual rules," he replied. "Tomorrow is the last day of the local exhibit, so it's our last chance. I for one wouldn't want to miss seeing your quilt given pride of place among the other entries."

"I wouldn't want to miss it either," said Sylvia fervently.

Later, over dinner, their father and aunties worked out a plan for the next day's travels. Richard and the cousins were dismayed to learn that they would be attending school as if it were any other Tuesday. "When you take first prize in a contest, you can miss school too," Uncle William replied over their protests.

Sylvia could already see the wheels turning in Richard's head as he pondered how he might do that, but in the meantime, he wasn't about to let this opportunity slip by. "Please, Father?" he asked. "It's not because I want to skip school. I want to see the quilt show. Really."

Uncle William smothered a laugh.

"Not this time, Richard," their father said. "I know you want to honor your sisters' achievement, but you need to get a good education if you want to run Bergstrom Thoroughbreds someday."

From her pinnacle of joy, Sylvia suddenly felt her heart plummet. Richard was the youngest of the siblings, the youngest of all the cousins living at Elm Creek Manor, and yet their father expected him to run Bergstrom Thoroughbreds someday? Richard loved horses, but it was Sylvia who worked at the stables nearly every day, who observed her father and uncle when they met with prospective customers, who had devoted as many years to learning the family business as she had to any of her school subjects. Two fillies she had helped raise had sold in April, earning what her father had called a windfall profit. And yet her father intended Richard, not her, to take over for him someday.

Sylvia almost shuddered from the cold shock of it: Father chose Richard because Richard was a boy. That had to be the reason. It couldn't be because her brother was more clever or better with the animals or more trustworthy, because that wasn't so. For as long as she could remember, she had assumed that one day, when she was all grown up and her father retired, she would take his place behind the big oak desk in the library, and more important, in the stables and the training rings and on the road, selling their fine horses to the most discriminating clients in the country. And now, on a day that should have been so joyful, to find out at the dinner table that this had never been the plan—

"What do you think, Sylvia?" Great-Aunt Lucinda prompted.

"What do I—" Sylvia's mouth was dry. "What do I think about what?"

The grown-ups chuckled. "She can't think of anything but that prizewinning quilt," said Great-Aunt Lydia indulgently. "Who could blame her?"

Sylvia managed an apologetic smile. They explained the plan again, since she had missed it the first time. Tomorrow, Uncle William and Aunt Nellie would stay home to work and to mind the younger children. Great-Aunt Lydia and Great-Aunt Lucinda would accompany Sylvia, Claudia, and their father to Harrisburg.

"I'm going to stand beside your quilt and boast about my exceptional grand-nieces to everyone who pauses to admire it," declared Great-Aunt Lydia. "You think I'm teasing, but I'm not."

"I want to view the exhibit to size up the competition you'll face in the regional round," said Great-Aunt Lucinda. She smiled as she said it, but Sylvia knew she was absolutely serious.

The next day, the sisters and their proud escorts traveled by train to Harrisburg, where they caught the trolley for the brief ride south to Market Square, on the eastern bank of the Susquehanna River. Claudia seemed a bit overwhelmed by the bustle and traffic, hesitating before she stepped off the trolley and seizing their father's hand as they made their way along the sidewalk, but Sylvia thrilled to the sights and sounds of a city so much bigger and busier than quiet, scholarly little Waterford. She craned her neck in a vain attempt to see everything at once, the tall buildings, the cars, the businessmen with briefcases and ladies with their shopping bags and all sorts of uniformed tradespeople with their wagons and pushcarts.

When her gaze fell upon the Sears building on the corner at 6 South Market Street, she darted ahead of the others and then stopped short to take it in, breathless from excitement. The building was five stories tall, the tallest four of light gray stone, the lowest of a marble so dark gray it was almost black. White awnings shaded the broad picture windows that ran the length of both sides, and rectangular signs above them announced "Sears, Roebuck and Co." in bold white lettering on black. Even from a distance Sylvia could glimpse enticing displays of clothing, housewares, toys, and modern appliances behind the glass. She felt a brief pang of sympathy for Richard, who would have admired every newfangled gadget he saw and would have besieged their father with questions about each one and how it worked. Maybe that was why their father preferred him to take over Bergstrom Thoroughbreds—his daring, his enthusiasm, his insatiable curiosity.

Sylvia shoved the thoughts aside as her family crossed the street and entered the store, a brightly lit, well-organized pageant of abundance. Sylvia rose up on tiptoe and looked this way and that for Chain of Progress until Claudia glared and murmured, "Stop acting like a country bumpkin."

"Stop acting like a country *mouse*," Sylvia countered, since Claudia was still clinging timorously to their father's hand.

Since the quilts were nowhere in sight, Great-Aunt Lydia approached a young, elegantly dressed saleswoman and asked where they might find the exhibit. When the saleswoman learned that two prizewinning quilters stood before her, she smiled with genuine pleasure and offered to escort them to the temporary gallery on the second floor.

With the elegant saleswoman in the lead, her high heels clicking authoritatively on the marble floor, they made quite a parade through men's and ladies' fashions and upstairs to housewares, where shelves and tables had been moved aside to make room for several aisles of quilt stands. "First things first," the saleswoman said to Sylvia and Claudia over her shoulder, offering a grin as she beckoned them along. "Let's see your champion quilt."

Suddenly, they turned the corner and beheld Chain of Progress, raised on a dais at the focal point where the aisles ended, hung a few inches higher than the second- and third-place quilts flanking it. Sylvia stopped short and drew in a breath, amazed. Arranged so impressively, their quilt looked even lovelier than she remembered, strikingly modern in design and yet rooted in tradition, with harmonious colors and exquisite quilting that added depth and texture to the whole.

Then Sylvia's gaze went to the lower right corner, and the bright blue First Place ribbon attached there. Claudia seized her hand and squeezed it, and Sylvia squeezed even harder back. She felt so proud she thought she might burst into tears, but she put on a tremulous smile instead. A quick glance took in several dozen people strolling at their leisure through the exhibit, and, true to her word, Great-Aunt Lydia mentioned to any who paused in front of Chain of Progress that her very talented grand-nieces had made it. Most responded politely, pleased to meet a relative of the winners, and the friendlier ones came over to congratulate Sylvia and Claudia. One older woman shook their hands and asked them to autograph a sales flyer she had picked up in housewares. Smothering laughter, they consented.

Suddenly, a man in a slightly rumpled suit appeared in front of them. "Carl Higgins, *Harrisburg Telegraph*," he announced, just as a flashbulb popped blindingly somewhere over his left shoulder. "So, which of you girls is Miss Claudia Sylvia Bergstrom?"

Sylvia, distracted by the spots dancing before her eyes, only shook her head, but her sister promptly replied, "I'm Claudia. This is Sylvia."

Sylvia heard pencil scratching on paper. "So you worked together?"

"Yes," Claudia said. "I'm only fifteen and my sister is only thirteen. If we combine our ages, we're still younger than most of the other participants."

Those were *her* words, Sylvia thought, too surprised to claim them. "That's a good one," the reporter said, grinning. "Say, would you mind if we take a picture of you two girls with your prizewinning quilt?"

Claudia agreed for both of them. She took Sylvia's arm firmly and steered her to one side of their quilt, and then took her place on the other. Flashbulbs popped again, but Sylvia was getting used to it, so when the reporter asked them a few more questions, she was able to reply as well as Claudia did.

When Sylvia's vision cleared, she explored the exhibit, admiring the best of the other entries, remembering to keep her face expressionless if she passed before one she did not care for, because one never knew if the quiltmaker or her best friend stood nearby, heart sinking at every frown or dismissive word. Her mother had taught her to be courteous at quilt shows, to say aloud nothing that she would not want someone to declare about her own quilts. Later, within the family circle, the Bergstroms might discuss what they loved or disliked or found peculiar about the quilts they had seen, but they never did so where a careless remark might cause hurt.

But on the homeward-bound train later that day, after they had studied all the quilts selected to represent the best of the Harrisburg entries, Sylvia and Claudia had very little criticism to share. Quite the opposite was true. The second- and third-place quilts, which would be moving on to the regional round with Chain of Progress, were different in style and theme from their own but equally beautiful and well crafted. In Sylvia's opinion, several quilts that had not won a ribbon also deserved recognition. She honestly couldn't have narrowed down her favorites to only three, and she wasn't sure how the judges had been able to do so.

"They used specific judging criteria, remember?" said Claudia, brandishing their own scoresheet. "Every quilt was evaluated and given a score for beauty, color—"

"I know," said Sylvia, a bit impatiently, wishing she could make herself understood. "I just think it very easily could have gone another way, if even one of the judges had felt slightly differently about one or two things. We could have come in third, or tenth, or thirtieth."

"But we didn't," said Claudia, eminently reasonable.

Yet her smile faltered, and Sylvia knew they shared the same thought.

The whirlwind of attention they had received at the local exhibit had been flattering, but although they had claimed first prize, the excellence of the other entries was humbling. And they knew the competition was certain to be even fiercer at the regionals.

11

September 2004

Sylvia didn't need to ask Matt twice to step away from his preparations for the launch of Elm Creek Orchards long enough to inspect the water-stained patch on the attic wall. With his years of experience working for his father's construction firm, he understood well the potentially dire consequences of ignoring a leaky roof.

"It could be worse," Matt reported when he met her in the library afterward. She was well aware that in Matt parlance, this meant the roof was in rather bad condition but was not in danger of imminent collapse. "The south wing seems intact, but I found two additional leaks in the west wing. Do you know when the roof was last replaced?"

"I have no idea," Sylvia replied, taking a seat on the sofa in the center of the room, squaring her shoulders as if to brace herself for worse revelations yet to come. "It would have been before I inherited the estate, to be sure. My sister may have taken care of it sometime in the past few decades when she was in charge, but given the state of the rest of the manor when I returned—" She shook her head and shrugged. "I assume it's long overdue."

"Looks that way to me." Matt sat down in one of the armchairs on the opposite side of the coffee table. "I'll get in touch with my father and ask him to recommend a roofer, someone who can start work soon and won't charge us a fortune. Fair warning, though, even if they give us a friends and family rate, it's going to be expensive."

Sylvia's heart sank, even though she had expected as much. "Our insurance won't cover it?"

He shook his head. "If the roof had been damaged in a hailstorm, maybe, but most home insurance policies won't cover a roof that's more than twenty years old. In our case, that wouldn't matter anyway, since the damage isn't due to a single storm but simply age and wear. I'm afraid we're going to be paying out of pocket for a new roof, and . . . that's a very big roof."

"I assume we'll also need to clear out the attic before the work begins."

"Yeah," said Matt, "but at least that part we can do ourselves, for free."

Sylvia inhaled deeply and rose, resisting the impulse to wring her hands as she paced the length of the room. The tall diamond-paned windows were open to the fresh autumn breezes, and she was exceedingly grateful for the forecast, which called for clear sunny days for the rest of the week. She had never dreaded the threat of rain as she did now.

Matt was watching her expectantly, so she returned to the sofa, although she braced her arms on the back of it rather than sitting down. "There's nothing for it but to fix it, and the sooner the better. Consult your father and choose the most skilled and reliable contractor you can find. When you have an estimate, let me know—and let Sarah know too, so she can figure out how best to pay for it." She couldn't bear to imagine how this new expense would strain their already stretched-thin budget. Elm Creek Orchards couldn't possibly sell enough apples to cover it, not in half a dozen seasons. "Let me know when you need me to sign a contract and write a check."

"I'm on it," said Matt, rising. "We'll get it done, Sylvia. It's going to be okay."

She certainly hoped so. She managed a smile and waved him on his way.

When she was alone, she clasped a hand to her brow and closed her eyes to ward off a headache. The need to generate additional revenue had suddenly taken on new urgency. If only she had listened to Sarah earlier—but she hadn't, and no amount of chiding herself would change that. Now she must make up for lost time.

She left the library in search of Sarah, and eventually found her in the playroom minding the twins. "Sarah, dear," Sylvia called, raising her voice to be heard over Caroline, who was striking a rainbow-hued toy xylophone with a wooden mallet in merry abandon. "Could we arrange a time, preferably soon, to meet to discuss your revenue-generating proposals in more detail?"

Sarah glanced up from her seat on the braided rag rug and smiled. "How about now?" she asked, placing a hand upon the xylophone bars to mute them somewhat.

"Now works for me," Sylvia replied.

After enlisting the ever-reliable Gretchen to watch the twins, Sylvia and Sarah reconvened in the library, where Sarah produced her folder of notes, reports, and bullet-point lists. As soon as they settled into their usual seats on opposite sides of the coffee table, Sarah made her pitches anew, clearly and concisely presenting the pros and cons of each proposed venture.

This time Sylvia listened, truly listened, wholeheartedly committed to solving their cash-flow problems instead of futilely wishing them away. She was still reluctant to raise tuition except as a last resort, and a decision to expand the camp season would require more thought and thorough discussions with the other members of the faculty. On the other hand, a corporate sponsorship program for Quiltsgiving offered certain advantages she'd overlooked before. It would cost very little to implement, and they could begin as soon as they wished, without disrupting any other aspect of the business. Yet with the second-annual event only two months away, they would have to move quickly if they intended to generate any revenue from the program this year rather than waiting for the next.

"I'll send out a group email to see what the other Elm Creek Quilters think," Sarah said. "If everyone's on board, I'll put together a list of potential sponsors. Quilt-related companies in particular should be interested in providing financial support or in-kind donations in exchange for increasing their audience reach and raising their brand awareness among our sizable customer base."

"My goodness, that sounded very businesslike," teased Sylvia.

"Too much jargon?"

"I understood every word," Sylvia assured her. "And since you'll be speaking with corporate folks soon, I suppose you ought to practice the lingo."

"One caveat—we may already be too late to get sponsorships from national corporations before November," said Sarah. "Typically, local small businesses have the flexibility and independence to make decisions quickly, but larger corporations often require a long lead time and a formal proposal process."

"I see. Yes, that would make sense." Sylvia paused to think. "Well, we mustn't let our late start keep us from making the attempt. Some small, local businesses may offer support in abundance, and some large corporations may pleasantly surprise us. We'll never know unless we try."

Flashing a grin, Sarah bounded up from her armchair, sat down at the oak desk, and woke the computer. While she swiftly composed an email to the Elm Creek Quilters, Sylvia went upstairs to the nursery to ask Gretchen what she thought of the plan. "It's a splendid idea," Gretchen murmured as she rocked a very drowsy Caroline on her lap; James was curled up on a quilt on a window seat, already asleep. By the time Sylvia returned to the library with Gretchen's vote, Gwen and Diane had both replied to the group email enthusiastically endorsing the plan, a very good start indeed.

As Sylvia and Sarah waited for their other friends to chime in, they decided to begin putting together the list of potential sponsors. At the very top were vendors from whom they purchased sewing supplies, followed immediately by quilt magazines and websites where they regularly ran ads for Elm Creek Quilt Camp. Before long, Sylvia shifted her focus to local businesses that benefited from the campers' presence in Waterford—cafés, craft stores, gift shops—while Sarah concentrated on major accounts in the quilting world, such as sewing machine, thread, cutting mat, and acrylic ruler manufacturers. By suppertime they had accumulated the names of an impressive number of potential sponsors. As they headed downstairs, they agreed that in the morning, they would complete their lists by filling in any missing contact information. The next step would be to draft a letter of request, which they would tailor to each individual company before sending.

"I spoke to my dad, and he put me in touch with a roofer based in Grangerville," said Matt when they had all gathered around the refectory table in the kitchen. It was Andrew's turn to cook, and he had prepared his specialty, grilled chicken with baked potatoes. "They're old friends. He's coming by tomorrow afternoon to inspect the roof."

"That's good news," said Sylvia, relieved. "How fortunate that he's available so soon."

"My dad implied that this guy owes him a favor," said Matt, allowing a grin. "Also, I think the size of the job appealed to him."

"I bet it did." Sarah leaned over to serve James some mashed potatoes. "When you told him the square footage, his eyes probably lit up with dollar signs on springs, like a cartoon character."

"That would explain the wacky cash register sound effects in the background."

"Oh, you two," Sylvia scolded playfully. She knew they were trying to lighten the mood, so the least she could do was go along.

"Are you sure we couldn't do the repairs ourselves?" asked Andrew, directing the question to Matt, but glancing to Joe for support. "Matt has years of construction experience, Joe's an expert woodworker and can build just about anything, and I put a new roof on my house in Michigan back in the day."

"Don't even think about it," said Gretchen, fixing Joe with a level gaze. "You are *not* scrambling around on a dilapidated roof three stories off the ground, not with your back."

"I wasn't planning to," said Joe mildly, helping himself to more chicken.

"Neither are you, dear," Sylvia told Andrew firmly. "This isn't attaching shingles to the roof of the market stand in the orchard. And I've seen photos of your old house in Michigan. It was a ranch, and you were likely forty years younger when you replaced that roof."

"Thirty," said Andrew.

"Even so."

"I appreciate the offer, but we definitely need a professional crew for this job," said Matt diplomatically. "I'm not licensed for this sort of work, and our insurance wouldn't cover it if something went wrong. Besides, I need your help with the orchard, and you wouldn't have time to do both."

"Fair enough," said Andrew, with a good-natured shrug.

Sylvia and Gretchen exchanged a look across the table, relieved. Sylvia appreciated her husband's frugality and work ethic, but not everything at Elm Creek Manor was meant to be a do-it-yourself project.

The conversation shifted to Anna's happy news, and from there, inevitably, to her eventual departure from Elm Creek Quilts. That topic was too melancholy to linger upon long, so they returned to the subject of the orchard and the many tasks yet to complete before their grand opening. They had just finished dinner and were tidying up when the phone rang.

Gretchen, who was nearest, answered. "Elm Creek Quilts," she said pleasantly, and then she brightened. "Hello, Summer. How is school going?" She paused, listening. "Oh, I'm so glad to hear it. And yes, I'll tell the others." She lowered the phone and announced, "Summer supports the corporate sponsorship plan. Also, Sylvia, she'd like to talk to you."

"Certainly." Rising, Sylvia came around the table and accepted the phone from Gretchen. "Hello, dear. What can I do for you?"

"That's the wrong question," Summer teased. "I'd like to do something for you."

"Oh? That would be lovely, as long as it doesn't involve climbing on the roof."

"What?"

"Oh, the roof needs to be replaced, and Andrew thought that he, Joe, and Matt could do it themselves. Gretchen and I talked them out of it." She waved a hand, dismissing the idea. "What did you have in mind, dear?"

"I thought you might be missing your World's Fair quilt," said Summer. "How'd you like to come for a visit? I'd really like you to see Union Hall's new dedicated restoration and cleaning room, where Chain of Progress is getting the five-star treatment."

"My goodness. It sounds like you're running a luxury spa for quilts."

Summer laughed. "That's not far from the truth. So, what do you think? I'd love to show you around."

Sylvia paused to think, but she didn't need long. She hadn't seen Union Hall since the gala grand opening of the quilt gallery in August, and the renovations to the rest of the historic building had likely come a long way since then. "I'd be delighted," she said. "When did you have in mind?"

"I'm free tomorrow afternoon if you are."

"Tomorrow?" She would miss the roofer's inspection, but perhaps that was just as well. It would be impossible to concentrate while the roofer climbed around overhead, and she would rather spend the time touring Union Hall with Summer than pacing anxiously in the library, glancing up sharply at every unexpected scrape and thud. "As a matter of fact, tomorrow afternoon would be ideal."

The next day, Sylvia spent the morning working on the sponsors list with Sarah, but after lunch, she hitched a ride downtown in the Elm Creek Quilts minivan with Sarah and Gretchen, who were taking the twins to story hour at Waterford Public Library. Sarah dropped off Sylvia at the town square in the historic district, and from there it was a pleasant stroll along the public green to Union Hall.

In her youth, Sylvia had known the stately Greek Revival building as a popular community center and headquarters for the Waterford Historical Society. It had only been the previous autumn, however, when she had learned that her Bergstrom ancestors had played a very significant role in its construction during some of the bleakest months of the Civil War. Thanks to some diligent historical research by Sarah and Agnes, a fascinating story once entirely forgotten had been brought to light.

In 1862, men of the Elm Creek Valley who had enlisted in the Union Army had written home with shocking tales of the hardships they endured, not only the dangers of the battlefield, but their daily struggles with inadequate clothing and shelter, poor rations, and scarce medical supplies. Determined to provide for their soldiers' needs, the women on the home front—including Sylvia's great-grandmother Anneke and her great-grandfather's sister Gerda—arranged shipments of essential supplies, but this was a costly endeavor. In order to raise money to build a venue of their own where they could host fundraisers, the Union Quilters, as the group of friends called themselves, embarked upon an ambitious plan to create a quilt called the Loyal

Union Sampler. From 121 six-inch patchwork blocks contributed by quilters from throughout the Elm Creek Valley, the Union Quilters created an exquisite sampler and offered it up in a raffle, earning enough money to begin construction on Union Hall. After Union Hall opened the following year, the Union Quilters hosted many successful fundraisers in the hall's theater, garden, and galleries, with the proceeds benefiting local soldiers from the 49th Pennsylvania Infantry Regiment, the 6th United States Colored Infantry Regiment, and the Veterans' Relief Fund, which provided for the wounded soldiers of the Elm Creek Valley and their families.

Although at the time the Union Quilters received national acclaim for their ambitious venture, their story was lost to history until the Loyal Union Sampler was discovered in a trunk in Union Hall little more than a year ago. By then, the once-lovely building had fallen into disrepair. What should have been a jewel of the historic district had become a long-neglected eyesore, a magnet for vandals, graffiti, and litter. It was common knowledge among the local schoolchildren that it was haunted. After an unscrupulous local real estate developer, Gregory Krolich of University Realty, contrived to have the property condemned so he could buy it, demolish it, and build lucrative condos on the site, the Waterford Historical Society fought back. With Elm Creek Quilter Agnes leading the way, they established Union Hall's historical significance and convinced the city council and zoning commission to rescind the condemnation order.

But saving the historic building from the wrecking ball was only the beginning. Union Hall required extensive renovations and repairs if the historical society was to achieve its ambitions—first, to preserve the structure, and eventually, to host a museum of local history. Even as the repair work had commenced earlier that spring, the Waterford Historical Society had launched a capital campaign in which Summer had taken on a crucial role. The beautiful east gallery on the second floor had been one of the first rooms to be renovated, and when it was finished, Agnes had proposed organizing an exhibit of quilts that were particularly significant to local history. Admission fees and donations would raise much-needed cash, and a grand opening gala would kick off the capital campaign in fine style while generating excellent publicity for the historical society's preservation efforts. In June, when Summer had come home unexpectedly from the University of Chicago, hoping to finish her overdue master's thesis amid the comforts and creative inspiration of Elm Creek Manor, Agnes had promptly hired her to be the exhibit's curator.

From June through August, Summer had acquired fascinating quilts for the Union Hall exhibit, including the Loyal Union Sampler, which had proven invaluable to understanding the building's historical significance; an extraordinary Log Cabin quilt pieced by Gerda Bergstrom in the years after the Civil War; and, the most recently created piece, Sarah's Sampler, a twelve-block sampler Sarah had made during her first quilting lessons with Sylvia. Back in August, when Sylvia and Agnes had suggested including Sarah's Sampler in the exhibit, Sarah had demurred. "I'd be mortified to have the public see my first quilt, with all its beginner's mistakes, displayed in a museum alongside true works of art," she had said, her cheeks flushing pink with embarrassment.

"And why shouldn't the quilt be imperfect?" Agnes had asked. "We all know that history has never been perfect. It's in the imperfections where the true story emerges."

Sarah had appreciated the kind words, but she'd had another objection. "I moved to Waterford only eight years ago—well, eight and a half. None of my quilts ever played a role in local history."

Here too her friends had disagreed. The other Elm Creek Quilters reminded her that the quilting lessons that had brought about the sampler had also kindled the friendship between master quilter Sylvia and Sarah, her younger apprentice. Their friendship inspired the creation of Elm Creek Quilts, which had affected, and was continuing to affect, local history in countless wonderful ways. Thus persuaded, Sarah had agreed to loan her quilt to the exhibit until the weather turned cooler and she and Matt needed it back on their bed. That time was nearly upon them, as Summer had reminded Sylvia when she asked to borrow the World's Fair quilt to fill the soon-to-be empty place on the gallery wall.

Sylvia had attended the gallery's grand opening gala in August, but as she approached Union Hall now, she marveled anew at the changes the Waterford Historical Society's team of volunteers and expert renovators had brought about in just a few short months. All of the buildings in the historic district sat fairly close to the street, but Union Hall boasted a small front lawn, lush green and freshly mowed, enclosed within a formerly rusty wrought-iron fence that had been painted a striking obsidian black. Every trace of graffiti had been scrubbed from the building's white stone walls, the broken windows had been replaced, the hedges had been neatly trimmed, and the once-creaky front gate swung open smoothly and silently when Sylvia unlatched it. She followed the cobblestone walk to the limestone staircase that climbed to the shaded porch, each stair slightly concave in the middle, worn from the footsteps of more than 140 years' worth of visitors. Passing between the tall, whitewashed columns supporting the two-story pediment, she crossed the porch, approached the tall double doors, and entered the building through the one on the right.

The foyer was smaller than the one that welcomed guests to Elm Creek Manor, but it too was splendid, with a gleaming gray-blue marble floor, marred only by a faint path of scuff marks. High above the scarred floor, elegant crown molding echoed the Greek key patterns of the ceiling medallion, which encircled a tiered candle-style chandelier with tapered bulbs. Directly across the foyer from the front entrance, a wide doorway led into a theater, where a red velvet curtain had been hung and rows of plush seats were being installed. Other doors along the foyer walls led to various hallways, offices, and meeting rooms, some of which, Sylvia assumed, were still in a state of remodeling disarray. If she needed any proof, from elsewhere in the building came the sounds of unseen hammers banging, power tools buzzing, and voices calling out questions and commands.

To Sylvia's right, a curved staircase climbed gracefully to the second floor, its banister and balustrades newly restored and polished to a soft gloss, the rich cherrywood fairly glowing in the light of the chandelier. Just as Sylvia grasped the banister, she heard a familiar voice call out from above, "You came!"

Sylvia glanced up to find Summer awaiting her on the second-floor landing, clad in slim-fitting jeans and a blue batik blouse that suited her rich auburn hair beautifully. "Hello, dear," Sylvia replied, smiling up at her young friend as she ascended. "I'm here for my appointment with the quilt spa."

Summer laughed. "You might be on to something with this quilt spa idea, but maybe something for the quilters themselves would be better. Massages for weary hands, soothing manicures for needle-pricked fingertips, and so on."

"Perhaps we should add that to Sarah's list of revenue-generating schemes," said Sylvia, a bit breathless as she reached the top of the stairs. "We could make arrangements with a local salon to come to the manor, or we could shuttle our campers to them. The salon would benefit from the additional customers, and Elm Creek Quilts could take a percentage as an agent's fee." She gave her head a little shake. "Goodness, listen to me. Now Sarah has me doing it."

Summer studied her for a moment, her expression warm and understanding. "There's nothing wrong with seeking creative solutions in unexpected places. That's essentially how Agnes came up with the idea for a quilt exhibit as a fundraiser for Union Hall."

"I'm very glad she did, and I'm pleased I'll soon have not one but two quilts included in it." Sylvia glanced around, admiring the fresh paint and gleaming hardwood, evidence of the repairs that had been completed since her last visit. "Now, where is this restoration and cleaning room you mentioned? I'd love to see how Chain of Progress is faring."

"It's coming along beautifully." Summer beckoned Sylvia to follow her past the gallery, where the open doors offered enticing glimpses of the quilts inside. If Sylvia had more time, she'd love to take another look around the exhibit, her third tour, but that would have to wait for another day if she hoped to catch the end of story time at the library with the twins.

Summer led Sylvia to a door at the end of the hall that opened into a spacious room overlooking the front of the building. The windows let in ample natural light, but it appeared that some sort of plastic material covered the glass. "That's UV blocking film," Summer explained, noticing Sylvia's curious gaze. "It protects fabrics from fading. It protects our skin from harmful rays too, but we installed it for the quilts rather than ourselves."

Sylvia nodded thoughtfully, her gaze traveling around the room. Near the door, a panel with numerous keys and a large, admirably legible display suggested that a state-of-the-art climate control system had been installed. Sylvia would have marveled at the expense, except she recalled that one of the Waterford Historical Society's board members owned a home improvement store, and he had been very generous with in-kind donations. Four sturdy flat worktables were arranged in the center of the room, with ample space for movement all around and a padded cover on top of each to protect delicate fabrics placed upon them. At the near end of the room, Sylvia counted several storage cabinets and shelving units, while the far end appeared to be set up as a dedicated area for documentation and photography, which Sylvia presumed would be essential for cataloging and recording the condition of the quilts and other artifacts before and after conservation. To her right, along the wall from the door almost to the corner, wheeled carts were neatly lined up, some loaded with cleaning tools and equipment, including lint brushes, soft bristle brushes, and mini vacuum cleaners especially designed for fragile textiles. Other carts held essential repair and conservation supplies, such as fine needles, cotton thread, fabric patches, boxes of acid-free tissue paper, and other tools for mending and stitching.

"This is a quilt restorer's dream," Sylvia marveled, taking it in. "How did you put all this together? I thought the Waterford Historical Society had limited funds, hence the need for all this fundraising."

"They do," said Summer. "Nearly all of what you see here is secondhand. A very generous alumna of one of the Penn State branch campuses donated a small fortune so they could completely renovate their textile museum. They bought all new equipment and furniture, and they didn't need their old stuff anymore. I snapped up most of this on the cheap at the university's annual surplus auction."

"For 'old stuff,' it looks quite serviceable." Sylvia nodded approvingly as she took in the scene, very much impressed. "Well done, Summer."

Summer smiled and offered a little shrug. "All in a day's work. In a way, it was that Penn State alumna who made all this possible."

"I suppose she did." Sylvia offered a wry smile. "I only wish Elm Creek Quilt Camp had its own very generous alumna who'd donate a small fortune to take care of *our* renovations. I confess I'm dreading to receive the roofer's estimate."

"Maybe it won't be as bad as you think." Summer paused, considering. "What about Julia Merchaud?"

"Julia? What about her?"

"Isn't she a generous alumna with a small fortune? Actually, in her case, it's probably a huge fortune."

"Oh, I see," Sylvia said, with a little laugh. "For a moment I thought you were recommending her as a roofer."

Whatever the size of her fortune, Julia Merchaud was certainly the most famous celebrity ever to attend Elm Creek Quilt Camp.

The actress, the winner of five Emmys and a Golden Globe, was best known for her roles as Grandma Wilson in the acclaimed television drama *Family Tree* and as Mrs. Dormouse in the classic, beloved children's film *The Meadows of Middlebury*. Currently she was starring as Sadie Henderson in the PBS historical drama *A Patchwork Life*, which had recently embarked on its fifth season. Looking back, Sylvia had to smile when she remembered how aloof Julia had been when she had first arrived at Elm Creek Manor, taking her meals in her room rather than in the banquet hall with the other campers, skipping the Candlelight welcome ceremony. She had come to quilt camp somewhat reluctantly to learn quilting skills for a movie role, but although she had mastered the techniques, the part had ultimately gone to a much younger actress. Fortunately, Julia had told them, the sting of that indignity had faded long ago, and she had come out ahead in the end. She had made wonderful new friends at quilt camp, she had learned to quilt at the studio's expense, and she had avoided working with "that dreadful hack of an ageist director," as she put it. Since her first visit, Julia had returned every year to reunite with her best quilting friends, and she had become quite an accomplished quilter along the way.

"Not as a roofer," said Summer, amused. "As a donor. She is very generous, you know. When she attended our grand opening gala, and guests were mobbing her for her autographs and photos, she turned it into a fundraiser on the spot. She smiled and posed for photos and signed autographs graciously all evening, in exchange for donations to the Waterford Historical Society capital fund."

"I'm sure Julia is very generous, dear, but I was speaking in jest. I would never expect a wealthy benefactor to rescue us from our financial woes. Only hard work and ingenuity will do that." Sylvia thought for a moment, then added, "And good luck. We could certainly use some of that."

Summer shrugged. "It wouldn't hurt to ask."

"It most certainly would," Sylvia retorted. "It would hurt me. It would wound my pride terribly."

"But if it would save Elm Creek Manor, and if Julia were willing—"

"We are not going to lose Elm Creek Manor," said Sylvia firmly. "Don't you worry about that. Our quilt camp is wonderfully successful, and we'll be creating new revenue sources soon. Julia Merchaud is welcome to attend quilt camp as often as she likes, but I will not ask her for a handout."

Summer looked as if she might argue the point, but she gave a little sigh and nodded. "If that's not an option, Elm Creek Quilts would probably be eligible for a small business loan."

Sylvia shook her head. "Thank you for the suggestion, dear, but I have a horror of debt. If you had grown up during the Great Depression as I had, you'd understand."

"I think I do understand—that is, as well as anyone who didn't live through it *can* understand." Summer gestured toward the center of the room. "Let me show you your quilt." She led Sylvia to one of the worktables, where Chain of Progress had been spread out, smooth and neat, sides straight and corners square. "We cleaned it thoroughly, and Agnes and I mended a few torn seams. We also detached a ribbon that had been pinned to it. Here's something a bit odd: the ribbon was pinned to the *back* of the quilt, not the front. Otherwise you and I probably would have seen it when you first showed me the quilt."

"Oh, yes, of course," Sylvia gasped. "Our Ribbon of Merit!"

"Yes, those were the words printed on the center of the rosette."

"Claudia and I were so proud of that ribbon." Sylvia shook her head in wonder. "I thought it had been lost years ago."

"Not so." Summer studied Sylvia, curious. "Do you know why it was pinned to the back of the quilt rather than the front?"

A memory stirred. "Yes, yes. Of course. The judges had pinned it to the front of the quilt in the border, but Claudia didn't want pinholes in her Odd Fellows Chain blocks. I had entirely forgotten."

"We saved the ribbon, of course." Summer tucked a strand of auburn hair behind her ear and bent to open a drawer beneath the table. "The pin left some rust stains on the fabric, but I'm happy to say that we were able to remove them."

From the depths of the drawer, she withdrew a small soft object and placed it in Sylvia's open palm. Sylvia drew in a breath slowly as she gazed at the long-lost Ribbon of Merit, a green satin rosette with a trailing double ribbon, the words printed in gold ink in the center announcing the honor it signified. "I almost can't believe it," she murmured. "I also saved the blue ribbon my sister and I were awarded for taking first place in the local contest at the Harrisburg Sears, but I haven't seen this ribbon in more than fifty years."

"You could take it home with you, and reunite the pair," said Summer, "or, if you like, we can display them on the gallery wall next to your quilt."

"Oh, I rather like that idea," said Sylvia. "It's not that I want to boast—"

"It's not boasting," Summer assured her. "Those ribbons are important historical artifacts. They help tell the story of your quilt while explaining its significance to local history. Your achievement is a credit to the Waterford quilting community, and it ought to be celebrated."

"After all this time? Does it still matter, really, what two teenage girls did so long ago?"

"Of course it matters. Think of the young quilters you'll inspire. Imagine how you would have felt at that age, if you had heard about two sisters who had dared to enter a national quilt contest and had won ribbons and honors."

Sylvia thought for a moment. "I would have wanted to do them one better," she admitted. "You might not believe this, but I had a competitive streak back then—"

Summer tried unsuccessfully to smother a laugh. "Oh, I believe it."

"Don't be sassy, dear. Seeing a prizewinning quilt made by girls my own age would have pushed me to improve my skills until I could win a blue ribbon too." Sylvia paused for a moment, thinking. "All right, then. You may display the quilt and the ribbons too. Let's inspire all those young quilters to reach for something that seems beyond their grasp. Maybe they'll discover they can attain what they seek after all, and if not, they'll learn from the attempt."

She certainly had, all those decades ago, and she wouldn't want those lessons to be wasted.

12

May–June 1933

The morning after the Bergstroms' excursion to Harrisburg, Sylvia set out for school filled with a dizzying mixture of elation and anxiety. Even as she boarded the bus and endured the jolting ride into Waterford, she imagined the elegant Sears saleswoman directing uniformed workers upstairs to the temporary gallery, where they would gently remove Chain of Progress from the display stand, roll it carefully in paper, and pack it into a padded crate for shipment. She tried not to dwell on the potential calamities that could befall the precious quilt on its journey east to Philadelphia, but just crossed her fingers and wished for clear skies, smooth roads, and cautious drivers.

The bus hadn't even traveled half a mile before Claudia had shared the news of their first-place finish with nearly all of the older students. Eventually Sylvia overheard enough to realize that Claudia was giving everyone the impression that she had made the quilt almost entirely by herself. Sylvia's temper smoldered but she didn't call out her sister, knowing that an embarrassing scene on the bus would tarnish the win. Her own friends knew the truth, as did her family, and Sylvia resolved to be satisfied with that. Still, as word spread through the school, when teachers stopped her in the halls and asked her to pass on their congratulations to her sister, she couldn't resist politely correcting the misunderstanding.

"What happens next, Sylvia?" one of her friends asked her at lunchtime. The other girls at their table leaned in, hanging on every word.

"The top three quilts from all the local Sears stores in our region have been sent to the one in Philadelphia," Sylvia explained, lowering her voice dramatically, enjoying the way her friends' eyes widened in anticipation. "That means not only the entire state of Pennsylvania, but also Maryland, New Jersey, New York, Ohio, West Virginia, and . . ." As she ticked them off on her fingers, the last one came to her just in time. "And North Carolina. I think a few mail-order houses belong to our region too, so there may be more than one thousand quilts in the Philadelphia competition."

"One thousand quilts," her friend Phyllis marveled, shaking her head in wonder.

"Will your first-place finish in Harrisburg give you an edge in the regionals?" another friend asked.

"Don't I wish," said Sylvia. "No, I suppose it's more fair this way. It's a clean slate for everyone, same rules, different judges."

"And tougher competition?" Phyllis prompted.

Sylvia felt a nervous flutter in her stomach. "I'm sure of it. This round of judging will take place tomorrow. After that . . ." She shrugged and tried to smile. "We'll just have to wait for the results to be announced. The top three quilts in each region will move on to the final round in Chicago. That's where the grand prize quilt will be chosen."

Her friends quickly assured her that she had nothing to fear. She was *so* talented, and her quilt was *so* beautiful, that it would surely sail through the regional round and on to the finals. Their encouragement lifted her spirits, but she couldn't help thinking that none of her friends had seen Chain of Progress except in the very early stages, when she had brought a few appliqué blocks to school to work on during the lunch hour. Nor had they seen a single stitch of any of the quilts exhibited at the Harrisburg Sears. She loved her friends for their unshakable belief in her, but they really didn't understand just how challenging the regional round was going to be.

Sylvia knew, but she refused to be daunted. The judges in Harrisburg believed her quilt deserved to move on to the regional round, so she must believe it too. Yet she badly needed a distraction from the tedious, nerve-wracking wait for the results to be announced, and in the middle of English class, an idea came to her.

Later that afternoon, as the Bergstrom siblings and cousins walked down the forest road from the bus stop to the manor, Sylvia fell in step beside Richard. "How much homework do you have today?" she asked.

He glanced up at her, curious and eager. "Not much. Why?"

"Do your homework first," she said, before he could volunteer to skip it. "When you're finished, meet me in the stables. I promised to help Paulie and Eugene do a footing check of the riding arena. I thought I'd ask Father if you can tag along."

He brightened. "Really?"

"Yes, really. Unless you don't think you're old enough?"

"Oh, I'm definitely old enough." Richard drew himself up to his full height, shoulders back, chin lifted. "I've been old enough for years."

Sylvia hid a smile, amused. "Homework first, though. You know the rules."

He nodded earnestly to show he understood, his eyes bright with anticipation. Although he hung around the stables nearly as much as Sylvia herself, he was permitted to help with only the simplest, least dangerous tasks. Until their father was convinced he had mastered those, Richard wouldn't be entrusted with greater responsibilities, but that didn't mean he couldn't begin shadowing Sylvia. Maybe a taste of more skilled work would whet his appetite, and he'd work harder to prove himself trustworthy and capable. That was what Sylvia hoped, anyway. If their father intended to put Richard in charge of Bergstrom Thoroughbreds, Sylvia must do everything she could to make sure he was prepared—for the horses' sake even more than for her brother's.

Back home, she asked her father if Richard could shadow her, leaving out the part about how she knew he intended to name Richard his successor instead of her, and how terribly disappointed she was. Her father gave her a long, searching look before he consented. Later, in the riding arena, Richard proved himself deserving of Sylvia's faith in him. He listened carefully to every instruction, observed the grooms closely, and asked questions respectfully without interrupting their work. Sylvia was pleased and impressed, and before she went to bed that night, she made sure to stop by the library and tell her father so. He was preoccupied with work, but nonetheless he rewarded her with a tired smile. "You're a good role model for him, Sylvia," he said, making her glow with pride.

Upon waking the next morning, though, she immediately felt her stomach tie itself up in a knot. Throughout the day, in Philadelphia, Boston, Atlanta, Chicago, Minneapolis, Memphis, Kansas City, Dallas, Seattle, and Los Angeles, three masterpiece quilts from each city would be honored with ribbons and prize money, and more important, they would qualify for the final round of the competition at the World's Fair. Sylvia hoped with all her heart that Chain of Progress would be among them.

All day long, she tried her best to focus on her classes and friends, but every so often, something would remind her of the judging taking place in far-off Philadelphia. Perhaps at that very moment, she would think, her heart giving a sudden thud, the judges were examining Chain of Progress, standing back to assess the overall effect of color and design, drawing nearer as they mulled over the theme, peering closely to evaluate the size and uniformity of the quilting stitches, the creativity and beauty of the appliquéd scenes, and the accuracy of the pieced blocks. The judges would find much to admire, but they would also inevitably find fault. In the end, it would all come down to the points awarded in each category, how many the Bergstrom sisters earned compared to their rivals.

Chain of Progress didn't have to claim first prize this time, Sylvia reminded herself as she walked from history class to algebra, hugging her books to her chest. All their quilt had to do was finish in the top three to advance to the finals. That would be enough—no, more than *enough*, it would be marvelous. In Chicago the judging would begin anew, and there, in the Sears Pavilion on the fairgrounds on the shore of Lake Michigan, surely their inspired interpretation of the Century of Progress theme would give them an advantage.

But first Chain of Progress had to make it through the regional round—and Sylvia had to make it through that maddeningly long school day, and another, and perhaps even another, until she and Claudia received the judges' verdict.

Finally, the dismissal bell rang. Sylvia packed her satchel, bade her friends goodbye, and hurried off to meet the school bus. She was descending the front stairs when she spotted Claudia standing perfectly still on the sidewalk below as other students milled around her. It took Sylvia another moment to realize that her sister was not standing alone. An older boy—straight light brown hair, a pale round face growing redder by the moment, shoulders slightly stooped from the weight of his overstuffed knapsack—was speaking to Claudia, or rather, struggling to speak. Suddenly he thrust a small bouquet tied with a white ribbon into her arms and dashed off down the sidewalk.

"What on earth?" Sylvia murmured, so thunderstruck she abruptly halted on the stairs, causing a momentary traffic jam until someone nudged her from behind, setting her in motion again. Claudia had not moved by the time Sylvia reached her, except to bury her nose in the pretty blossoms and gaze after the boy, her cheeks flushed.

Frowning, Sylvia too watched as he disappeared into the crowd. "Wasn't that Susie Midden's brother?"

Claudia closed her eyes, inhaled deeply, and sighed as if she'd never smelled lovelier flowers. "Yes," she said, a mysterious smile playing at the corners of her mouth as she continued toward the school bus. Her quick strides implied that she hoped to leave her younger sister behind.

But Sylvia was faster and easily caught up to her. "What's all this about?" she asked, gesturing to the bouquet. "Why would Susie Midden's brother give you flowers?"

Claudia threw her an exasperated look over her shoulder as she stepped onto the bus. "His name is Harold, and he wanted to wish me good luck in the quilt competition."

Astonished, Sylvia snapped out a laugh as she followed her sister onto the bus. "He could have just said, 'Good luck, Claudia. Hope you win.' Why shove flowers at you?"

Claudia halted and whirled around to face her. "He didn't *shove* them at me. He's shy and he couldn't—" Claudia inhaled deeply and gazed heavenward for a moment before fixing Sylvia with a pitying gaze. "I wouldn't expect you to understand. You're too young." With that, she continued down the aisle to join her friends, who erupted in squeals and giggles at the sight of the bouquet.

"Oh, for crying out loud," Sylvia muttered under her breath. She felt strangely humiliated, as if she had been caught doing something she should have left behind in childhood, like playing with dolls or going to bed before sunset. Her cheeks burned as she plopped onto the seat beside her friend Phyllis in the middle of the bus, not so far back to be in range of Claudia's lofty mockery, but not near the front with the little kids either.

"What's wrong?" Phyllis asked, giving her a searching look. "Are you worried about the quilt contest?"

"No—I mean, yes, I am, but it's—" Sylvia frowned and jerked her head in Claudia's direction, then slouched in her seat, arms folded over her satchel on her lap. "She's impossible sometimes."

Phyllis glanced back at Claudia, then turned around to face forward as the bus pulled away from the curb. "Does your sister have a boyfriend?"

"She'd better not," Sylvia said, raising her voice in warning, though not loud enough for Claudia to actually hear. "Our father wouldn't like it."

Phyllis studied her, curious. "No offense, but it sounds like *you* wouldn't like it."

To be honest, she didn't. She didn't like reminders that Claudia was two years her elder, always entitled to do everything first. Now it seemed as if Claudia was growing up and away from her, receiving pretty flowers and gazing dreamily at boys—at bashful, silent *Harold Midden*, for goodness' sake, when so many other, worthier boys admired her. If any boys admired Sylvia, it was because she was an excellent rider, was always willing to help them with their math, and would gladly join in a kickball game if they needed more players. She couldn't imagine any of the boys at their school wanting to give *her* flowers, not that there was anyone in particular she hoped would one day shove a ribbon-tied bouquet at her. So why was she so disgruntled?

At home, the aunties admired Claudia's bouquet and replied to her bashful explanation with gentle teasing. Later, when their father and Uncle William returned from the stables to wash up for supper, they didn't glance twice at the vase of flowers in the alcove in the hall. As the family seated themselves around the table, Claudia didn't mention that a boy had given them to her, nor did the aunties, and the men didn't think to ask. Sylvia waited for the truth to come out, anticipating a stern reprimand from their father and tearful protests from her sister. It would serve Claudia right for acting so smug on the school bus. But the revelation never came, and Sylvia finished her meal in silence, disappointed.

In the morning she again woke with a knot in her stomach, but the uncomfortable sensation faded as the school day passed. There were even long stretches of time during her most interesting classes when she didn't think about the contest at all. On Saturday morning, she felt only the slightest twinge, and that disappeared as she kept herself happily occupied exercising and tending to the horses. Richard helped her with some of the grooming before he ran off to play, but mostly she was on her own, riding on the bridle trails or in the round ring, her every thought for the horses, with none to spare for anything else.

When she returned to the manor in the early afternoon, breathless and happy but ravenous since she had missed lunch, she washed up hastily and went to the kitchen, hoping Great-Aunt Lydia had set something aside for her. She stopped short at the sight of Claudia slumped at the refectory table, arms folded, head resting upon them. An envelope and a couple of unfolded pages lay just out of reach, as if Claudia had shoved them away in anger or misery.

Sylvia's heart plummeted.

She drew in a shaky breath, seated herself at the table opposite her sister, and gathered up the scattered pages. One appeared to be a press release, which she only skimmed enough to learn that 1,700 quilts had been submitted in their region's semifinal, and that the top three, one honorable mention, and a selection of other entries would be exhibited at Sears's Roosevelt Boulevard store in Philadelphia during the first week of June before being sent on to Chicago. The prizewinning quilters' names and the titles of their quilts were also listed, but Sylvia barely glanced at those, except to confirm what she had already guessed. When she sighed, Claudia raised her head long enough to give her a woeful look before resting her head on her arms again.

The second page was a brief, sincere letter from the contest officials thanking Miss Claudia Sylvia for participating. Many truly excellent quilts had been submitted, the judges' task had been extremely difficult, and they regretted to inform her that her quilt had not placed in the top three. It would, however, be included in the regional exhibition, a testament to its exceptional artistry.

Sylvia heaved another sigh, folded the pages, and returned them to the envelope. "At least we didn't come in last place."

"How do you know that?" asked Claudia, her voice muffled.

"I don't think they'd include our quilt in the regional exhibit if we had."

Claudia groaned and sat up. "Last place or tenth place, what's the difference? We didn't make the top three. We're out of the competition."

Sylvia's throat constricted. Somehow, hearing her sister say it aloud made it much more real. "We did our best," she said, but the words rang hollow. "We took first place in Harrisburg. We won ten dollars for the family."

"I wanted to win so much more."

"I know. I did too."

They sat there for a long moment, heavyhearted, but at the sound of someone bustling into the kitchen, they instinctively sat up straighter and glanced toward the doorway. "Goodness, girls," Great-Aunt Lydia said, planting her hands on her hips and regarding them with mild concern. "You two look like you each lost your best friend."

"That's not what we lost," Claudia replied glumly.

"I know, dear," said Great-Aunt Lydia as she joined them at the table, "but you girls made it further along in the competition than most who entered, and that's something to be proud of. You're young. You'll have many more quilt shows in your future."

"Not like this one," said Sylvia.

She expected her great-aunt to assure her that she was mistaken, but instead Great-Aunt Lydia nodded. "No, not like this one," she acknowledged. "This one was unique. But there will be others, and you shall make the most of them."

Somehow that made Sylvia feel the tiniest bit better.

She even laughed, later, as the family gathered for supper, when Richard flung his arms around her waist, peered up at her anxiously, and said, "I'm sorry you lost, Sylvia. I would've picked your quilt for first place."

"I'm sure you would have," she replied, stroking his hair out of his eyes and kissing him on the top of the head, "which is why they wouldn't have chosen you as a judge."

Throughout the meal, the family expressed such sympathy and encouragement that Sylvia's spirits were nearly restored. She wouldn't admit it aloud, but it was a relief to know the results at last, even though they weren't what she had hoped for, rather than waiting anxiously through another day. And to see that her family wasn't disappointed in her at all—in fact, they seemed really quite proud of her and Claudia—was tremendously uplifting.

Then, when they were finished eating, their father rose and planted his hands on the table in a way that commanded everyone's attention. "First-place ribbons aren't the only honors worth celebrating," he declared. "Claudia and Sylvia worked very hard on their quilt, and they dared to compete with far more experienced quilters. They didn't win, but their quilt was still chosen for the regional exhibit. I believe we should go see it, to show everyone how much we appreciate the honor."

Claudia gasped.

"Really, Father?" Sylvia asked. "Philadelphia is so far away."

"Yes, really," her father replied, a hint of amusement in his voice. "And it's not that far by train. We could do it in a day."

"That would be a long day," said Aunt Nellie, shaking her head.

"Who gets to go this time?" asked Richard, hopeful, his expression pleading.

"Whoever wants to," their father replied. "We'll go on Saturday, one week from today, so no one will miss school."

The younger children clapped their hands and cheered. Uncle William grinned and whooped right along with them, but Aunt Nellie threw Father a look of amused exasperation, as if she wished he'd consulted her first.

But in the days that followed, as the travel plans came together, Aunt Nellie not only permitted Sylvia's cousins to join the party, but she decided to come along too. In the end, only Great-Aunt Lydia declined. Someone must prepare lunch for the workers, and she was perfectly content to stay behind. "Bring me home a souvenir," she said, with a lighthearted wave to suggest that anything would do.

A week later, after rising early to complete the morning chores before breakfast, the rest of the Bergstrom family boarded the first train to Philadelphia. The younger children were so excited they could hardly sit still, despite the frequent quiet, firm admonitions of Great-Aunt Lucinda and Aunt Nellie that they mustn't disturb the other passengers. But Sylvia scarcely noticed their fidgeting and lively chatter. Her gaze was fixed on the lovely scenery passing by her window—the rolling, forested hills, hazy green with the young foliage of spring; breathtaking vistas of the river valleys; scattered farms with patchwork fields and cows grazing near red barns. For a time the train followed the course of the Juniata River, its meandering waters sparkling in the morning sun, until it spilled over into the broader, majestic Susquehanna, which tumbled over boulders and around narrow islands as it flowed southeast. At Middletown, the train left the river behind and turned eastward, passing verdant farmland and small towns, with the occasional glimpse of a gleaming black horse-drawn buggy swiftly moving down a country road, a cloud of dust rising in its wake.

Eventually, hours after their departure, they reached the outskirts of Philadelphia. The city skyline was visible in the distance whenever the train rounded a bend and angled Sylvia's window toward it. The train followed the winding course of another river—the Schuylkill, Sylvia's father told her—which flowed through steep green riverbanks lined with parks and factories and houses. The train slowed as it entered the city proper, offering glimpses of redbrick colonial buildings and cobblestone streets just around the corner from smooth, paved boulevards and modern structures of limestone and glass.

At last the train pulled into the 30th Street Station, which had opened only that year. When the family disembarked and made their way to the vast main concourse, the children stopped short and gazed around, awestruck. "Is this the biggest building in Philadelphia?" Peter asked, craning his neck to take in the striking brass pendant chandeliers suspended in two parallel rows from the red, gold, and tan coffered ceiling, which looked to be about a hundred feet above the creamy gray marble floor. Tall, translucent windows lined the walls, bathing the travelers seated on the double-sided benches of oak and marble in warm, natural light.

"Not the biggest, or even the most famous," said Uncle William, placing his hand on his son's shoulder and guiding him forward. "There's Independence Hall, the Philadelphia Museum of Art—"

"Can we see those too?" Elsa asked, catching up to her father and taking his hand.

"Depends," said Uncle William, smiling down at her. "If we have time."

By then they had made their way to the far end of the room, where they passed through towering marble pillars to the exit. Outside, Sylvia turned about in place on the sidewalk admiring the city scene until Great-Aunt Lucinda called, "Sylvia, don't fall behind!" Turning with a start, Sylvia gasped to see her great-aunt gesturing urgently from the doorway of a city bus, which the rest of the family had already boarded. Sylvia darted over and climbed aboard just before the doors closed.

After the long train journey, Sylvia was reluctant to settle in for another ride, but thankfully it was only a few more miles to the intersection of Adams Avenue and Roosevelt Boulevard in the northeastern part of the city. When the bus reached their stop, the children scrambled from their seats and out the door ahead of the adults, scattering on the sidewalk and trying to look in every direction at once. "Stick together," Aunt Nellie called as Great-Aunt Lucinda swiftly counted heads to make sure they were all present. Only when she was certain no one had been left behind on the bus did the family walk down the tree-lined street toward the Sears building.

Sylvia was astounded by the size of it. She had expected something like the Harrisburg Sears, maybe a little larger because Philadelphia was a larger city, but this was a vast, nine-story redbrick Gothic edifice the span of a city block, with a fourteen-story clock tower in front. Inside, several large signs directed customers to the Century of Progress quilt exhibit, but Sylvia would have known which direction to turn simply by following the crowd. So many eager attendees were entering the exhibition space that Sylvia could not see very far ahead of her family. She craned her neck and tried to bound up on tiptoes as they made their way forward, but she couldn't glimpse so much as a single block of a single quilt.

Then, all at once, the crowd parted in front of her. She halted so abruptly that Richard bumped into her from behind. "Sorry," he said, but she could only nod in reply, transfixed. She had attended many quilts shows in the Elm Creek Valley, but she had never seen so many gathered together in one place, rows and rows of quilts hanging neatly from metal rods fixed between tall footed poles. As her gaze took in the hundreds of works on display, it occurred to her that maybe their inclusion in the regional exhibit was not such a rare distinction after all. She quickly brushed the thought aside.

Sylvia found herself trailing behind Claudia as the family began to tour the exhibit, wandering down one aisle and then another, often pausing to admire a particularly striking work. A lovely Double Wedding Ring that had taken first prize in the Hackensack local contest boasted exquisite, intricate quilting and some of the most perfectly matched seams Sylvia had ever seen, aside from her mother's handiwork. Beside it was a lovely Mariner's Compass quilt from West Virginia, with thirteen maroon, navy blue, and tan pieced blocks alternating with twelve light blue setting squares, the rows framed by a double border of Flying Geese and quilted all over in a stylized pattern resembling cresting waves on a stormy sea.

"Mama, look," Alice exclaimed, seizing Aunt Nellie's hand and tugging her across the aisle for a closer look at a pretty gingham Grandmother's Flower Garden quilt. Sylvia understood why her cousin was so delighted—Aunt Nellie had used the same traditional pattern to make the quilt upon Alice's own bed. A placard next to the quilt noted that its maker hailed from New Jersey and that the quilt had claimed second prize in its local contest.

"Well, that is curious," mused Great-Aunt Lucinda.

Sylvia glanced away from the Grandmother's Flower Garden to find her great-aunt studying the next quilt over, a square New York Beauty pieced from orange, yellow, and ivory solid cottons. "What's curious?" she asked, drawing closer.

Great-Aunt Lucinda indicated the lower left-hand corner. "The maker's initials are quilted into the ivory triangle here, and just below that, she recorded the date—nineteen thirty-two."

"Are you sure?" Sylvia craned her neck to see, and sure enough, the four digits were there, stitched into the quilt with thread barely a shade darker than the surrounding fabric. "She finished her quilt last year?"

"So it would appear."

"That doesn't seem fair." Sylvia frowned at the telltale number.

"The rest of us started our quilts in January, and we had to race to meet the deadline. This lady just had to brush hers off and leave it at her local Sears. It probably took her more time to fill out the form."

"I'm sure she's not the only one who submitted a quilt she'd finished before the contest was announced," said Great-Aunt Lucinda, casting an appraising glance around the room. "I don't recall anything in the rules against it."

"I don't either." Sylvia thought for a moment. "They did say that the contest wasn't intended as an exhibition of heirloom quilts, but I guess last year is recent enough. Maybe we should have submitted my mother's Elms and Lilacs quilt after all."

Great-Aunt Lucinda regarded her fondly. "You don't really think that. You might have taken top honors, but that wouldn't have been any fun. Wouldn't you have missed the challenge of creating something new, something better than anything you've made before? What about the excitement and the suspense of racing to meet a deadline without knowing whether you'll succeed? I'd take the enjoyment you two girls had over a grand prize ribbon any day."

"I'd rather take both," Sylvia admitted, and Great-Aunt Lucinda laughed.

The Bergstroms wandered the aisles, sometimes in one large group, but more often in pairs or trios, as some lingered to admire a particular quilt while others moved on to something more appealing farther ahead. Eventually Sylvia and Claudia arrived at a central circular dais where the top three quilts in the Philadelphia regional contest had been given pride of place. Sylvia very much admired the third-place quilt—Autumn Leaves by Edith Snyder of Buffalo, New York—a lovely design with a central autumnal appliqué motif surrounded by four concentric rectangular borders, solid fabric strips alternating with ones appliquéd in winding semicircular vines lush with small, almond-shaped leaves.

But when she moved around the dais and paused before the

second-place quilt, she felt her heart thud and her breath catch in her throat.

The quilt that had claimed second prize was a Century of Progress theme quilt. In fact, it was only the second theme quilt she had seen in the exhibit so far, with a white muslin outer border, a Sawtooth inner border, and a central appliqué medallion split horizontally by a band embroidered with the phrase "Century of Progress." In each of the four corners was a Tea Leaf block, each block's twelve appliquéd marquise-shaped leaves perfectly aligned, the tips sharp and sides flawlessly curved. Above the horizontal band was a meticulous appliqué portrait of a man on horseback riding alongside a covered wagon pulled by a team of four horses. The section below the embroidered band was adorned with an image of the Earth as if it were viewed from the heavens, North and South America visible as green calico continents on a blue sateen ocean. Above and to the left of the globe was an airplane, its propeller pointing toward the Earth at a forty-five-degree angle, as if it had soared to the stars and was now homeward bound.

She felt Claudia seize her arm. "Goodness gracious. Is this supposed to represent progress in transportation?"

Nodding, Sylvia swallowed, a bit queasy. "It's much different than my design would have been." Before she'd scrapped her original idea, she'd planned to depict many different vehicles. This quiltmaker—Mrs. George Leitzel of Northumberland County—had captured the idea of progress in only two scenes. Simpler, but maybe more effective.

Claudia tsked her tongue scornfully, then quickly glanced over her shoulder to make sure no one had overheard. "This quilt is nice enough, but I like your idea better," she said in an undertone.

"Maybe I should've stuck with it," Sylvia murmured back, sick at heart. "She used a transportation theme and won second place, while we—"

"No, you've got it all wrong," said Claudia, shaking her head. "If we'd turned in a transportation quilt too, we might still have won at Harrisburg, but here, we would've looked like copycats. The judges would've taken off points."

"Or maybe Mrs. Leitzel would have looked like the copycat, and *she* would've lost points, and *we* would've taken second instead."

"No, it's much more likely that we *all* would have looked unoriginal, and both quilts would have lost points. The third-place quilt would have moved up to second and the honorable mention would have taken third." Claudia fixed a level gaze on her, full of all the elder-sister authority she could muster. "We wouldn't have won anyway, so deep breath, chin up, and no tears, at least not until we're back home."

"I wasn't going to cry," Sylvia retorted in a whisper, but she did feel close to it. She gulped a breath, put on a pleasantly interested expression, and took one last long look at the transportation quilt before turning away. She couldn't help wondering if her decision to change her theme had cost her and her sister a shot at the grand prize.

The same thought must have occurred to Claudia too, Sylvia thought as she followed her sister around the dais to view the first-place quilt. It was good of her to be so nice about it—good, and wholly unexpected.

A throng of admirers had gathered in front of the regional winner, so the sisters had to linger patiently at the back until other viewers had seen their fill and moved along. When the crowd finally thinned, Sylvia realized why they had been so transfixed. The first-prize quilt was a marvel, radiant in five hues of gold, a single block encompassing the entire surface of the quilt, except for four narrow borders arranged in a gradient of light to dark from the center out, creating the illusion that the quilt's edges were receding into shadow. The focus element was a variation of the traditional Sunflower pattern, or so Sylvia surmised, with a dark gold circle at the center, from which radiated twenty-four medium-light gold kites. Each of the long points was separated from the others by a wedge comprised of a smaller, dark gold kite flanked by two medium-gold kites. Triangles with curved bases attached to the dark gold center and other, smaller kites between the triangles enhanced the impression of a bright sun surrounded by radiant beams. The quilting was as masterful as the piecing, elaborate feathered wreaths and plumes adding texture and dimension, especially in the lightest gold sections surrounding the central medallion.

Sylvia spotted Great-Aunt Lucinda and Aunt Nellie standing in front, so she made her way around other spectators to join them. "It's gorgeous," Aunt Nellie breathed, her gaze fixed on the quilt as she shook her head in wonder. "This masterpiece might take the grand prize in Chicago."

"It is stunning," Great-Aunt Lucinda allowed, but Sylvia detected an undercurrent of puzzlement in her voice. "Yet . . . I'm sure I've seen this quilt before."

Aunt Nellie put her head to one side, considering, her gaze never leaving the quilt. "In the Harrisburg display, perhaps?"

"No, this quilt definitely wasn't in Harrisburg," Sylvia broke in. She would have remembered. If it had been, it very well might have nudged Chain of Progress from first place into second. She read the object label mounted on the wall next to the quilt and said, "It's called Sunburst, and it was made by a lady from Hyndman, Pennsylvania."

"Never heard of it," said Claudia, peering up at the quilt.

"I believe it's southwest of Elm Creek Manor, southeast of Pittsburgh, near the Maryland border," said Aunt Nellie. When they all glanced at her in surprise, she offered a modest shrug. "I got straight A's in geography in school."

Sylvia read through the object label again. "It says here that the quiltmaker submitted it to one of the mail-order houses, where it took first place. If she'd delivered it in person to her local store instead . . . maybe she would have entered it in the Harrisburg contest."

"Well, I for one am heartily glad that she didn't," said Claudia fervently.

"That makes two of us." The sisters exchanged a look, enough for Sylvia to see that Claudia too realized that they were even luckier than they had realized to have taken first prize in the local round. If one or two or more quilters had tried their luck in Harrisburg instead of another store or a mail-order house, the sisters could have been shut out of the top three altogether.

Before long, they stepped aside to allow other admirers a closer look at Sunburst. "I don't know why that quilt looks so familiar, but it does," Great-Aunt Lucinda said quietly as they turned the corner. There, halfway down the aisle, they at last found Chain of Progress. Sylvia felt a warm rush of affection for their quilt, as if she had run into an old friend in a crowd of strangers.

"Oh, my goodness," Elsa exclaimed, darting ahead and reaching the quilt first. "Claudia and Sylvia, look! You won a ribbon!"

The sisters hurried to join her. Sure enough, pinned to the bottom right-hand corner they discovered a green satin rosette with a trailing double ribbon. "Ribbon of Merit" was printed in gold ink in the center.

"Congratulations, girls," sang Great-Aunt Lucinda, coming up between them to put her arms around their shoulders, drawing them close to her sides in a quick hug. "A well-deserved honor."

"My cousins made this one," Alice informed a random onlooker proudly, pointing to the ribbon and then to Sylvia and Claudia.

Nearly everyone within earshot turned to look, and soon a small crowd had gathered around them in front of their quilt. Several viewers offered congratulations, and one white-haired lady shook their hands and declared that she was delighted to see young ladies keeping the traditional arts going in these modern times. Claudia, smiling radiantly, quickly won over the crowd, accepting praise and answering questions graciously. Sylvia was content to let her sister claim the spotlight. She stepped back a bit, and then farther, until curious onlookers passed between her and her sister and she could pretend she was just another face in the crowd.

"Excuse me, young lady," someone said just behind her. "Did I hear correctly? Are you Miss Claudia Sylvia Bergstrom?"

She turned to find a balding gentleman in a dark pin-striped suit regarding her from beneath raised eyebrows. He carried a briefcase, and a badge pinned to his lapel indicated that he was a contest official. "I'm Sylvia Bergstrom, sir," she replied. Indicating Claudia with a nod, she added, "That's my sister, Claudia."

"Very good to meet you, Miss Bergstrom. Congratulations on your selection for this exhibit, and on winning a Ribbon of Merit. As you can see, the competition was quite fierce."

"Thank you, sir. We're truly honored."

Opening his briefcase with a quick snap of a latch, he searched around for a moment and withdrew a white envelope. "I intended to mail this with the others, but since you're here, you might as well have yours now and we'll save the postage." He handed her the envelope. "Your scoresheet, complete with judges' remarks. I'm told they can be quite instructive to quiltmakers who wish to improve their craft."

"Thank you, sir," she said, looking the envelope over quickly before slipping it into her skirt pocket. The end stuck out a bit, so she placed her hand over it protectively. "I'm always grateful for advice."

That wasn't exactly true. Sometimes advice was really annoying, especially when she hadn't asked for any. But she had clearly given him the right answer, for the gentleman's smile broadened. He offered her a gracious nod and wished her a good day before continuing on his way.

Sylvia looked to Claudia, who was still enjoying her place at the center of attention. Maybe they were meant to read the judges' comments together, but Claudia wouldn't appreciate being dragged away from her fans and Sylvia was too curious to wait.

Darting a look toward her family to make sure they weren't

watching, she stole off down the aisle, found a quiet corner alone, and carefully tore open the envelope. She withdrew the judges' scoring sheet with trembling hands, her heart pounding. She *wanted* to know their professional opinion of her quilt, and she *didn't* want to know. She closed her eyes for a moment, took a deep, steadying breath, and began to read.

Chain of Progress had scored well for design, receiving nearly perfect marks for suitability and beauty. For color, it had received a perfect score of thirty points, fifteen each for beauty and harmony. They had lost two points for materials, maybe because the judges could tell they had used what they'd had on hand instead of purchasing new fabrics, but Sylvia was only guessing. The score for workmanship hit her like a gut punch: ten out of fifteen for beauty of quilting, six out of fifteen for perfection of stitching. For general appearance, they had earned seven points out of a possible ten.

Sylvia braced herself and read the comments written in stark black ink below the scoring table.

The insightful and original interpretation of the Century of Progress theme was remarkably well done, the judges noted. The appliquéd scenes, while not flawlessly sewn, were cleverly constructed and visually appealing. The quilting was inconsistent over the entirety of the quilt; many stitches were absolute perfection, but certain sections indicated a far less accomplished hand at work, with larger stitches unevenly spaced. Ultimately, the skill element most in need of improvement was basic piecing, including greater attention to seam allowances, distinct points, alignment of pieces, and proper sizing and fitting of borders to avoid wavy edges. Since the quilt did not demonstrate mastery of these fundamental techniques, the overall appearance of the quilt was diminished, despite the truly excellent handiwork evident in the appliqué and most of the quilting.

"Oh, no, no," Sylvia murmured, heartsick. The judges might have guessed that more than one person had made the quilt, but even if they hadn't, they couldn't have drawn a clearer distinction between Sylvia's contributions and Claudia's. Claudia would be devastated. She would blame herself for their quilt's elimination from the contest— and to be honest, she wouldn't be entirely wrong.

Sylvia would have to warn Claudia to brace herself before reading the judges' remarks, unless—

Unless she didn't.

Claudia hadn't seen the contest official hand Sylvia the envelope. As far as anyone else knew, it was tucked away in a mailbag elsewhere in the building, awaiting delivery to the post office. Claudia wouldn't be expecting it to arrive at Elm Creek Manor for days, and when it didn't, she would probably assume it had been lost in the mail. Eventually, with any luck, she would forget about it. They both already knew what mattered most—they had won a ribbon but were out of the running for the grand prize. What more did Claudia really need to know? Mere minutes ago, when Sylvia had been struck by dismay and doubt at the sight of that other transportation quilt, her sister had refused to let her second-guess herself or accept blame for their failure to take a top prize. How could Sylvia repay her with a mean-spirited jab now? It would be far better to protect Claudia's feelings, as Claudia had tried to protect hers. That's what a truly kindhearted, loving sister would do.

Quickly Sylvia returned the paper to the envelope, folded it in half, and tucked it deep into her skirt pocket so not even a tiny corner was visible. Let Claudia's memories of the Sears National Quilt Contest be of two ribbons, ten dollars, whirlwind trips to Harrisburg and Philadelphia, and a crowd of well-wishers and admirers congratulating her on a job well done. Why spoil it for her?

Sylvia made her way back to her family, feigning nonchalance, hands clasped demurely, glancing to her right and left at the lovely quilts on either side of the aisle. She arrived just as the crowd around Claudia was dispersing. Sylvia felt a pang of sympathy and affection for her sister, whose eyes were bright, her cheeks flushed, her smile so full of genuine joy as it hadn't been in—

As it hadn't been in more than three years, when their grieving began.

Just then, Great-Aunt Lucinda glanced Sylvia's way. "Where have you been?" she asked. "You missed all the fuss. I lost count of your quilt's many admirers."

"I was admiring other people's quilts," Sylvia replied, gesturing vaguely over her shoulder. "Claudia seems happy."

"Oh, yes." Great-Aunt Lucinda's gaze shifted to her for a moment. "As happy as one can be when one's quilt wins a ribbon yet doesn't move on to the final round. Oh, well. Nothing ventured, nothing gained. At least she'll have a delightful story to share with the folks back home."

"That's what's most important, right?" said Sylvia, nodding perhaps a bit too emphatically. Great-Aunt Lucinda regarded her quizzically until Claudia joined them, still beaming.

As for Aunt Nellie, she was looking a bit frazzled as she tried to keep an eye on all three of her children as they darted from one dazzling quilt to another. Eventually she gave up, gathered the entire family together in front of Chain of Progress, and firmly suggested that they remain in a group for the rest of the tour. Everyone willingly agreed, and they spent another hour strolling through the exhibit, taking in the marvelous display of color and pattern until they had reached the end.

By that time everyone was famished, so they made their way to an Italian restaurant down the street, where they feasted on spaghetti and meatballs and warm fragrant bread dipped in olive oil and Parmesan. They were nearly finished when Great-Aunt Lucinda suddenly gave a start. "I know where I've seen that quilt before," she declared, sitting back in her chair and giving the table a little slap.

"Which quilt?" asked Richard, reaching for the bread basket. "We've seen thousands today."

"Not thousands," said Alice, reasonably.

"Sunburst," said Great-Aunt Lucinda. "It's a kit quilt."

Aunt Nellie's eyes went wide. "No. It couldn't be. Really?"

Great-Aunt Lucinda nodded. "It is. I've seen the advertisements in the Needleart Company catalog. I'll show you when we get home."

"What's a kit quilt?" asked Sylvia's father.

"It's essentially a quilt in a box," said Aunt Nellie. "They're popular—not in our household, but among quilters who want to save time, or who don't trust their own creative instincts."

"Or," said Great-Aunt Lucinda magnanimously, "quilters who are perfectly capable of making their own original quilts from scratch, but they see a photo of a quilt they absolutely love and want to reproduce it exactly."

"I suppose," Aunt Nellie allowed. "Either way, a quilt kit takes much of the artistic choice and labor out of the process. Instead of designing a quilt, choosing the fabrics, tracing the templates, and cutting out the pieces oneself, one could order the required fabrics in harmonizing colors with the cutting lines already stamped on the back. Some kits even spare the customer the bother of cutting out the pieces by offering die-cut pieces."

"So all the quilter has to do is sew everything together, like assembling a jigsaw puzzle?" asked Uncle William.

"To finish the top, that's essentially right," said Great-Aunt Lucinda. "She'd still have to quilt it, of course. I remember now. In the catalog, the pattern was called the Rising Sun Quilt. It was offered in sateen, gingham, or cleona cloth, depending upon the customer's budget, in four complementary shades of pink, orchid, violet, or yellow."

"Yellow, like the one we saw today," Richard chimed in.

"Yes," said Great-Aunt Lucinda. "Like Sunburst."

Elsa wrinkled her nose. "Entering a kit quilt in a quiltmaking contest sounds like cheating."

Sylvia was inclined to agree, but Great-Aunt Lucinda shrugged. "The rules didn't forbid using commercial kits or patterns. Evidently the contest organizers hold technique and perfection of stitching in higher regard than originality."

Sylvia could have told them that. Her hand involuntarily went to her pocket, where the envelope was still safely concealed. What should she do with it when she got home? Burn it in the fireplace? No, she might want to read it again someday. Hide it? Yes, but it would have to be someplace Claudia would never think to look and no one else might accidently discover it.

After lunch, the family boarded another bus that carried them back the way they had come, and then a few blocks farther east, to Independence Hall. They spent more than an hour exploring the historic landmark, which Sylvia enjoyed very much; her only regret was that there was no time left afterward to visit the Philadelphia Museum of Art. Instead the Bergstroms hurried back to the 30th Street Station to catch the train for their return journey home.

As the train rumbled along, north out of the city and then west, Sylvia gazed out the window while the younger children chattered for a while before leaning back against the seats or on each other's shoulders to rest. She was aware of the adults murmuring earnestly among themselves, but she thought nothing of it until her father came over to where the children were seated and beckoned Sylvia, Claudia, and Richard to draw closer.

"You children were so well-behaved on this adventure that I thought we four might have a go at another," he said quietly, glancing to their cousins, who dozed nearby. "We earned more than I expected from the sale of those two fillies last month, and since Sylvia helped raise them, she deserves a say in how we spend the windfall. After school lets out for the summer, what do you say we travel to Chicago to see the World's Fair?"

13

September 2004

Sylvia knew the roofer's estimate would be staggering when Matt encouraged her to sit down before he handed her the paperwork. Even then, settled comfortably in an armchair in the library while he and Sarah watched her intently from the opposite sofa, she felt her throat constricting as she read through the itemized list of necessary supplies and estimated labor hours. The grand total at the bottom delivered the final blow in stark boldface.

"Goodness gracious me," she said, letting her hands fall to her lap, still clutching the papers gingerly, as if she expected them to burn her fingertips.

Sarah gave Matt a sidelong look. "You offered her a chair. Maybe you should've offered her a stiff drink."

"Oh, nonsense. You know my idea of a stiff drink is a cup of hot tea with extra caffeine." Sylvia removed her glasses, closed her eyes, and pinched the bridge of her nose, hoping to nip a headache in the bud. "Needless to say, this is more than what I expected, if not quite as bad as I'd feared. Matt, I trust that you and your father looked over these numbers. Do you consider this a fair estimate?"

"It's more than fair," said Matt. "I wish they'd had better news for us. But there's one more reputable local company I know of from when I worked at Landscape Architects. I could ask them for an estimate too."

"Let's do that. I'm inclined to go with your father's recommendation, but it can't hurt to get a second opinion. Maybe another roofer will tell us he can simply patch the leaks rather than replace the entire roof."

Matt shook his head. "If he said that, I wouldn't believe him. Asphalt shingles are meant to last fifteen to thirty years. If we don't replace them now, we'd have to replace them soon anyway."

"In that case, putting off the repairs will only cost us more in the end." Sylvia passed Sarah the paperwork over the table. "Sarah, assuming this is the best rate we can get, will we be able to pay for it?" She shook her head and managed a laugh. "What a question. We'll have to, somehow. We can't leave the roof as it is, and simply cross our fingers and hope it doesn't collapse on us."

"It's in no danger of collapsing anytime soon," Matt hastened to reassure her. "The roofer said so himself. Even so—"

"Time is of the essence," Sylvia finished for him. "Well, Sarah? What do you think?"

Sarah paged through the estimate, brow furrowed in concentration. "I'm fairly confident our savings will cover this, but there won't be much left over. How much, exactly, I won't know until I consult our banker and our financial advisor."

"And while Sarah's doing that, I'll get in touch with the other roofer about a second opinion," said Matt.

"Very good." Sylvia breathed a sigh of relief. Nothing was fixed yet, far from it, but she felt better knowing they had a plan. "Oh, one other thing. Matt, after you schedule that appraisal, please leave the rest of this roof business to me and Sarah. You still have so much to do before we open the orchards to the public. I don't want you to feel pulled in all directions."

"I appreciate that, but it's really not a problem," Matt assured her. "Thanks to Joe and Andrew pitching in, we're right on schedule to launch Elm Creek Orchards at the end of the week. I'll still be the point person with the contractor too. If all goes as planned, we'll have a new roof by Quiltsgiving."

"Speaking of Quiltsgiving," said Sylvia, turning back to Sarah, "as soon as you sort out the accounts, I think you should resume working on the corporate sponsorship program with all speed."

"Absolutely," said Sarah. "But that means I won't have much time to plan and prepare for the event itself. Anna will take care of food service—assuming she feels up to it, of course—but I'm responsible for registration, accommodations, and programming. What would you think about delegating room assignments and programming to Gretchen, Agnes, and Diane?"

"I think that's an excellent idea. Should we call in Gwen and Summer too?"

Sarah shook her head. "At this point in the semester, their schedules must be packed, and Summer also has her work at Union Hall."

"Oh, yes, of course. In that case, count on me to assist wherever I'm needed most, whether that's sending out the letters to potential sponsors, helping our friends organize Quiltsgiving, or minding the twins so you can work uninterrupted."

"Or helping me sell apples?" said Matt, grinning. "What if it turns out you're needed most in the orchards?"

"Matt," said Sarah, shaking her head, "don't tease."

But Sylvia smiled, amused. "Yes, Matt, I'll even step behind the counter of the market stand and sell apples, if that's what it takes to get a new roof on Elm Creek Manor and keep Elm Creek Quilts out of the red. You forget that one of my first jobs on this estate as a girl was mucking out stables. I can certainly handle peddling fruit."

The meeting ended there. Matt left to call the second roofer on his cell while Sarah took her seat at the oak desk and opened the accounting software on the computer. As for Sylvia, she decided to make her phone calls from the kitchen so Sarah would have peace and quiet in which to calculate the ever more precarious state of their finances.

Sylvia reached Agnes first. Her former sister-in-law was so eager to take charge of Quiltsgiving that she offered to come over that very afternoon and get started.

"Tomorrow is soon enough," Sylvia assured her. Though every day counted, she didn't expect her friends to drop what they were doing and rush over on a moment's notice. "I still have to bring Gretchen and Diane on board. If they agree, then you three can work out where and when you'd like to meet."

"Let's share the work and save time," said Agnes. "You speak with Gretchen, and I'll call Diane and explain that it's all hands on deck for Quiltsgiving."

Sylvia agreed and thanked her. They had no sooner hung up when the phone rang again. Sylvia quickly picked up. "Hello?"

"Hi, Sylvia. It's Summer. Um—" She hesitated. "Two things. First, don't be mad."

"Oh, dear. What conversation ever ended well that began, 'Don't be mad'?"

"This one will," Summer quickly assured her. "At least, I hope so."

"Don't leave me in suspense, dear. You didn't misplace Chain of Progress, did you?"

"Of course not!"

"Then whatever it is, it can't be that bad." Nevertheless, Sylvia braced herself.

"Remember the other day when we were talking about how a generous alumna in possession of an impressive fortune might want to donate some of it to us?"

"That's not exactly how I remember the conversation, but for the sake of argument, yes."

"Well, yesterday Julia Merchaud emailed me with a question about one of the quilts she saw in the Union Hall exhibit. Did you know that she's not only one of the lead actors in *A Patchwork Life*, but also a director and an executive producer?"

"Good for Julia. I'm sure she's excellent in every role." Patience, Sylvia counseled herself. "Summer, what did you do?"

"I might have mentioned that Elm Creek Quilts is dealing with some unexpected financial setbacks, including, most recently, the urgent need to replace the manor's roof."

"*Might* have mentioned?"

"Okay, *definitely* mentioned."

"Oh, Summer." Sylvia sat down in the nearest booth and clasped a hand to her forehead. "I told you I didn't feel comfortable going hat in hand to our former students."

"And I didn't. Really. Julia asked me how things were going with Elm Creek Quilts these days, and I told her the truth—without divulging any confidential information, of course."

"One might argue that our company's financial status is confidential."

"Of course it is," said Summer, contrite. "I should have realized that. I've become so used to asking for donations to Union Hall that I didn't think it through."

"I understand, dear. You only meant to help. However, unless you hear otherwise from me, please don't solicit donations. Elm Creek Quilts simply isn't set up to take on new investors." Sylvia paused. "Just out of curiosity, what did Julia say?"

"Nothing yet. She hasn't replied to my email."

"Oh, I see." With any luck, Julia had accidently deleted it unread, and that would be the end of it. And yet Sylvia felt a tiny sting of disappointment despite her relief. If Julia Merchaud had graciously offered to pay for the roof repair, Sylvia would have been tempted to accept, although she would have insisted that it be in exchange for free visits to Elm Creek Quilt Camp for life. "What was the second thing? You said there were two."

"Right. I'm happy to say that the cleaning and restoration of Chain of Progress is almost complete, and the Ribbon of Merit is ready to display. There wasn't really much to do with the ribbon, except a light dusting and the removal of the rusty pins. I've also finished writing a draft of the object label."

"That's excellent news. Does this mean you'll be hanging the quilt in the gallery soon?"

"I expect to by the end of this week. When you last visited, we discussed displaying your first-place ribbon from the local round in addition to the Ribbon of Merit from the regionals. Were you able to find the first-place ribbon?"

"I confess that in all the uproar about the roof, I entirely forgot. But I know right where it should be."

"Oh, good. May I come by this evening to pick it up?"

"Certainly. Why don't you come for dinner too? Gretchen is making spinach lasagna." Then Sylvia thought of something else. "Did your mother ever mention my box of keepsakes?"

"Keepsakes from the quilt contest? I don't think so. What did you save, besides the ribbon?"

"An assortment of things, not only from the quilt contest but also from our trip to the Chicago World's Fair. The first-place ribbon, of course, but also programs, tickets, newspaper articles published after the contest, and so on. I showed them to your mother when I first told her about the contest. I believe those mementos were what inspired her to write her article. Would you like to see them?"

"I'd love to," said Summer. "I'd welcome more details to include in the object label. Maybe we'll even find a few other things to display in the gallery. I'll bring a salad to dinner. Is there anything else you'd like?"

"Just your company, dear, and your mother's if she's free."

Gwen wouldn't be, unfortunately, due to a late seminar on campus, but Summer promised to arrive in time to help set the table.

Sylvia spent most of the intervening hours in the library. First, she gathered up all the essential information about Quiltsgiving to pass on to Gretchen, Agnes, and Diane. After that, she worked on the list of potential sponsors and proofread Sarah's solicitation letter. Sarah spent some of that time in the library too, poring over their accounts, placing calls to their banker and their investment advisor, and so on. They both kept at it until about a half hour before dinnertime, when Sylvia suggested they head down to the kitchen to see if Gretchen needed a hand. They found Summer already there, chatting with Gretchen as she set the table, plates and napkins and cutlery neatly placed upon a red-and-white-check tablecloth.

Sylvia and Sarah had just begun to pitch in when Joe and Andrew came in from outdoors with the twins, their little hands dirty, hair tousled and tangled, and faces sticky with apple juice. "We were playing in the orchard, and they wanted a snack, so they shared an apple," said Andrew sheepishly as Sarah met them at the doorway. "I guess we should have checked with you or Matt first. I hope we didn't spoil their supper."

"No, not with only half an apple apiece," Sarah assured him, lifting Caroline to her hip and taking James by one sticky hand. "I hope they weren't any trouble?"

"Not at all," said Joe. "What do they say, 'It takes a village'?"

"Well, I'm very lucky to have all of you for my village," said Sarah as she whisked the twins off to wash up.

Sylvia had just finished filling the water glasses when Sarah returned with the children, hands and faces scrubbed clean and hair combed, James in a different shirt entirely. Soon thereafter, Matt came in from the orchards, and Gretchen set the lasagna on the refectory table, deliciously fragrant with rich notes of tomato, onion, basil, and oregano. Everyone took their usual favorite seats, and soon the kitchen was humming with talk and laughter as they all shared their news of the day and their plans for the next. After the delicious meal was finished, they lingered at the table over coffee and tea, but eventually the twins grew restless and the party broke up. Sarah and Gretchen took the children off to the nursery for a little more play before bedtime, while Matt, Andrew, and Joe stayed behind to clean up the kitchen. Sylvia and Summer headed upstairs to the library, where Sylvia's World's Fair mementos awaited.

"Let's see," Sylvia murmured, planting her hands on her hips and surveying the bookcases from the center of the room. "We're looking for an engraved tin box. It should be on one of these shelves. Why don't we each take a side and work our way down?"

Nodding, Summer went to the far corner of the room and began scanning the bookcases on the east-facing wall. "You don't recall where you put it?"

"It *was* more than two years ago, dear," said Sylvia, taking up the search on the west wall. "Also, I wasn't the one who shelved it. Your mother did, after she finished writing her article. Before then, the box was stored in the attic, lost amid the clutter like so many other things."

"Was it in the same carton as the quilt?"

"That would have made sense, but no, it was tucked away in a drawer in that antique walnut bureau about halfway down the west wing. It used to be in my grandparents' bedroom. Do you know the one I mean?"

"Yes, I do. I can't imagine how anyone managed to haul it up the attic stairs."

"My father and Uncle William managed somehow. I always rather liked that bureau, but when my aunt Nellie agreed to let my cousin Elsa have the bedroom it was in, she preferred more contemporary furniture—although I suppose even that furniture is antique now." Sylvia paused, taking in the expanse of bookcases fondly. "So many lovely books. When I was a girl, I vowed that I would read them all someday."

"All of them? Even—" Summer removed a heavy tome from a shelf. "*The Cultivator and Country Gentleman, Devoted to the Practice and Science of Agriculture and Horticulture at Large, and to all the Various Departments of Rural Economy,* volume sixty-one, from eighteen ninety-six?"

"Now you understand why I never fulfilled that vow."

"If you're certain you'll never read this," Summer mused as she returned the book to its place, "you might be able to sell it online. I could set you up with an eBay account."

"A what account? Oh, eureka!" Sylvia exclaimed, rising up on tiptoe to retrieve the familiar tin box from a high shelf. Any higher, and she would have needed a stepstool.

She brushed off a fine layer of dust as she carried the box to the coffee table and settled herself in an armchair. Summer had already hurried over to the sofa opposite, and she leaned forward in anticipation as Sylvia lifted the engraved tin lid.

Inside, on top, was the bright blue first-place ribbon Sylvia and Claudia had won in Harrisburg. Sylvia removed it, admired it for a moment, then handed it to Summer. "If you turn it over, you'll see a tag on the back identifying the winner as Claudia Sylvia Bergstrom." She smiled and shook her head. "How clever we thought ourselves, employing an alias when we filled out the entry form and confirmed that our quilt was 'of the contestant's own making.'"

"Contestant's, singular?"

"That's right. We freely admitted that we'd had help quilting the top by adding a line that said, 'Quilted by the Bergstrom Family' or something like that." Sylvia laughed lightly, amused by the memory of her younger self. "I was so needlessly anxious that we might be disqualified if the judges discovered that Claudia and I had collaborated on the top. As it turned out, most of the quilts at all levels of the competition weren't the work of one individual quilter, so we were in good company."

"The contest was announced in January and the deadline was mid-May," said Summer, setting the ribbon carefully on the sofa beside her. "You'd almost *have* to collaborate."

"Almost. Some especially industrious quilters did indeed make their quilts entirely by themselves, from start to finish. And some entered pieces they had completed before the contest was announced."

"Really? That was allowed?"

"The rules stated that entries needed to be *recently* made, which I suppose was open to interpretation. Here, see for yourself." Sylvia carefully sorted through the mementos, found the pamphlet with the official rules, and handed it over. "I recall seeing quilts both in Philadelphia and in Chicago that predated the contest itself. I wouldn't have known except their makers had included the completion dates on the fronts of their quilts, usually in embroidery or quilting stitches in a border. The earliest date I saw was nineteen thirty-one."

"It's so cool to see the actual official rules you and Claudia read when you decided to enter the contest," said Summer, her gaze fixed on the pamphlet. "May I include this in the display too? I'll mat and frame it, so it'll be protected."

Sylvia consented, and then she settled back to watch, amused and pleased, as Summer continued examining the contents of the tin box as if she were excavating a treasure trove. She removed each item and studied it in turn—brochures, ticket stubs, programs, photographs, booklets offering patterns for several of the prizewinning quilts, and yellowed newspaper articles from around the country featuring local quiltmakers whose entries had made it to the regionals or the finals.

"Are any of these articles about you and your sister?" Summer asked, holding up one by two corners and skimming it for their names.

"No, although Claudia and I both thought our regional win would make the papers, since a reporter interviewed us in Harrisburg. A photographer took a picture of us with our quilt too, if I recall correctly." Sylvia shrugged. "I admit we were rather disappointed. Perhaps I saved these articles to prove that I wasn't a poor sport, and that I could celebrate other quilters' successes and fame, not only my own."

Nodding thoughtfully, Summer set the article aside and continued delving into the tin. A few items she placed carefully on the sofa with the ribbon and official rules pamphlet to take to the gallery. The others she arranged on the table in orderly rows, none of the edges overlapping. Sometimes a keepsake would evoke a vivid memory, and Sylvia would share its story, but mostly she let the mementos speak for themselves.

When Summer had emptied the tin, Sylvia regarded the assortment, puzzled. "Are you sure that's everything?" she asked, and Summer checked again and nodded. "I don't see the regional judges' scoresheet. It should be in an envelope—a plain white business envelope addressed to Claudia Sylvia Bergstrom here at the manor, but with no stamp or postmark. There was a crease down the middle where I folded it so it would fit in my pocket."

"I don't see anything like that," said Summer, glancing through the items on the sofa beside her, then checking to see if anything had fallen on the floor around them or beneath the table.

Sylvia's heart sank. "I don't understand. I know I saved it." She paused to think. "When I brought it home, I hid it from my sister in a safe place. Later, though, after I had accumulated these other mementos and I decided to store them in this tin, I would have sworn I put the envelope in here too."

"Wait." Summer studied her, curious. "You hid the scoresheet from your sister?"

"Yes, and I'd do it again. The judges praised my work and found fault with hers, and she would have been devastated. She would have blamed herself for our quilt not making it to the finals, and I wanted to spare her that."

Summer looked dubious, but she nodded acceptance. "Maybe you should check the original hiding place. Do you remember where it was?"

"Yes. There was a loose baseboard in my childhood bedroom with a narrow space behind it. I used to hide notes and journals there, things I didn't want Claudia to find." Then she thought of something else. "Is it possible your mother forgot to return that envelope with the rest of these mementos when she was finished writing her article?"

"It's possible. I'll ask her when I get home."

But when Summer phoned later that evening, she explained that Gwen had searched her files for the article, but she had not found an envelope that met Sylvia's description. Nor did she recall ever having seen it, or the scoresheet, and she was certain she would have remembered such a compelling artifact. Nor did Sylvia find it when she searched her erstwhile secret hiding place in her childhood bedroom, which held only a woven bookmark, a few coins, and a postcard a school friend had sent her from the Poconos in 1938.

Sylvia could not explain why the loss of the scoresheet troubled her so much. Decades had passed in which she had not given a fleeting thought to the judges' comments, or to the World's Fair quilt itself, for that matter. Perhaps it was because she did not care to think of herself as someone who had become aged and forgetful, and now she had little choice but to consider that possibility. She simply could not account for her memory of seeing the envelope among her other Century of Progress souvenirs, since it obviously was not with them anymore.

As she lay in bed that evening beside her dear Andrew, trying to fall asleep, one worry nagged at her more than any other.

Sylvia had been absent from Elm Creek Manor for fifty years after her first husband and younger brother were killed in the war. She had found it absolutely impossible to remain on her ancestral estate after her irreparable falling-out with her sister and Harold Midden, whom Sylvia held responsible for her loved ones' deaths. When she had fled, overcome by grief and despair, she had taken only a single suitcase, leaving behind many cherished belongings, including the engraved tin box.

In Sylvia's absence, Claudia could have found it, and she could have discovered the envelope tucked inside among the other mementos. If she had read the judges' comments, she would have known that Sylvia had read them too and had deliberately concealed them from her.

What would Claudia have thought then? Would she have believed that Sylvia had been trying to protect her? Or would she have resented her younger sister for assuming she couldn't bear the judges' evaluation, denying her the opportunity to decide for herself whether to dismiss their criticism or learn from it?

When Sylvia slipped that envelope into her pocket so many years before, she had acted with the best of intentions. The World's Fair quilt had marked a singular moment in the sisters' relationship, a rare instance when they had put aside their rivalry and had worked together in hopes of achieving something extraordinary. Even during their long estrangement years later, from time to time Sylvia had reflected upon those months and found comfort in remembering that she and her sister had been able to come together once, and perhaps someday they would again.

But if Claudia had indeed discovered the truth Sylvia had withheld from her, she would have remembered those months of creative collaboration very differently. To her, the World's Fair quilt would have become just another relic of their fractious, broken sisterhood.

14

June 1933

At twilight, Sylvia and her family arrived home to Elm Creek Manor in a cool, steady rainfall to find that Great-Aunt Lydia had a tasty supper waiting for them. Though the aromas were enticing and Sylvia was famished after their long, full day, the judges' review weighed her down so heavily it could have been etched on stone. As she took her place at the table between Claudia and her cousin Alice, it was an effort not to fidget or frown, but her impatience to race upstairs and hide the envelope was no match for her appetite. Soon she was enjoying fresh-baked rye bread alongside a dish of sausage, potatoes, and onions cooked in apple cider with caraway, and she chimed in eagerly as her siblings and cousins recounted their adventures for Great-Aunt Lydia. It was all so pleasant that for minutes at a time Sylvia would forget her unhappy secret entirely, but then she would shift in her seat on the bench, the envelope's sharp corner would poke her annoyingly through the cotton lining of her skirt pocket, and she would remember.

After the meal was finished, she and Claudia cleared the table and helped tidy up the kitchen while the younger children wandered off, yawning, to get ready for bed. Only after the floor was swept and the dishes dried did Sylvia at last steal away to her bedroom, where she hid the envelope behind the loose baseboard next to the wardrobe. She was certain—fairly certain—that protecting her sister from the judges' blunt criticism was a kindness, but if she had second thoughts after some time had passed, she could pretend that the review had only just arrived in that day's mail.

A few days later, something did arrive from Philadelphia—a sturdy, well-sealed carton with "Sears, Roebuck and Co." stamped on the sides and the lid. Claudia was the first to answer the knock at the front door, but Sylvia flew down the stairs to join her just as the deliveryman was departing after hauling the parcel into the foyer.

Richard had heard the doorbell too. "I'll get the box cutter," he called out from the upper balcony.

"No!" Sylvia and Claudia shouted back to him in unison, alarmed. Sylvia could well imagine her brother attacking the box with the sharp blade, sending up a shower of shredded fabric and batting.

Claudia hurried off to the west sitting room where she had left her sewing basket and returned a few minutes later with scissors and Great-Aunt Lucinda and Aunt Nellie too. Wielding the scissors with care, Claudia opened the carton while Sylvia hovered anxiously nearby, ready to take over should her sister bungle the job. Fortunately Claudia managed perfectly well on her own, and when the box was finally open, she beckoned Sylvia forward to assist. Together they removed the soft bundle tucked inside, unfurled it between their outstretched arms, and admired their World's Fair quilt, safely home once more and none the worse for the journey. Even with the folding creases, which would fall out eventually, Chain of Progress was without question a remarkable quilt—ambitious, modern, and bold. It seemed to Sylvia that the faults the judges had found weren't really all that evident unless a persnickety person was deliberately searching for mistakes. All the more reason not to make Claudia feel worse about her truncated triangle tips and poorly matched seams than she probably already did, or so Sylvia told herself.

"Oh, no, look!" Claudia wailed. "They left the ribbon pinned to the front of the quilt."

"And why not?" said Great-Aunt Lydia. "All the better not to lose it in transit."

"The pins might leave holes in my Odd Fellows Chain blocks," said Claudia. "Let's move the ribbon closer to the middle."

"No, don't," Sylvia protested. "I don't want pinholes in my appliqué blocks either."

"Fine. We'll pin it to the back." Without waiting for a reply, Claudia passed her edge of the quilt to Aunt Nellie, who held it for her while Claudia carefully unfastened the green Ribbon of Merit and secured it to the back instead. Sylvia figured it was rather pointless to display a ribbon where no one could admire it, but Claudia was right about avoiding pinholes in the top, and Great-Aunt Lydia was right too, about keeping ribbon and quilt together.

"What will you girls do with your prizewinning masterpiece now?" Aunt Nellie asked, smiling.

Sylvia honestly hadn't given it any thought. She had hoped Chain of Progress would be on its way to Chicago at this point.

Claudia put her head to one side and scrunched up her pretty features, thinking. "Maybe Sylvia and I could take turns using it on our beds?"

Sylvia felt a pang of fear for her meticulously stitched appliqués. "I don't think that's a good idea. You don't even want anyone to sit on your Sunbonnet Sue quilt, and we'd have to be even more careful with Chain of Progress."

"What, then?"

"Your World's Fair quilt is an award-winning work of art," said Great-Aunt Lucinda. "It doesn't belong on a bed. It should be displayed on a gallery wall."

"But we don't have a gallery," said Claudia.

"No," said Great-Aunt Lydia, "but we do have a ballroom and a banquet hall."

Sylvia turned to Claudia and saw her own question reflected in her sister's eyes. The ballroom was grander, but the banquet hall was elegant too. The family used the banquet hall more frequently, not only on holidays but whenever they entertained guests in numbers too great to fit around the refectory table in the kitchen. Although it was true that the Bergstroms welcomed guests for dinner less frequently than they had before the Great Depression, they hadn't hosted a single ball since well before the girls' mother's last illness. The ballroom was rarely used at all anymore, except when the children needed to run around and the weather was too foul for playing outside.

"I think the banquet hall would be best," said Sylvia.

"Me too," said Claudia, nodding. "More people will see it, and more often."

"It's decided, then," said Great-Aunt Lydia. As the eldest member of the family, when she used that particular tone, her wish was their command.

When Sylvia's father and uncle were informed of the plan, they sent Paulie, the hired hand most adept with tools and carpentry, to install brackets and a hanging rod on the banquet hall's southern wall, near the door leading into the ballroom. Sylvia begged Paulie to let her help hang the quilt, and when they finished, Chain of Progress looked so splendid there that she lingered to admire it long after everyone else had dispersed. In the days that followed, she gladly took any opportunity to pass through the banquet hall, even if it was the long way around. The World's Fair quilt really did look as if it were in a museum gallery. It wasn't the Sears Pavilion on the shore of Lake Michigan, but it was a place of honor all the same.

Ordinarily Sylvia loved school, but for the first time ever she joined Richard in counting down the days until the end of the semester and summer break. Although the thirty Sears National Quilt Contest finalists would not be displayed at the fair until after the ten regional exhibits concluded, the Century of Progress International Exposition was already in progress. Sylvia wished she could have attended the grand opening on Saturday, May 27, but she made do with the detailed descriptions that appeared in the *Waterford Register*, with a map of Chicago at hand so she could find the unfamiliar locations the reporters mentioned.

The momentous day had begun with a glorious parade down Michigan Avenue, from the Near North Side south to Soldier Field, a stadium overlooking the fairgrounds. Thousands of spectators watched the grand procession either from the crowded sidewalks or from above, through the windows of the tall buildings lining the parade route. Troops from all branches of military service, equestrian teams, veterans' associations, cadets from local military academies, and proud Boy Scouts strode along to the musical accompaniment of marching bands, bright with lively brass and woodwinds and drums. Gleaming black automobiles escorted dignitaries, including the governor of Illinois, the mayor of Chicago, a bishop of the city's Protestant Episcopal diocese, and Postmaster General James Farley, who was President Franklin Delano Roosevelt's official emissary to the fair. Representing Chicago's thriving, diverse immigrant and first-generation population were members of international social clubs clad in the traditional attire of their ancestral homelands—Italy, Ukraine, Sweden, Norway, Greece, Spain, Belgium, and many others, the kilted Scots accompanied by the skirl of bagpipes.

After the parade of nations came five enormous floats richly draped and canopied with strawberry-red velvets and silks, conveying in stunning luxury the Queen of the Fair and her fifty ladies of honor, chosen in a national competition sponsored by the *Chicago Tribune* for their beauty, grace, and poise. The queen, described breathlessly by an admiring reporter as nineteen-year-old, golden-haired, violet-eyed Lillian Anderson of Racine, Wisconsin, wore an ivory satin gown with an Elizabethan collar and "yards upon yards" of purple velvet train. In one hand she clasped a scepter glittering with pearls and rhinestones, and in the other, two gold medals, one for the postmaster general and one for him to deliver to President Roosevelt, splendid mementos of a historic day. The queen's ladies of honor also wore ivory silk gowns, as well as broad-brimmed strawberry-red latticed hats. "Be assured, brethren," the reporter noted, "these girls make as easy an eyeful as ever you took."

"Honestly," Sylvia muttered, rolling her eyes and turning the page.

While Claudia sighed longingly over the descriptions of the queen and her court and their lovely attire, Sylvia was captivated by the astonishing ceremony that had taken place later that evening when the fairgrounds were illuminated for the first time. As twilight descended, the crowds waited expectantly, entertained by the stirring music of choir and symphony orchestra. The waxing crescent moon shone, and Mars and Jupiter appeared, and all eyes turned to the southeastern sky, eagerly searching for the red giant star Arcturus in the constellation Boötes. Arcturus was so far away that the light from its rays took forty years to reach Earth across the vastness of space—which meant that the starlight visible from the western shore of Lake Michigan on the first night of the Century of Progress Exposition had departed Arcturus during the previous Chicago World's Fair, the 1893 World's Columbian Exposition.

Four observatories working in unison—Yerkes in Williams Bay, Wisconsin; Harvard in Cambridge, Massachusetts; the University of Illinois at Urbana; and Allegheny, in Pittsburgh—captured Arcturus's rays, then used photoelectric tubes and amplification equipment to operate a relay closing circuit in the telegraph line. A radio receiver tuned to the broadcast of the ceremony from the fairgrounds notified each observatory's operator when to project the star's light upon their electric eye, closing their local circuit to the wire. This set in motion a complicated system of relays and series circuits that eventually acquired enough power to flip a master switch at the fairgrounds in Chicago, which turned on a sweeping searchlight atop the Hall of Science. The searchlight cast its beams upon each of the other buildings, one by one, triggering photoelectric cells installed on their façades and causing their own lights to turn on. From star, to observatory, to searchlight, to each building, the fairgrounds gradually became illuminated to the accompaniment of rising cheers and cries of astonishment from the tens of thousands of witnesses. Afterward it was said that everyone present believed they had observed a scientific miracle, and Sylvia desperately wished she had been among them.

She took heart, though, knowing her turn would come soon.

At last school ended for the summer. A few days later, in the evening after supper, Sylvia, her siblings, and her father packed their suitcases and left Elm Creek Manor in a scramble of hugs from the aunties and woebegone looks and pleas for souvenirs from their cousins. Uncle William drove them to the station in Altoona, where they boarded the Broadway Limited for Chicago. It was quite late by the time the train pulled away from the station, but Richard was eager to see the Horseshoe Curve, so their father let them watch from the observation car until they passed through the famous ascending curve through the Alleghenies. Then he ushered them back to their sleeper car, where Sylvia and her siblings prepared for bed and climbed into their bunks, still insisting they were much too excited to sleep even as the rocking motion of the railcar lulled them into slumber.

They woke the next morning in time to freshen up and breakfast in the dining car before the Broadway Limited pulled into Chicago Union Station a few minutes before ten o'clock. Their father hailed a cab to take them about a mile southeast to the Stevens Hotel on Michigan Avenue, where he had booked two adjoining rooms. Barely five years old, the Stevens was said to be the world's largest hotel, with three thousand guest rooms, a barbershop, a pharmacy, a candy store, a five-lane bowling alley, a 1,200-seat movie theater, and an eighteen-hole miniature golf course on the roof. What impressed Sylvia most was the view from her window, the broad stretch of greenery, walking paths, and monuments of Grant Park right across the street and the vast dark blue expanse of Lake Michigan beyond it. If she stood at the far left side of the center window and peered southeast at a particular angle, she could just glimpse three impressive structures her father told her were Adler Planetarium, Shedd Aquarium, and the Field Museum.

"That's where we'll find the north entrance to the fairgrounds," he remarked, and her heart seemed to skip a beat.

"What do you say, kids?" her father called out from the connecting doorway after they had unpacked their suitcases and claimed beds, Sylvia and Claudia in one room, he and Richard in the other. "Shall we rest for a bit and see the fair later, or—"

"See the fair *now*," Richard shouted, seizing their father's hand and tugging him, laughing, toward the hallway door.

Sylvia and Claudia scrambled to follow them.

Soon they were descending in the elevator, stepping out onto the busy sidewalk, and crossing the street to Grant Park. Following the broad sidewalk between Shedd Aquarium and the Field Museum, they entered the fair through the Twelfth Avenue gate, turned right onto the expansive Avenue of Flags, and paused to take in the scene, enthralled. Sylvia knew from her reading that the fairgrounds extended three miles southward from where they stood and covered more than four hundred acres, but those numbers had not prepared her for the expanse of brightly colored, very modern structures; or the throngs of bustling fairgoers, smiling or laughing and exclaiming aloud with the same excitement Sylvia felt rising in her own chest; the enticing smells of unfamiliar foods, the lively strains of distant music, the bright sunshine, or the brisk wind off the lake, tugging at her hair ribbon and tossing unruly strands into her face.

Ahead and to the left was the Administration Building, the first of what appeared to be dozens of futuristic buildings lining the long avenue. The venue constructed for the 1893 World's Columbian Exposition had been called the Great White City for the buildings' classical architecture and glowing white walls illuminated at night by thousands of incandescent bulbs. What Sylvia beheld now was something else entirely—astonishing structures with angular, soaring towers, bold geometric forms, and smooth surfaces, most without visible windows. Even more striking than the modern architecture was the color scheme, a palette of twenty-three bright, intense hues that had inspired the fairgrounds' nickname, the Rainbow City. Almost every building within sight boasted several different colors, and Sylvia couldn't decide if the effect was energizing or jarring. She supposed she'd reserve judgment until after nightfall, when the rays of Arcturus turned on the newfangled lights that, by daylight anyway, appeared to be strange glass tubes accenting prominent features of each building. Sylvia had heard of these gaseous tubes, the so-called neon lights, but she had never seen them in action. She was curious to see what all the fuss was about.

Behind the Administration Building, Sylvia glimpsed a long lagoon running parallel to the shore, dividing the fairgrounds into the lakefront, where her family stood, and Northerly Island, a section that appeared to extend into Lake Michigan, connected to the mainland by bridges on both ends and a third in the center. In the far northeastern corner of the island, Sylvia could make out the curved dome of Adler Planetarium, and, moving south, several more modern, multi-hued buildings and the midway. High above the center bridge on opposite sides of the lagoon rose a pair of steel towers more than sixty stories tall, connected by the looping cableway of the Sky Ride. Each of the ten "rocket cars"—gondolas on a strong traction cable—could carry thirty-six passengers on a leisurely four-minute round trip more than two hundred feet above the fairgrounds. Sylvia had read that the Sky Ride offered incomparable bird's-eye views of the fair, and on a clear day, one could see four states. She was eager to see the fairgrounds from high above, but even on familiar, solid ground everything about the fair was vibrant, and not just because of the bright colors. Every sight and sound evoked an electric frisson of excitement and discovery. Sylvia felt it, and she was sure the bustling crowds all around her did too.

"What would you like to do first?" asked their father, casting an appraising look around.

"I want to ride the Sky Ride," Richard exclaimed, pointing toward the towers. "After that let's go to the Enchanted Island to see the world's largest model train display, and next let's go see Fort Dearborn, and then the Hall of Science, and then—" Abruptly he fell silent and turned to his sisters, chagrined. "But maybe you want to see the quilt show first?"

"Yes, please," Sylvia quickly replied, before her sister or father could demur. "The Sears Pavilion is closer, so it makes sense to start there."

"Why don't we split up?" Claudia suggested. "Sylvia and I can see the quilt show while Father and Richard tour the Hall of Science. We can meet you there when we're finished, and we can all go on the Sky Ride together." When their father hesitated, dubious, she added, "I promise I'll keep an eye on Sylvia."

"For the last time," Sylvia burst out, "I'm thirteen. I don't need you to keep an eye on me."

"In this crowd, so far from home, maybe you do." Her father studied them both for a long moment. "If you both agree to keep an eye on each other, I'd allow you to go off on your own for a while."

The sisters exchanged a quick glance. "Agreed," said Claudia, and Sylvia nodded.

"All right, then." Their father glanced at his wristwatch. "Meet us in front of the Hall of Science in two hours. Can you find your way?"

"I have a map," Sylvia assured him, taking it from her pocket to prove it.

With a final caution to stick together, their father and Richard set off down the long avenue.

"This way," said Sylvia, glancing at the map and pointing to the right. "It's that building, the one on the corner."

Making their way past the Court of Honor at the intersection with Fourteenth Street, the sisters approached the tall majestic Sears Pavilion they had seen so often in advertisements for the quilt contest and in newspaper articles about the fair. In the center rose a tall rectangular tower, with a gleaming dome on the roof and "Sears Roebuck and Co." proudly displayed at the top of each of the four sides. Two wings about a quarter of the height of the tower stretched out in opposite directions parallel to the front façade, and a shorter wing jutted out to the rear. Unlike the more brightly colored buildings all around, the Sears Pavilion was mostly white, with a pair of dark blue horizontal stripes outlining the wings, the square base of the tower, and the round pedestal of the dome. Three quarter-circle supports on the ground level and two tall narrow pillars one story above flanking the main entrance were adorned in the same shade of blue, solid rather than striped. Instead of stairs, a pair of long wide ramps descended on opposite diagonals from the main entrance in the center. The grounds were beautifully landscaped with small evergreens, flowering trees, and perennials, and as the sisters drew closer, Sylvia glimpsed fairgoers strolling on rooftop gardens.

Ascending the nearest ramp and passing through one of the tall glass front doors, Sylvia and Claudia found themselves in a busy guest services area, where signs directed visitors to restrooms, telephones, complimentary parcel-checking facilities, and a telegraph office.

"There," Claudia said, grasping Sylvia's arm and nodding to a large banner off to one side of the main reception desk. "We'll find the quilts upstairs."

"But where are the stairs?" Sylvia asked, just as she saw the painted arrow indicating the way.

They headed down the main corridor, weaving in and out of the crowd, taking care to stick together. On the walls, a series of dioramas depicted the history of retail sales from 1833 to the present, and through one wide doorway, Sylvia glimpsed an enormous relief map of the United States. Over the loudspeaker system, a man with a rich pleasant baritone told the story of the Sears, Roebuck company from its origins as a mail-order house selling watches and jewelry to its current status as a thriving nationwide network of department stores and mail-order houses offering nearly every imaginable household good one could possibly desire.

The mellifluous voice faded behind them as they ascended to the second floor. "We mustn't be jealous," Claudia murmured as they joined the throng of smiling women chatting happily with their companions as they made their way toward the wide gallery entrance through which enticing glimpses of colorful fabric were visible. "Mother would have been proud of us just for making it to the regional round."

"Of course she would have been," replied Sylvia, so surprised that she halted, obliging the amiable crowd to shift around them. "We should be proud of ourselves too. Mistakes and all, Chain of Progress is the finest quilt either of us has ever made, alone or together. I bet most of the finalists, maybe all of them, have been quilting since before we were born. When we're as experienced as they are, we could be master quilters, just like whoever won the grand prize here, just like Mother and our aunties."

Claudia regarded her, uncertain. "Do you really think so?"

Sylvia was more confident in her own chances than her sister's, but now was not the time to get specific. "Of course. We just need to practice, and to learn as much as we can." She inclined her head toward the gallery. "This is a great place to start. These are the thirty best quilts in the country, right?"

"The thirty best quilts in the country that were entered in this contest," Claudia amended.

Sylvia knew her sister was thinking of their mother's masterpieces.

"Fair point. Either way, we can learn from them." Honesty compelled her to add, "I don't know whether I can *not* be jealous, though. I really wanted our quilt to be here today."

"So did I." Claudia sighed and squared her shoulders. "Well, just do your best to be a good sport, and I will too. Come on. Let's go learn something."

They entered the gallery, and in the two hours that followed, they strolled through the exhibit, first pausing before each quilt at a distance to take it all in, then drawing closer to study particular details—a quilter's dynamic color choices, or her impressively precise piecing, graceful appliqué, or intricate quilting. When they came upon the three finalists from the Philadelphia region, they were rather surprised to see that none boasted a ribbon, not even for honorable mention. Then again, Sylvia thought, it couldn't have been easy to choose the three finest quilts from such a splendid array. She couldn't even rank a top three among her own favorites.

One quilt titled The Spectrum, the first-place winner from the Los Angeles regional, resembled a swirling, rainbow-hued star with a white sun at the center, vibrant with color and motion. Sylvia was awestruck by the flawless appliqué of a quilt called Bleeding Hearts, which featured twelve identical blocks, each with a lavender woven basket filled with dark pink bleeding hearts, yellow-and-white daisies, and blue forget-me-nots amid green foliage. The blocks were set on point with alternating setting squares of a delicate pink cotton, the same background fabric as the appliqué blocks. The entire surface was lavishly quilted with feathered plumes and crosshatch, all the way to the edges of the scalloped border.

Several other quilts also featured stunning floral appliqué, including two Sylvia knew her mother would have adored. The first, Iris, was the second-place winner from the Atlanta regional. It reminded Sylvia of her mother's Elm and Lilacs—although her mother's quilt was superior in both design and craft—with a central bouquet of dark and light gold irises in various stages of bloom from bud to full flower with intertwining sage-green stems and leaves. The outer border was made up of twenty-two individual iris plants, their flowers facing the center of the quilt, with a graceful scalloped edge bound in sage green. The second quilt, one aisle over, was Louisiana Rose, the second-place winner from the Dallas regional. The pattern reminded Sylvia of the popular Whig Rose, but more graceful and with a modern flair. Sixteen blocks of stylized roses in three shades of pink and two of green were arranged in a straight setting and encircled by a twining green vine adorned with leaves and rosebuds. In the lower left corner, the quiltmaker had appliquéd her monogram and the date, 1930, revealing it to be yet another quilt completed before the contest was announced. Yet as exquisite as Iris and Louisiana Rose were, neither had claimed a ribbon.

"There's something I don't understand," murmured Claudia as they lingered to admire Louisiana Rose.

"Why such a marvelous quilt didn't break into the top three?" Sylvia murmured back, shaking her head in bewilderment. "I don't understand either. I can only imagine how magnificent the winners and the honorable mentions must be, if the judges found them better than this."

"That's not it," said Claudia. "I mean, yes, I'm certainly expecting to see the most wonderful quilts ever made after seeing those that *didn't* win, but—" Brow furrowing, she glanced around and shook her head. "Where are all the theme quilts? I've seen only two, the transportation quilt from the Philadelphia regional, and the Blazing Star with the appliquéd scenes from the fairgrounds."

Sylvia paused to think. "You're right. That doesn't make any sense. There were dozens of theme quilts in Harrisburg and Philadelphia. And maybe some were just traditional pieced quilts with 'Century of Progress' embroidered on them so they would qualify as a theme quilt, but most were really quite clever and original."

"That's what I thought too. Most of them were as good as Chain of Progress."

"I don't know about *that*," said Sylvia. "But either way, why did so few of them make it through to the finals?"

Claudia shrugged. "I have no idea. We thought the judges would prefer theme quilts—"

"*I* thought so," Sylvia reminded her, a knot of apprehension tightening in her chest. "You thought a traditional quilt, perfectly made, would impress the judges most."

"Maybe I thought so at first, but I changed my mind."

"Only because I persuaded you."

"No, because it made sense. But why would Sears give their quilt contest a theme at all if they were just going to ignore it later? Why offer bonus prize money if the first-place winner is a theme quilt?" Claudia's eyes went wide. "Unless the top three quilts and the honorable mentions *are* all theme quilts. We haven't seen them yet. Maybe they are."

"I doubt it. Wouldn't there *have* to be more theme quilts among the other twenty-five for that to be so?" Sylvia drew in a breath sharply, realizing the truth only as she spoke it. "The people who organized the contest and wrote the rules aren't the same people who judged the quilts. The regional judges preferred traditional styles. They didn't *reward* quilts that included the theme. They *marked them down* for it."

"We don't know that for sure."

"Maybe not, but doesn't it seem likely?"

"Maybe. I don't know." Claudia placed her hand on Sylvia's shoulder and looked her straight in the eye. "Either way, this isn't your fault. Our theme isn't what kept us from advancing."

That was very likely true. Sylvia knew what the judges had said about Chain of Progress, knew where they had found fault—but she could never tell Claudia the truth, not ever. Claudia was being so loyal and encouraging, and Sylvia couldn't spoil it. Even if Claudia secretly believed they had lost because of Sylvia's stubborn insistence they make a theme quilt, she wasn't saying so. She was trying to spare Sylvia's feelings, and Sylvia had to repay her in kind.

Soon thereafter, they reached the heart of the exhibit, where the three winning quilts had been given pride of place on a raised platform in a well-lit alcove. Sylvia and Claudia had to wait until a crowd of admirers moved on before they could approach, but when they were able to view the quilts without obstruction, Sylvia found herself both impressed and bewildered. The third-place quilt was a flawlessly pieced, elegantly quilted red-and-white Delectable Mountains quilt, with a central sawtooth triangle design encircled by ten concentric borders—an exceptional rendition of a straightforward pattern requiring only straight seams, with no curves or set-in angles. The second-place winner was another floral appliqué quilt, Colonial Rose, beautifully made but neither as pretty nor as complex as Louisiana Rose, in Sylvia's opinion.

The grand prize–winning quilt gave Sylvia pause. It was a beautiful quilt, perfectly pieced and gorgeously quilted, with exceptional stuffed work that added pleasing dimension and texture, but otherwise, it too was a rather straightforward design. The title given to the quilt was Unknown Star, but Sylvia knew the block as Blazing Star, a variation of the popular LeMoyne Star, with each of the eight rhombus star points composed of four smaller, similar pieces. Two shades of gray-green and one small-scale floral print had been used to make the forty-two blocks, which were arranged in straight sets of seven rows of six blocks each, with no sashing, and only a narrow solid border of the darker gray-green.

"Hmm," Claudia murmured as she studied it.

"It's perfectly made," Sylvia offered. "I think I could search all day with a magnifying glass and not find a single flaw."

"The stuffed work is very impressive," Claudia noted. "It really sets off the quilting. I'm sure the judges loved that."

Then they exchanged a long, silent look, and Sylvia knew they shared the same thought: Unknown Star was a beautiful quilt, no doubt about it, but did it really deserve the grand prize?

They stepped aside to make room for other viewers. "Why, it's perfectly ordinary," Sylvia heard an older woman exclaim before a companion quickly hushed her.

It wasn't perfectly *ordinary*, Sylvia thought as she and Claudia moved along down the aisle. It was perfectly *lovely*. Mrs. Roosevelt would surely be pleased to receive it. How proud and honored the quiltmaker must be to know that her quilt would soon grace an elegant room in the White House, where dignitaries from around the world might see it!

Sylvia and Claudia said little as they viewed the last of the quilts. "I would have given the second-place quilt the grand prize," Claudia murmured as they left the gallery.

"It was impressive," Sylvia allowed, "but I would have given first place to Louisiana Rose."

"That one was quite lovely too." Claudia hesitated, began to speak, paused, and tried again. "You're not sorry we entered the contest, are you?"

"Of course not," said Sylvia. "Why? Are you?"

"What I mean is, do you wish we had each made our own quilt?"

For a moment Sylvia imagined herself beaming proudly, a first-place ribbon pinned to her sweater as she graciously handed a grand prize–winning quilt to Eleanor Roosevelt at the White House. But the image quickly faded. "No," she said emphatically as they exited the Sears Pavilion. "We took first place in Harrisburg. That's amazing, and missing out on the finals doesn't change that. I never would have done that on my own."

Claudia gave her a sidelong look as they descended the southerly ramp. "Only because you wouldn't have finished in time."

"Not only because of that," Sylvia countered.

She watched Claudia from the corner of her eye as they walked down the avenue toward the Hall of Science, waiting for her to admit that she wouldn't have accomplished so much on her own either.

But her sister said nothing.

15

September 2004

When the estimate from the second reputable local roofing company came in, it was even higher than the one from the firm Matt's father had recommended, and their crew wouldn't be able to begin work until March. Out of options, and unwilling to dread rainy forecasts in perpetuity, Sylvia had little choice but to sign the first company's contract. As she paid the deposit, she took a deep breath and said a silent prayer that their accounts wouldn't be entirely depleted after they paid off the balance.

Their financial advisor would know for certain, so Sarah booked the first available appointment even though the timing was less than ideal—the afternoon before the grand opening of Elm Creek Orchards. Sarah invited Sylvia to accompany her to the meeting, but Sylvia's afternoon was fully booked with back-to-back phone calls to potential corporate sponsors for Quiltsgiving. So Sarah entrusted the twins to Gretchen and set off alone.

Later, when Sarah returned, she found Sylvia in the kitchen wrapping up her last phone call of the day. "Could you join me in the library for a bit?" Sarah asked as soon as Sylvia hung up.

"Certainly," Sylvia said, scooting out of the booth. She followed a pensive Sarah upstairs, heart sinking. If Sarah had good news, she would have shared it over a cup of tea in the kitchen, and she would have been smiling.

"Give it to me straight," Sylvia said after they closed the library doors behind them. She took her usual seat on the sofa and watched her younger friend expectantly.

Sarah sank into one of the opposite armchairs and set her satchel on the floor beside it. "We have enough in our savings account and money market to cover the roof replacement," she said, her expression strained. "Thanks to some ingenious juggling of funds, we'll also have enough left in our checking account and emergency fund to pay our bare-bones operating expenses for the next four months."

"Goodness." Sylvia felt lightheaded from relief. "That's better news than I expected."

"Bare-bones," Sarah repeated distinctly, grasping the armrests and squaring her shoulders. "Four months. That means utility bills. Groceries. Off-season salaries. Gas for the minivan. It does *not* mean advertising and publicity for next year's camp season, or class-room supplies to replenish what we used up this year. We'll also need to postpone our scheduled maintenance, and that includes the pro-fessional servicing of the longarm sewing machine, replacing the ballroom carpeting, and repainting the west wing guest rooms."

"Oh, I see." Sylvia rested her chin on her hand, thinking. "Well, I'm no stranger to belt-tightening and making do. We'll get by." Un-less another catastrophe struck, heaven forfend. She dared not voice the thought aloud.

"That's the bad news." Sarah allowed a small smile. "The good news is that we aren't flat broke. We won't have to take on debt."

"Very good. That means any income we earn from the orchard and the corporate sponsorship program can go straight to paying expenses. If we're lucky enough to have anything left over, we can replenish our savings."

Sarah nodded. "Agreed. To that end, I plan to open registrations for our next camp season early, so we can start bringing in those deposits. Also, Matt and I have agreed to defer our salaries until this rough patch is behind us."

"Surely that's not necessary," Sylvia protested. "None of the Elm Creek Quilters would expect you to make that sacrifice. You're raising two young children. You need an income."

"We're getting free room and board, and we *will* draw our salaries in full, eventually. Just not now. It's less than ideal, but it won't be for long." But Sarah's smiled faded and she averted her eyes, as if she didn't quite believe her own words.

Next she withdrew a folder of documents from her satchel and spread them on the table between them. Clearly and calmly, she showed Sylvia exactly how much of their money remained, how it was dispersed, and which funds Sarah and their financial advisor intended to move from this account to that one in order to make the most of interest rates and to reduce their tax burden. Listening intently, Sylvia tried to emulate her younger friend's unperturbed manner, but it was mere pretense. Mindful of her age and the all too swift passage of time, Sylvia had taken great comfort in knowing that Elm Creek Quilts was fiscally sound and would thrive even after she was gone. She had never been blessed with children, but she loved Sarah and Matt as if they were her own, and they considered her the twins' honorary grandmother. She had hoped to leave the McClures not only financially secure, but prosperous. Now all of that was in doubt, and she had precious little time to put things right.

Later, over dinner, Matt offered a cheerful, heartening update about the next day's launch of Elm Creek Orchards, a welcome reminder to Sylvia that she would not have to weather the storm alone. Quite the contrary. She was surrounded by clever, hardworking, faithful friends who would help her find solutions where at first glance she may have seen none.

After the meal and the preview of the next day's events, her spirits felt so restored that instead of retiring to her room to sew and brood, she invited Andrew to accompany her on a walk through the orchard. The evening was cool enough for a sweater, and after so many long summer days, sunset around seven o'clock felt surprisingly early. Yet the western sky was still rosy pink as they set out, and Andrew carried a flashlight in case they needed it to illuminate the return journey.

"I've been thinking about my sister quite a lot lately," Sylvia confided as they set off hand in hand through the tantalizingly fragrant rows of apple trees, verdantly leafy and heavy with luscious ripe fruit, decadently abundant.

"Claudia?" Andrew gave her a quizzical glance. "Because Summer's been getting your World's Fair quilt ready for the exhibit?"

"Yes, I'm sure that's why." Sylvia fell silent for a long moment. "You know better than anyone how harshly I've judged my sister and her husband for running Bergstrom Thoroughbreds into the ground all those years ago."

"I wouldn't say you've been too hard on them." Andrew squeezed her hand gently. "I know you blame yourself too. If anything, you've judged *yourself* too harshly."

"I can't say that I agree. If I hadn't fled Elm Creek Manor, I could have taken charge of the business. I could have prevented Claudia and Harold from nearly bankrupting the estate." Sylvia sighed and shook her head. "But we'll never know what might have been, will we? I left, and I stayed away for fifty years. In my absence, the estate declined."

"That wasn't your fault."

"Perhaps, but maybe it wasn't theirs either." Sylvia halted and gazed up at the darkening sky. "I understand now what it feels like to be land rich but cash poor. I had some sense of that during the Great Depression, but I was only a child then. Though times were hard, I always trusted that my father and aunties would provide for me. But after the war, Claudia and Harold were essentially on their own, with an estate to manage and a business to run and no one to advise them."

"Most people would've considered themselves lucky to have so much," said Andrew, frowning. He was the kindest man Sylvia knew, but his heart had hardened irrevocably against Harold decades ago. Andrew had no sympathy to spare for him. "Harold had it pretty good, if you ask me. A beautiful bride, a fine home, a place in his wife's family business—not to mention that *he* got to come home from the war, when many better men didn't."

Sylvia felt a pang. "You don't need to tell me that," she said, a catch in her throat. "My husband and my brother—"

"I know. I'm sorry." Andrew cupped her cheek with his hand and held her gaze, contrite. "I just can't forgive him for what he did. For what he failed to do."

She placed her hand over his. "You might feel better if you could. Not for his sake, but for yours." When Andrew returned a stubborn scowl, Sylvia sighed and let her hand fall to her side. "Yes, Harold came home from the war to a lovely bride and a livelihood, but he knew absolutely nothing about raising horses. Claudia understood little more than he did about running a business. She hadn't spent her life since childhood shadowing our father, learning all she could, loving every part of it, in hopes of taking her place in the company someday."

"No, that was you."

"That was me." Sylvia reached up and plucked an apple from the nearest tree, polished it on her sleeve, and bit into it, savoring its crisp sweetness. "To be perfectly honest, Bergstrom Thoroughbreds never fully recovered from the Great Depression. It's been rather unfair of me, all these years, to have expected Claudia and Harold to turn a profit, invest wisely, and properly maintain the estate. It was too much for them to manage. They simply didn't know how."

She held out the apple to Andrew, who took it from her, brow furrowed, but did not take a bite. "Are you saying that you forgive them? Maybe they were in over their heads, but if not for Agnes, they would have sold off the entire estate. There would have been nothing left for you to come home to."

"I'm saying I *understand* them," Sylvia replied. "At least, I understand my sister. I've judged her too harshly for selling off acres of Bergstrom land when Bergstrom Thoroughbreds failed and she had no other income." Glancing around, Sylvia surprised herself with a laugh. "No other income indeed—that's not at all true. Even in the worst of times, Claudia kept an acre or two of this orchard going. I've seen her old records. She managed a small harvest every year and sold the apples to local grocers and a cider mill. Her profits were modest, but they were enough to pay the property taxes, keep the power on, and put food on the table."

"So the orchard saved Elm Creek Manor once before."

"My sister saved Elm Creek Manor," Sylvia corrected him. "All this time I've blamed her for everything she lost. I never truly appreciated her for all she saved." With a sweep of her arm, Sylvia gestured, taking in every part of the estate. "Now I have all this—the orchard, the manor, Elm Creek Quilts, and you. And I intend to hold on to it, whatever it takes, come what may. I'll pass it all on in the fullness of time and not a day sooner."

"I believe you," said Andrew, clasping both of her hands in his and drawing her closer. "And I'll be here beside you, come what may."

His eyes were full of love and tenderness as he bent to kiss her.

The next morning, Sylvia woke to a perfect autumn day, clear and sunny, with a brisk nip in the air that put a lively spring in her step as she washed, dressed, and hurried down to breakfast. Her darling Andrew, a perpetual early riser, already had coffee brewing. Sarah and Matt were feeding the twins and going over their daily schedule in a rapid shorthand that Sylvia could barely follow. Gretchen and Joe were sitting at a booth nearby, finishing up their scrambled eggs and toast. That looked rather tasty to Sylvia, so she headed to the fridge and the breadbox, pausing as she passed the refectory table to rest a hand on Andrew's shoulder and kiss his cheek. A frisson of excitement and anticipation filled the room, and by the time Sylvia sat down with her breakfast, the conversation had turned into a strategy meeting. Matt reminded everyone of their assignments, Gretchen chimed in with important, last-minute details that no one else had remembered, and Andrew broke in now and then to assure everyone that everything was well in hand and it was going to be a great day.

Matt was nearly finished when they heard the low, musical tolling of the front doorbell. Andrew rose to answer, and he soon returned carrying a crystal vase with a gorgeous autumn bouquet of blue delphiniums, blush and yellow roses, and burgundy smoke bush leaves.

"How lovely," Gretchen exclaimed as a bemused Andrew set the vase in the center of the table. "Who sent it?"

"And who is it for?" asked Sarah.

"There's a card on that bamboo stick in the middle," said Joe, gesturing.

Sylvia was nearest, so she deftly plucked the small white envelope from the bouquet. "It's to 'My dear friends at Elm Creek Orchards,' from Julia Merchaud!"

An exclamation of surprise and delight went up from the table. "How thoughtful of her," said Gretchen.

"Save that card," teased Matt. "That autograph might be worth something."

"It's definitely worth something—to us," Sarah admonished him playfully. "A heartfelt message from a loyal camper always is."

"I'm not parting with this at any price, so autograph collectors will have to look elsewhere," Sylvia declared. "There's more. 'Warm congratulations and all best wishes for your grand opening. Your friend and admirer, Julia.' Oh, dear."

"'Oh, dear?'" Sarah echoed. "What's wrong with that?"

"Nothing at all, but she added a P.S. She wants me to call her tonight to let her know how our premiere went—that's what she called it, a premiere—and to discuss a small matter of business."

"What sort of business?" Andrew asked.

Sylvia flipped the card over, but Julia had not elaborated on the back. "She doesn't say."

"Maybe she wants to buy apples for an upcoming red-carpet event," Matt joked, but there was a hopeful look in his eye. "We could ship to Hollywood."

"If she wanted to buy apples, I think she would have said so. It's more likely to be something quilt related." Sylvia slipped the card back into the envelope and creased the flap shut for emphasis. "I'll find out soon enough. Matt, please carry on."

Matt nodded. "Just a few more things," he promised.

Sylvia sipped her coffee and followed along, but Julia's note remained a distraction no matter how firmly she tried to forget it. She tucked it into her pocket, and that helped a bit—out of sight and almost but not quite out of mind.

Matt had just finished his checklist and Sylvia was carrying her breakfast dishes to the dishwasher when they heard the back door open and someone, or several someones, enter.

"Another bouquet?" said Andrew, surprised.

"Early orchard customers?" Matt wondered aloud.

Joe shook his head. "Not if my road sign did its job."

"Customers would knock," said Gretchen. "So would a florist."

"Good morning," Agnes sang out, her blue eyes merry behind her pink-tinted glasses as she led Summer, Gwen, and Anna into the kitchen. Anna and Summer both carried large white bakery boxes that almost certainly contained something delicious. "Happy grand opening day!"

"Thank you, dear. We intend to make it so," said Sylvia, smiling. "Have you come to pick apples?"

"We came to help, of course," said Summer, setting her pair of boxes on the refectory table. "Diane would have come too, but she said something came up at the last minute."

"We brought along a little treat to inspire you." Anna smiled indulgently as Joe lifted the lid of the nearest bakery box and peeked inside. "Help yourself, everyone."

"*Little* treat, indeed," said Gwen, heading for the coffeepot. "You're looking at twelve dozen homemade apple cider doughnuts, made from scratch in my sadly underused kitchen by our own Chef Anna."

"Doughnut!" James cried, scrambling down from Sarah's lap and racing toward the boxes. In two strides Matt caught him and swept him up in his arms, mere moments before the toddler might have pulled one of the boxes off the table, spilling the precious contents all over himself and the floor.

"The twins can split one doughnut," Sarah told Matt firmly. "Better yet, I'll have half, and they can split the other half."

"Do I have to split one with someone?" asked Joe, admiring the neat rows of golden-brown, cinnamon-sugar-sprinkled treats nestled within the box he had opened.

"Anyone over the age of ten may have a whole doughnut," Agnes proposed. "Anyone over the age of eighty may have two."

"Hear, hear!" said Sylvia, the only one among them who qualified for the latter.

"We'll probably work up our appetites today, but this is still a lot of doughnuts for our little group," Gretchen noted.

"Eight per person minus one for the twins sounds about right to me," remarked Gwen, taking a napkin from the basket on the counter and deftly plucking a doughnut from the box with it.

"They're not all for us," said Anna, laughing. "I thought we could offer them at the market stand, one free doughnut for each of our first one hundred customers."

"Do you really think we'll have so many?" asked Agnes, a bit anxiously.

"I'm sure we will," said Andrew stoutly.

"Of course. I didn't mean to suggest we wouldn't," said Agnes quickly, with an apologetic smile for Matt.

Matt took her unintentional gaffe in stride. "An hour ago I was hoping for twice that many customers," he said, shrugging. "Now, if they don't show, we can console ourselves with delicious leftover doughnuts. Either way, we win."

"I can always make more doughnuts," Anna reminded him. "Keep hoping for huge crowds. That's what I'm doing."

"Fingers crossed," said Sarah cheerfully, brushing cinnamon sugar from her daughter's chin.

Sylvia was too full from breakfast to manage more than a nibble from Andrew's doughnut, but that yummy morsel inspired her to wrap a whole one in a napkin and tuck it in the breadbox to enjoy later. Then, with little more than ninety minutes to go before Elm Creek Orchards opened to the public, everyone set off to their assigned tasks, with Matt quickly directing their unexpected extra helpers wherever they were needed most. Summer traded places with her mother so she could assist Sylvia with arranging the red wagons near the market stand. It wasn't long before Sylvia found out why.

"Chain of Progress will be ready to display as soon as I finish writing the object label," said Summer as they left the kitchen at the tail end of the group and headed into the rear foyer. "I've written a draft, but somehow it doesn't feel complete."

"Oh? What do you suppose is missing?"

"For one thing, the controversy surrounding the grand prize winner is so intriguing that I'd love to include that as well." Summer shook her head, bemused. "You know, considering how many quilters entered the contest, it's mindboggling to me that the woman who claimed the grand prize didn't put a single stitch into the quilt submitted in her name."

"It seems too strange to be true, doesn't it?" said Sylvia, following her young friend outside. "The truth didn't come out to the wider quilting world until the nineteen eighties, after some diligent quilt historians researched the story. At the time of the contest, the press proclaimed Margaret Caden to be 'America's Greatest Quilter,' but everyone in her hometown of Lexington, Kentucky, was well aware that she didn't know which end of a needle to thread."

Summer fell in step beside Sylvia as they crossed the parking lot. "She didn't sew, but she owned a quilt shop, right? I'm sure I read that in one of your news clippings."

"It was a high-end gift shop, not a quilt shop, although Margaret and her sisters did sell handmade quilts, fabrics, and patterns. They also quilted their customer's tops and made custom quilts." Sylvia gave her head a brisk shake. "I don't mean that they did the sewing and quilting themselves. Margaret took the orders and delegated the work to seamstresses for hire. These were usually rural women whose farms were struggling or whose husbands had lost their jobs in the Great Depression. They took in sewing to make ends meet."

"Do you think that's the method Margaret Caden used to create Unknown Star?"

"Oh, certainly. It's well documented that she sent the fabric and pattern to one woman, who pieced the top. Others added the beautiful stuffed work and that exquisite, sixteen-stitches-to-the-inch quilting. She paid each of the quilters-for-hire a modest fee for their labor as she always did, no more than a few dollars apiece. Shamefully, she refused to share any of the prize money with them after she won."

"That's the part I just don't get," said Summer as they crossed the bridge over Elm Creek. "The Caden family was quite wealthy, and the quilters-for-hire were poor. The grand prize was an enormous sum in those days, so there was more than enough to go around. Margaret got all the fame and glory. Why not reward the people who actually did all the work?"

"I suppose she figured she'd paid them the wages they'd agreed upon, and her obligation to them ended there." Sylvia tsked disapprovingly. "I'll never understand why she wasn't more generous. Then again, from what I've read, she was a hard, no-nonsense woman, gracious to her customers among the elite, tightfisted and curt with the help, intimidating to those less fortunate than herself."

"Charming."

"Hardly."

"Still, you'd think she would have wanted to stay in the quilters' good graces," said Summer. "Any one of them could have come forward and confessed the truth to the contest officials at Sears, or to the press. I can't imagine Margaret would want anyone to know that although she signed the entry form declaring that the quilt was entirely of her own making, her only contribution was the design and the materials."

"But the quilters couldn't have come forward, could they? Not if they wanted to keep working for the Caden family. They couldn't afford to offend Margaret and lose their livelihoods. They had little choice but to let her take credit for their lovely handiwork, keep their complaints to themselves, and be content with the little pay they did receive. I'm sure they also thought no one would take the word of a few poor women from the countryside over that of the respectable, dignified Miss Margaret Caden."

"That's so unfair."

"Indeed it is." They had reached the other side of the bridge, where Sylvia paused to think. "Years later, when they no longer feared retaliation, some of the women who had worked on Unknown Star did come forward and tell their stories to the quilt historians, who in turn shared what they had learned in their research papers and books. Sometimes the quilters' children or grandchildren were the ones who spoke up, offering their own memories of those months when their mothers or grandmothers or aunties toiled so diligently and created such beauty. However, even if the quilters had come forward soon after Unknown Star won the grand prize, I don't think it would have mattered to the judges or to the general public."

"Really? Why not?"

"Because then, as now, quilting was often a communal pastime. It was quite common for one or more people to make a top and then pass it along to someone else to quilt and bind. Usually whoever designed and made the top, or made the top from a commercial pattern, was considered to be the quilt's creator." With a shrug and a smile, Sylvia resumed walking toward the red barn. "If you ask me, the rule that an entrant's quilt must be entirely of her own making wasn't taken very seriously in the Century of Progress contest. It revealed a certain lack of familiarity with quiltmaking traditions and customs on the part of the rule writer."

Summer gave her a sidelong look, a smile playing on her lips. "You and your sister certainly thought so."

"And yet we were anxious enough to sign the entry form with a silly alias."

"Still, even if it *was* acceptable for Margaret Caden to claim credit as the quiltmaker because she designed the quilt and selected the fabrics herself, I still say she was out of line not to share the prize money with the women who actually made it."

"I couldn't agree more," said Sylvia emphatically. "She and her sisters continued to profit from their success after the contest too. Within a few months they were selling patterns for it both in their shop and through mail-order. Although they changed the quilt's name from the rather dull 'Unknown Star' to the more evocative 'Star of the Bluegrass,' they took care to identify it as the grand prize winner from the Sears Century of Progress contest."

"And as if ribbons, prize money, and sales profits weren't enough," Summer remarked, "she also had the honor of having her quilt presented as a gift to First Lady Eleanor Roosevelt."

"Oh, but Margaret didn't consider that an honor at all," Sylvia exclaimed. "According to a family member who was interviewed years later—Margaret's nephew's wife, or some such—Margaret didn't like Eleanor Roosevelt. She was very displeased when executives from Sears presented Unknown Star to Mrs. Roosevelt at the White House."

"But she knew all along that the grand prize quilt would be given to the First Lady," said Summer, incredulous. "Everyone knew. It was in the official rules."

"Maybe Margaret didn't think she would take first place and she wouldn't have to worry about it. In any case, eventually she commissioned an identical quilt to replace the one she had been obliged to give away."

They had reached the red barn, but Summer paused at the entrance and regarded Sylvia curiously. "And no one today knows what became of the original Unknown Star?"

Sylvia shook her head. "Apparently not. Mrs. Roosevelt might have taken it with her when she left the White House, or perhaps she gave it away. Maybe it suffered the fate of many a quilt and was worn threadbare over the years, until it was eventually used for rags or discarded."

"As a historian and an archivist, I find it unbearably frustrating that no one kept a record of it. Laws about presidential gifts weren't established until the nineteen sixties, but this was a very significant quilt. It was the grand prize winner of the largest quilt competition in history. How do you lose track of something like that?"

Sylvia spread her hands and shrugged. "I don't know, dear. Unfortunately, to many people, a quilt is just a very nice blanket."

Summer groaned. "Shame on them."

"Indeed." Sylvia sighed. "Maybe the quilt will turn up someday. Maybe you'll be the one to find it, and you can display it in your exhibit at Union Hall."

"I'd love to find it, but it wouldn't belong in my exhibit."

"Oh, yes, of course. Local history only." Sylvia gestured for Summer to proceed her into the barn. "Has this helped, dear? With writing your object label, I mean."

"Definitely. I should be able to finish it tonight. Would you like to come by Union Hall tomorrow and see Chain of Progress in the gallery?"

"I'd love to." Sylvia followed her younger friend to the fleet of little red wagons lined up along the wall just inside the door. "It will have to be after Elm Creek Orchards closes for the day, however. In fact, it might be better to wait until Monday. It's likely I'll be needed here to help out throughout the weekend."

Summer grasped one wagon handle in each hand, her expression suddenly pensive. "Do you really think so? Will the orchard bring in that many customers?"

So much depended upon the success of Elm Creek Orchards that Sylvia had to believe it. "I hope so," she replied honestly. "I don't know what more we could have done to ensure its success. But success doesn't always come quickly. It's possible we might get off to a slow start this weekend, and we need weekends without rain so that people will come pick. But with any luck, word of mouth will spread, and we'll see more customers every weekend after that."

"Who knows?" said Summer as they pulled the rattling wagons behind them from the barn to the road and on to the new parking lot. "By the end of the harvest season, Elm Creek Orchards could be the biggest thing in Waterford since—well, since Elm Creek Quilts."

"We'll find out soon," Sylvia replied, smiling to conceal the sudden nervous flutter in her stomach.

The hour swiftly passed as Sylvia and Summer made several round trips from the barn to the market stand, where they lined up the wagons, fully repaired and freshly painted and gleaming in the sunshine. Meanwhile, their friends were bustling about too, calling out encouragement to one another, trading jokes to conceal their apprehension. It was entirely possible that they would see only a handful of apple pickers that day, or none at all. But Sylvia resolved not to worry. If they had a disappointing launch, they would gather around the refectory table, figure out what went wrong, and come up with a new plan. Sometimes progress was two steps forward, one step back. Together they would find their way ever forward.

Sylvia was in the market stand helping Anna arrange the first box of doughnuts on the counter facing the parking lot when she heard a car's horn honking in the distance. "What on earth?" she murmured, gazing toward the woods, where the road disappeared into the shade of the trees. Suddenly a car emerged—Diane's car, she realized a moment later. It was followed by another, and then two more, and then a veritable parade.

"Places, everyone," Matt called, picking up James just as the boy made a run for it toward the nearest apple tree.

"On it," said Sarah, taking Caroline with her to her station beside the large sign explaining the orchard's policies, ready to offer help to anyone with questions.

"We still have ten minutes until we open," Gretchen exclaimed, scrambling to join Sylvia in the market stand.

"Those two dozen cars filling the parking lot say otherwise," Gwen called back, grinning. "Make that three dozen."

Soon at least half of the parking lot was filled. Women, couples, and families with small children piled out of them and made their way up the hill to the market stand, Diane in the lead. "I brought my book club," she called out, waving merrily, oversized sunglasses and blond curls giving her the air of a movie star on a country vacation, a pose worthy of Julia Merchaud herself. "And most of the Waterford Quilting Guild, and a few other friends."

"A few?" Sarah teased, shifting Caroline to her other hip.

"You heard me." Diane paused to glance behind her to the crowd now streaming up the hill. "Actually, I don't know most of these people. They must have seen the ads or heard about it from friends."

Sylvia's spirits soared. "Whatever or whoever brought them, they're all very welcome."

Gwen tossed Diane an apron, which she deftly caught with one hand. "Are you just going to stand around looking pleased with yourself or are you going to pitch in?"

"I can do both," Diane said airily, tying on the apron. "Can I work the cash register?"

"Be my guest," said Matt, looking rather dazed as he watched the rapidly filling parking lot. "I think I might need to go manage the traffic flow." Passing James to Andrew, he hurried down the hill.

"We aren't going to have enough doughnuts," Anna predicted, chagrined, as they began welcoming customers and distributing bags for them to fill.

"That's all right, dear," Sylvia assured her, very glad indeed that she had set a doughnut aside for herself earlier. "I'm more concerned that we might not have enough apples!"

As eager customers passed between them, bags in hand and questions newly answered, Sylvia caught Sarah's eye, and they shared a smile—joyful, relieved, and full of anticipation for all that the day would bring.

16

July–December 1933

Sylvia visited the Sears Pavilion twice more during the four days her family spent at the World's Fair. Her father and brother joined her and Claudia on their second tour. "Your quilt is nicer than any of those," Richard told his sisters afterward, ever loyal.

"If we'd made it through the regionals," Claudia replied forlornly, "I think we would have placed in the top three."

Sylvia shot her sister a sidelong glance, enough to see that she was serious. "I'm not so sure," Sylvia said, though she smiled at Richard to thank him for the praise. "The competition looks pretty fierce to me."

"We'll never know, will we?" Claudia sighed dramatically. "I only wish I knew what the regional judges didn't like about our quilt."

"I'm sure they liked it," said Sylvia quickly. "They just liked other quilts more."

"Yes, but why?"

Sylvia shrugged and turned to Richard, eager to change the subject. "Where to next?"

His face lit up. "Adler Planetarium," he declared, seizing her hand

and pulling her after him at a trot. She was more than willing to leave Claudia's uncomfortable questions behind.

On their last day in Chicago, Sylvia ventured once more to the gallery, alone, while the rest of her family explored the Homes of Tomorrow exhibit. This time she lingered in front of her favorite quilts as long as she wished, studying fine details she had missed before, learning all she could from one quilter's intriguing artistic choices and another's expert technique.

In the end, although the grand prize winner was still not her favorite quilt among the finalists—Louisiana Rose had fended off several impressive challengers to retain that status—she understood better why Unknown Star had so enchanted the judges. Although the pieced design was rather ordinary, the quilting was flawless, a uniform sixteen-stitches-per-inch over the entire surface, and the exquisite stuffed work distinguished it from all other contenders. What she still didn't understand was why more Century of Progress theme quilts had not qualified for the finals. If it were up to her, the two-hundred-dollar bonus would have been awarded to the best theme quilt regardless of whether it had claimed the grand prize, if only to recognize the extraordinary artistic effort that went into the creation of each one.

As she left the Sears Pavilion, Sylvia found herself unexpectedly at peace with the regional judges' decision not to send Chain of Progress on to the finals. Although it truly was the finest quilt either Sylvia or Claudia had ever made, she had to admit that it wasn't the equal of the quilts she had admired that week. Someday, Sylvia vowed, she too would make masterpieces deserving of national recognition, but she wasn't there yet. She had much to learn before she could be considered a master quilter.

Later that evening, she and her family strolled along the boardwalk enjoying the splendid view of Lake Michigan as they awaited the glorious illumination of the fairgrounds at dusk. Sylvia's father offered to buy each of them a souvenir of their choice, something special to take home as a memento of their grand adventure. Richard chose a model train, a replica of the colossal Burlington Engine No. 3000, one of three railroad cars on display outside the Travel and Transport Building. Claudia selected a lovely blue-and-white silk scarf from the Japanese Pavilion, a scatter print decorated with an artistic interpretation of the star Arcturus, encircled by a border of concentric fine lines in different shades of blue.

"What would you like, Sylvia?" her father prompted as they left the Japanese Pavilion with Claudia's scarf folded neatly in a flat, rectangular box fastened with an artfully tied silk ribbon.

Sylvia knew exactly what she wanted. Two days before, when her family toured the Electrical Building, she had observed a demonstration of an ingenious new sewing machine called the Singer Featherweight 221. The small, gleaming black device was fully electric powered, sparing the sewist the fatigue of working the treadle with her foot. Unlike older electric models, which were made of heavy cast iron or steel, this new version was fashioned from aluminum, weighing in at only slightly more than eleven pounds. It was also fully portable, not mounted in a cabinet but stored in a cunning black carrying case no bigger than a hatbox, with compartments for the power cord and various useful attachments sold separately. The Featherweight 221 sewed like a dream, producing a flawless straight stitch in a fraction of the time it would take even an accomplished seamstress to sew by hand. In honor of its debut at the World's Fair, each Featherweight on sale at the Singer Manufacturing exhibit was adorned with a striking red-and-gold oval commemorative badge on the uprise. The center emblem, in brass, was two crossed needles set upon a stylized S resembling a curved strand of thread, with a curved floral plume below and the phrase "The Singer Manfg. Co." in an arc above. Framing the emblem was a border of ruby red bearing in brass lettering the slogan "A Century of Progress Chicago 1933."

Sylvia could not imagine a more wonderful souvenir of the World's Fair—unique, beautiful, and useful—if not for the jaw-dropping price of $125. She could buy a hundred silk scarves like Claudia's for that, or several entire model train sets for Richard. Asking her father for one was simply out of the question, especially considering how much he had already spent on their marvelous adventure. And the more Sylvia *did* consider how much he'd likely spent, the less she wanted him to spend another penny.

"I can't think of anything I really want," she told him, scrunching up her face and shrugging helplessly. "I already have the mementos that will best help me remember the fair—the maps, brochures, tickets, programs, all the things I've been collecting this week."

Her father regarded her, curious. "Are you sure, Sylvia?"

She nodded vigorously. "I'm sure." From behind their father's back, Claudia caught her eye and glared, but Sylvia pretended not to notice. No doubt Claudia would have forgone a souvenir too, if she'd known Sylvia was going to be so sensible and frugal, but Sylvia hadn't known either until the moment arrived. She certainly hadn't done it to make Claudia look bad.

She could only hope that Claudia figured that out for herself when her temper cooled.

Richard too was unhappy that Sylvia hadn't chosen a souvenir, but for entirely different reasons. "It's not fair that we got presents and you didn't," he fretted on more than one occasion as they enjoyed their last hours of the fair, and as they made their way to the train station the next morning. "Even our cousins are getting the postcards and photo booklets we picked out for them, but you won't have anything special to remember our trip by."

"I don't need anything more," Sylvia assured him as they settled into their train car. "I couldn't forget this week if I tried. It's all been so wonderful."

Richard pulled a face, clearly skeptical that a collection of papers every fairgoer could take home for free would suffice as a souvenir. Sylvia laughed, ruffled his hair, and settled back to gaze out the window at the passing scenery as the train left Chicago behind.

Back home once again, Sylvia, Claudia, and Richard enthralled their cousins and charmed their aunties with tales of their adventures at the World's Fair. Great-Aunt Lucinda prompted both sisters for more details about the prizewinning quilts, while Great-Aunt Lydia was more curious about the new Featherweight 221. She seemed tempted, but in the end, frugality won out. "That's too much to spend when I have a perfectly good sewing machine already," she said, dismissing the notion with a wave of her hand.

Sylvia nodded agreement, relieved that she had known better than to ask her father for such an expensive gift.

As the days passed, Sylvia realized she truly had chosen the very best souvenirs to capture all that she had seen and done at the World's Fair. Her only regret was that she hadn't collected more of the bookmarks, flyers, and postcards the various exhibitors had offered free of charge to everyone.

It was a few weeks later when she suddenly realized that she'd already saved other keepsakes she could add to her collection. Swiftly, before anything could be inadvertently tossed out, she swept through the manor gathering up other ephemera—the pamphlet Aunt Nellie and Uncle William had brought home from the Harrisburg Sears listing the official rules, her final quilt sketches, the full-page announcement of the contest from the January Sears catalog, and several newspaper clippings about the contest and the fair she had saved over the previous few months.

One afternoon, she was sitting on the nursery floor admiring her collection when Claudia entered. Her sister took a long look at the various items spread out in a semicircle around her and the crumpled paper bag in which Sylvia stored them, an eyebrow quirked in mild disapproval. Claudia left the room without a word, only to return soon thereafter carrying something behind her back. "Your collection has outgrown that old bag," she said, revealing a flat pasteboard box, which she handed to Sylvia. "You're welcome to use this instead."

When Sylvia glanced at the lid, she recognized the elegant embossed emblem of the Japanese Pavilion and knew it was the same box that had held Claudia's souvenir silk scarf. "Thank you," she said, surprised and touched. It would have been greedy to ask for the silk ribbon that had once tied the box closed, so she didn't. "This will be perfect."

"When we receive the judges' comments from Philadelphia, you can keep that in the box too." Claudia sighed and rolled her eyes. "*If* we ever receive their comments."

Sylvia busied herself with gathering up her souvenirs and placing them neatly in the box. "Does it really matter at this point?"

"Of course it matters. I'd like to know just how close we came to making it to the finals."

"I don't think the judges' comments would tell us that. They'd only tell us what we did wrong, not how we ranked overall." Sylvia placed the lid on top and scrambled to her feet, the box clasped to her chest. "Anyway, whether we came in fourth place or fortieth, it's probably better not to know."

Claudia wrinkled her nose. "How would it be better?"

"Because it doesn't matter," Sylvia exclaimed. "Who cares what the judges thought? There's nothing we can do to change their minds now. We did our best and we took first at the local level, and we should just be happy with that."

"I am happy with that." Claudia regarded her, bewildered. "You don't have to get so excited. I'm sorry I brought it up."

But Claudia wasn't sorry enough to *stop* bringing it up. Whenever she came upon Sylvia perusing her collection, she would admire the souvenirs for a moment and then, invariably, she would wonder aloud why they had never heard anything from the regional judges. "Maybe a letter was in the delivery carton with the quilt and we accidently threw it out along with the wrapping," she mused one day in late September.

"That could be," Sylvia replied, knowing very well that it wasn't.

"Maybe it was lost in the mail," Claudia said one rainy afternoon in mid-October. "Maybe we should write to the Philadelphia Sears and ask if they kept a record of our scores and the judges' remarks."

"I wouldn't bother," said Sylvia, fighting to hide a pang of worry. "They probably threw out all that paperwork long ago. But if you want *me* to tell you how you could improve—"

"No thanks," Claudia said sharply, and Sylvia breathed more easily, relieved—until the next time a glimpse of her box of souvenirs reminded Claudia anew of the mysteriously absent scoresheet.

Eventually Sylvia so dreaded prompting her sister's memory that she began keeping the pasteboard box out of sight, admiring her collection only when her sister wasn't around. One day in mid-November, she was surreptitiously sorting through the box in the library near the fireplace when her father entered, carrying something beneath his arm. She had jumped at the sound of the door and had swiftly begun gathering her souvenirs together, but she heaved a sigh when she realized her father was alone.

"There you are," her father said when he spotted her. "Aunt Lucinda said you might be up here."

"I finished my homework already," she assured him, continuing to gather up her souvenirs, although in a less panicky fashion than before.

He nodded absently as he approached, which told her that wasn't why he was looking for her. "Have you added anything new to your collection lately?"

"No, not since that newspaper clipping cousin Elizabeth sent from California." Sylvia offered him a quick, rueful smile as she placed the lid on the box. Or rather, she tried to. The box wasn't very deep, and it was so full that the lid didn't really close, but merely balanced upon the items inside. "I don't think I'll find much more to add after this. The contest hasn't been in the news much since the World's Fair closed."

"I suppose that was bound to happen," her father said. "Maybe that's just as well. From the look of it, your collection has outgrown that box. Perhaps you need a more suitable chest for your treasures."

With that, he smiled and passed her the object he was carrying beneath his arm. It was a lovely engraved tin box, lightweight and spacious enough to hold all her treasures, with a snug-fitting lid to keep them safe.

"For me?" asked Sylvia, dumbfounded, turning it over in her hands, admiring it from every angle. "Where did you find such a pretty thing?"

"A grocer from Woodfall traded it to me for a peck of our apples." Her father gestured, smiling. "Go on. See if everything fits."

Eagerly she carried both boxes to the coffee table and quickly transferred her mementos from the pasteboard box to the tin. Everything fit neatly inside, with room to spare. "It's perfect," Sylvia declared, leaping up to fling her arms around her father. "Thank you so much."

"Of course," he said warmly, laughing a bit from surprise as he returned her hug and kissed her on top of the head. "It's not much. It's just tin, you know. It isn't silver."

"I don't care. It's perfect. It's exactly what I wanted and I didn't even know it until I saw it." Sylvia returned to the table to pick up the tin box and hold it close. "Does that make sense?"

"Perfect sense. Sometimes I feel that way about things too."

"But sometimes there are things I've wanted so much for so long that I can't remember ever *not* wanting them, things like—" Abruptly Sylvia halted, biting her lips together before she said too much.

"Go on," her father prompted, peering at her quizzically. "What do you want, Sylvia?"

She shook her head fiercely and looked away, ashamed of the heat she felt rising in her cheeks. "It doesn't matter."

"It looks like it matters to you very much." He sat down on the sofa and patted the cushion beside him. "Come here. Have a seat."

Reluctantly, Sylvia sat beside him, fixing her gaze straight ahead and clutching the tin box on her lap.

"Sylvia," her father said gently. "What is it you want?"

She inhaled deeply, bowed her head, and murmured, "I think you'll be mad."

"I see. Then you must be referring to that little Featherlight sewing machine we saw at the fair."

She was so surprised that she whirled to face him. "No, not that! Although it's true I *would* want one if it wasn't so expensive. And it's called a Featherweight, not Featherlight."

"Featherweight. Of course." He put his head to one side and held her gaze. "If not that, then what? You can tell me. I promise I won't be angry."

Before she could think better of it, Sylvia blurted, "I want to run Bergstrom Thoroughbreds with you and Uncle William someday. I was hoping to take over for you when you retire like you took over for Grandpa David. But you're turning everything over to Richard, and I think that's only because he's a boy, and that's not fair."

Her father's brow furrowed as she spoke, and he looked deeply bewildered. "Why would you assume I intend to turn everything over to Richard?"

"Because of what you said when he wanted to go with us to the Harrisburg Sears to see the quilts." When her father shook his head, uncomprehending, she added in a rush, "You said he needed to get a good education if he wanted to run Bergstrom Thoroughbreds someday."

"I see." Her father sat back and ran a hand through his hair. "And you've been feeling awful about that ever since?"

Sylvia pressed her lips together and nodded, afraid that if she tried to speak, a sob would come out instead.

"Oh, Sylvia." Her father sighed, put an arm around her shoulders, and pulled her close in a hug. "I never meant that Richard would run the business alone. Of course you'll all have an equal share, you and your siblings and any of your cousins who want to play a part."

She felt tears of relief gathering. "Really?"

"Yes, really. I thought you understood that. Why else would I be teaching you everything I know about how to care for the horses and how to manage the business?"

She thought for a moment. "I don't know," she said in a small voice.

"Well, I'll tell you why. I wanted you to be able to run Bergstrom Thoroughbreds when you grow up—as long as that's what you want to do."

She seized one of his hands in both of hers and squeezed it. "It *is* what I want to do."

"You don't have to decide now—"

"Yes, I do. I mean, I already did. Years ago, when I was still little."

He laughed softly and ruffled her hair. "Let's see how you feel when you finish school. The whole world will be open to you then. You can be anything you want to be."

"I already know," she insisted. "I want to run Bergstrom Thoroughbreds and I want to be a master quilter. I can do both."

"I'm sure you can," he said. "But you're still young, honey. You might decide to marry, and you might move away to follow your husband wherever his profession takes him."

Sylvia shook her head fiercely. "I could never fall in love with anyone who doesn't love horses. When I marry, *if* I marry, my husband would have to live with me here at Elm Creek Manor and help me and Richard run Bergstrom Thoroughbreds."

A smile quirked in the corners of her father's mouth. "I see. And if this hypothetical husband doesn't agree to this arrangement?"

"Then I wouldn't marry him."

Her father's laughter rang out, warm and clear. "All right, then. Just be sure to give the poor fellow fair warning ahead of time. But you said he would help *you and Richard* run the business. What about Claudia?"

"I don't think she'll want to," said Sylvia frankly. "She's afraid of horses. Maybe she'll be the one to get married and move away with her husband."

"Fair enough, but what if she wants to stay here at Elm Creek Manor?"

Sylvia mulled it over. "She can be in charge of the orchards. The orchards are her very favorite part of the estate—besides the manor, of course."

"Of course," her father echoed. "Well, this sounds like a fine plan. We'll see how you feel about it in a few years, and how your siblings and cousins feel. They'll have a say in the future of Bergstrom Thoroughbreds too, if they want it. There will always be a place at Elm Creek Manor for any Bergstrom who calls it home."

"Really? Always?"

"Always. I promise."

Weeks passed. Sylvia kept the precious tin box on a shelf in her wardrobe, out of her sister's sight. Most days she remembered to check the *Waterford Register* for news of the contest, but by early December, when she realized that she hadn't seen anything in ages, she ruefully concluded that there weren't likely to be any more articles. Her collection was complete, and she was content.

Then, a few days after Christmas, Claudia came running into

the west sitting room where Sylvia was sketching blocks for a new quilt. "Did you see this?" she exclaimed, brandishing the newspaper, which Sylvia had ignored that morning in favor of a new novel she had received on Christmas morning.

"See what?" said Sylvia, setting her sketchpad and colored pencils aside. Bounding up from her chair, she craned her neck to see as Claudia folded the newspaper open to the proper page. She drew in a breath as her gaze fell upon the headline. "'Margaret Rogers Caden's Prize-Winning Quilt Is Presented to Wife of President,'" she read aloud. Below the headline was a photo of Eleanor Roosevelt holding an edge of Unknown Star. She was flanked by two men in dark suits, one of whom was holding another edge of the quilt. The First Lady's astute gaze was fixed upon the section of the quilt between her hands, and the camera seemed to have captured her in midsentence, as if she had been praising the excellent handiwork.

"Read the rest of it," Claudia urged, an edge to her voice.

Sylvia threw her a curious glance before she read on.

A tribute was paid to the needlework of Southern women by Mrs. Franklin D. Roosevelt when she complimented Margaret Rogers Caden, of Lexington, on the beauty of her hand-made quilt, which won first prize in the recent Century of Progress contest sponsored by Sears, Roebuck and Company.

The quilt, a variation of the eight-point star, was presented to Mrs. Roosevelt a few days before Christmas by representatives of the big merchandising firm. During the period of a Century of Progress it had been on display in the Sears building with prize winners from all sections of the country, many of them copies of priceless old heirlooms that have been preserved to this day.

The South, and Kentucky particularly, walked away with the lion's share of honors, including the $1,000 first prize and

several regional prizes. The ability of Southern women to
reconstruct the life of their ancestors in quaint little patches
and minute stitches—

"Quaint little patches?" Sylvia echoed.

"I knew you wouldn't like that part."

"And why are they only talking about Southern women? Women—
and girls—from all over the country participated."

"Your guess is as good as mine." Claudia tapped the page twice to
prompt Sylvia to continue reading.

—in quaint little patches and minute stitches was apparent
in almost every quilt submitted by this group. They ably
demonstrated the fact that in the midst of all that a century of
progress has changed, quiltmaking is one domestic craft that
has never been allowed to die.

"What?" Sylvia exclaimed, aghast. "'Allowed to die'? He sounds
disappointed! Why would anyone say such a thing?"

She didn't wait for her sister to prompt her but braced herself and
read on.

Twenty-five thousand women worked 5,600 hours to finish the
quilts entered in this $7,500 contest, and more than 500 judges
were required to pick the winners in the various districts.
Second prize of $500 went to Miss Mabel Langled of Dallas,
Texas, and the third award of $300 to Mrs. Freida V. Plume of
Evanston, Illinois.

Sylvia glanced up from the page, shaking her head. "The picture
is very nice, and some of the facts are interesting, but what was the
point of those mean little digs?"

Claudia shrugged and shook her head. "They don't give the reporter's name, but I bet this was written by a man who resented having to write about quilts instead of something like, I don't know, politics or business."

"If you ask me, if someone hates something simply for what it is, they shouldn't be allowed to review it for the newspaper." Sylvia studied the photo again. "I wonder why Mrs. Roosevelt is pictured with the two men from Sears instead of Mrs. Caden. Shouldn't the quiltmaker be in this photo?"

"Maybe the men didn't invite her along."

"Can you imagine taking first place in the biggest quilt competition ever, and then not even getting to go along when your quilt is presented to the First Lady at the White House?" Sylvia shook her head, incredulous. "I would've gone anyway. I would have walked right into that room and said, 'Good day, Mrs. Roosevelt. I'm the girl who made that lovely quilt you're holding. Please accept it with my compliments, and give my best to your husband, the president.'"

Claudia was smiling, but she was shaking her head too. "You can't just walk into the White House, not without an appointment."

"Well, I would've insisted that those fellows from Sears take me along."

"For all we know, they invited Mrs. Caden but she declined. Anyway, it's not the nicest article, so I guess you don't want it for your collection?"

"Are you joking? Of course I want it."

Sylvia darted back to her chair for her sewing scissors, and when Claudia handed her the newspaper with an amused smile, she carefully cut out the article—every line of it, even the annoying reference to the death of quilting.

Then, just as she was leaving to take the clipping upstairs to her room, Claudia remarked, "I bet the judges made sure Mrs. Caden received their comments about Unknown Star. As for the rest of us—"

"I'm so sick of hearing you go on and on about that," Sylvia exclaimed. "Maybe it was lost in the mail. Maybe they never sent it. What does it matter? Would you please just forget it?"

Claudia gaped at her. "Gosh, Sylvia, there's no need to shout. Sorry to bore you. I won't mention it again."

"Good," Sylvia snapped, stalking from the room.

She hurried upstairs to her bedroom, took the pretty tin box down from the top shelf in her wardrobe, and set the new article on top. As she replaced the lid, she realized that her sister would never stop wondering about the missing scoresheet as long as Sylvia's collection was there to remind her of it. Claudia never mused aloud about the contest when she wore the silk scarf she had brought home from the World's Fair. Yet something about Sylvia's souvenirs provoked her, time and again.

Sylvia wished she had never hidden the judges' comments. After the regionals, she had meant to spare her sister pain and embarrassment, but if their places had been reversed and Claudia had tried to keep the truth from *her*, Sylvia would have felt humiliated and furious. What Sylvia *should* have done was to warn Claudia to brace herself, and then she should have handed over the scoresheet and waited quietly while her sister read it. Afterward, if Claudia had been angry or sad or bewildered, Sylvia should have been there to listen, to comfort, and to reassure her. Later she could have offered to help Claudia improve her skills where the judges had found fault. If only Sylvia had done all that instead, Claudia would have gotten over the hurt by now, and she might even have learned something from the criticism that would have helped her improve her quilting.

When Sylvia had hidden the scoresheet months before, she had told herself that if she had second thoughts later, she could simply produce the letter and claim that it had only just arrived. But now that she *had* changed her mind, she felt trapped, powerless to undo her mistake. Claudia would want to see the envelope, and the absence of a postmark would immediately reveal that it had not come by mail. If Sylvia claimed she had thrown away the envelope, Claudia would likely search the rubbish bin for it, and when she didn't find it, she would know Sylvia was lying.

There was nothing Sylvia could do to fix her mistake. She didn't see any possible way to confess the truth without creating an enormous fuss, getting into trouble with her father and aunties, and making Claudia feel even worse about everything. Sylvia had decided to keep a secret from her sister, and now she had to *keep* keeping it, probably forever.

The sisters weren't supposed to enter each other's bedrooms without permission, but Sylvia granted Claudia entry often enough that Claudia was bound to glimpse the tin box from time to time, if the wardrobe door happened to be left ajar. That meant Sylvia couldn't keep her collection in her bedroom any longer.

She paced the length of her room, clutching the box, weighing her options. Eventually she stole down the hall and around the corner to a bedroom that had gone unused ever since her Great-Uncle George and his family had moved to Harrisburg years before. No one ever entered except during spring cleaning, and that was only to air out the room and dust the furniture, not to search bare shelves and peer inside empty drawers. Quietly, Sylvia eased the door shut behind her, crossed the room, and tucked the tin box into a high, narrow drawer of a large walnut bureau, which was empty except for a few mothballs and a single cotton handkerchief. Claudia would never stumble upon it there, but Sylvia could visit her collection any time she wanted.

She felt enormous relief as soon as she returned, unobserved, back to her room, but as the days passed, another worry began to nag at her. The judges' scoresheet still resided in the secret hiding place behind the loose baseboard in her bedroom. If Claudia or anyone else in the family happened to nudge it with a foot in precisely the wrong way, it would topple over, revealing everything concealed within the narrow space.

And so on another evening when she found herself alone, Sylvia retrieved the envelope from behind the baseboard and swiftly, silently carried it off to Great-Uncle George's old bedroom. Just as she was about to remove the tin box from its high, narrow drawer, she heard footsteps approaching. In a panic, she shoved the envelope to the far back of the drawer behind the box rather than tucking it inside with the rest of the collection. Without a sound, she slid the drawer closed, then ducked out of sight behind the bed until the footsteps passed. When she was as certain as she could be that no one lurked outside in the hallway, she eased the door open, darted glances to the left and the right, and fled back to her own room.

In the weeks that followed, she returned occasionally to peruse her collection of World's Fair souvenirs in solitude, but she never read the judges' comments again. The envelope was forced farther and farther back into the high narrow drawer every time she slid the tin box into its hiding space.

Eventually the weeks between visits became months, and then years.

Sometimes, for as long as Chain of Progress was displayed in the banquet hall, Sylvia would remember her box of souvenirs and make a mental note to go through it again, but she usually forgot before she got around to it. Years later, when the quilt was taken down so the banquet hall could be painted, and another, newer prizewinning quilt was hung in its place, Sylvia found herself unexpectedly relieved.

The World's Fair quilt that had once filled her with pride had become an uncomfortable reminder of a secret she never should have kept—and one she wished she could forget.

17

September 2004

The grand opening of Elm Creek Orchards succeeded beyond their most hopeful expectations—except for Matt's, perhaps, since he had anticipated success from the very beginning. As customers paid for their heavily packed bags of fragrant apples, many cheerfully promised to encourage their friends to visit soon. Others, studying the seasonal calendar Matt had posted on the market stand, were overheard planning to return to harvest other varieties when they ripened later that fall.

After their last customers departed—a full twenty minutes after closing time, they were so busy—Matt inspected the orchard while Sylvia and the rest of the crew restocked bags, put away the red wagons, and tidied up the market stall and the nearby grounds. When everything was in order, they returned to Elm Creek Manor for a delicious autumn pasta supper that Anna deftly threw together with two boxes of cavatappi from the back of the pantry, some leftover roasted vegetables, and a wedge of Pecorino Romano, a gift from a grateful camper whose family ran an Italian deli in Pittsburgh. Despite their fatigue, they were so pleased, relieved, and thankful for how the day had unfolded that they lingered at the table over empty plates, chatting and joking and wondering aloud about what tomorrow might bring.

It was only much later, after the dishes were cleared away and their visiting friends had departed, that Sylvia's gaze fell upon the beautiful bouquet on the table in the rear foyer. All at once she remembered that Julia Merchaud was expecting her to call.

"It might be too late to trouble her," Sylvia mused as she and Sarah finished tidying the kitchen. The sun had already set, and she was tempted to enjoy a soothing cup of herbal tea before turning in a bit early. She would need a good night's sleep if Elm Creek Orchards was even half as busy tomorrow as it had been on opening day.

"It's three hours earlier in California," Sarah reminded her as she set off to help Matt put the twins to bed. "Anyway, I think Julia would stay up late for you. She sounded eager to talk."

Sylvia could only imagine why. She didn't like the thought of making Julia wait by the phone, so she put on the kettle and fixed herself a cup of lemon ginger tea. As it steeped, she settled into her favorite booth with her teacup and the cordless phone and dialed Julia's number.

The actress herself answered on the second ring. "Sylvia, darling," Julia greeted her, her voice warm and mellifluous. "How was your grand premiere?"

"Very grand indeed," Sylvia replied, "as befitting that gorgeous bouquet you sent. Thank you, dear, on behalf of us all."

Sylvia proceeded to tell her about the day, and when she finished, Julia sighed wistfully. "I do wish I could have been there. You make it sound like such fun."

"Oh, it was, but it was hard work too."

"I don't doubt it for a moment. Unfortunately, I think the harvest will be over by the time I return to Elm Creek Manor."

"This year's harvest will be, but not to worry. The Zestar and

Ginger Gold will be ripe and ready for picking when you and the other Cross-Country Quilters arrive for your annual reunion next August."

"As a matter of fact," Julia remarked, teasing out the phrase to build anticipation, "I'm hoping to return much sooner than that."

"Oh?"

"Yes, which brings me to that small matter of business I wanted to discuss with you."

Sylvia sipped her tea and settled back against her seat. "Now you've piqued my curiosity. What can I do for you?"

"First, the good news. Filming will begin on the sixth season of *A Patchwork Life* early next year."

"Congratulations! That's very good news for all of us. Sarah, Gretchen, and I gather around the television in the parlor for a watch party every week without fail. We've very much enjoyed this season's episodes, especially the premiere."

"Thank you," Julia replied, clearly very pleased. "Actually, I directed that one."

"Well done, dear. And the bad news? It's hard to imagine how there can be any."

"If only that were true." Julia sighed, a comic lament. "The bad news is that many members of our cast and production crew need to refresh their quilting skills. We've also recently signed on new actors who have never quilted before, and they absolutely must learn before we begin filming."

Sylvia nodded to herself, fairly certain she knew where the conversation was going. "And you thought it would be wise to send them to quilt camp?"

"Yes, but I'm afraid we can't wait until your regular season. March would be too late for our production schedule. Our performers need to look like experts on-screen, and that means intensive training—and the sooner they begin learning, the better."

"But if March will be too late, how can Elm Creek Quilts help you?"

"As it happens, I've heard that you're considering expanding your camp season into the fall."

"Oh, you've heard that, have you?" said Sylvia, amused. "From Sarah or Summer, I assume. It's true we're considering it, but we haven't made a final decision. If we do move ahead, it wouldn't be until next season."

"I had something a bit earlier in mind. What would you say to a practice run in November—and yes, I do mean *this* November? I'm thinking twelve or so guests for a one-week stay. In the mornings, your teachers would offer classes in quilting fundamentals. The afternoons would be devoted to practice sessions, with an instructor or two on hand to offer assistance and advice. We'd want your usual fabulous meal service, of course, but you needn't arrange any evening programs. If we want entertainment, we can provide that for ourselves."

"My goodness," Sylvia murmured.

"So, what do you think?"

"I think—" Sylvia paused to take a deep, bracing drink of tea. "I think it all sounds . . . very intriguing."

"But doable, though? And maybe even fun?"

"Yes, indeed, but this is rather unexpected. I'd need to consult the other Elm Creek Quilters to make sure they'd be willing and able to participate."

"Sarah and Summer are already on board."

"Of course they are. If I didn't know better, I'd suspect this was all their idea, and you're only going along with it to send some work our way."

"Not at all. Summer *did* tell me about your financial difficulties, but I had already decided that quilting lessons for our cast and crew were long overdue. But while we're on the subject of finances, I should mention what our producer has budgeted for our quilt camp excursion."

Julia then blithely listed what they were prepared to pay for their week of quilt lessons, meals, and accommodations—a figure so stunning that Sylvia wondered if someone had mistakenly tacked an extra zero onto the end. It would entirely pay for the roof replacement, with enough left over to substantially replenish their emergency fund.

"I—I hardly know what to say," Sylvia stammered. "It's very generous of you—"

"It's not generosity. I'd expect to pay that price anywhere considering the services we require, but I'd much rather work with Elm Creek Quilts. You're the very best at what you do."

"Thank you. I'll be sure to pass along the compliment." Sylvia thought quickly. "As I said, I'll need to discuss it with the others—"

"Of course."

"But I'm sure we can accommodate your group."

"Excellent," Julia exclaimed. "When you're all set on your end, call me back and we'll discuss specific dates and whatever paperwork you need us to sign. I'd prefer to pay up front if that works for you, so we don't have to fuss with the studio's accounting department later."

"An up-front payment would work very well for us too," said Sylvia, through a catch in her throat. "I'm grateful, Julia. This truly is a windfall in our hour of need."

"No, it isn't," Julia countered cheerfully. "It's a job. I'm not mailing you a suitcase full of cash. Trust me, you and your staff are going to be earning every penny. I won't name names, but some of my colleagues are terribly clumsy with a needle."

"If you say so," said Sylvia, tears of joy in her eyes. "But thank you very much all the same."

They promised to speak again soon. After the call ended, Sylvia sat for a long moment in wonder, mulling over Julia's proposal.

Then she finished her tea in one gulp and hurried off to tell Sarah and Gretchen.

The next morning, Elm Creek Orchards welcomed even larger crowds than the previous day. The little red wagons were such a hit that Gretchen and Sylvia made plans to search garage sale listings for more. Much later, when they gathered around the kitchen table for a tasty supper of Anna's brown rice and lentil soup and apple cider bread, the Elm Creek Quilters discussed Julia's proposal and quickly agreed to accept. Even Maggie chimed in over the phone to say that she thought it was a wonderful idea, and if the cast and crew's visit coincided with a break in her touring schedule, she'd love to teach for them.

After the meal, everyone pitched in to make quick work of tidying up the kitchen. Summer and Gwen were the last to depart. "Are we still on for your gallery tour tomorrow?" Summer asked Sylvia as they were heading out the door.

"Oh, yes, I wouldn't miss it," Sylvia replied. "Matt has errands downtown, so he offered to drop me off at Union Hall at nine o'clock sharp."

"Your quilt fits in beautifully with the exhibit," Summer told her, smiling over her shoulder as she descended the back stairs to the parking lot. "I hope you'll be pleased."

"I'm sure I will be," Sylvia replied.

Later that evening, as she and Andrew were heading upstairs to bed, Sylvia found her thoughts turning nostalgic as she imagined her World's Fair quilt in the lovely new gallery at Union Hall, enjoying pride of place in an exhibit dedicated to artworks with a significant connection to local history. What would Claudia have thought if she could have seen Chain of Progress hanging there in the place of honor? She would have been excessively proud, no doubt. She would have preened with pleasure to observe passersby admiring their quilt and the two ribbons it had won. Any remarks she might have overheard would surely be thoughtful and flattering, unlike those the regional judges had—

Suddenly Sylvia gasped. "I know where it is! It was never lost. It's been there all this time."

Andrew glanced up from his seat on the edge of the bed. "What's been where?" he asked, removing his slippers and setting them on the floor. "What are we talking about?"

"The judges' scoresheet from the regional round of the Century of Progress Quilting Contest." Sylvia snatched up his slippers and held them out to him. "Come along, dear. I need your help. You're taller."

"I feel like I walked in on the middle of a conversation." Obligingly, Andrew put his slippers back on again, rose, and tightened the belt of his robe. "Where are we going?"

She took his hand and drew him after her into the hallway. "To the attic."

"The attic? Now?"

"No time like the present. Curiosity will keep me awake otherwise."

"Well, we can't have that," said Andrew good-naturedly as he followed her down the hall and up to the third floor. There he led the way up the narrow attic stairs so he could open the trapdoor and switch on the light for her. "This place is a pack rat's dream," he said, glancing around at the boxes and trunks and furniture. "It's going to take days to clear it all out before the roofers can get to work." He threw her a look of mild alarm. "Don't tell me you mean to get started tonight."

"Goodness, no." She made her way through the clutter to the walnut bureau, beckoning him to follow. "Tomorrow afternoon will be soon enough. For now, I'm only searching for one particular thing."

"And that is?"

Rising up on tiptoe, Sylvia opened the high, narrow drawer on the left and reached into it, but even though she stretched as far as she could, her fingertips touched nothing, not even the back of the drawer. "An envelope," she said, stepping aside, "but you're going to have to be the one to find it, if it's there. Would you, dear?"

Nodding, he took her place and reached into the narrow drawer. "Here's something," he said, brow furrowing thoughtfully. "It's stuck. It's wedged between the drawer and the back of the bureau." Working his arm back and forth, he gave the stubborn object one firm tug, and then another, and then it came free.

Sylvia held her breath as Andrew withdrew his arm from the bureau and revealed a creased, yellowing envelope in his grasp. "Oh, my word, that's it," she murmured. When he handed it to her, she removed the paper tucked inside, unfolded it, and strained to read the faded ink. Though the light was dim, she could make out enough to confirm that it was indeed the scoresheet from the regional round of the Century of Progress quilting contest, hidden so well so long ago that it had been lost even to herself.

A bit breathlessly, she explained to Andrew what the paper was, and why she had hidden it. "The judges' comments are even harsher than I remember," she said, shaking her head. "I was expecting quite the opposite. I thought perhaps I had overreacted all those years ago, that my dismay back then was simply a naive girl's misunderstanding of constructive criticism."

"Memory is funny that way." Andrew craned his neck to read along with her. "Wow. Those judges didn't pull any punches. Claudia would have taken this badly, not that I'd blame her. This might have convinced her to give up quilting altogether."

For a moment, Sylvia was too surprised to speak. "That never occurred to me," she replied when she found her voice again. "Do you really think so?"

Andrew shrugged. "Didn't you tell me she stopped making jam after she came in last place at the Elm Creek Valley Fair two years in a row?"

"Oh, my goodness. You're right." Sylvia pressed a hand to her chest and inhaled deeply. "What a shame it would have been if she had given up quilting. She would have missed out on something that offered her so much enjoyment and satisfaction through the years. And she did improve, with practice."

"Then it's just as well she didn't know what the judges said about her piecing."

"Maybe so." Sylvia paused to mull it over. "You know, I've always thought I was wrong to keep this from her. I feared I had denied her the opportunity to benefit from a professional critique. In her place, I would have wanted to know the truth, even if it was this bad. But now—" She shook her head, folded the paper, and returned it to the envelope. "Now I think . . . perhaps it wasn't such a terrible mistake after all."

"It definitely wasn't terrible," Andrew said earnestly, squeezing her shoulder gently. "Your intentions were good, and I've always believed that counts for something."

Sylvia placed her hand upon his and thanked him with a look that conveyed all she could not say.

On the way back to their bedroom, Sylvia and Andrew stopped by the library so she could leave the judges' scoresheet in the engraved tin box. That was where it belonged, among the other souvenirs that a certain young, ambitious quilter, optimistic about progress and her own future, had collected and cherished so long ago.

The next morning, when Matt dropped Sylvia off at Union Hall, Summer must have been watching from the window of the restoration and cleaning room, for she was right on time to open one of the tall front doors for Sylvia even as she was still climbing the limestone front stairs. "Welcome back," Summer called to her, smiling. "I just finished hanging the last item in the Chain of Progress display. You'll be the first to see it."

"The last item?" Sylvia echoed as she proceeded Summer inside into the elegant foyer. "You must mean the ribbons."

Summer shook her head and led Sylvia up the elegant curved staircase. "No, not the ribbons. Those went up on the first day, right after the quilt and the object label."

Sylvia paused, resting her hand on the cherrywood banister. "If not the ribbons, then what?"

Summer paused too, but only long enough to smile brightly at Sylvia over her shoulder. Then she continued up the stairs, and Sylvia, mystified, followed.

The doors to the bright spacious gallery were open when they arrived, but Sylvia spotted only one docent and a security guard inside. Glancing about, she gasped in recognition and pleasure when she spotted Chain of Progress on the long wall to her right. Summer had hung it next to another twentieth-century quilt Sylvia was particularly fond of, an exquisite, autumn-hued Cleopatra's Fan variation. It reproduced in exquisite piecing the beautiful mosaic tile of the historic First Bank of Waterford building, which had been razed in the 1970s to make way for condos. That was before the town's historic district had been established; such wasteful, tragic destruction would never happen in Waterford now.

Sylvia's breath caught in her throat as she approached her World's Fair quilt. She had seen it displayed in several remarkable settings—on a dais of honor at the Sears store in Harrisburg; among the finest regional submissions at the impressive Sears headquarters in Philadelphia; and in the banquet hall of Elm Creek Manor. This new display moved her as none other, for it not only recognized her and Claudia's achievements but also honored the quilt as a significant artifact of local history, deserving inclusion among other beautiful historic and artistic treasures.

Sylvia wished with all her heart that Claudia were there to see it too.

Her gaze traveled over the surface of the quilt, which Summer and her colleagues had restored to exemplary condition. Then she turned to the object label, which hung in a lovely wooden frame Joe had made, and to the two ribbons beside it. Yet as Sylvia drew closer to read the description Summer had written, she stopped short at the sight of another framed document above the ribbons. It was a photo reproduction of a newspaper article, two columns of text beneath a photo, and if she was not mistaken, the two familiar teenage girls pictured could only be—

"Oh, my goodness," she breathed.

The masthead revealed that the article was from the May 25, 1933, edition of the *Harrisburg Telegraph*, written by Carl Higgins. "Waterford Sisters Take First in Sears Quilt Contest" the headline announced.

Sylvia read the first paragraph, enough to confirm that it was indeed the article she and Claudia had so eagerly anticipated but had never seen. She turned to Summer in wonder. "Where in the world did you find this?"

"In the archives of the Waterford College Library," Summer said. "I didn't find anything in the *Waterford Register*, but when I searched the Harrisburg newspapers, there it was. Are you surprised?"

"Surprised? I'm absolutely—" At a loss for words, Sylvia shook her head and turned back to the article. "I'm flabbergasted. Astounded. Oh, we *did* make the newspaper after all! Claudia would have been so thrilled, and so proud."

"And rightly so," Summer said, her eyes warm with affection and shared happiness. "When I first asked you if I could display your World's Fair quilt in this exhibit, you almost declined because you didn't think it was significant to local history. You said that your 'small success didn't even merit a few lines in the Waterford newspaper.' Remember?"

Sylvia did, vaguely. "That sounds like something I might have said at the time."

Summer laughed. "You said it. I remember distinctly. You didn't believe me then, but with this evidence from the historical record—"

She gestured to the framed article. "*Now* are you convinced that your World's Fair quilt is important?"

"Absolutely," Sylvia assured her, smiling. "Well done, dear."

As Summer laughed and applauded in celebration, Sylvia turned back to the World's Fair quilt, her heart full. Indeed, Chain of Progress did belong in this exhibit among so many other historical treasures significant to local history, just as her enthusiastic young friend insisted. But more important yet was the role the quilt had played in her own history—hers, and her shared history with her sister.

Despite their squabbles and artistic disagreements as they had sketched and planned and sewed, their collaboration truly had marked a turning point in their relationship. They had learned to work together despite their differences, they had celebrated their achievements, and they had supported each other through disappointment. In the years that followed the Century of Progress Exposition, Sylvia and Claudia had quilted together often, making quilts for fundraisers and gifts and for no special reason at all, simply to create something beautiful that provided warmth and comfort in a world much in need of both.

For years Sylvia had focused so much on what had driven her and Claudia apart that she had not properly reflected upon all that had drawn them together. But as she admired their World's Fair quilt, so proudly and beautifully displayed in the Union Hall gallery, she felt her lingering bitterness and regret diminishing, replaced at long last by love, understanding, and forgiveness.

It was time to leave the heartache of the past behind, and to carry the best of her memories forward into a future bright with hope and promise, stitched together with compassion and bound in love.

ACKNOWLEDGMENTS

My sincere thanks to Maria Massie, Max Moorhead, Sophie Weiler, Rachel Kahan, Emi Battaglia, Martin Wilson, Deanna Bailey, Alexandra Bessette, Elsie Lyons, and everyone at William Morrow who contributed to *The World's Fair Quilt*. Geraldine Neidenbach, Marty Chiaverini, and Michael Chiaverini read multiple versions of the manuscript, and I appreciate the insightful comments and questions they offered. I'm grateful as well to Nick Chiaverini, whose wonderful instincts for storytelling helped me navigate through narrative tangles.

For readers who are interested in learning more about the Sears National Quilting Contest at the Century of Progress Exposition, I highly recommend *Patchwork Souvenirs of the 1933 World's Fair* by Merikay Waldvogel and Barbara Brackman, and *Soft Covers for Hard Times: Quiltmaking and the Great Depression* by Merikay Waldvogel. Please note that I disregarded historical accuracy by having Sylvia admire the Singer Featherweight 221 during her visit to the World's Fair in 1933. The Century of Progress commemorative edition did not debut until the exposition reopened in the summer of 1934.

Most of all, I thank my husband, Marty, and my sons, Nick and Michael, for their enduring love, steadfast support, and essential encouragement. I couldn't have completed this book without you. All my love, always.

ABOUT THE AUTHOR

Jennifer Chiaverini is the *New York Times* bestselling author of thirty-five novels, including critically acclaimed historical fiction and the beloved Elm Creek Quilts series. Her works of nonfiction include seven collections of quilt patterns and original designs featured in *Country Woman*, *Quiltmaker*, *Quilt*, and other magazines. In 2020, Jennifer was awarded an Outstanding Achievement Award from the Wisconsin Library Association for her novel *Resistance Women*. In 2023, the WLA awarded her the honor of Notable Wisconsin Author for her significant contributions to the state's literary heritage. Jennifer graduated from the University of Notre Dame and earned her MA from the University of Chicago. She, her husband, and their two sons call Madison, Wisconsin, home.